# Death at the C

Adrian Magson is an experienced author of crime and spy novels, including the Harry Tate series and the Inspector Lucas Rocco crime thrillers. He also has countless short stories and articles in national and international magazines to his name plus a non-fiction work: *Write On! – the Writer's Help Book*. Adrian lives in the Forest of Dean, and rumours that he is building a nuclear bunker are unfounded. It is in fact, a bird table.

# Also by Adrian Magson

*Smart Moves*

## Inspector Lucas Rocco

*Death on the Marais*
*Death on the Rive Nord*
*Death on the Pont Noir*
*Death at the Clos du Lac*
*Rocco and the Nightingale*
*Rocco and the Price of Lies*

## The Gonzales & Vaslik Investigations

*The Locker*
*The Drone*

# Death at the Clos du Lac

Adrian Magson

**CANELO**

First published in the United Kingdom in 2013 by Allison & Busby

This edition published in the United Kingdom in 2021 by

Canelo
31 Helen Road
Oxford OX2 0DF
United Kingdom

A CIP catalogue record for this book is available from the British Library.

Print ISBN 978 1 80032 504 3
Ebook ISBN 978 1 80032 245 5

Look for more great books at www.canelo.co

Printed and bound in Great Britain by Clays Ltd, Elcograf S.p.A.

*For my parents, who showed me France.*

*And Ann, of course, who knows where Rocco lives*

# Chapter One

*Spring 1964 – Picardie, France*

The man was standing on the bottom of the therapy pool in the Clos du Lac sanitarium, his white cotton shirt billowing out like gossamer in the clear, blue water. Staring up through the glass-panelled roof at a pale, three-quarter moon bathing the world in an eerie light, his expression was one of deep melancholy. But that may have been because his face was some way beneath the surface, and breathing was a thing of the past. *Garde Champêtre* Claude Lamotte's rubber-soled boots crunched with grit as he moved along the side of the pool for a closer look. Behind him a woman in a nurse's uniform was sobbing quietly, reluctant to come closer. Somewhere in the distance a door creaked open and shut repeatedly, a lonely drumbeat in the night.

The combination of sounds and atmosphere, more than the sight of the body, caused the hairs on the back of Claude's neck to stir uncomfortably. Responsible for policing the area around Poissons-les-Marais in rural Picardie, he was accustomed to moving around the lakes and rivers and marshes in the small hours, inured to the sometimes sinister mists and dark waters and sudden unexplained rushes of hidden movement in the night. But a death in this place, a supposedly secure haven of luxury and quiet, was something else entirely.

He propped his shotgun in the corner by the door and sniffed at the chlorinated air. It reminded him of his army days and the enforced swims with fellow conscripts every morning. The only difference then was they never had to contend with finding corpses in the water. Not real ones, anyway.

He shivered in spite of the clammy warmth, and gripped his flashlight for reassurance, irritated by the spider-touch of fear crawling up his back. Maybe this was what the training had been all about: finding stiffs in pools and remaining calm.

Signalling to the nurse to stay back, he forced his breathing to settle and knelt with a grunt by the edge of the water. A residue of cold moisture from the ribbed tiles soaked through his heavy cord trousers. At this level he could see every detail of the pool and its grisly contents, lit by a number of underwater lights spaced along one side. A faint mist was lifting off the surface as the colder air from outside met the warmer temperature inside. He debated shedding his jacket and boots and going in. Maybe there was a trace of life left in those staring eyes, a remote chance that he could keep that thread going.

Then a glance at the man's feet decided him against it. He felt a cold tremor go through him. '*Merde!*' The word slipped out unbidden, and he glanced guiltily at the nurse. 'Sorry.'

A large metal milk churn was resting on its side on the tiled bottom of the pool. It was attached to the dead man's ankles by a heavy chain, the links bright and glistening against the dark of his trousers. Holding the chain in place was a padlock. According to the nurse, from the time she'd noticed the lights on and had come to investigate, to when she had finally rushed out of the pool house to seek help, the man must have been in there for at least twenty minutes, probably longer. Even if Claude could get the chain off, it would take a kiss of life of which only God himself would be capable to bring the man back from whatever dark and distant place he'd gone to.

'A telephone. I need to call this in.' He had to get Lucas Rocco here. He'd make sense of it. He was an experienced investigator, accustomed to this kind of stuff.

He stood and followed the nurse as she hurried away to a desk near the entrance to the pool house. The movement made his stomach lurch, and he fought against the urge to let it all go. He'd seen his share of fights, stabbings, shootings and the gut-churning results of car crashes and agricultural accidents over the years. But nothing like this. It seemed worse, somehow, in a setting associated with health, to see death standing here so casually, so cavalier and blatant.

There was no answer from Rocco's house in the village of Poissons a kilometre away, so he rang the office in Amiens and left a message. The duty officer recognised Claude's voice.

'The inspector's been called in to an unexplained death in the town centre,' he said. 'I'll get a message to him. Is it urgent?'

'Very,' Claude breathed. 'Tell him I've got another dead one for him, even more unexplained. And he'll need Doctor Rizzotti and his swimsuit for this one.' Rizzotti was the Amiens area's forensic representative, a self-confessed amateur seconded from his role as a GP to fill a post vacant now for two years. But the doctor was good, and Rocco had faith in his abilities.

Claude had no wish to return to the pool, but he felt bad leaving the dead man alone. Not that the poor soul would notice, of course, but it just felt wrong. Besides, as first man on the scene, Rocco would want his opinions, so he walked back across the tiled floor and knelt once more by the edge of the water.

He focused on the knuckles of the man's right hand, just breaking the surface. The fingers, with a sprouting of coarse, dark hairs, were locked into a fist, gripping a thin, helical steel wire running up to a boxed wheel device sitting on an overhead cable stretched across the pool. He followed its length, wondering at its purpose. The cable was held at each end of the pool house by steel plates bolted to the walls, with a wire running out to the box. The down-wire was taut, he noted, and the only thing keeping the body upright.

He heard a scuff of footsteps and found the nurse standing nearby. Her face was a pale oval, the expression unchanged since he'd seen her running out of the building earlier. He didn't know her name, although he'd seen her in the village once or twice, at the co-op store. A handsome woman with a nice figure. Or maybe it was the uniform. She was lucky he'd been passing, otherwise she would have had to call for help and wait for a team to arrive from Amiens. She had clammed up now, though, he noted. Probably shock.

'I'd put some coffee on, if I were you,' he suggested kindly. The activity would keep her occupied until Rocco and the others got here. 'And if you haven't done it already, wake your boss because this place is going to be invaded.'

'My boss?' Her eyes flickered uncomprehendingly, edging towards the body in the water with reluctant fascination, then away again.

Claude let it slide. 'Coffee,' he said again. 'Make it a big pot.'

—

Less than half a kilometre away, a dark figure waited for the moon to slip behind a cloud, before emerging from the cover of a hedgerow and walking with a confident stride along the edge of the lane leading away from the Clos du Lac. The narrow route was little used in daytime, even less at night, but the man believed in taking simple precautions.

He was dressed all in black, from flexible, rubber-soled boots to the woollen cap covering his head, practically invisible to anyone unless they took him by surprise. But that wasn't likely to happen. Even so, he stopped periodically to test the air around him, using skills gained over many years to seek out the presence of others. All he heard was the faint, mournful shriek of a fox drifting on the night air, and a flap of wings in the trees nearby. Satisfied he was unobserved – by humans, at least – he moved on.

He reached a small, dilapidated barn at the side of the lane and stepped inside. He moved easily in the dark, having scouted the place in daylight two days earlier to study the layout and memorise any obstacles. The air was thick with the smell of old straw and mould, and he felt his nostrils react to the dust in the atmosphere.

He reached out and located the moped parked against the wall of the barn. From a pannier on the back he took a slim flask and opened the cap. The aroma of coffee with a lacing of cognac took over from the smell of straw. He poured a measure and drank it quickly, savouring the warmth spreading through his gut. He wanted a cigarette, too, another craving, but it was a risk too far. He would save it for later.

The moped held a second pannier, this one containing a collapsible net and rod, and a box of bait. But he was no fisherman; they were props, simple distractions in the unlikely event that he was stopped by a patrolling policeman or spotted by a farmer with insomnia. Fishing without a permit was easily excused, given the right amount of reasoning and charm and a willingness to apologise. As he knew all too well, the success of a mission was in the preparation, not simply the execution. He smiled at the play on words. Tonight's job had been just that – an execution. And it had gone as planned, if a little convoluted at the end. But he didn't mind that; it added to the frisson he still gained from a task done well. Tomorrow was the next phase, and undoubtedly the most important part of the plan. However, that was for others to deal with. His skills lay more in the role of a troubleshooter – a fixer of problems.

He replaced the flask and checked his watch using a flick of a flashlight. The glass over the face showed a tracery of fine scratches. Plenty of time to get clear. He had to be back on his way to Paris before sunrise. Seconds later he was wheeling the moped out of the barn and along the lane, heading for a route deep into the countryside that connected eventually with a back road out of the area, and his car.

Once he was certain he was well beyond earshot of the Clos du Lac, he jumped on and pedalled at a steady pace, travelling a full half-kilometre before engaging the engine.

He smiled to himself and placed his feet together on the central rest, enjoying the quirky feeling of using such a bizarre mode of transport away from a killing.

# Chapter Two

Inspector Lucas Rocco studied the dead man in the pool. His gaze lingered for a moment on the chain around the ankles, before following the wire upwards just as Claude Lamotte had done, running from the water to the overhead cable, then to each end of the pool house where the supporting cable was fastened to the walls by strong steel brackets.

'One day I'll get a dry one,' he murmured, looking back at the body. 'Someone who just curled up in a bed and died normally. No water, no canal, no ponds or lakes. Just a layer of dust and a spider or two for company.' Water, it seemed to him, had been an overriding feature of sudden deaths around here ever since his posting from Clichy, in Paris, the year before, and he was wondering if the region possessed some kind of deathly affinity with the stuff.

'What is this place?' he asked Claude. He'd seen the building at a distance, but there was nothing at the front to inform outsiders, no signs advertising its services, no indication of a specific function, save for an air of tranquillity and quiet purpose. It was simply a large stone mansion with an outbuilding housing this pool, set inside high stone walls covered in ivy, located down a narrow lane in the Picardie countryside.

Claude moved closer. 'They call it a sanitarium,' he replied softly, as though wary of disturbing the dead man.

'Used to be owned by a local landowner with fingers in shipping. He decided to make it into some kind of health retreat for his rich friends, but sold it before the war. Nobody knows who owns it now.' He pulled a face. 'They don't answer questions, only employ outsiders and never get involved in the village save for the odd visit by one of the staff. Even the lane outside is marked private, although it's not really; it's to discourage visitors.'

'How did you get here so quickly?'

'Stroke of luck. I was on the trail of a poacher along the canal and came up here to get a better view. This is on high ground, and you can see down the slope all the way to the canal and the lake beyond if you stand in the right place. Anyway, as I came through the gate, I heard a scream and saw her running out of the house, yelling her head off at me. Bloody scary at the dead of night, I can tell you.'

'You should try Clichy,' said Rocco. 'Happens all the time there.' Clichy in north-west Paris had been his base until he was posted to this rural region. He still missed its vibrant air of activity and tension, although less and less the longer he was here. He sometimes wondered if he was being sucked into the atmosphere of country living, having his edge slowly rubbed away.

He gathered up the tails of his long, black coat and squatted by the edge of the pool. The water was a pleasant shade of light blue, destined, no doubt, to draw people in and make them feel relaxed. But the glow of the underwater lights caught a trace of pink hanging around the dead man's hand like fine strands of hair. Bending closer, he saw traces of torn flesh on the fingers and palm. The dead man had been fighting frantically to pull himself out.

Difficult to do with two hands, he decided; impossible with the other hand tied by rope to the chain around his lower legs.

He'd never seen anything quite this inventive in Clichy.

'I left word for Dr Rizzotti,' he said softly. 'Nobody comes in here until he's had a look.'

Claude nodded. He was already carrying a coil of rough string to tie off an approach to the body. Rocco and the doctor had established a clear understanding between them that a crime scene should not be tainted by unnecessary traffic, and everyone was clear on the procedure.

Rocco looked up at the cable structure holding the dead man upright. 'What the hell is that thing?'

'I asked the nurse earlier. She said it was invented by the original owner to help his daughters to swim, but they learnt like most kids by jumping in the lake. Since then it's been used for helping residents who don't have the strength to keep themselves buoyant. Therapy, they call it. Didn't help this poor soul much, did it? Can't we use it to pull him out?'

'Not with that milk churn tied to his feet.' Rocco stood up. 'And he wouldn't notice the difference now, anyway. I need to speak to the nurse and whoever runs this place.' He looked around, puzzled by the quiet. 'Where is everybody?'

'No idea. It was like this when I arrived. The nurse can probably tell you. She's in the kitchen in the main building.' Claude gave him directions. 'Her name's Dion. I didn't ask her first name. She's a bit fragile.'

Rocco smiled grimly. 'Don't worry. I won't use a rubber hose on her unless she becomes difficult.' He had a sudden thought. 'Is Alix at home?'

'Yes. You want me to call her?' Alix was Claude's daughter, and a recent addition to the local police as a *gardienne*. In a burst of policing initiatives across the country, one of which had led to Rocco being transferred here, she had been recruited to help with sensitive cases involving women and children. Rocco had a feeling her skills might be needed before the night was out.

'Yes, please.'

He left Claude and walked out of the pool house across the yard to the main building. Through the entrance, which was open, he passed through an impressive foyer with marble columns and hung with elegant chandeliers. The walls were panelled with dark wood, no doubt courtesy of its original designer and unchanged by the current owners. The kitchen occupied a section of the lower floor at the rear of the mansion, and was furnished with a range of professional equipment in stainless steel. The room was cold and lacking in character, and he reflected that in his short time in Poissons, he'd seen milking parlours with more warmth.

A woman in nursing whites was sitting at a large wooden table, staring into a glass of amber liquid. She was attractive, with strong features and dark hair tied in a bun. No wedding ring.

'Mademoiselle Dion?' Rocco felt he was looming over her; it wasn't difficult with his height and broad shoulders, so he sat down across from her. She didn't stir or acknowledge his presence, and he guessed she was in shock. There was probably a professional as well as a normal humane cause for concern in what she had discovered, but he had to establish a connection with her before she shut down completely.

'If you've got any coffee and another one of those,' he said softly, nodding at the glass, 'I've had a long night.' It reminded him to check his watch. With the previous case he'd been to – a bizarre case of suicide, or so it seemed – he'd lost track of time. It was coming up to five in the morning and a spring light was already showing through the windows over the fields at the back.

The nurse seemed to shake herself. She stood up. 'Of course. I'm sorry...'

'Lucas Rocco,' he said. 'Inspector of police. I'm here to help.'

She nodded and turned away, picked up a percolator and poured him a cup of black coffee. Then she fetched a glass and poured a shot of cognac. She placed both on the table in front of him, gesturing at a box of sugar cubes and a small jug of milk.

Rocco picked up a newspaper from the table. Etienne Maintenant, the foreign minister, was shown boarding a flight to Peking and waving to the cameras like a film star. The headline was stark:

> France confirms diplomatic relations by sending foreign minister and trade delegation to China! The dawn of a new era for French trade?

Minister Maintenant, Rocco thought dryly, looked a little uneasy at the top of the steps leading to the aircraft door, as if he thought he might be on a one-way trip and desperately wanted to change his mind at the last moment.

'Quite a development,' said the nurse, nodding at the newspaper and sitting back down.

'We live in interesting times,' Rocco agreed, scanning the faces but seeing nobody he recognised. Nurse Dion showed no sign of having recognised his paraphrasing of the alleged Chinese curse. He picked up the glass. It was both too late and too early for it, but he showed willing by taking a sip. It was better quality than he'd expected; maybe they kept it for staff emergencies. He poured the rest into his coffee. His relaxed approach worked, and Dion took a sip from her own glass, wincing as she swallowed.

'So tell me,' he said, 'who did you call?'

She frowned. 'Call?'

'Yes. You're a professional, I can tell. In a place like this, there must be standing orders to call someone in case of emergencies. Who was that?'

'Director Drucker. I called him. He should be here soon.' She looked nervous and he wondered why. With help coming from various quarters, she should have been feeling reassured. 'Where did you train?' he asked. It was a distraction question only, but might prove useful. She looked about forty, at a guess, which meant she would have been old enough to be involved in the war, had she wanted to be. If so, she would be tougher than she seemed right now.

'In Brest,' she said vaguely. 'Other places, too. Wherever I could get work.'

'Places like this?'

'Hospitals, mostly. Why are you so interested in me?' She looked pale but somehow in control, as if a core of durability lay beneath, sustaining her. She was tough all right.

'I'm interested in everybody and anybody,' he replied, and sipped his coffee. 'I'm also interested in why nobody else is around. As I understand from Officer Lamotte, you screamed loudly enough when you discovered the body to have attracted a lot of attention.'

'Scream?' She looked defensive. 'I did not. I was calling out.'

'Of course. Who for?'

She stared levelly at him. 'For anyone... for help – I saw a man entering the driveway and didn't know he was a policeman until he told me. I was probably panicking a little. Shouldn't you be getting the man out of that pool?' She brushed a stray strand of hair from her face, her starched uniform rustling crisply in the silence.

'We will, soon enough.' He changed tack. 'What's the dead man's name?'

There was a lengthy silence, then she said, 'I can't talk about that.'

'What?'

'I'm sorry. I can't tell you. I have instructions. You'll have to speak to Director Drucker.'

'I will, of course. But let me tell you something, Mademoiselle: in the matter of a murder investigation, my instructions supersede any that you might have.' He breathed easily. 'Let me start again. Why is there nobody else here, and who is the dead man? Two very simple questions. Take them in any order you wish.'

Dion said nothing for a moment, then shrugged. 'I am the only one on duty tonight. There was... there's nobody else. A relief nurse when required, and two cleaners on rota – but that's it.'

Rocco jumped on the hesitation. 'You were going to say something else. What was it?'

'Nothing.' She twisted her fingers together, then appeared to relent. 'We have a security man, but I don't know where he is. He arrived for his shift yesterday evening, but I haven't seen him since. I called, but he didn't come.'

'And his name? Or is that something else you can't tell me?'

'André Paulus.'

At last. 'Good. Now, how many patients do you have here?' Rocco was amazed at the lack of activity. Surely someone else had heard the commotion? And could a man have been overpowered and chained up like this, then manhandled into the harness and dropped into the water without arousing attention?

She shook her head. 'I can't discuss that, either.'

'Are they sedated? Is that it?'

Her eyes flickered in alarm. 'What makes you say that?'

'It's a fair assumption, isn't it? A sanitarium in the middle of the night, a murder and a scream – pardon me – a shout. And no reaction from the other residents. What other reason would there be? Unless they're locked in their rooms.'

'It's not like that.'

'Really?'

He let the silence build. Now he'd got her talking and knew she wasn't going to fall apart in front of him, he could apply some pressure. Yet something told him it wasn't going to be that easy. She acted as if she was scared of someone. But it clearly wasn't him, or the police.

So who, then?

# Chapter Three

'I'm sorry. Really. But you have to understand—'

'What's going on here?'

Rocco turned. A short, stocky man had entered the kitchen and bustled up to the table with an air of fussy self-importance. 'This is a private facility and you should not be talking to my staff without authorisation.' He emphasised this by shooting a hard look at Dion, as if she were at fault, his gaze lingering on the drink glasses. 'Gilles Drucker. Director of this establishment.'

Rocco said nothing. He sipped the last of his coffee and counted to five. Then he stood up.

In any room, standing at two metres tall and dressed all in black, Rocco looked down on most people. To this man he must have appeared like a giant. With his impressive width of shoulders and short scrub of black hair, Rocco knew he was no baby face.

'That's good, Mr Drucker,' he said, and watched as the man swallowed hard and moved back a step. Drucker was a dandy, wearing a smart suit and highly polished shoes, and a handkerchief poking out of his right jacket sleeve. And where his imperious manner clearly worked here most of the time, it looked like suffering a sudden failure. 'Have you seen the reason I'm here?'

'I… no. Not yet.' Drucker flapped a hand. 'Inès – uh, Dion told me about it.'

'Good. Follow me.' Rocco turned and walked away, but not without making sure that Drucker didn't say anything to the nurse. He led the man at a fast pace through the main building and across to the pool, where Claude was tying off a makeshift string barrier to prevent anyone walking inside. Just before they entered the pool house, a car's headlights swept across the entrance and a vehicle stopped in the car park area.

'That must be Alix,' said Claude.

Rocco said to Drucker, 'Wait here.' Then walked over to meet Alix as she stepped from the car.

'What can I do to help?' she said. She was wearing a freshly pressed uniform and looked surprisingly alert for the time of morning.

Rocco gave her directions to the kitchen. 'A nurse named Inès Dion found a body in the pool. Sit with her, draw out anything you can. She's been told to button it by the short-arse in the suit behind me, but before I get heavy, see what you can find out. In particular, I'd like to know where the security guard, André Paulus, beds down when he's not here. I want to talk to him, find out where he's been.'

Alix raised an elegant eyebrow. 'So I get to talk to the nurse. Women's work, is it?'

'Actually, yes. Didn't you know some of the best inter-rogators throughout history have been women? You're not going to let the side down, are you?'

He nearly laughed at the tightening of her lips. No doubt she would get her own back soon enough.

He walked back to the pool entrance and led Drucker inside.

'Stay between the string lines,' he instructed him, 'and don't go too close to the edge. Tell me what you see.'

Drucker cleared his throat and took out his handkerchief as a line of perspiration sprang up across his forehead. He mopped his brow, then stepped forward as if walking across a minefield, and moved closer to the pool's edge.

While waiting for Drucker to react, Rocco looked at Claude. 'You never trained as a diver, I suppose?'

'Me? Hell, no. Dry land is hard enough. Why?'

'Because sooner or later we're going to have to get someone to go in there and cut the body free of those chains.'

Claude nodded. 'Couldn't we drain the pool?'

'No.' Drucker had heard them. 'It takes approximately seven hours to drain completely. The pipes are a very small bore. Besides, we would get complaints from the locals because it drains into the canal.' He shrugged. 'Fishermen don't like the chemicals in the water.'

'I know a man who'd go in there,' Claude suggested. 'He'd do it easy.' He knew all manner of strange people, some with slightly shady backgrounds.

'Friend of yours?'

'Well, not a friend, exactly. Local lad. Got lungs like a porpoise. He can stay underwater after most people have passed out.' He sniffed. 'He's good with locks, too.'

'Get him in here but don't tell him why.'

Claude nodded and disappeared to make a phone call. 'Well?' Rocco looked at Drucker. The director was standing by the pool trying not to look sick. He was flapping his handkerchief around as if attempting to dispel the aura of death, but Rocco sensed it was something of an act.

'He's one of our residents. I can't believe this. Why would he do it?'

'You think it was suicide?' Rocco stared at him. The man was in denial.

'I don't know. I thought maybe...' He flapped his hand again towards the water and up at the pulley.

'He was murdered,' Rocco said bluntly. 'Somebody put him in that contraption and dropped him in the water with the milk churn chained to his legs. As it filled with water it pulled him down. No way back up from that. Odd item to have handy, though – a milk churn.'

'There are two or three about the place,' Drucker murmured vaguely. 'They're purely ornamental, left by the previous owners.'

'So who is the dead man?'

'We don't have many residents, you understand,' Drucker continued as if he hadn't heard the question. 'That's why we don't need many staff, especially at night. It's a small facility, but effective. Too big and we wouldn't be able to give each one the care they need.'

'How many exactly?'

'Five at the moment. Never more than six.'

'How do they get here?'

'They're referred.'

'By whom?'

Drucker shrugged. 'By a specialist... or a doctor, often working with a magistrate or judge. The usual thing.'

'What kind of specialist?'

'I can't tell you that. It would violate the terms of privacy.'

Rocco kept his calm. Sooner or later this man would run out of rules to hide behind. 'All right. What about this particular patient? Who referred him?'

'I still can't tell you.'

'Why not? He's dead.'

'If I tell you what kind of specialist, it would indicate the nature of the patient's problem.' Drucker looked affronted at the very idea. 'That would be unethical.'

'So would me throwing you in the pool alongside him with weights tied to your ankles,' Rocco growled. 'So don't tempt me.' He leant towards Drucker, and the director nearly toppled back into the pool. 'I'm investigating a murder, not discussing ethics or your patients' medical ailments. Now. Give. Me. A. Name.'

'*All right.* Wait. Wait.' Drucker took a small card from his pocket and scrabbled for a pen. He wrote down a number and a name, and gave the card to Rocco. 'I'm sorry, Inspector, but that's all I can give you.' He slid past Rocco and headed for the door at a near trot.

Rocco glanced at the card. Drucker had written down a Paris telephone number and a name. Marcel Levignier.

'Wait.' Rocco turned. 'Is this the dead man?'

Drucker stopped immediately, skidding slightly on the tiles. 'No. It's a number we call if there are problems,' he muttered. 'But that's all I'm allowed to tell you. In any case, you won't have to call Levignier; he's already on his way. He'll be an hour – perhaps a little longer.'

'You called this in?'

'Yes.'

'Before coming here?'

He hesitated. 'Yes. It's standard operational procedure.' He turned and scurried away, his back rigid.

Rocco watched him go. The man was behaving like a frightened rabbit. But a rabbit with a big and scary older brother.

*Standard operational procedure.* The words had an unmistakably official air. He wondered why he found that so sinister.

# Chapter Four

'Inspector Rocco?' A tall, lean man in a dark-blue suit stepped out from a Citroën DS and walked across the car park. Above their heads a flock of small birds was in full song, lending the scene a surreal air. Two other men followed at a distance, scanning the inner courtyard of the Clos du Lac and staring at the birds as if they were intruders. They had the hallmarks of policemen, only much better dressed.

Rocco nodded. He'd been alerted to their arrival by Claude, on station in the small lobby at the front door. Claude was holding his shotgun in the crook of his arm, the over-under barrels pointing down and gleaming in the morning light.

'Marcel Levignier,' said the new arrival, eyeing Rocco carefully and shaking his hand. He had deeply tanned skin and dark hair peppered with hints of grey at the temples. He looked fit and his handshake was firm; to Rocco the signs of a former military man.

'Welcome to paradise,' said Rocco. 'You have a rank?' Levignier looked surprised. 'Why do you assume that?'

'I rang the number Drucker gave me. Your department is located within the Interior Ministry. In my experience, there are people in the Ministry who value rank over title. And you don't look like a civilian.'

Levignier smiled without humour. 'I'll take that as a compliment. But you read it well. I was a *commandant*, although I don't have cause to use it much now.' He glanced sideways at Claude, standing a couple of paces away. 'Does he have a permit for that thing?'

'Of course. It goes with the job.'

'All the same, I'd prefer to have it locked away. Would you—'

'On what grounds?' Rocco interrupted him. This wasn't going to go well if Levignier was intent on establishing pissing rights.

'On the grounds, Inspector, that this building is under the control of the Interior Ministry, and we are assuming command of events here. That includes who carries a weapon... and who does not.' He nodded at one of his men, who stepped forward and reached down to take Claude's gun.

Claude responded by tilting the weapon so that the tip of the barrel nestled firmly into the man's crotch. The man froze, as did his companion.

Claude smiled. 'I can hit a sparrow on the wing at two hundred metres every time. You honestly think I'd miss your tiny *couilles* at this range?'

'He's a cop,' explained Rocco to Levignier. 'Like me, he only gives up his gun to a direct superior.'

Levignier hesitated, then flicked a hand for his men to back off. 'Very well. But you had better call *your* superior because you are now off this investigation. Good day, Inspector.'

'Well, in that case, good luck,' Rocco told him. 'I hope your men are experienced in underwater recovery. Will you take the dead man all the way back to Paris in your DS?'

Levignier brushed past him without a word and walked into the main building, followed by his men. Drucker was waiting just inside the door, feet shifting nervously on the tiled floor of the foyer.

Rocco glanced at Claude. 'Wait here in case Rizzotti shows up. I won't be long.'

He walked across to the pool house and picked up the telephone on the desk. It clicked automatically onto an outside line. He dialled the office number in Amiens and asked for *Commissaire* Massin. It was just after seven-thirty, but the senior officer was an early starter.

'What is it, Inspector?' Massin's voice was crisp and faintly suspicious in tone. But then, with Rocco it usually was. The two shared a history going back to the war in Indochina, when Massin had suffered a crisis of confidence in the battlefield, and Rocco had been forced to escort him to safety. Finding on arrival in the Amiens region that Massin was his new boss had not been welcome news for either man. But they were working on it.

Rocco gave him a summary of events. When he mentioned the name Levignier and the Ministry, he felt a chill come down the line.

'You had better do what he says, then.' Massin's decision was as speedy as it was predictable. He rarely stood up to the Ministry attack dogs, preferring to let others take the heat, another point of contention between them.

'But it's a murder,' said Rocco. 'It's our job, not theirs.'

'I hear what you say, of course. And I agree. But you won't win on this one. Levignier is very established within the Ministry. He will have the backing of senior figures and his brief gives him considerable power.'

'You know him?'

'I know of him, but only by reference and reputation. What does he do?'

'He runs the Internal Security Directorate. That is all I know. All I need to know.'

Rocco sighed. He'd heard of them. No wonder Massin was jumpy. The vast and multi-layered Ministry of the Interior based in central Paris was responsible for internal security in France, and the ISD was its internal police watchdog, plugging holes and rooting out problems wherever they existed. Working separately from the normal security and intelligence departments, Levignier's team worked on finding rats in the woodpile and isolating threats to the stability of the government and the status quo. It gave them great reach and power, but rarely made them any friends.

'Why would they be interested in a death in a sanitarium?'

'I have no idea, Inspector. Levignier's work spans the police, intelligence, the military and other departments. Best leave it alone, I think. One death, even as odd as this one, is not worth fighting over. Get your man Lamotte out of there and leave it to Levignier to sort out, if that's what he insists on doing.'

Rocco put the phone down and walked across to the poolside to take a last look at the body. He was reluctant to let this matter go, but he could recognise when a fight wasn't worth having. Yet…

'Who put pussy in the well, d'you think?'

Rocco spun round. A man in a bathrobe and slippers was standing behind him, staring into the water. He was in his fifties, fat and balding, with deathly pale skin and liver spots across his head. He looked half asleep, his eyes crinkled at the edges, and yawned. 'Dear me, poor old

Simon. What's he doing in there? He couldn't swim, you know. He told me. Hated water. Don't know what made him use that bloody device. I wouldn't, if you paid me.'

'Simon?' Rocco heard voices approaching outside. 'Simon who?'

'Simon Ardois. At least, that's the name he used. Can't rely on that here, though. It's the house of smoke and mirrors, know what I mean?'

'Not really. Tell me.'

He gave Rocco a sideways look, like a big child about to tell a lie. 'Well, nothing is what it seems here. Same with the people.' He leant forward and whispered, 'Lots of secrets in this place, let me tell you. But I've got a few of them tucked away.' He winked conspiratorially and laid a finger along the side of his nose, the dramatic co-conspirator. Then he yawned again and looked about as if surprised to find himself here. His eyelids drooped suddenly, and he shook his head.

'Where did you come from?' Rocco asked him.

'From my room. I was looking for the kitchen. I need coffee. I woke up, but had trouble getting out of bed.' He squinted. 'What was all the shouting about? Lights on everywhere, too. Bloody place is usually so quiet. Too quiet, in fact. Not last night, though. Couldn't have been Simon, though, could it? Sounded more like a woman's voice.' He nodded at the dead man. 'He'd have blown a few bubbles but not much else, eh?' He giggled, his jowls wobbling. 'Sorry – that's in bad taste.

These damned drugs are terrible; destroy everything in the end, including one's sense of decorum.'

'You're on drugs?'

'Yes. To help me sleep, they say. We're all on them. Don't know which way is up most of the time. And don't get me started on the physical side effects. Some nights I can't even pee in a straight line.' As he scratched at his chest, his bathrobe moved aside slightly, revealing a small tattoo of a tiger between his neck and shoulder. It was a style Rocco had seen before, in backstreet tattoo parlours in Paris, and further back, in Indochina during the war. This man didn't look like any soldier, however.

'What's your name?' Rocco asked. The voices were closer now, just outside the building. Someone – it sounded like Drucker – was arguing about security.

'I can't tell you!' The man looked shocked, if slightly stupefied. He smiled coyly. 'You'll get me into trouble, asking me questions like that. Naughty man.'

'But you do have a name.'

'Of course I do. Tell you what, you can call me Stefan – only don't tell the Gestapo I said that, otherwise I'll get into trouble.' He giggled again and suddenly seemed to realise what Rocco looked like. 'Christ on a bike, you're big, aren't you? Oops – see? Told you.' He looked mock-sheepish and smiled dreamily. 'What's your name, then?'

The voices had entered the building. Rocco took Stefan by the arm and said softly, 'I'm Lucas Rocco. Tell you what, let's not tell anyone we spoke.'

Stefan winked and patted Rocco's hand. 'Good idea. Very decent of you. Pity about poor Rotenbourg, though, eh?'

'Rotenbourg?'

'Yes. Him in the water.'

'You said his name was Ardois.' The man looked confused. 'Did I?'

'Earlier, you called him Simon Ardois; now you just called him Rotenbourg. Which is it?'

'I didn't. We don't know each other's names. You must have misheard me. I—'

He was prevented from saying anything more by Drucker bustling through the door, followed by Levignier and one of his men. They saw Rocco and stopped.

'You need to keep a closer eye on your patients,' Rocco said sternly. 'This one was looking for coffee and nearly went for a swim instead.' He left Stefan with them and walked back to join Claude, wondering what kind of drugs they pumped into people like Stefan to keep them docile and rendering them stupefied at the same time.

Alix was with her father, looking flustered.

'One of those men told me to get lost,' she muttered. 'Claude, too. Can they do that?'

'Looks like they just did. Claude, call your diving friend. He won't be needed just yet. Alix, did you get an address for Paulus?'

Alix nodded. 'He rents a small place about seven kilometres from here.' She handed him a page from her notebook with an address written down. 'I think they might have a thing going, her and the guard.'

'What makes you say that?'

'She got a bit defensive when I asked her about him. I told her I just wanted to make sure he was all right. She reckoned it's out of character for him to disappear like that, and in any case, Drucker can check on his work throughout the night.'

'How?'

'Paulus carries a time-stamp register. He has to insert a key from a series of boxes around the building every hour. The register stamps the time on a card, and Drucker checks them religiously every morning. She doesn't like

Drucker. Calls him a lapdog.' She smiled. 'That was the polite expression.'

'Good work.' He was already harbouring thoughts about Paulus. His disappearance halfway through a shift could mean one of two things: either he had deliberately gone missing to allow someone free rein to enter and do his business undisturbed… or Paulus himself was the killer. But he didn't want to jump to conclusions. 'Anything else?'

'She trained in the General Military Hospital in Brest.' She paused. 'Actually, the way she said it, I don't think she ever left.'

'What do you mean?'

'It was the way she talked, as if she's still attached to the military in some way. Paulus, too – she mentioned something about Drucker being the only civilian in the place apart from the patients. Why would that be?'

Rocco thought about it. He could think of one or two reasons, but he needed to make sure, whatever Levignier's instructions had been. 'Why indeed?'

# Chapter Five

The air along Avenue de Friedland felt cool and fresh after the warm, perfumed atmosphere of the exclusive *Salon Elizabeth*, and their first client of the day brushed a stray hair from her face and walked east towards Boulevard Haussmann. Her thoughts were on shopping, and meeting her husband for an early lunch. He had been tied up for several days in business negotiations, and she wanted to make sure that he took a break from work and relaxed, if only for an hour or two. Success, as she knew well, was too expensive if bought at the expense of one's health.

She caught a glance of her reflection in a window, pleased with the magic worked on her hair by Marcel, the *Elizabeth*'s chief stylist. She hoped her husband would approve, and gave a wry smile before moving on.

She came to a narrow street between elegant apartment buildings. A block of shadow was cast over the pavement and she shivered momentarily, glancing back to check before crossing, eager to be back in the sun. As she did so, a grey furniture van signalled and pulled alongside her, the driver holding up a clipboard and smiling.

She stopped. Another out-of-towner lost in the maze of city streets. It happened all the time and she sympathised. She waited for the driver to wind down his window. But instead of looking at her, he was now glancing up and down the street, frowning in concentration. Something touched her consciousness, that tiny part of the human instinct warning of imminent danger, and she heard the metal ping of a door opening, and the scrape of feet on tarmac. A movement to one side caught her attention, and a tall figure stepped out from behind the van.

'What are—?' Her words were choked off by an arm whipping across her throat. She felt herself lifted by another powerful arm around her waist, and a smell of male body odour filled the air around her. Then she was out of the sunshine and in the dusty, close interior of the van, and being thrust face down onto a mattress lying on the floor.

The van began moving.

'Lie still. Don't shout,' whispered the man holding her, his breathing hot in her ear. He smelt of onions and cigarette smoke, and she felt the smooth texture of a leather jacket against the skin of her neck. 'Be good and you'll live to see your fancy salon another day. Give us trouble and… well, you wouldn't want Robert to have to attend your funeral, would you?'

She lay still and was quickly bound with lengths of fabric tape, which she recognised as the sort used by furniture delivery men to lash goods to the sides of their vans. Then a soft cotton hood was drawn over her head. She realised that she still hadn't seen her captor's face.

'*I can't breathe!*' she cried, and shook her head violently as a rush of claustrophobia overtook her. 'You're making a mistake!' Then she recalled that the man had mentioned her husband's name. This was no error. With it came the cold chill of knowledge that the one thing Robert had feared, but that she had never truly believed possible, had finally happened: she was being kidnapped.

Her instinct was to fight. She had played a part in the Resistance during the war, mostly as a messenger and a carrier of weapons, sometimes ammunition and supplies. Young women were able to move about much more easily than men, although the risks had still been great. But the experience of battling the constant dread surrounding her back then had given her courage beyond her understanding, and the idea of being taken by the Germans had instilled in her and her colleagues the certain knowledge that to submit was to die. It was that early experience that she called on now.

She drummed her heels on the floor of the van, then lashed out with a kick, hoping to connect with the man who had torn her away from her freedom out there on Avenue de Friedland. The mattress absorbed all of her attempts to draw attention from outside, and her kicks were fended off with ease before her ankles were caught and held in a powerful grip.

'Enough,' said the man, as if he were chiding a troublesome child. 'You're wasting your time. Nobody will hear you from in here.' Seconds later, she felt the same fabric tape being used to tie her legs together, and she became immobile, waiting to see what would happen next.

Her breath was coming in short gasps as the van's movement began to rock her back and forth on the mattress. It absorbed some of the bumps, but she could feel the ribbed aluminium floor underneath and picture the road speeding past below. They had already made several sharp turns, but she soon lost all sense of direction or speed, and gave up trying. Instead, she focused on listening to sounds, hoping for something to indicate where they were. But soon that became a blend of noises and she gave that up, too. She could hear other traffic outside, but it was muted as if through cotton wool, and she guessed they had taken precautions to reduce any chances that she might call for help and attract attention.

'Why are you doing this?' she demanded. Engage him in conversation, she told herself. To communicate is to lower barriers, according to her husband, a practised and very successful negotiator. But there was no reply. Whoever her captor was, he either did not believe in unnecessary talk or had learnt the same lesson about communication.

She forced herself to breathe slowly, deeply, trying to regain a sense of calm, in spite of her fears. There was no point in becoming stressed to the point of exhaustion, and this entire episode had taken place with no shouts of alarm on the street, and with such ease that it spoke of practised skill. It was probable, therefore, that it had all gone unseen, with nobody the wiser that a woman had been snatched off the street and was now being carried who knew where by men who would no doubt soon make their demands clear.

She put her face down and continued breathing. Robert would soon have her freed, she was certain of that. For now, though, she had to survive.

# Chapter Six

'Should we be here?' Claude eyed the surrounding countryside as they pulled to a stop. They had driven in Rocco's car to a tiny village a few kilometres north of Poissons, leaving Alix on duty at the sanitarium as the local police presence.

Berlay hardly merited the title of village, consisting of a clutch of houses and two smallholdings strung out along a narrow dead-end road leading into open fields. No church, no shop, no bar. Lots of perfectly formed cowpats in the road, though, Rocco noted, so not much motorised traffic passed this way.

'Better than hanging around near Levignier,' Rocco replied. It struck him that if a man wished to hide himself away, this was as good a place to do it as any. Like dropping off the end of the world. Yet he wondered why Paulus would live here when there was so much more choice in Amiens or even Poissons. Maybe Alix had been right about him having a relationship with Ms Dion; they certainly couldn't ask for more privacy than this.

The cottage rented by Paulus was a single-storey plaster-and-lathe building with a corrugated metal roof and a rusted chimney stack. The structure looked lopsided, as if it was trying to melt into the landscape. And if Paulus was any kind of gardener, he'd put his talents on hold for a while: the grass was long, a once cultivated area with sticks for vegetables was overgrown, and the path leading to the front door was a barely visible trail of flattened stems.

Claude checked the chimney. 'No smoke. Could be out.' Rocco got out of the car and led the way up the path.

'Check the back,' he said.

He knocked on the door. It rattled, the sounds echoing back with the uniquely hollow aura of a deserted building. Above the keyhole was a handle with a simple thumb latch arrangement. He pressed it down.

The door swung open and he stepped inside. They were too late.

Whatever Paulus had or had not done at the Clos du Lac, his part in the proceedings was now over. He was lying slumped in an armchair, head thrown back, a mass of dark blood across his chest, soaked into his shirt. None on the floor, though, or the chair, Rocco noted.

Paulus was a big man, somewhere in his forties, with a no-nonsense brush-cut and the beginnings of a day-old growth of beard. He had probably been good-looking in life, but he now looked softened and somehow twisted in death, his mouth open and wrenched to one side. He was dressed in dark trousers and shoes and a dark-blue shirt, but no tie. Almost a uniform. The watch on his wrist was a utilitarian model, probably steel, of the kind favoured by military men for simplicity and robustness.

Rocco bent close to examine the chest area. Paulus had been shot twice at close range at the base of the throat. He went behind the chair and gently eased the body forward. It felt cold and the stiffness of rigor mortis was on its way. No exit wounds and no blood. Low charge rounds.

The work of a professional.

Claude came through the front door and joined him. 'Nothing to see round there – Mother of God!' He crossed himself.

Rocco checked the room carefully. It didn't take long; it was a living room-cum-kitchen combined and held a table, two chairs, the armchair, a heavy metal range and a rustic oak dresser with a collection of household bits and pieces on the shelves instead of crockery. He saw nothing that would be of any help: a couple of paperback novels, scattered newspapers, magazines, pens, a large flashlight battery, some keys, a few coins and some new socks still clipped together. The twin cupboards underneath held a selection of saucepans and heavy plates, cups and bowls, with an assortment of tinned goods, two bottles of wine and half a stale baguette. Not unlike his own collection, he reflected; just enough to get by, a single man's idea of the basics in life.

He walked through the only door into a small bedroom. The air smelt stuffy. There was a double bed with rumpled bedclothes and a single, ancient wardrobe. A few clothes hung from a rail inside: shirts, trousers and a couple of jackets. And a woman's blouse, plain white.

The single shelf held a pair of women's panties, folded and resting on brown paper alongside a small, floral washbag. The bag held a small bar of soap, a tin of tooth powder and a toothbrush and a small jar of face cream.

A woman's overnight kit. Alix had been right.

'Do you think he could have done it – the murder back at the Clos?' Claude had followed him in and was standing by the door looking back at the body.

'Possibly. As a night security guard he'd have had access to all areas of the building. He would have had plenty of opportunity to get into the patient files, too, if he needed.'

'And he might have known how to operate that pulley thing.'

Rocco nodded. 'That, too.' And from what Stefan had said, if the patient was drugged to the eyeballs, as most of them were, he wouldn't have had any trouble fitting him into the harness.

But why end up dead afterwards? A killer killed? It didn't make sense.

He checked through the jacket pockets in the wardrobe. Nothing there. He went through the rest of the room, then walked through and checked Paulus's trouser pockets, careful not to disturb the body. Nothing there, either. No cash, no wallet. Then he had a thought. He checked the belt. It looked like service issue, the leather in good condition apart from a two-centimetre stretch just above the left hip, where it was slightly distorted and shiny.

Paulus had been wearing a hip holster. So where was it now?

He stood back, puzzled. The place was clean. Too clean. 'We need to call this in,' he said, and led the way out of the house.

'There's no car,' Claude observed, stubbing his toe on a well-worn rut at the edge of the lane where a vehicle had been parked. 'So how did he get around?'

'He was killed somewhere else,' Rocco said. 'No blood spillage and no signs of a struggle. The car will have been dumped.'

He drove fast past the collection of houses, and saw no sign of the inhabitants. They were probably out in the fields by now, working. He'd send someone back later to see if anyone had heard or seen anything.

As they hit a straight stretch, another car approaching from the opposite direction sped by, kicking up a column of dust. It was a dark Renault saloon with two men inside.

'Cops,' Claude said, turning to look back. 'Somebody beat us to it. Shouldn't we go back?'

Rocco shook his head. 'No. Not cops.' More of Levignier's men, he was certain of it.

The vultures were gathering.

They were halfway back to Poissons when Claude suddenly slapped his knee in frustration. 'Hell, I must be getting old. What an idiot!'

'What?'

'The nurse – Dion. I thought she was screaming for the police when I first heard her.'

'Yes. So?'

'I just realised – she wasn't calling the police. She was calling *him* – the dead man: Paulus.'

# Chapter Seven

'We have all reasonable grounds for taking this over as a murder enquiry.' Rocco was in Massin's office, having driven straight to Amiens from Berlay. Also present were his deputy, *Commissaire* Perronnet, tall, aloof and keeping his own counsel as usual, but ready to support Massin, and Captain Canet of the uniformed branch. Slightly flushed of face and stocky, with a well-developed stomach, Canet was genial enough and inclined to favour action rather than talk. Massin had listened to what Rocco had reported, before calling in the other two in for a council of war and despatching a clean-up team to the Paulus cottage, including Dr Rizzotti.

'You're probably right, Inspector,' Massin agreed smoothly. 'But I've already had instructions from Paris.' He gestured at the telephone on his desk. '*Commandant* Levignier is in charge of the investigation regarding all matters related to the Clos du Lac – including the subsequent death of the security guard. If required we are here in a support role only.'

'That's just my point,' Rocco argued carefully. 'The murder of Paulus took place outside the sanitarium. It's a civilian matter, which places it within our jurisdiction.'

Massin said nothing, but looked at the other two officers for their opinions. Perronnet wagged his head from side to side, signalling indecision. Canet nodded and patted his stomach subconsciously. 'I agree with Rocco, sir. The second murder might be connected with the sanitarium, but it did happen outside. We have to have some autonomy, surely.'

'That may be true, Captain. But we don't know where the shooting took place. We have only a brief examination of the scene at the Paulus residence to go on, although,' he tipped his head towards Rocco, 'I'm not suggesting you're wrong, Inspector.' He chewed his lip.

'We should not ignore the question of jurisdiction,' Perronnet conceded reasonably, drawing a startled look from the other three. He was not well known for voicing any opinion in contradiction to Massin. 'What I mean is,' he hurried on, 'what if other deaths were to occur – although God forbid that they do, of course – involving people related to this place but unconnected with the first murder? Where do we draw the line? And we are bringing the body of Paulus back here, are we not?'

Rocco sighed inwardly at the convoluted argument and wondered whether Perronnet wasn't merely playing an even field, trying to remain uncommitted in what could become a prolonged argument. But he decided not to let the opportunity offered go by.

'I agree,' he said. 'We could end up being expected to clear up the mess with none of the authority to investigate the cause.'

Massin nodded slowly. 'I can see I'm outnumbered.' He chewed on his lip in thought, then tapped his desk with the tips of his fingers. 'Very well. I will go back to the Ministry and let you know what their response is. But don't be surprised if they lock us out. This Clos du Lac is clearly a government facility, so we should not expect them to allow access too easily.'

'I'd like to know what kind of facility,' said Rocco. 'Drugged patients, armed security, and the presence of three Ministry men within hours of a death?'

'Yes, well, if you'll excuse the untimely reference, don't dive deeper than you can swim, Inspector,' Massin warned. 'They may not be your favourite people, but they carry a lot more influence and weight than anyone in this room. Push too hard and you might find yourself assigned to some hellhole of an island in the Pacific.'

Outside in the corridor, Rocco nodded at Canet. 'Thanks for the support.'

Canet smiled. 'Don't worry, I'll expect you to return the favour one day. Frankly, I like to see the Ministry noses put out of joint now and then; there are some, like Levignier, who treat the uniformed branch like second-class citizens most of the time. Be good to win a point back now and then.'

Rocco headed for his desk to clear some paperwork. On the way, he spotted the muscular outline of Detective René Desmoulins coming down the corridor. He was one of the best investigators in the region, and Rocco trusted him implicitly.

'You busy?' he asked.

Desmoulins smiled shyly, smoothing his thin moustache. For something he was so aware of, it never seemed to progress much beyond a heavy fuzz, but Rocco admired his determination.

'Nothing I can't drop. Why?'

'I want you to find out everything you can on an André Paulus, former or serving naval cop. Try the records office in Brest.' He ran through the little that he knew from nurse Dion. 'Did he leave the navy, if so, were there any problems – the usual background stuff?'

Desmoulins nodded, committing the details to memory. 'Will do.'

Rocco left him to it and went to his desk. It wasn't long before he got a call from Massin.

'You've been given authority to investigate the Paulus death,' the senior officer told him. 'But that's all. Anything inside the facility is strictly off-limits.'

'That was quick,' Rocco said. 'Has Rizzotti had a look at Paulus's body yet?'

'He has. I have him with me. Come to my office and he can tell you himself.'

Rocco climbed the stairs and found Canet and Perronnet were there, too. Rizzotti grinned when he saw Rocco.

'You're still dragging them in for me to play with, I see,' he said, referring to Rocco's talent for finding corpses. He was a pale individual with thinning hair and wire spectacles, and seemed completely at home when poring over bodies or evidence that needed his opinions.

'Your report, please, Doctor,' Massin said softly.

'Of course. Well, it's very simple. The deceased was shot with two nine-millimetre rounds to the upper chest.' Rizzotti looked at their faces. 'Anyone want the full medical details? No? Well, that's it. Whoever did it was very clever, however. Neither round exited the body, yet I found nothing solid to have impeded them.'

'Meaning?' Massin urged him.

'Meaning that whoever killed him used reduced-charge cartridges to restrict the range.' He nodded at Rocco. 'As I learnt from Inspector Rocco, it's a method used by professional assassins for close-quarter kills. The lack of blood at the scene would appear to confirm some care was taken in the execution,' he winced at the unintended pun, 'although it's probable the shooting occurred outside the premises. But wherever it happened, there are clear signs of powder burns around the entry wounds, to the clothing and the flesh, suggesting that the killer was standing close to the deceased when shooting him. As near as I can estimate, death occurred during the night, sometime between midnight and 6 a.m.'

'If he was killed elsewhere,' said Canet, 'why not leave him? Why would they bother dumping him back at the house?'

'Now that,' Rizzotti gave an expansive shrug, 'science – even my limited version of it – cannot tell you. Perhaps where he was killed was inconvenient for the killer. But that's up to Inspector Rocco to find out.' He smiled at Rocco as he handed over the baton.

'There has been a suggestion,' said Massin, waving his thanks to Rizzotti, 'that the killing might be a simple case of jealousy. He was rumoured to be involved with the nurse, Dion. Levignier has suggested that might be an avenue worth pursuing.'

Rocco nearly laughed. 'Levignier said that? He can't be serious.'

'You don't think it's an explanation worth exploring?'

'Only if Dion was also involved with a jealous hitman. Rizzotti's right – this has the hallmarks of a professional kill. A jealous lover wouldn't take all the personal effects the way it was done here. Neither would they bother hauling the body back to the house. And Paulus disappeared in the middle of his shift; it's too much of a coincidence that it just happened while a murder was taking place at the Clos. He either left his post under his own steam or was forced. Then shot.'

'I heard another suggestion,' Perronnet put in. 'That Paulus might have been involved in the first killing in some way. He may have been paid to leave the building in order to leave the way clear, but for some reason became surplus to requirements. It's a possibility.'

'Where did that one come from?' asked Rocco.

'I forget. One of Levignier's team, I believe. It was a passing remark.'

Rocco wasn't surprised. It was a reasonable assumption, but all too easy – and far too quick. He sensed an attempt to sidetrack them. Somebody in the Ministry had seen the potential problem in denying access to a normal murder investigation, and was tossing these suggestions out as a concession, a meagre bone to a dog.

'I need access to Inès Dion,' he said. 'She's a material witness to what happened.'

'That has already been agreed. But the director, Drucker, will be there at all times. And you should take another officer with you. I suggest *Gardienne* Poulon, to avoid any unfounded accusations of pressure.' Massin's voice hardened. 'Make no mistakes, Inspector, and remember what I said: you have been given reasonable access, but do not abuse that permission. You should also not forget that you have other cases to investigate, such as a shooting not far from Poissons. The report is on your desk, I believe.'

'I'll behave myself,' Rocco replied. 'Scout's honour.'

He turned and left before Massin could make a comeback. He'd never been in the scouts and doubted they'd have accepted him. But Massin wouldn't know that.

He scooped up the report marked urgent from his desk and scanned it on the way around the building, finally locating Alix Poulon in the basement, knee-deep in paperwork. She looked glad of a diversion and dropped what she was doing immediately.

'What are we doing, exactly?' she asked, as they walked out to Rocco's car.

'First we're going to sort out two troublesome brothers who've been shooting at each other. Then we're going hunting.'

# Chapter Eight

The lunchtime crowds were out in force as two men strolled along the east side of Place de la Concorde in central Paris. Steering clear of the Obelisk in the centre, a focal point for the bulk of tourists, they kept to the outer perimeter, automatically scanning the people around them for familiar faces.

Both men were dressed in suits and ties, gleaming white shirts and polished shoes, the quality indicating a position above the ordinary rank and file of office workers and bureaucrats populating the area. Neither man had any legitimate reason not to be there, but being seen together, while not illegal or sanctioned, could give cause for interested speculation among those who knew them.

On their left was a stone wall topped by a balustrade and trimmed hedge around the Tuileries Garden, a good place for a private chat. But the shorter of the two men indicated the broad pavement leading down to the north bank of the Seine. The road here was blocked to traffic and quiet.

'Less likely to be noticed along here,' he commented briefly. 'And we can hear ourselves speak, too.'

His name was Josef Girovsky, and he was a fourth-generation Pole who had never been further east than the Alps. He had the square build and thick, grey hair of his forefathers and the smooth, coiffed appearance of a man of money – something those forefathers would have given their right arms for. Whenever his name appeared in the national press, which was rarely, he was referred to as an industrialist, even a capitalist, with a chain of businesses and joint ventures around the world, from engineering to finance, from farming to fishing fleets. But he preferred the title of investor, for that is what he was. He invested in anything that made money, and he was very good at it.

He was also ruthless about increasing his reach for more.

'So where's Levignier?' he asked. 'Why couldn't he come like he usually does?'

'What's the matter – are you worried about being seen with me?'

His companion was tall and slim, with thinning hair and a chillingly direct gaze. He possessed a lazy smile that rarely left his mouth yet never quite managed to touch his grey eyes. And he had about him a stillness that made other men very wary indeed.

'If I knew who you really were,' Girovsky muttered with a touch of acid, 'I might. But you haven't told me yet.'

'Because you have no need to know who I am. I'm simply a functionary – a messenger. I work for Commander Levignier.' In fact, the tall man was known mostly by the name Delombre, which he enjoyed for its double meaning; his work was predominantly in the shadows, so therefore entirely appropriate. At other times, when it suited him, he used other names, each fictitious and disposable, like a cheap suit. He worked a decent rifle shot away from where they were now walking, in the depths of the Ministry of the Interior in Place Beauvau, in a department few people knew about, and which Girovsky only knew of at arm's length.

'What happened at the sanitarium?' he asked. 'I received a rambling message from Drucker. He's not supposed to contact me. What does he hope to gain?'

Delombre gave a small sigh. 'I know. He panicked when he couldn't contact us, so he chose you instead. It's the people we have to work with, you see.' He smiled without humour, his cold eyes resting for a long moment on the Pole. 'Don't worry, it's being taken care of.'

'The same way the guard was taken care of? I don't like the sound of that.'

'If you don't have the stomach for the answers, you shouldn't ask the questions.'

Girovsky's head swivelled at the abruptness of the response. 'What does that mean?'

'Think about it. I'm sure you'll understand eventually.'

'I don't like your attitude.'

'That's too bad.' Delombre stopped, forcing Girovsky to halt and face him. He waited for a pretty young woman with a student's satchel over her shoulder to go by, his gaze drifting down to slim, bare legs, lightly muscled, then said, 'Do we continue with this or not? Because we can always abandon it and close it down, you know.'

Girovsky gasped. 'You don't have that authority!'

'Not directly, not here and now. But I know somebody who does. Only…' He hesitated and stared up at some pigeons flying overhead, their wings a muffled beat of panic.

'Only what?'

'I'm not sure you'd like the consequences of our stopping things right now simply because you don't approve of our methods. And I'm pretty sure your business colleagues would be very cross with you. Actually, speaking of them, I'm surprised you weren't on the flight to China with the rest of the trade party. Were you not invited?'

Girovsky's face coloured at Delombre's mischievous tone, but he held himself in check. He cleared his throat, the action of a realist faced with little alternative. 'My presence is not required at this stage, that's all. I have colleagues on the trip, naturally, but it was not thought… necessary for me to go until the talks have progressed further.'

'I see. You mean the others know how to use their chopsticks.' Delombre yawned, ignoring the other's protest. 'Still, I know what it's like to live in the shadows, being shunned by polite society.' He chuckled, and Girovsky grunted angrily at being the object of this man's sarcasm. His press coverage over the years had not been entirely kind, due to both his ancestry and his business methods, and he therefore operated behind the scenes where the media was concerned. The opening trade talks involving the Chinese government were a prime example, and one where he was forced to take a back seat for the time being.

'Very droll.' He straightened his jacket. 'I must go – I have appointments. Tell Levignier that we must continue, of course. I'm concerned, that's all. There's a great deal riding on this project, and the Chinese won't wait while we sort out our internal problems. If they sense trouble, they'll pull out and take their business elsewhere. We can't have that.'

'The Chinese.' Delombre's lips twitched. He turned to stare across the city rooftops at the hazy shape of the Eiffel Tower in the distance. It looked glorious in the sunlight and he wished for a moment that he was over there, enjoying watching the pretty girls with their skirts gusting in the breeze rather than here with this toad of a man. 'Yes, we mustn't upset them, must we?'

'I hope not. The country needs them. They are the future. You see – in twenty years' time they'll be the world's new powerhouse economy.'

'So everybody keeps telling me.' Delombre didn't like business people; they were greedy and boastful of their achievements and unable to see that not everything came down to money. But with the exchange of words had come a subtle shift in positions, with the Pole now holding the higher ground simply because he was right. For now, anyway. 'What else are you worried about?'

'The policeman who intervened – Rocco, is it? I hear he's pushing for answers.'

'You hear too much. You want to watch that – it could be dangerous.'

'It's what I pay people for: to keep me informed. It's how I run a successful business. Information is power.'

'Well, rest assured, that problem is being dealt with, too. Rocco's a country cop with pretensions of greatness; he'll back off or give up, whichever offers the easiest solution. Word has already gone down the line to cut him off. The case is on its way to being closed.'

'How so? There's a body. Two bodies.'

Delombre smiled this time, his face creasing. It still didn't reach his eyes. He checked his watch, a sturdy, businesslike model covered with fine scratches, each one of which could tell a tale. 'Actually... that's not quite correct. Not now. We couldn't do anything about the guard, not after Rocco found him. But the other one has... disappeared. For good.'

Girovsky's look of surprise was overtaken by relief. 'I see. Good.' He glanced around them before asking, 'What about the... the business today? I haven't heard anything on the news. Did it happen?'

'It's done, that's all you need to know. What did you expect – a fanfare and a public announcement?'

'No, I assumed there would be some... outcry, I suppose. Did nobody notice?'

'If they did, it was kept very quiet. After all, we wouldn't want to panic the nasty kidnappers, would we? And before you ask, don't bother. She is not your concern.'

'As you wish. What about the other patients?'

'The prisoners, you mean.' Delombre allowed a brief moment of cynicism to show at the terminology. 'They were there for a reason, each one of them. That doesn't change and it certainly doesn't concern you, either. The only one who did is no more. So forget him. Forget *them*.'

Girovsky blinked, but forged on, his tone resentful. 'They were common criminals, weren't they? Deviants.' His mouth twisted. 'Why they were getting special treatment is beyond me.'

'It was hardly special. Or are you suggesting that a bullet for each of them would be the better option – and save the state a few francs into the bargain?' He tapped Girovsky on the chest, making him flinch. 'Now that *would* be messy, don't you think, shooting prisoners? If it caught on it could lead to all sorts of excesses. Although,' he chuckled without humour, 'I grant you, it might be much cheaper in the long run.' He chewed his lip. 'Come to think of it, you own an armaments company, don't you? God in Heaven, you'd even make money out of that. Now that's what I call clever.'

Girovsky said nothing, but his expression showed what he would like to do with this pushy government functionary who treated him with so little respect.

'Are we clear on everything else?' Delombre's eyes were touched with glints of colour, as if filled with an inner fire. Another shift had taken place, each man finding their position in the order of things, and remembering that, like it or not, they needed each other.

'Do what you have to.' Girovsky's voice was calm, flat, resigned. 'Tell Levignier that.'

Delombre lifted an eyebrow and leant forward slightly for emphasis. He said softly, 'We always do what we have to, Mr Girovsky. You should bear that in mind.'

# *Chapter Nine*

'I know this place.' Alix leant forward and stared through the window of Rocco's Citroën as they approached a ramshackle farmhouse and a collection of tumbledown buildings down a narrow single-track lane. They were just a few kilometres from Poissons, but the village could only be reached from here by a circuitous route. 'I was out here only a week ago.'

The place was owned by Thomas Portier, one of two brothers. His younger sibling, Hervé, owned the farm adjacent, just visible across the fields. A report had been filed about shots being fired. At first the brothers had claimed they had been sport shooting at targets in the back fields. But then Hervé had been admitted to hospital with gun pellets embedded in his shoulder, and the truth had slowly emerged.

'They've been squabbling over the division of land for years,' she explained. 'Their father left Thomas a bigger share because he's older, and it's been eating away at Hervé ever since. Claude said it's been going on for years. He's been out here more than once to keep them apart, and I came out last time – but that was only to make sure the government vet didn't get shot when he came to run a regular test on their animals for disease.'

'Well, they've escalated their argument up the scale from squabbling,' said Rocco. His mind was still half on the Clos du Lac affair, but this job had been dropped on his desk by Massin and he couldn't ignore it. 'Somehow we've got to put a stop to it before they kill each other – or anybody else. Any suggestions?' He pulled to a halt and cut the engine, then took out his service weapon and checked the magazine.

'Short of actually shooting them both, you mean?' Alix eyed the gun with raised eyebrows. 'A bit extreme, I'd have thought.'

He gave a grim smile. 'Never go into a situation where guns are involved without being prepared. If they're ready to use them on each other, they've already crossed one line; I wouldn't want to be next.'

Alix nodded and took out her own gun and checked it, releasing the magazine and reinserting it with easy familiarity before sliding the gun back into its holster. She nodded. 'Ready.'

They climbed out and walked across a rough gravel area to the house. Up close, it was clear that it was in need of more than just running repairs, with broken and missing tiles and peeling paint on the shutters and windows. The chimney was skewed precariously to one side as if waiting for the next strong wind to knock it down through the roof, and a collection of rubbish was scattered across the front of the property, completing an air of desperation and neglect. A line of barns and outhouses stood behind the house, along with an assortment of ancient farm equipment, a trailer made from an old lorry chassis and the customary large dung heap being picked over by a bunch of mildewed chickens.

On the house roof itself, a line of nervous pigeons stared down at the newcomers and shuffled along the ridge tiles like a badly rehearsed chorus line.

The door opened before they reached it and a large man with a grey beard and a belly stepped out, hostility in every bone. He was dressed in traditional blues and rubber boots, with white chest hairs sprouting from a grubby check shirt. Rocco judged him to be in his late sixties.

'What do you want?' he demanded, and stared at Alix. 'Come back to show off your uniform again, have you?' He sneered at Rocco. 'Who's your boyfriend?'

Rocco stepped forward and said, 'My name is Rocco. Inspector of police. You are Thomas Portier?'

'Yes. So what?'

'Is your brother around?'

'Not on this property, he isn't.' Portier gave a lopsided grin. 'Haven't you heard – we don't really get on.'

'So I gather. In fact, you don't get on so much, you shot him.'

'Rubbish.' Thomas waved a work-calloused hand. 'It was an accident, like I already told your lot. He happened to be standing on the edge of my land when I shot at a polecat. Serves him right. Anyway, he retracted the charge against me this morning, so there's no case.' He stepped back and began to close the door, but Rocco jammed his foot in the way.

'Where is he now?'

Portier let the door open fully. 'I don't know. Who cares? He's probably over at his dump of a house on the other side of the field, watching us through field glasses and hoping you've come to re-arrest me.' He jerked his head sideways, and Rocco looked to where the upper windows of a house showed just above a dip in the ground.

'Would he come here if we asked him?'

'I doubt it.' Thomas turned and reached round the edge of the door. When he drew his arm back, he was holding a shotgun. He had a glitter of something malicious in his eyes. 'I hope he does – then I'll give him another taste of this. Now, if you don't mind, I've got work to do, so piss off – and take the little girlie with you.' He snapped the barrels shut with a loud click.

Rocco sighed. This one could run and run until somebody ended up dead. Probably somebody like Alix or Claude, called out to do their duty and running into a long-standing bitter feud between two men who would never give way.

'I'm sorry to hear you say that.' He took out his own gun and pointed it down at the ground, then pulled the trigger twice in quick succession. The reports were shockingly loud and scared up the clutch of pigeons on the roof in a rush of flapping hysteria and falling plumage.

Thomas stared, wide-eyed, and swallowed. But the gun barrels dropped. 'Are you crazy?'

'Far from it. I know at least three cops who would have already shot you dead for pulling that trick.' Rocco stepped forward took the shotgun from him, and handed it to Alix. 'Consider it a lesson for the future. Now, let's wait for your brother to get here, shall we? Something tells me he won't be long.'

Sure enough, moments later, they heard the whine of a 2CV engine, and a small grey car came barrelling across the open fields towards the farmhouse, trailing a spiralling cloud of dust and grass fragments and veering from side to side.

Rocco nodded for Alix to walk out and show her uniform. He knew Hervé was nursing buckshot wounds, but he didn't want to take the chance on the man being as quick-tempered as his brother, and to come out of his vehicle shooting.

The car stopped and a younger, carbon copy of Thomas climbed out and walked urgently across the yard, leaving two dark-brown spaniels jumping up and down in the back. He was dressed in boots and rough corduroy pants, with a greasy peaked cap on his head and a leather jacket. One arm was held tight in a sling.

Rocco was relieved to see that his other hand was empty.

'What the hell's going on?' the newcomer yelled. 'Have you shot my idiot brother?' He gave a bark of laughter when he saw Thomas still standing, and nodded slowly when he spotted the gun in Alix's hand. 'That explains it. He pulled that on you, didn't he? He thinks he lives in the Wild West.' He stopped alongside Alix and shook his head. 'So what brings you out here, officers? I dropped the charges, although I'm beginning to wish I hadn't, now.'

'You stole my cow!' Thomas shouted, his face going deep red and revealing the extent of the passions between the two men simmering not far beneath the surface.

'Why would I do that? You think I want your disease-ridden bags of bones?'

'Because you're greedy and always have been. You resent everything about me and you're a thief into the bargain!'

Rocco stooped and picked up the two shell casings from his gun and dropped them in his pocket. Then he checked the magazine, making a series of loud clicks in the silence and deliberately ignoring the two men. They watched him, their argument momentarily suspended.

He put the gun away. 'This has got to stop. I've got two murders to investigate, and a backlog of other cases, so I'd appreciate it if you two would sort out your differences without resorting to open warfare.' He looked at Hervé. 'Did you steal his cow?'

'No! He's lying, as usual. Go count them if you like.' He pointed at his bandaged arm and added quickly, 'He shot me for no good reason!'

'You were on my land, that's reason enough for me,' Thomas retorted, but some of the wind had gone out of him.

Rocco said to Hervé, 'How many?'

'What?'

'How many animals have you got, as a matter of interest?'

'He's got twenty-six,' muttered Thomas, 'because I went over and counted them last night while he was lying in hospital playing the wounded soldier. He only had twenty-five before. Go on, ask him.' He glared at Hervé. 'Or are you claiming a case of divine intervention made your herd grow by one overnight?'

Hervé pulled a face. 'I've always had twenty-six and you know it.'

'Really?' It was Alix, stepping forward to join in the conversation. 'Are you sure about that, sir?'

'Huh?' Hervé looked puzzled. 'What do you mean?'

'I came up here and visited both farms about a week ago with the government vet – to make sure he was safe. I had nothing else to do, so I helped him fill out some forms while he did his tests.'

'Well, good for you. So what?'

Hervé, Rocco noted, was suddenly looking sullen, and rubbing his injured shoulder.

'I distinctly recall you having twenty-five heads, and your brother having thirty-six. You and I counted yours together and you signed the form to confirm it.'

'So I made a mistake. What are you going to do, lock me up for having a lousy memory?' He gave a snort, but it lacked conviction.

'See?' Thomas crowed, pointing at him in triumph. 'I knew it – he was lying! I want my cow back, officers!'

Rocco raised a hand to shut them both up. 'Seems to me we have something of a trade-off.'

Both men looked at him. 'What?' muttered Thomas.

'Thomas can be charged with using a firearm to intimidate two officers performing their duty, and Hervé can face a charge of cattle rustling.'

'There's no such charge,' Hervé blustered. 'That's cowboy stuff from films.'

'Yes, there is. It's under an old land and properties act, I grant you, but it's still enforceable and carries a prison sentence. Quite a stiff one.'

Hervé looked stunned and his mouth snapped shut like a trap.

'The gun charge,' Rocco continued, 'is definitely current and also carries a prison term. Would you like me to arrange a shared cell? Or I can drop both charges on your personal assurances that you will stop arguing… and Officer Poulon and I can get on with finding out who murdered two people just over the hill from here.'

'You've got it.' Thomas was the first to speak. 'I promise.'

Hervé nodded. 'Yes. Me, too.' He spat on the ground. 'Rustling. I can't believe it.'

'Shake hands on it,' said Rocco.

'Mother of God, do we have to?' Hervé began, then saw the look on Rocco's face. He stepped over and the two brothers clasped hands.

'So who killed who, then?' said Thomas, scratching his belly. 'I didn't hear anything about a murder.'

'Probably the same person who drove down the lane and dumped a piece of shit moped on my land,' Hervé murmured. 'Mind you, what kind of murderer rides a moped, eh? Not exactly Jacques Mesrine's style, that's for sure.' He grinned at his brother and got a wink in reply at mention of the notorious gangster.

Rocco stared at them. It was as if the argument and shooting and the misappropriation of a cow had never taken place. He said to Hervé, 'A moped. When was this?'

'Sometime last night. I heard a motor, figured it was somebody taking a shortcut up the lane. Some still do, though not often. Never thought anything more until I got up this morning and took a walk across the field. The machine was lying in the ditch just inside the fence. I wouldn't have seen it if it hadn't been for one of the dogs. Whoever left it there would have had quite a walk, though, if they were heading for the road to Amiens.'

'Have you moved it?'

'No. I was planning on going back when I had time. Why?'

'Because I need to inspect it. It might have been used in the crime.' After getting directions across the fields, Rocco repeated his warning about prison sentences and left the two men standing together in the yard.

'Hey,' yelled Thomas. 'What about my gun?'

'You'll get it back in a few days,' Alix replied, stowing it in the boot. 'They're like kids,' she muttered, as they got back in the car. 'Do you think it will last?'

'I don't know. Probably not. Just be careful if you're ever called back out here. And don't forget your gun.'

'Right. Is that correct, about the rustling charge? It's on the books?'

'No idea. We never had much call to worry about it up in Clichy.'

# Chapter Ten

The moped was lying upside down in a ditch, just as Hervé had described. Rocco squatted down beside it and noted the worn tyres and scarred paintwork of the frame and mudguards. It had long ago experienced its first flush of newness, yet in this area even old machines like this had a value. Then he noticed the panniers, almost masked by an overgrowth of grass and weeds at the bottom of the ditch. He slid down further and hauled at the wheels until he could wrestle it up the short bank and lay it down on the grass for a closer inspection.

Alix undid the straps on the uppermost pannier and took out a net with a folding handle and a fishing rod composed of several short pieces with interlocking joints. Last came a box with dried bait on one side and a selection of hooks, weights and floats on the other.

'Looks like somebody had a bad day's fishing,' she suggested.

'If he did,' Rocco replied, 'it would have ended up in the lake or river, not out here.' He lifted the moped so that Alix could get at the other pannier, which revealed a flask but nothing else.

Alix used her handkerchief to lift it out, then opened the top and sniffed at the contents. 'Coffee, with something else. Could be brandy. It's still warm.'

Rocco lowered the moped and stood back. He didn't know about the bike, but why on earth would someone dump a perfectly good set of fishing equipment – especially in an area renowned for its fishing enthusiasts?

He walked over to the entrance to the field and climbed the gate, jumping down on the other side. 'Where does this lead?' he asked Alix. He'd never had cause to come here, and had only a vague idea of their location on the map.

Alix pointed to the right. 'Poissons that way, about four kilometres, and a road to Amiens the other, about three. This lane is hardly used ever since the Clos du Lac pretty much stopped people going down it, other than a few older locals and farmers with fields further along.'

'So somebody could have come from the Clos on the moped, and met up here with a waiting car?'

She nodded and joined him on the lane. Rocco walked fifty metres one way, towards Poissons, scanning the verge. The grass was long, but untouched, and he soon gave up. It was evident that nothing had stopped here in a long time.

'Here's something.' Alix was standing just a few metres beyond the gate, where the verge was wider, beneath the shade of a crab-apple tree. Rocco walked back and stood alongside her.

Twin tyre tracks showed clearly in the grass, with the stems flattened or bent, and at one point there was a deep rut where a patch of softer ground had given way beneath the vehicle's weight. Rocco felt the soil underneath with his fingertips. There was a definite tyre-tread pattern here, and he guessed it was from a car or small van rather than a truck. Whether the details would be enough for Dr Rizzotti to make anything of, he wasn't sure. But it was a start. Somebody had been here just before or just after a murder had been committed. And that spelt opportunity. All he had to do now was find motive and who might have benefitted.

He stood up and walked across the road, trying to read the scene from a distance. If the driver had been careful, he could have driven down from the direction of the road leading to Amiens and left his car here where it wouldn't have been noticed, then used the moped, perhaps slung in the back of a van, to travel the short distance to the Clos du Lac. After completion of his task, he could have ridden the moped back here, disposed of it in the ditch, then driven calmly away, with nobody any the wiser other than hearing engine noises in the night.

# Chapter Eleven

The Clos du Lac looked unnaturally quiet when they drew to a stop in the car park; unnatural in the way that deserted buildings have no warmth, no sense of human occupation, no vibrancy. Even the birds had fallen silent. There was no sign of Levignier or his men, and the pool house was closed, with a chain and padlock through the double handles barring the way inside.

With a sense of foreboding, Rocco led the way through the main entrance. The air was cool inside, the sounds of their footsteps echoing off the tiled floor. He looked round. No sign of a bell to signal their arrival, so he walked along the corridor towards the kitchen where he'd first seen nurse Dion.

A woman in an apron was sitting at the table, drinking coffee. A mop and bucket stood nearby. The woman looked up and brushed at her cheek. She was plump and rosy-cheeked, with greying hair, and looked faintly lost.

'Can I help you?'

'I'd like to see nurse Dion or Director Drucker, please,' Rocco said politely. 'Tell them it's Inspector Rocco.'

The woman put down her coffee cup and stood up. 'Sorry – I wish I could. But there's nobody here.' Rocco frowned. 'Where are they?'

'If I knew that, I'd tell you.' She waved a hand around. 'I got here fifteen minutes ago, ready to put dinner on for the evening as usual, and do a bit of cleaning. But the place was empty. Everyone's gone. Looks like I'm out of a job.'

'What about the patients?'

She sat down again with a sigh, as if her legs had failed her. 'Them, too. All gone. Do you believe in flying saucers and… what do they call it – alien abduction? I never did, until now.'

Rocco looked at Alix. 'Wait here. I'll be back.' He left the kitchen and raced up the stairs, following the corridor through to the back and checking rooms as he went. Some showed signs of recent occupancy, with bedclothes thrown back and wardrobe doors flung open. Other rooms were stripped bare and cold, evidently unused. Everywhere else had an air of hasty evacuation.

He found an office. It looked bare of anything helpful; a desk, two comfortable visitors' chairs, two filing cabinets and a bookcase. But no paperwork of any kind.

He ran back downstairs and checked the ground floor rooms. A library, a large lounge area, a games room with a pool table and two smaller rooms he guessed were reading areas, both looking out to the rear of the building.

All empty.

He turned and went back to the kitchen. The woman and Alix were sitting in silence.

'Do you have telephone numbers for Dion or Director Drucker?' he asked.

The woman pursed her lips. 'Never needed them,' she replied. 'Someone's always here normally. Except today. I just cook and clean. What's been going on – and why's the pool chained up?'

'There's a problem with the water.' Rocco had a thought. 'How did you get here?'

'My husband dropped me off, same as always. I live in Fonzet. I'd come on my bike, but my back's playing up. What kind of problem?'

'A patient drowned in it. If you can leave your name and address with *Gardienne* Poulon, we'll be in touch.' He smiled at her look of concern. 'I'm sorry this has happened, but it's a surprise to us, too.'

He walked out of the building to his car, took a tyre iron out of the boot and went over to the pool house. The chain was strong but the door handles weren't. One of them ripped out of the wood and he was inside.

There was no sign of the body.

He walked around the pool area, but found nothing to show what had happened here, save a large wet patch on the tiles where they had hauled out the body. Whatever heating was in the place had not yet dried the area completely.

'They worked fast,' Alix murmured, coming to stand alongside him. She was eyeing the length of chain and the milk churn lying on the bottom of the pool. The steel wire still hung in the water, but it had now been moved closer to the edge, no doubt once the chain had been unfastened. 'The cook's gone. She called her husband and he's going to pick her up. Who did this?'

'Levignier,' said Rocco. He knew instinctively that the body was gone for good, spirited away God and the ISD alone knew where. 'He employs some very resourceful people.'

—

As they walked back towards the main building, a small Renault drew up in the car park. Nurse Dion climbed out and stood watching them. She was rubbing her eyes and looked very pale. Rocco guessed she must have heard about Paulus.

'Sorry, Inspector,' she said, walking over to join them. Her eyes were red-rimmed and she was clutching a white handkerchief. 'Have you been waiting long?' Her voice sounded rubbed raw with emotion. 'Director Drucker told me to take the afternoon off, but… I need something to do.' She looked towards the main building, then at the empty car park, and frowned. 'What's going on? Where is everybody?'

'That's what we'd like to know. When did Drucker tell you to take off?'

'This morning, just before noon. What about the patients?'

'All gone.'

Her jaw dropped. She gestured towards the road. 'I saw a woman walking away. Was that Mrs Sevrier, the dinner cook?'

'Yes,' Alix said. 'She didn't know anything, either.'

'But I don't understand. Where would they all go?'

'That's what I'd like to know,' Rocco said carefully. 'But first of all, I'm sorry about Mr Paulus. We're hoping to find out what happened to him. Can we talk somewhere?'

'Of course.' She turned and led them through the entrance and into a darkened side room lined with bookshelves. She closed the door and pulled back the curtains, flooding the room with light.

'Those other men wouldn't tell me what happened,' she said, looking between them. 'You'll tell me, won't you?'

'I'm sorry,' Rocco said carefully, and explained what he and Claude had discovered at the house outside Berlay, keeping strictly to the facts.

She said nothing for a few moments, merely nodding slightly as if absorbing the news and consigning it to a safe place. Her expression was unreadable. Then she sat down heavily on a sofa, her expression collapsing into one of utter confusion and loss.

'Why didn't they say?' she whispered. 'Levignier and the other two – they were with Director Drucker all morning. I heard them mention André's name but… they stopped talking when they saw me.' She looked at Rocco. 'All they said was that he was dead and that it should not concern me. Why would they say such a thing?'

'Did Drucker know of your friendship?' Alix asked, sitting next to her.

Dion bunched her handkerchief and wiped her eyes, which were brimming over. 'There's no need to be quite so diplomatic,' she whispered. She tried hard to smile, but it didn't quite come off. 'We were having a relationship, André and I. And yes, Drucker knew. It's impossible to keep any secrets in this place.' She laughed bitterly. 'Ironic, when you think about it. The whole place is built on secrets of one sort or another.'

Stefan had said much the same thing. '*Lots of secrets in this place…*'

Rocco waited to see if she would enlarge further. There was a moment in most investigations when a tipping point was reached that could change the entire nature of an enquiry; it could be at any time in the proceedings, with no warning. But it usually hinged on a simple revelation, a careless or unexpected word, a change of attitude. Rocco knew that point had been reached. Dion was ready to talk.

'We still don't know why he was killed, or who is responsible,' he said calmly. 'But I believe it is connected with the death of the man in the pool.'

'Why do you think that?'

'Well, most killings usually have a motive driving them. Anger, fear, greed, hate... even love, occasionally. But nobody in this area knew him well enough; like me, he was brought in from outside.'

Alix said, 'Had he made any acquaintances here – people he might have mixed with outside of work?'

'No. He liked to keep to himself... when we weren't together, anyway. He was a very private man. Very conscientious, too.' She looked at Rocco. 'That's why I don't understand why he would have disappeared like that. He never believed in taking time off when he was on duty. Something must have happened to make him leave his post.'

'Something did. Or someone.'

# Chapter Twelve

She stared at him. 'You're suggesting he left deliberately?' Her face flushed quickly and she looked alarmed at the idea.

'No. I'm not. But he was a trained security man, wasn't he?'

'How do you know that?'

'I was in the army in a previous life. And now I'm a cop. I know the type.'

'I see. Well, he was a naval policeman until he suffered a back injury in training. He was transferred to other duties. Still security but… onshore.'

'Other duties?'

'I can't talk about that. You'll have to take my word for it.'

'So he was still serving?'

'Yes.'

'And you?'

A brief hesitation, then, 'Yes. Me, too.'

'You were engaged here *because* you were in the military?'

'Yes. Nobody told us why – only that it was important work.' She gave a lift of her shoulders. 'I was thinking of going into civilian nursing, anyway. It seemed a good move to make, for the experience.'

'What about André?'

'He arrived one day not long after one of the patients went missing. You've heard of closing the door after the horse has gone? Well, that's what it was.'

Rocco nodded. Standard military practice the world over. Most armies ran training courses in it – or should have. 'Was he armed?'

'Yes. He was sent here to improve security. When a couple of new patients were checked in and they couldn't get a reliable guard, he was asked to stay on.' Her eyes misted up, and Rocco guessed that it probably hadn't been a hard decision for Paulus to make. She was an attractive woman to be around. 'Best time I ever had, meeting him.' She wiped angrily at her face and looked at the ceiling.

There was a short silence, and Rocco wondered at the kind of work that could get a military-trained guard killed and frighten his lover into silence. What made this place so important that the Internal Security Directorate should assign a military cop to guard the doors?

Was it to keep people out... or to keep them in?

'You're saying that André was conscientious, never cut his duties?'

'No, he never did.' She lifted her chin. 'I know what you're thinking – and I don't blame you. But we never compromised our work and he wouldn't have walked away willingly. He wasn't like that.'

'When was the last time you saw him?'

'Some time after two this morning – ten past or so.'

'You sound fairly sure. Was he here in the building?'

This time the blush was nothing to do with anger. She looked away and said, 'He was with me.'

'Upstairs?'

'Yes. I... I fell asleep... and he went off to do his rounds.' So, they'd been having a little private time when everything was quiet. Rocco couldn't fault that. For every soldier the world over, the credo was the same: when things were quiet and under control, you catnapped, ate or relaxed, because one thing was certain – it never stayed that way for long.

'Did he know anything about the patients... about Ardois, for instance?'

'You know the name? Who told you that? It's cla—' She stopped speaking, eyes wide.

'Classified? Is that what you were going to say?'

'No.'

'I think you were. You should know that now I have a name, I can start asking questions. You might as well tell me, save us both a lot of time.'

'Really? Will that help André? Will it bring him back?'

'No. I'm afraid it won't do that. But if I can find out why he was taken away and killed, why Ardois was murdered, it will help shift any element of blame away from André. Why was Ardois here?'

A few seconds went by, then she gave a small sigh. 'André didn't know anything about him, only that he wasn't really ill. Anybody could see that.'

'So why was he here?'

'I have no idea. All I do know is Ardois wasn't his real name. It was a file name, to be used while he was a resident here. Everybody has one; it comes with them. When they move on the file name is destroyed and they're given a fresh one. I've no idea why – something to do with confidentiality, I suppose.'

'Does that happen a lot?'

'Over the past year, probably four times.'

Four patients moved in and out of a small government-controlled facility, all with names that weren't their own.

It sounded improbable, but Rocco had heard of stranger things.

'Do you know his real name?'

'No. They don't tell us. But I heard Drucker mention it once when he was on the phone.' She frowned, trying to remember it. 'Sorry – it's gone. If it comes back I'll let you know. Other than that, all I have is their current medical regime and background notes in case of emergencies.'

'They're all on a regime?' Alix asked.

She gave a wry smile. 'If you can call it that. They're on various medications, some stronger than others. Mostly it's sedatives, to keep them calm.'

'To shut them up, you mean? Keep them under control?'

'Yes. Once they're down, they don't move.'

Not quite the case with Stefan, Rocco thought, and asked her about him.

She pulled a face. 'Stefan's different.'

'How?'

'He's highly manipulative, very clever and loves to play games. He pretends to swallow his pills, but doesn't always do it. Then he wanders the corridors at night, poking around. But he's harmless.' She looked at Rocco and explained, 'I know a bit of his history. He's a genuine case. He had a series of nervous breakdowns and his family used their influence to get him in here and away from outside pressures. His family has connections. He's not like the others.'

'Did he tell you that?' In Rocco's experience, serial manipulators never dropped the habit. Like habitual criminals, it was in their blood. Stefan had even been able to work his magic on him for a short while.

'Yes.' She looked doubtful. 'I shouldn't have believed him, should I?'

Alix glanced at Rocco and he nodded. There was really only one main question to ask.

'You said he's not like the others,' she said, and placed a gentle hand on Dion's. 'How are they different? The dead man, for example. It won't go any further, I promise.'

Dion hesitated, then shook her head angrily. A teardrop flew from one cheek and she brushed a hand down her face, smearing her make-up. 'It doesn't matter now, does it? They've gone. But André didn't kill him. You have to believe me. He just wouldn't.'

'We believe you,' Rocco said. He doubted a military man like Paulus would have chosen anything so elaborate; if soldiers decided to kill, it was usually short, sharp and brutal. He changed tack to lower the tempo. 'Let's go back to last night. Did you see or hear anything?'

'Like what?'

'Cars going by… voices… a knock at the door?'

'No. It's always so quiet here. We never hear anything.'

'What about the patients? Have they said anything about last night?'

'Not to me. Stefan said he'd talked to a nice man, though. I thought he was imagining things. He does that a lot. Was it you?'

'Yes.' He wondered whether Drucker was going to turn up and spoil things, and went back to his original question. 'So, who were the other patients?'

Dion stood up. 'I'll show you.' She walked out of the room and they followed.

She led them to the office Rocco had seen before. 'Drucker keeps everything locked away. He's obsessive about secrecy and doesn't trust anyone.' She reached under the desk and took out a key. 'He doesn't know I found this, though.' She went over to one of the filing cabinets and unlocked it, and swept open the top drawer.

It was empty.

'Looks like someone got there already,' observed Rocco.

'I don't understand.' Dion looked stunned. 'It was full only yesterday. All the patient records were in there, arranged alphabetically. The staff files, too – everything.' She checked the lower drawers but they were also empty. Then she used the key to open the other cabinet. The same. 'Why would they do that?'

'It's what they do.' He took a turn around the room. It was standard security behaviour if a place became compromised: cleanse the scene thoroughly and leave nothing behind. But why here? What were they hiding?

'What do we do now?' said Alix.

'We keep looking,' he said quietly, and picked up the telephone. He rang the office in Amiens and got through to René Desmoulins. 'Can you get away?' he asked him. Desmoulins relished getting involved in investigations with Rocco, and had a usefully rebellious streak when it came to dodging authority and cutting corners.

'Just tell me where and when.'

'Now. But quietly.' Rocco gave him directions and cut the connection, then handed the handset to Alix. 'Can you get Claude here?'

'Of course.' She looked at him knowingly. 'You're planning something.'

'We're going to search this place,' he told her, 'starting with the patients' rooms and working our way down. Desmoulins can help when he gets here, and Claude can do the outside.' He looked at Dion. 'You probably shouldn't be here for this. But thanks for your help.'

She shrugged. 'I've got nothing else to do until I contact my base for instructions. Is what you're going to do legal?'

'I don't have the authority to do it, if that's what you mean.'

'Fine. Count me in.' She gave a half smile, reached into her jacket pocket and took out a packet of cigarettes. 'I'm not normally allowed to smoke on the premises,' she said, and lit up, then blew out a mouthful of smoke with relish. 'Drucker would have me transferred on the spot if he knew. But who's going to stop me now?' She gestured towards the door. 'I'll show you where everything is. And if we're going to break the law together, Lucas, my name's Inès.'

# Chapter Thirteen

It took them two hours to comprehensively search the entire house, even with Desmoulins helping. And Rocco knew that even in this time, they were probably only scratching the surface. The building was a rabbit warren of rooms and corridors, although with Inès's help they were able to isolate or disregard a number of places where access had been denied to patients. But it was still a long job, moving furniture and checking a number of what could have been obvious places of concealment. Rocco had considered getting in more manpower, but figured they would only get in the way.

'What are we looking for?' asked Desmoulins, as they were checking the layout of rooms on a fire escape panel in the office and using it to mark the areas covered. The detective had arrived not long after Rocco's call and, with his powerful build and energetic attitude, looked ready to tear the building apart with his bare hands.

'Anything hidden,' said Rocco. 'The people here were kept locked in or sedated. To all intents and purposes they were prisoners. And prisoners hide things.'

'Like what?'

'Things they value; items they might normally ignore, but which become trophies. It's like a game, where scoring a point over the authorities becomes part of their life. After all, what else do they have to do?' He glanced at Inès, who looked surprised by the comment, but nodded.

'That's correct,' she said. 'Stefan was the worst, but they all did it to one degree or another. Food, fruit, books, items of cutlery, documents – even personal things left lying around by the staff. They never intended to keep them, but having them was a sort of victory. We'd find them, take them back… and they'd take something else.'

'What did Stefan hide?'

'Anything and everything. The man was like a big child – a jackdaw. He had his fingers into everything, especially at night. If we didn't lock a room, he saw it as his to explore. I was forever retrieving stuff that didn't belong to him.' She sighed. 'It was quite sad, really. Most of them probably wanted some attention. It was their way of getting it.'

'Documents.'

She looked at him. 'I'm sorry?'

He tried to recall Stefan's exact words. 'I met Stefan in the pool house. He said something like, "*There are lots of secrets here… but I've got a few of them.*" It was an odd thing to say, not as if it was just food or cutlery he'd picked up. I think he meant papers. Documents.'

Inès frowned. 'But the only documents here were kept in the office, which was always locked. Drucker was paranoid about it.'

'Could you swear to that – twenty-four hours a day?'

She hesitated, then shook her head. 'No. I suppose not.'

'Fine. Then that's what we're looking for.'

'That narrows it down, at least,' Alix suggested. 'We concentrate on Stefan's room.'

'I wish it was that easy.' Rocco looked at Inès again.

She pulled a face in agreement. 'He loved hiding stuff away from his room,' she said. 'That way he could claim it wasn't him, and he could watch while we took the place apart whenever something went missing. He enjoyed the game. As I said, he was like a big child.'

—

Claude wandered in after doing a thorough search of the grounds, to find Rocco, Desmoulins, Alix and Inès taking a break.

'You need to see this,' he said, nodding behind him. 'I found a door open at the back of the pool house and footprints leading away across the garden towards the lane.'

Inès looked up. 'That can't be right; that door's never unlocked.'

'Well, it is now.'

Rocco stood and followed Claude outside, leaving the others to continue the search. Daylight was beginning to fade and the countryside around the sanitarium was sinking into the soft folds of evening. The ground at the back of the pool house fell away down a sloping garden to a hedge overlooking the lane. Beyond that, a field ran for some two hundred metres down to a large lake, gleaming in the last of the light. It was surrounded on the far side by tall poplars, in a pattern too regular to be accidental, and he guessed it had been the wealthy owner, wanting the lake to be framed for the delight of friends and family.

'The canal runs by just before you get to the lake,' Claude told him. 'It's in a fold in the ground, so you can't quite make it out from here.' He turned to his right and pointed at the ground, where a faint line could be seen through the grass. 'Somebody walked across here. I thought at first that it could have been a member of staff or the guard, Paulus. But the trail only goes one way, across to a hedgerow on the far side. I wouldn't have seen it in direct sunlight, but the falling light helps show it up. Come this way.' He set off on a parallel line with the trail and with one hand pointing it out as he walked. They were now on a parallel course with the lane.

He was right, Rocco realised; in normal sunlight this wouldn't have been noticeable. They arrived at the hedgerow, a gnarled, ancient tangle of briar and rose-wood. Claude turned down the slope for a couple of paces, then stepped into the hedge where a natural gap had occurred.

'See this?' He pointed at a thick piece of rosewood where a pale gash showed against the darker coloration. 'And here.' Another gash. Both cuts had separated a main stem of the hedge, leaving just enough space for someone to squeeze through the tangled growth.

Claude lifted his arms and pushed through, and Rocco followed. They were in an open field of overgrown, lush grass, and a dark line showed the continued trail leading down the slope towards a fence at the bottom.

'He headed for the lane down there,' said Claude. 'It runs along just the other side of that fence. Come on.'

They followed the trail, which ended at a wire fence, and a deep, seemingly man-made pit in the ground over-looking the lane.

'An old German gun emplacement,' Claude explained. 'There were several on the roads around here, meant to cut off the retreat to the coast.' He skirted the pit and hopped over the fence, then skidded down the bank to the lane and turned away from the house. A few minutes later, he stopped and pointed at an ancient corrugated metal structure at the side of the road. It was a small barn, rusted and full of holes, the thin metal of the walls beginning to flake away.

Rocco followed Claude inside. The air was musty and cold, and the place probably hadn't been used for many years. Not by farmers, anyway. A couple of bright-yellow sweet wrappers were on the ground by the door, alongside some old cigarette butts. The wrappers were dried out and brittle. Kids, he figured.

The floor was a compounded layer of ancient straw, dried grass and cow droppings. Against one wall was a collection of old metal farm implements, among which he identified a feeding trough, bent and battered out of shape. Elsewhere, weeds, brambles and nettles had pushed their way through the walls and sprouted to almost shoulder height, untroubled by any competition for space.

'See here?' Claude knelt just inside the entrance, and pointed at a small patch of dirt, where the imprint of a tyre had been left in the surface.

'A motorbike?' said Rocco.

'Small one, maybe. More likely a moped.' He reached down and touched a dark spot. 'Oil.'

'How old?' Rocco could follow basic trails, but Claude was much better at this kind of thing.

'We'll soon see.' Claude bent and blew gently at the dirt. After a moment, some of the looser dust shifted, filling in some of the lighter tread marks. He looked up. 'If these imprints were more than a couple of days old, they'd have filled in by now. I'd say last night.'

Rocco stood back and surveyed the barn. 'But a moped?' He tried to picture a professional hitman using such a lowly form of transport. It didn't quite fit. Yet he'd once arrested a gang killer in Paris who had used a bicycle for the simple reason that it didn't stand out. Until he was caught, he was absolutely right: who ever took notice of a man on a bike?

'Didn't you say you were following a poacher before you heard the scream?'

Claude nodded. 'I was, but he was on foot, following the line of the canal. He wouldn't have come this way. And there's only one set of tracks. If this was a regular poacher's hideout, he'd have left more traces.'

Rocco went back outside and looked both ways along the lane. If this had been the killer, he would not have wanted to run the risk of going back past the house. 'Where does this lead to?'

Claude puffed out his cheeks. 'Just open fields. It's a while since I've been up there. It runs out of proper road after a couple of kilometres and becomes a track. Old Bertrand owns most of the land up there, but he gets to it from the other end.'

'So it's not a dead end?'

'Not really. The track loops through the fields and meets up with another road. It wouldn't be quick, but a moped could make it easily enough.'

'But he'd be unlikely to meet anyone coming the other way?'

'Not a soul.'

'And once he was on that road?'

'You name it. Locally, Amiens, Bapaume – anywhere north. Double back and he'd eventually hit the road to Paris.'

'That's what I was afraid of.'

# Chapter Fourteen

The woman lifted her head. She needed water. She had been lying motionless for what now seemed a lifetime, too scared to move, unable to see. And hearing anything above the drumming noise of the van in motion was impossible. Even the noise of other traffic, just metres away, might as well have been on another planet, it meant as little to her. The constant juddering motion and the smell of exhaust fumes filtering through the hood over her head had made her nauseous at first, but she had fought hard to overcome it.

Now the van had stopped moving and the man in the leather jacket had climbed out. There was silence at first after the door slammed shut, then she heard voices nearby and a grunt of laughter. Beyond that, however, there was nothing. Wherever they had stopped was devoid of the normal life sounds such as cars, children, machinery – even birdsong.

She tried to work up some spittle by holding her mouth open, but nothing came. Sucking her teeth merely highlighted just how dry and thirsty she was. So she rolled onto her back and lifted both feet in the air, then brought her heels down as hard as she could. Maybe that would bring the man on the run.

But the noise was muffled by the mattress. She shimmied down by dragging herself along with her heels, aware that her skirt was being hiked up around her thighs, but she was beyond caring. She was close to choking; if she didn't get some moisture in her throat soon, she was going to suffocate.

She stretched out her legs and heard the rasp of leather on the metal floor. At last. With that she lifted her feet again and slammed them down hard. It made a satisfying booming sound. She did it again and heard an exclamation from outside. Quickly she moved back to her original position before the man came in and saw her.

The van rocked and a door opened, letting in a gust of cooler air. She heard breathing nearby, and a faint squeak of leather as the man moved. She could smell cigarette smoke on him, overlaid with male sweat and unwashed clothing.

'I need some water,' she said, keeping her voice under control. 'Please – I'm choking in here.'

The man didn't reply, but she heard him moving around close by, then the clink of a spring stopper being loosened on a bottle.

'Sit up,' he told her. 'But don't try anything silly or I'll slap you.'

'No. I promise.' She felt herself shrink. It was the first distinct threat that he'd made.

She felt his hand beneath her shoulder, then she was sitting upright and her back began aching at the unaccustomed position. She couldn't feel where her skirt was positioned, and hoped her legs weren't bare.

'I'm going to loosen the hood,' he said, 'to put the bottle underneath. But I'm not taking it off. You'll have to drink as best you can.'

'Please,' she said softly. 'Take it off, just for a moment. I need to see daylight.'

There was a short silence, then he said, 'Fine. Don't drink. Your choice.'

'No, wait!' Panic took hold of her. The thought of not drinking was horrifying. Her throat was as dry as paper, and scratchy from having to breathe forcibly under the hood. If it closed up altogether... she didn't want to even think about it. 'Please.'

She felt the hood loosened, and a subdued flood of light came in and made her wince. Then she felt a rough hand touch her throat and the cool touch of glass against her chin. Almost sobbing with relief, she waited patiently while the man lifted the bottle and a rush of water filled her mouth. She choked instantly, and coughed, half the water falling across her chest and soaking the inside of the hood. But it was like the best nectar in the world, even though it had a slightly metallic taste.

'More,' she gasped.

'Slowly,' the man said. 'Ready?'

She nodded with almost shameful gratitude, and the man repeated the process, carefully dribbling water into her mouth until she turned her head aside and coughed. As she did so, she caught a glimpse of a western-style boot. It looked new, with burnished, stitched leather and a silver tooled point on the toe. 'Thank you,' she murmured. 'Thank you.'

He helped her lie down again and made sure the hood was tight, then moved away. 'Remain still,' he told her, 'and you'll have food later. But don't bother trying that trick again to attract attention. Where we are, nobody but God can hear you.'

Then he was gone and the door slammed shut behind him, leaving her alone once more with her thoughts and fears.

Several kilometres away, a team of undercover police officers was quietly scouring the area around Avenue de Friedland and the *Salon Elizabeth*, trying to pick up a trace of how a woman could disappear off a main Paris thoroughfare so easily without anyone noticing. They were under strict orders not to disclose who they were looking for; the instruction having come from high in government circles. It had been judged best not to alert the press in order to avoid panicking the kidnappers – if indeed the woman had been taken against her will.

'Let's not fool ourselves,' Divisional Inspector Leon Drueault, given overall charge of the task, had told his three hand-picked men, 'this isn't going to end well.' He had wide experience of such crimes and knew that women of certain years did not simply disappear from a comfortable life of luxury imagined by many but enjoyed by few, and run off into the hills with a wandering shepherd or their favourite plumber. And this woman had even less reason to go anywhere, for she was loved by her husband above all things. Well, a cynic might argue with that, but if press publicity was to be believed, she certainly seemed to come higher on his list of values than his many businesses, which took up most of his waking life.

Until now.

'Her husband,' Drueault had continued, 'could reach for a phone and have the president himself join a search team if he so wishes. He's that important. He could take on his own private army – and probably already has – to track her down if he thinks we're not doing enough. But we've managed to hold him back by convincing him that rash action will only get her killed. So don't screw this up and don't get noticed. Get out there and find what happened, when and how. Somebody must have seen something. Anything.'

'So what's wrong with using the press this time?' asked Captain Paul Detric, the team leader. He had worked on many such cases and knew that there had been times when a press campaign had resulted in the early release of a kidnap victim. He was also aware that it had failed on more than one occasion, with tragic results.

'This is not like other cases,' Drueault had replied calmly. 'If someone's taken this particular woman, it's not simply for money. They could have done that at any time. She uses Avenue de Friedland like you and I use the *Métro*.'

'So why now?' asked Sebastien, one of the other men. 'It might help us to know.'

It was a fair question. But not one Drueault was prepared – or even allowed by his superiors – to answer. He shook his head. 'I can't tell you. Just know this: if we balls this up, she will most likely die. The kidnappers aren't going for cash or diamonds or any of the usual stuff. If they took her, it's got to be for something far more important.'

'You know what that is?' asked Detric, probably the only one of the three who could.

'No. And I haven't asked. Some things we don't need to know. We just do our jobs, right?' He looked at them each in turn, Detric, Sebastien and Ivrey, the third man, until they nodded agreement, confident that if any three officers could find a single trace of the woman, these three would. Then he nodded towards the outside world. 'Go find her.'

# Chapter Fifteen

Rocco and Claude arrived back at the Clos du Lac to find the small search party gathered around the kitchen table. Piled on the surface was a collection of food packets, sweets, several assorted bits of cutlery, a pair of nail scissors, a small silver clock, a man's leather belt, a lipstick, two magazines and a bundle of papers held together by a clip.

'The lipstick's mine,' said Inès. 'It went missing a few days ago. I knew it must have been Stefan, but he just grinned like an idiot and denied it.'

'Where was it found?'

'In an air vent in one of the back rooms, along with those.' She pointed at the papers.

'The rest of the rubbish was dotted all over,' said Desmoulins. 'Nothing exciting, though, unless you can see anything relevant.'

Most of the papers were to do with running the sanitarium, from copy orders for supplies, compliment slips, old, blank letterheads, some unused envelopes, several pages of official instructions regarding the maintenance of the building, even a slim manual for operating an electric mixer.

The magazines were a surprise. Copies of an American photographic monthly, they were expensive and their presence was sufficiently unusual to warrant further examination. They looked well-thumbed, proof no doubt that they had been attractive enough to an inveterate jackdaw to want to hide them away from anyone else. Rocco put them to one side; he'd take a closer look later.

Among the papers was a letter addressed to Drucker. It was on Interior Ministry letterhead (Employment Section) dated two months ago, confirming a percentage increase of salary to an unspecified amount. The significant fact for Rocco was that it gave Drucker's home address. He put that to one side also.

Another letter was addressed to Paulus. It was also on official letterhead, this one from the Interior Ministry (Defence Section), confirming his change of role from that of a serving NCO in the naval military police and taking on a short-term contract (to be extended if and when deemed necessary and depending on satisfactory performance) assigned to the Clos du Lac facility. This role was general security of the establishment and its residents, with authorisation to carry his naval-issue sidearm. His reporting line was daily to Director Drucker, and weekly direct to the Interior Ministry (Defence Section). A telephone number was underlined. A short paragraph at the end emphasised specific duties to watch patients S. Ardois and J. Tourlemain.

'The names sound made up,' Desmoulins commented.

The letter went on to request that Paulus report any unusual behaviour in the area, contacts between patients, and to take 'all necessary action in the event of access to the patients by outsiders'.

'Sounds a bit extreme,' said Alix. 'What were they frightened of?'

'Actually, it sounds like the military,' said Rocco. 'A rule for everything so that everybody knows where he stands.' He glanced at Inès. 'What's so special about Tourlemain?'

'I don't know.' She looked mystified. 'He's one of the men who came here not long after André arrived. The other one was…' She stopped, blinking rapidly.

'Ardois?' Rocco suggested.

'Yes. They arrived at about the same time.'

'So André was watching them both?'

'Yes. How do you know?'

'It makes sense. You said he was sent here after one patient went missing and shortly before another two arrived. If they had two more to watch over, who better than a military cop to do it?'

'They must have been worth the effort,' Desmoulins put in. 'And the way one of them was killed, that sort of proves it. Can we trace them back?'

'No.' Inès shook her head. 'We never know their back history, why they're sent here or where they're from. And not their real names.'

'Or where they're going?' She nodded and Rocco wondered at that. 'Somebody must know. You can't just shift people around the country without some degree of planning.'

'But why would you?' said Alix. 'What kind of people have false names and no back story?'

'Spies.' Desmoulins looked at them. 'Spies operate undercover, without contacts or a real history. Not even their families know what they do.'

'I can think of another group.' Rocco stood up. He'd had a wild idea, but it needed corroboration to make it fly. And preferably the real identity of at least one of the former inmates. That made him pause: why was he thinking of them as inmates? Prisons had inmates, not sanitaria.

'Where are you going?' said Desmoulins.

Rocco picked up the letterhead with Drucker's home address on it, and on impulse, the American photography magazines. 'Hopefully, to a man who might have some answers. Even if I have to click his teeth together.'

–

Drucker's home address was a neat house in the eastern suburbs of Amiens. It sat on a raised garden, with a garage underneath and had the air of a model, as if created by a giant. Drucker was obsessively tidy, Rocco thought, and must spend all his off time trimming the grass and polishing the slate chips filling every bit of space not covered by lawn or driveway.

He knocked on the door. No answer.

He tried the garage door beneath the house. It opened and swung up with a ping of metal springs to reveal an empty space. No tools, no rubbish, hardly a speck of oil on the concrete floor. In the far left-hand corner was a single door. He walked across and opened it. The aroma of polish was sucked into the garage. Something sharper, too, vaguely familiar, but not a cooking smell. Perhaps Drucker ate out a lot.

He stepped through the door. Immediately in front of him was a small cellar space, empty save for some cardboard boxes and a stack of newspapers. A flight of tiled steps ran up to a wooden door. He walked up and stepped into a hallway, also tiled. Silence.

The kitchen held the most basic equipment but that was all. The place was stripped of anything personal. No food in the cupboards, no personal clutter, a room barely used. The same elsewhere; no clothing left lying around, nothing in the bathroom save for a heavy smell of disinfectant, and in the living room, not even a lost sock or an envelope tucked down the back of the sofa. The bedroom contained an empty wardrobe, the door hanging open, a dresser and bedside cabinet, all empty, and a double bed with one pillow. Unless there was a Mrs Drucker, and she or her husband had neck problems, it meant Drucker lived alone.

He checked the rubbish bin at the rear of the property. It contained two empty bottles of floor cleaner and a wet rag.

He checked the bathroom again. It was spotless. Not a grain of dirt, not a splash of soap, not a strand of hair. Just the smell of cleaning fluid. The kitchen, by contrast, although clean, had the quick-wipe appearance of most houses, done to a presentable standard, but nothing to impress the neighbours. Rocco could feel his antennae twitching. Something wasn't right. It centred mainly on the smell he'd picked up when he first came through the inner door in the garage, and now in the bathroom. The two empty bottles of cleaning fluid.

Why so much – and only in the bathroom?

He checked his watch. Too late now to get Rizzotti. Still, he picked up the phone on the kitchen wall, got the dialling tone and rang the station. He left a message for the doctor to come out and take a look first thing in the morning. Another pair of eyes might spot something he was missing.

Next he rang Philippe Poitrel, the mayor of Poissons-les-Marais, and asked if he had any information about ownership of the Clos du Lac. He'd only ever spoken to the man once, and found him a stuffed shirt. But he was punctilious about his responsibilities, which were the administration of the commune.

'I regret I cannot help you, Inspector,' said Poitrel, with the hint of a sniff. 'That building falls under central government control and I have no files relating to it. You will have to go to a higher authority than mine, I'm afraid.' He sounded faintly peeved, Rocco thought, affronted by having been overlooked in the chain of paperwork.

'Thank you, *Monsieur le Maire*,' he said politely, and hung up.

He went home. It had been a long day and he needed some sleep.

## Chapter Sixteen

He was woken early next morning by a knock at the door. It was his elderly neighbour, Mme Denis. Grey-haired and brusque, and dressed in a worn, grey-patterned dress and white apron, she made no attempt to come in, but thrust out her hand. She was holding a small basket of fresh eggs.

'You should eat breakfast,' she said. 'A nice omelette to start the day. My chickens are overproducing and I hate waste.'

He thanked her, seeing through the white lie, which was her way of being neighbourly. Taking the eggs was easier than arguing, and refusing them, along with the vegetables and fruit she occasionally left on his doorstep, was unthinkable. Local blood feuds had been started for less. Besides, she meant well and had his best interests at heart. She had helped ease his acceptance into the village, and had once saved him and Claude from a shooting, and destroyed an accusation of Rocco taking bribes. He wasn't about to overlook that kind of support.

'Tell your chickens their contribution is warmly appreciated.'

'I'll do that.' She turned to go, then hesitated. 'You had some visitors yesterday afternoon.'

'Did they say who they were?'

'No. They didn't stop. Just pulled up in the lane outside and sat there for a few minutes. Then they left.' She peered at him keenly, eyes narrowing behind her glasses. 'I know they weren't interested in me or my chickens, so it must have been you. You're not in trouble with foreign gangsters again, are you?' She was referring to his previous encounter with an English gang member – the one who'd offered the bribe.

'Did they look like foreign gangsters?'

'No. More like your bosses, actually. Smart suits and short haircuts. In a black Citroën DS.' She handed him a scrap of card with a car number written on it in a shaky hand. 'I wrote it down because I knew you'd ask.'

'You're getting good at this.' He took the card. The number wasn't familiar, but he could check it out. 'I should hire you as an investigator.'

Mme Denis' eyes twinkled. 'Well, live next door to a *flic* long enough and you start to develop a nose for trouble.' She turned and shuffled back down the path with a vague wave of her hand, duty done.

Moving to this house in Poissons-les-Marais the previous year after working the gangs and serious crimes beat in Paris and other centres had seemed like stepping back in time. At first the natives had been suspicious of the cop from Paris, and the quiet of the country-side had seemed almost threatening; almost as threatening as the unexploded ordnance scattered in the woods and the *marais* – the marshland – outside the village. Since then he had settled in more and was in danger of being almost accepted within the community. Another twenty-five years here should do it. His closest friends were Mme Denis next door, Claude Lamotte and his daughter Alix, and a family of fruit rats up in the attic. The latter were undemanding company, and there were times when he found the idea of living here long-term beginning to grow on him.

He went out to the water pump and filled the large jug, and put on some coffee. He looked at the eggs and decided an omelette wouldn't be so bad. He put some butter in a frying pan on his latest acquisition, a new gas stove, and began cracking eggs.

'Aha. I thought I could smell something.' It was Claude Lamotte, sniffing appreciatively and carrying a fresh baguette. 'Her next door been nagging you to eat properly again?'

'She means well.' Rocco held up two eggs and Claude nodded. He cracked them into a bowl and began to stir. Claude never refused food, day or night.

'Got a message from Philippe Delsaire,' Claude told him, drawing up a chair and breaking off two hunks of bread. Delsaire was the village plumber and man-of-all-trades. 'He's got the contract to connect the houses down here to the mains pipes along the road and needs access to your place to do the work.'

'He can have it anytime he likes,' said Rocco. 'Mme Denis has a spare key. I'll let her know.' The pipes had been laid along the road outside for months now; all Rocco and the other houses along here had been waiting for was completion of the job. At least it meant he could give up having to use the handpump to draw water.

'He's got two men to dig the trenches from the road to the house.'

'That's good, isn't it?'

Claude looked awkward, and Rocco said, 'Come on, spit it out.'

'Huh?'

'Say it. Something's on your mind.'

'Well, yes. You wouldn't know, being still new here, but the work will go a lot faster if you… you know, stand them a drink down at the café. The faster they complete yours, the sooner everyone else gets done.' He smiled briefly and cleared his throat.

'I see.' Rocco nodded slowly, letting him squirm. 'So, let me get this straight: I pay for drinks and everyone else benefits. They put you up to this, didn't they?' He was referring to the other residents along the street whom he hardly ever saw.

Claude puffed out his cheeks. 'Well, that's not exactly how it happened.'

'Fair enough.'

'Eh?'

'Yes.' A drink meant putting up a bottle or two behind the bar. 'I'll see to it. Tell him that includes Mme Denis, too. In fact, they should do her place first.'

Claude smiled with relief. 'She'll be pleased, but she won't like it.'

'I know. She's stubborn and proud. Don't worry – I'll talk to her.'

When the omelette was done, Rocco poured coffee for them both and they sat and ate in companionable silence.

Claude looked up at the ceiling, head cocked to one side. 'You haven't got rid of your neighbours, have you? I thought you liked them.'

'I do. They're harmless enough.' They had gone quiet recently, although he could hear them some nights, scuttling about like dry leaves whispering across the bare floorboards. 'They like to sleep late these days. Must be the warmer weather.'

Claude's eyebrows lifted and settled again, and he smiled. 'Have you ever seen what's up there?'

'Not yet. Why?'

'Well, some people use the term "fruit rat" for anything that lives in the roof space and eats fruit. I know people who've lived here all their lives and never seen one. But there's more than one species. You thought it was a *fouine*, fair enough.'

'Actually, I didn't. That's what Madame Denis called it.'

'Really? Well, there you go. She's probably never seen one, either. Mind you, if it is a *fouine* up there, it's not what I'd call cuddly. They have razor-sharp teeth.'

Rocco stared at him, thinking about the times he'd gone up to investigate the noises. 'How come you've never mentioned this to me before?'

'I didn't want to spoil your perception of life in the country. Nor did I want you blowing holes in the roof with your gun if you saw a big one. Some people can be funny about stuff like that.'

'Do you have them?'

'Sure I do. No idea what kind, mind you, but they're up there.' He shrugged. 'Live and let live, I say.'

'I'll try to remember that.'

'You're going native, you know that? Happens to all of us in the end. Any day now, you'll start changing those fancy black imported clothes for a set of working *bleus* from the farm supplies store and a packet of Gitanes.' He laughed at Rocco's scowl and wiped his plate with a piece of bread, popping it in his mouth with relish. 'You're getting good at this, too. You'll make someone a fine husband one day. You know Mme Drolet's still available, don't you? And she's on the hunt.' He fluttered his bushy eyebrows. 'Word is, she likes 'em big and tough.'

'Too bad,' Rocco growled. Mme Drolet had recently taken over the village co-op. She was a handsome, single woman with what Claude had once called the tendencies of a black widow spider, and seemed hell-bent on getting an invitation to cook Rocco supper. So far he had managed to resist her advances. 'Anyway, she's not my sort.'

'Of course she's your sort.' Claude grinned earthily. 'She'd keep you entertained at nights and do more than cook an omelette, I can tell you. Lots of warm, loving meat on those bones. We're all laying bets, you know – she'll have you in the end.' He smacked his hands together as if he were crushing an insect. '*Paff!*'

Rocco stood up and put the plates in a bowl of water. 'You and the rest of your degenerate friends should get out more,' he said mildly. 'What exactly did you want, anyway?'

'Ah, yes. I went over to see Bertrand yesterday evening – the farmer who works those fields beyond the Clos du Lac? His farm's not visible from the lane, but he says he heard an engine go by the night before last, about four-thirty. He thought it might have been a motorbike. Could be our man.'

Rocco nodded. It would fit with what they knew and the tracks across the grass. What it didn't tell them was the man's name. Or where he came from.

'You thinking of taking up photography?' Claude asked, picking up the two American magazines. 'Not really your thing, I'd have thought.'

'You're right and I'm not. They were among the stuff hidden at the Clos du Lac.'

Claude flicked through the pages, which included numerous examples of colour pictures and equipment available for the enthusiast. 'I'm no expert,' Claude commented, 'but this looks like professional-level equipment.' He turned the magazine over and added, 'Whoever Mr S. Devrye-Martin is, he must have plenty of cash. I couldn't afford the subscription for this, not on my wages.' He dropped the magazine back on the table. 'I might borrow them when you're done, though.'

Rocco was staring at him, his mind still on what he'd found at Drucker's place. Or rather, what he hadn't found. Then Claude's words clicked into place.

'What did you just say?'

'I said I might borrow them.'

'No, before that.'

Claude picked up the magazine again. 'Mr S. Devrye-Martin must be rich, to subscribe to this.'

'Let me see.' Rocco took the magazine and stared at the back. A small white label at the bottom of the page carried a name and address:

S. Devrye-Martin, Les Hirondelles, Rue de Nonancourt, Evreux 27000

S for Stefan? Or a fellow patient who'd lost their magazines to a human magpie? He thought it unlikely to be a member of staff, since the cost of imported publications like this would be considerable, especially with postage. And why send them via Evreux? It was something worth checking.

'Can you keep a friendly eye on the Clos du Lac?' he said, putting on his coat and jamming the magazines in his pocket. 'Just a passing glance now and then, in case anything happens.'

'Of course. What are you going to do?'

'Start looking under some stones. Official ones.'

# Chapter Seventeen

The woman came to with a start. She was shivering with cold and her buttocks and back ached unbearably where the mattress had failed to cushion entirely the ribbed surface of the metal floor. She coughed, her throat painfully dry where her breathing had rasped while lying on her back. She had no idea how long she had been asleep, but it must have been a long time. And no idea whether it was day or night. Instinct, though, told her it was daytime.

She tried to spit. There was a bitter taste on the back of her tongue. Bile, perhaps. Or was it something the man had put in the water? She shook her head. She was definitely light-headed, the same feeling she'd experienced after taking an occasional sleeping tablet.

She held her breath and listened. Not a sound: no voices, no movement, no traffic. Just the pounding of fear in her head. It must be morning, but how late? Or early. She had no way of knowing.

Was that a fluttering of birds somewhere close by? Instinctively she knew the van was inside a building – a shed, perhaps, or a warehouse. The birds were probably sparrows, nesting beneath the rafters. It was somewhere big enough, anyway, to take the vehicle, and removed enough from human habitation or a road to dull any noise.

The idea brought panic. Had they taken her outside Paris? If so, how far? What if they had run off and left her here, tied up like this and unable to escape? How long could she last before being found?

She forced herself to think rationally. She had been kidnapped, and kidnaps only ever happened for ransom. And the men who'd brought her in here and tied her up knew who she was – and who her husband was. That meant she had a value to the people who had taken her. So why would they simply run away and lose the chance of making a lot of money? It would be beyond stupid.

Unless they had been scared off by police activity.

She found it a struggle to sit up, groaning as her back and stomach muscles ached in protest. It reminded her of a camping trip many years ago in the Loire, when Robert had persuaded her to take a weekend away in a tent before they were married. It had been very daring then – even shocking. And the passion they had felt and exchanged that first weekend had not diminished, although it had left her with a wry memory of aching bones and, she recalled with a faint blush, even now, of scraped knees.

She lifted her hands and tried to remove the hood. But the man she had come to think of as 'Leather Jacket' had tied it securely at the back with some sort of drawstring, and she couldn't reach the knot. Then she tested her bonds. The tape was thick and unyielding, strong enough to hold heavy furniture and certainly impossible for her to break or move. She gave up and began to search the inside of the van by touch, starting with the area immediately around the mattress, and widening her probing until she was moving on her buttocks like a mermaid. From mattress to metal floor was a stark reminder of her plight, but she tucked the fears away and stretched out until she made contact with the side of the van.

Wood. A smooth grain, but she could just detect by feel the wavy lines in the surface. Plywood. She ran her hands across until she felt a join, and a horizontal line of nails or screws bisected by another line, this time vertical. The join between the sheets of ply was close, barely enough for her to insert a fingernail. She knocked on the wood with her knuckle. It made a dull sound, muffled and solid. So they *had* built a baffle. A simple layer of wood, with maybe something stuffed down inside.

She felt a cold shiver that had nothing to do with the temperature. This had been no random snatch of a chance victim, but a well-planned and prepared kidnap. They had known what they were going to do in advance.

This was where she was going to stay. The thought made her stomach heave and she had to swallow hard to avoid throwing up.

She steeled herself and continued her search, shuffling around the van on her bottom. Her skirt and slip began catching on the rough floor, but she ignored that; there was time for dignity later. She stopped now and then to listen. It would do no good to be caught looking for an escape, and would make her situation all the worse. It was a reminder that she was thirsty once more, and desperate for the feel and taste of water. Hungry, too, although that could wait.

She was close to what she thought might be the front of the van's interior when she heard a noise. A bang, a rattle of a chain, then footsteps. Hard heels on a concrete floor. Coming closer.

Without hesitation she rolled backwards, tumbling over like a child until she felt the mattress cushion her body once more. Quickly arranging herself as best she could, she lay waiting for the door to open.

But there was nothing.

*Coward*. The word came floating before her, as much a silent curse as self-accusation. So what if he found her sitting up, she asked herself? What could he do that he wasn't already doing? But she knew the answer to that. He could do far worse than simply keeping her trussed up like this. She didn't like to think about it, but thoughts of what had been done to other women flooded in on her, and she lay still, waiting.

Then the footsteps moved away, followed by a slamming door and the rattle of chains.

Silence.

—

Barely five kilometres away, in the district of Pantin, in north-east Paris, Divisional Inspector Drueault was sharing a brief meal with his men in a café near the railway station. They were tired and frustrated, but still upbeat.

They had found a trace.

'We nearly had her,' said Sebastien, chewing a hunk of bread. 'I'm bloody certain of it.'

Drueault nodded slowly, scooping up a forkful of fried potatoes. He wasn't about to let dismay lower the morale of the small group. They had to keep trying. 'Close, but not close enough. But that's better than anybody else would have done.'

Captain Detric had been the first to pick up a scent. After drawing a complete blank on Avenue de Friedland, the last place the woman had been seen, they had spread their search zone further out, looking for any signs of unusual activity. It was a huge task, but one Drueault believed would pay dividends. Digging deep in the normal way, by asking questions from house to house using uniforms and publicity bulletins, would alert the kidnappers and cause them to panic. But this way, merely asking those on the street if there had been anything odd or unusual lately in the everyday traffic in the area, would arouse nobody's suspicions.

First Detric had chanced on a street cleaner working near the Parc Monceau mentioning a delivery van turning into a side street along de Friedland, where he'd been assigned to cover for a sick colleague the previous day. The day of the kidnap. The van had turned in, then out again almost immediately. It had been early, when most shops had been about to open. But discreet enquiries had revealed that *Salon Elizabeth* had opened early that morning for two select clients. It had proved sufficient to give them an initial idea of the type of vehicle used, albeit very tentative. But later, Detric had talked to a shopkeeper who'd complained of a furniture van with a smoky exhaust late on the evening of the kidnap, pulling out of a side street where some demolition work had been going on, but where the site had been closed due to the demolition firm going bust.

The street was in the St Denis district, not a million kilometres from Avenue de Friedland.

The team would not have given this incident much thought had it not been for Sebastien mentioning at the next briefing a furniture van knocking over a parked bicycle and driving off. The witness hadn't got the licence plate, but had said all the police had to do was look for a van by following the trail of exhaust smoke. This had happened in the Livry area, further to the east.

Drueault had relied on his nose. Two delivery vans with bad exhausts were hardly unusual in this city – they had a hard life driven at ridiculous speeds by morons. But you followed whatever clues you had until they proved worthless or fruitful. Further, it made sense that if the kidnappers had gone anywhere, it would not have been further into the city centre, where there was too much risk involved of a random stop by police. Instead, they would probably have made for a prearranged location where the woman could be kept quiet and away from the public gaze.

But why use a delivery van – if that's what they were doing? Unless they were keeping on the move. He'd known it done before, to good effect. The advantage was that it put them ahead of any police cordon and nosy neighbours. The weakness in the idea was that constant movement put them at risk of being noticed, either because of the vehicle breaking down or a simple road traffic accident.

Then a report had come in from a council worker in Pantin, just a few kilometres further on, saying that a large truck had been parked overnight in the grounds of a war-damaged and disused church. The man had only noticed it because he knew restoration work would be starting there shortly and the truck had driven through a rope barrier to gain entry. When he'd wandered over to take a look, he'd been stopped by a man in a leather jacket, who'd claimed he was resting before continuing his journey.

Drueault fastened on it like a dog on a bone. Delivery van, furniture van, large truck… and using abandoned or unused sites to park up. And each sighting had been on a progressive line from Avenue de Friedland out through the north of Paris to here in the north-east. It wasn't much to go on, but better than anything else.

'When we're done here,' he said, finishing his meal, 'we spread out and keep asking questions in this area. Whoever they are, they aren't moving far. Find empty building sites, warehouses, bomb-damaged lots – anywhere a van can park up without attracting too much attention.'

His men nodded, quietly electrified by his positive manner.

## Chapter Eighteen

When Rocco got to the office, he looked up the number of the Evreux police and asked to speak to the captain of the uniformed branch. In his experience, the uniforms had a more detailed knowledge of their towns than investigators, who usually went where they were pointed and did not have the same depth of local network.

'Captain Franck Antain. May I help you?' The voice sounded brisk and efficient.

Rocco introduced himself, and said, 'I'm looking into some papers believed stolen from a resident of Evreux.' He gave the captain the address. 'Would you have any way of checking whether a Mr Devrye-Martin at that address goes under the name Stefan?'

'It's a local family, I know that much, Inspector,' Antain replied. 'I don't know all their names, but I can find out. What's the interest?'

Rocco decided to be cautious. 'Some personal belongings were handed in yesterday, and the name was on a magazine.'

'I'll have to get back to you. I know of the family, enough to know they are somewhat reclusive, to be honest, and don't encourage questions.'

'What's their background?'

'Land, mostly, which is a lot, around here and further south, and several houses here in town that I know of. I'm not familiar with all their business, but they used to have connections in various manufacturing areas, although I think that's all gone now. But they're not exactly short of cash or properties, you know? It's old money and they know how to keep it.' He said the last with a light chuckle.

'That's fine, Captain. Whatever you can find out, I'd be grateful.' He rang off before the captain could press him further, and went in search of Dr Rizzotti. He was in his office across the yard, as usual, immersed in a large medical treatise. He dropped the volume readily enough, and his verbal report on Drucker's place was brief, as Rocco had feared.

'Clean. Very clean. I'd hire him to do my place.'

'But?' Rocco felt slightly deflated. He'd been expecting something interesting, something he could get his teeth into.

'I've taken samples from the bathroom and sent them with the empty cleaning fluid bottles to the laboratory in Lille.'

'Samples?'

'Scrapings from between the tiles and around the skirting board.'

Rocco felt his ears prickle. 'Now why would you bother to do that?'

'Because only my mother-in-law uses cleaner on that scale. But she's a mental case, not a murderer. I can't be certain, but you're right in being suspicious about the bathroom. I've seen isolation rooms in clinics with more bacteria. If a special clean-up job was done, it can only have been for one reason.'

'Blood?'

'Most likely. Hopefully, if there is any in the samples, the laboratory will find it. Nobody's that good at eradicating all traces entirely. Well, except my mother-in-law.' He hesitated. 'I took a look at that moped found on the Portier farm. Nothing to help, I'm afraid. The machine was old, no identifying marks, and the panniers and fishing equipment were standard, store-bought items. I could ask for a fingerprint search, but after being outside in a ditch, it's likely there's nothing left.'

Rocco thanked him and went back to the main office. He handed the slip of paper with the car registration number that Mme Denis had given him to a sergeant in the records office and asked him to check it out. Then he walked along to the café on the corner, a favoured spot where the local cops went to drink, gossip, complain and try to act normal. Mostly they didn't quite pull it off.

There were several officers present, blue uniforms half camouflaged by a heavy fog of cigarette smoke. He nodded greetings and placed his order with the barman before finding a table in one corner where he could sit and think things over without being disturbed. The waiter placed a heavy cup and saucer of black coffee in front of him, then left him alone.

Rocco felt uneasy. He recognised the signs of a chase building, and wondered where it would lead. He usually found his tolerance for caffeine growing when he got into a case, and this was one of those times.

Running through what he had so far, he realised ruefully that it amounted to not very much. Someone, identity unknown, had gained access to the Clos du Lac and murdered an inmate, identity also unknown. A security guard, a serving naval cop assigned to the same establishment, had also been murdered at an unknown location, either to get him out of the way while the first murder took place, or because he'd been involved in setting it up and had been silenced because his services were no longer required. Gilles Drucker, the Clos du Lac's director, a man apparently obsessive about his duties, had since disappeared, along with the office records and complement of patients, numbering five, identities also unknown. And now a trio of men from an obscure security department within the Interior Ministry had been through the place and closed it down.

Rocco felt he was lagging behind the race. Along with the unknowns, he so far hadn't got a clue as to the who or why. With most murders, there was a selection of motives, and a few names of who would benefit from the killing. But all he'd got here was a vague suspicion or two. The most worrying part was that something about the events after the killings had been organised in a way that only someone with considerable clout could manage. Levignier and his men had been unexpectedly quick to arrive on the scene, and only a government department could have arranged for such an equally rapid and efficient removal of a body and the remaining patients. But proving it was another matter, especially when that government department had the means to remain well beyond the reach of anything Rocco could throw at them.

His immediate problem was how to prove or disprove ISD's involvement. He could hardly ring Levignier and ask him; the man would simply put down the phone and make a complaint to someone high up in the Interior Ministry. The next questionwas what precisely was the purpose behind the whole Clos du Lac set-up? Something had to make it worthwhile, even if only to one person. Yet nothing was springing to mind from the paltry evidence he had so far.

He finished the coffee. With such limited amounts of information, Massin would stand firmly in his way if he suggested approaching the Ministry. The Clos du Lac was clearly an official facility, and any cooperation from that end would be unforthcoming. But he was damned if he was going to let go of it yet.

Drucker. The man was at the centre of all this, if only because he probably knew more than anyone else. He'd had the paperwork, he knew the details, he'd seen the people. And the letter confirming his salary increase wasn't just because he dressed nicely.

He'd also called Levignier before attending the scene. A reflex action for a man with connections.

Back in the office, he found the sergeant waiting for him. 'That registration number's assigned to a fleet car in the Ministry,' the sergeant told him. He didn't need to say which ministry: in police parlance, there was only the one. 'I asked who would have been driving it, but they as good as told me to get lost. The usual thing, I'm afraid. You want me to try again?'

Rocco shook his head. 'Thank you, Sergeant. That's good work.' It would be a waste of time pursuing the matter. A large number of cars were used by various departments in the Interior Ministry, many of them on confidential business. Rocco had come up against their intransigence before when working in Clichy, after a vehicle had been towed away, leaving a hapless official or undercover officer stranded. The matter rarely got reported and never went anywhere.

He sat down at his desk, wondering how much of an interest Levignier and his men were going to take in his life. It was probably second nature to them, scooping up whatever information they could find. Without thinking, he dialled Drucker's number. He realised his mistake and was about to drop the phone back on its hook when he noticed something odd.

Silence. No ring tone. Nothing.

He got onto the PTT, the Post and Telecommunications service, and asked them to check the number.

'It's been disconnected,' the female operator told him.

'But I was there yesterday,' he told her. 'I used the phone myself.'

'Sorry, Inspector, that's all I can tell you.'

Rocco asked to be put through to a supervisor, who told him the same thing.

'I'm an inspector of police,' Rocco told him calmly, 'and I'm investigating a murder, and now,' he added, 'the sudden disappearance of this subscriber. Who authorised the disconnection?'

The supervisor sounded unimpressed, but agreed to check. He came back a few minutes later. 'I've got the job card here, but it doesn't tell me much. Just says to disconnect the line and withdraw the number.' He sounded faintly puzzled, and Rocco could hear the rustling of paper in the background. Then, 'That's pretty unusual, though. Can you hold on a minute?'

Rocco waited, the line crackling with static, until the supervisor came back and said, 'The order to withdraw the number originated from our Central Services Department in Neuilly. Beyond that, I can't help you.'

'Then give me the number in Neuilly.' He knew the area slightly, a mix of residential and commercial buildings in north-west Paris, with a growing influx of new businesses and government offices. It wasn't too far from his old base in Clichy.

The man gave him the number, but added, 'It won't do you any good, Inspector. I can tell you from experience that all instructions originating from Neuilly come under a government ordinance. Any details about the number are automatically marked as a closed file.'

'What are you saying?'

'The Neuilly office has a special function. It deals with all state subscribers and services, from the Élysée Palace on down. They even have their own team of engineers, all security checked and monitored. This disconnection order came from a government department, which means you'll need an act of legislation or a senior judge to unlock it. Sorry.'

He put the phone down. Another dead end. That left Inès Dion. Without Drucker, she was the one remaining constant in all this. She had been in a relationship with Paulus, the dead security guard, and she was still a serving member of the naval establishment. Did she know more than she was letting on? Or did she know more than she realised, some snippet that might unlock what was going on here?

He checked his notebook and found where he'd made a note of the number of the Clos du Lac. She might still be there. He dialled and waited. And waited.

No reply.

He put down the phone and went in search of Alix. She was back at her desk in the basement, processing paper. He asked her if she had got Inès Dion's address.

Without looking up, she said, 'Setting up a date, Inspector?' Then she glanced up and saw his expression. She apologised, flushing red. 'Sorry. Yes, it's here.' She checked her notebook and read out the details. It was a street in Amiens.

'Why do I recognise that?'

'It's a block of apartments and rooms attached to the military barracks, used by visiting personnel,' she replied. 'Inès told me she was allocated a room there while she was working at the sanitarium. Is there a problem?'

'If there is, I'm already too late.'

# Chapter Nineteen

Rocco decided to walk to the barracks and take a chance on catching Inès in. It wasn't far, out towards the eastern suburbs, and the exercise and fresh air would help him think. He checked in at the guard post and was given a pass and directions to Inès's room. The single rooms for visiting personnel were located in a separate wing of the barracks building set apart from the central offices by a low wall. He followed a stone walkway and entered the building through a glass-panelled door, following the signs up to the first floor.

There was no need to knock at Inès's door: it was open. He heard someone humming and looked inside. The floor was being swept by a woman in a grey cotton overall. A cleaning trolley stood just inside the door, loaded with sheets and cleaning items.

'Dion? She's gone,' said the woman, and checked a clipboard on the trolley. 'Yes, she checked out early this morning. I thought she was staying longer, but there you go – that's the military for you.' She smiled. 'My husband was in the army for thirty years. Hated every day of it. Killed him in the end.'

'I'm sorry to hear it. In action?'

Her look could have frozen a lemon. 'You could say that; he fell out of a second-storey window when a woman's husband came home.'

Rocco felt as if everything was getting away from him. 'I suppose you don't know where Dion went?' It was a vain hope, but he'd been lucky in the past with such chance remarks.

The woman smiled, the ice gone as quickly as it had appeared. 'Sorry. They don't tell us what they're doing.'

He walked back outside, then turned and went back in and showed the cleaning lady his card. 'I'm investigating a murder and need to get hold of Inès Dion. Was there anything left behind… any papers she might have disposed of?'

'Take a look, Inspector.' She flapped a hand towards the cleaning trolley out in the corridor. 'I just emptied the waste basket in the bag on the back.'

Rocco checked, but other than a magazine, some food wrappers and some toiletries Inès had clearly decided were no longer worth keeping, there was nothing.

He thanked the woman for her help and walked back to the administrative office and another brick wall.

'Sorry, Inspector,' said the manager, examining his card. 'We're not allowed to give out the private addresses of military personnel without a court order and instructions from the Defence Ministry. It's a matter of security. I'm sure you can understand.'

Rocco thanked the man and returned to the station in a dangerous frame of mind. He rang Captain Michel Santer, his former boss in the Clichy–Nanterre district of Paris.

'Before you start,' he told Santer, 'I'm planning on coming to the city, so name a restaurant and I'll let you know when.' Santer was constantly reminding him of the favours he had done Rocco, and the expensive meals he was owed as a result. The captain was probably one of his closest friends, and a man he trusted implicitly.

'God, touchy today, aren't we?' Santer said with a smile in his voice. 'Still, never let it be said that I can't be magnanimous.' His voice dropped. 'What do you really want, Rocco? Another favour, I'll bet. It usually is.'

'An opinion, that's all.'

'Ah, an opinion. Well, I've got lots of those, mostly uncomplimentary and uncouth, yet true, about detectives who disappear off into the countryside and forget about their old comrades. Go on, then.'

'There's a PTT office in Neuilly, called the Central Services Department. Know anything about it?'

'Ouch. That's a locked box, my friend. Why do you want to know about it?'

Rocco told him in brief about his conversation with the telephone service supervisor.

'Well, you can rest assured that the person you talked to was telling the truth. I know that office block and it's got more security than the president's private bathroom. You don't intend breaking in there, do you?'

'No. Nothing like that. Just checking that I wasn't being spun a line.'

'You weren't, take it from me. If that office issued an instruction to disconnect a number and eradicate the details, it came from somewhere not too far from the Place Beauvau.'

Back to the Interior Ministry. Wheels within wheels.

When he got back to the office, he was handed a message to call Captain Antain in Evreux.

'I've dug around as you asked,' Antain told him, 'and can confirm that there was a Stefan, listed as the elder son of Honoré and Maude Devrye-Martin, with a younger sister, Josette. Several cousins live in the area, too, mostly elderly and female. The family has been established here since 1730, and apart from various business dealings have been active in local politics, although they are less so now. The parents are both in their eighties and rarely seen in public these days. Josette lives in Switzerland. As I indicated to you before, the family is very private, wealthy, with extensive land ownership, much of which is leased out to tenant farmers in the region and further south.'

'Stefan's the name I have,' Rocco began, then stopped. 'You said "was" listed.'

There was a brief hesitation, then Antain said, 'Well, there we have a small problem, Inspector. According to our records, Stefan Devrye-Martin is dead.'

Rocco felt the air go out of him. 'How – and when?'

'Three years ago, in Thailand. A report lodged with us from that time states the cause as blood poisoning following a motorcycle accident. Apparently he didn't receive adequate treatment in time and infection set in. He died ten days later. Not uncommon in that part of the world, I understand.'

Rocco could confirm that. He reached across the desk and picked up the American photography magazines. He checked the issue dates on the front.

They were just two months old. 'There's no other S. Devrye-Martin?'

'No. Not even a woman's name. Sounds as if your information is wrong.'

'Yes, it does.'

Antain cleared his throat. He sounded unsure of himself, and his voice dropped a few notches. 'Actually, Inspector, this might not be relevant, but I don't actually come from here, you see, so I don't have a feel for all the local history. But when I asked around about Stefan, I hit something of a brick wall. It seemed as if people were reluctant to talk about him.'

'Who did you ask?'

'Colleagues, of course, an *avocat* who comes in regularly… one or two locals. It was only when I asked a friend who's lived here all his life that I actually got anywhere.'

'Go on.'

'Well, it seems there were rumours of a nasty scandal surrounding Stefan about ten years ago. It all blew up, but just as quickly blew away again after a barrage of lawsuits by the family closed it down.'

Rocco felt his pulse quicken. 'What sort of rumours?'

'Something about taking inappropriate photographs of children at a swimming pool. I say pool, but it was more of a public swimming area in a lake. A father who went looking for his eight-year-old son was charged with assaulting a man he said was using a camera to take pictures of children in a state of undress. I believe it was fairly relaxed around here then and young children changed clothes without bothering too much about covering up. Anyway, Stefan Devrye-Martin was treated by a local doctor for cuts to his head and his attacker was arrested.'

'What happened to him?'

'That's the odd thing: the case was later dropped when the accusations of assault against the father were withdrawn by the family. The local police captain at the time tried to press ahead with the investigation, because some of the children confirmed that Stefan had indeed been taking photos of them – and it wasn't the first time. My friend said Stefan was rumoured to be a bit soft in the head, so it was thought he wouldn't have known what he was doing was wrong. We have no way of confirming that, of course. In the end, the captain was overruled by a magistrate with, um, connections to the family.'

'Connections?'

'A cousin.'

'You sound almost sceptical, Captain,' Rocco observed.

'Well, if it had been me, I'd have made a fuss. But money talks, I suppose, as it always has. Not long afterwards, Stefan disappeared to the Far East and nobody heard anything more about him until the report came in of his death three years ago.'

Convenient, thought Rocco cynically. It wouldn't be the first time someone had been reported dead in an effort to foil justice. But was it relevant? And would a supposed dead man be stupid enough to come back and take out a magazine subscription in his real name?

'Was the body repatriated for burial?'

'There's nothing on record. I checked.'

Also convenient. It seemed on the surface to be a dead end. But Rocco wasn't so sure. Something about this business didn't sound right. Any family able to suppress an investigation of this kind had the reach and influence to do more, if they needed to. The idea raised his hackles enough to want to follow it through. And there was only one way of seeing if this had any legs or not. Visual confirmation.

'This is a long shot, Captain, but do you have a photo of Stefan on file?'

Another pause, longer this time. Then Antain said, 'Are you sure this is about stolen property, Inspector?'

Rocco hesitated. This was a sensitive issue, but he had no choice but to take a punt on the captain's professionalism. He explained that he was investigating a murder, and had been trying to be discreet in the process so as not to alarm the family unnecessarily. Antain hadn't seemed to mind the small lie, and even sounded impressed.

'I don't have a photo here – the family's very shy of publicity, as I told you. But I know the owner of the local newspaper. He might have one. Do you want me to ask?'

'I'd consider it a favour, Captain Antain. But be careful. If the family is connected, you don't want to make official enemies.'

'No problem. If there is anything I'll get it couriered to your office.'

That evening, Rocco called round to give Mme Denis the news about the pipes.

'I know,' she said grumpily, her chin jutting out. 'I heard. You think I want charity? Preferential treatment because I'm old? I don't need that kind of help, thank you very much.'

Rocco sighed inwardly. He preferred dealing with criminals – they were so much easier to negotiate with. You never needed to placate them, and if they got too bolshy, you could always threaten to lock them up for the night.

'I realise that,' he said. 'But if you were my mother, I'd do the same. Why keep pumping water when you can simply turn on a tap?'

'It's not the tap I object to, young man!' she snapped. 'It's the special treatment.' Then her face softened. 'I don't want people thinking I need your help.'

'Well, I need more eggs,' he replied. 'So, let's look on it as a trade. You get your pipes first, and I get to eat more omelettes. We both win. How's that?'

She scowled at him in suspicion and said, 'One moment.' Then she went inside. She returned moments later with a small basket of eggs. 'That's a down payment.' Then she slammed the door.

But not before he saw her face break into a smile.

# Chapter Twenty

'*Union leaders, businesses and members across the political spectrum are today calling for a new rationale regarding trade talks with the two Chinas. With opening discussions between French representatives and the People's Republic of China in Peking now under way, there has already been some dissatisfaction expressed by Peking at the very highest level at the ongoing negotiations with their political rivals in Taiwan. These negotiations were started some months ago at the instigation of industrial leader and magnate, Robert Bessine, and there are fears in Paris and the wider commercial community that these smaller, rival trade discussions, mostly focused around the supply of military and commercial aircraft being built by Bessine's own companies, could derail any progress on a much wider front in Peking.*

*General Secretary of the Confédération Générale du Travail, André Pallemart, has expressed concern that greatergains for workers across the industrial and commercial sector in France could be put at risk for the sake of what he called "warmongering production for private profit" – a direct attack on Bessine Industries and its charismatic leader. Elsewhere, Minister of Commerce and Industry Louis Bricusse has reinforced his support for exclusive talks with Peking, while Secretary of State Michel Combray has suggested that the Taiwan talks are "not in France's national interests". When asked for his response to these statements, Robert Bessine was reportedly unavailable for comment.*

*A spokesman has said that he is unwell but will respond shortly. In other news—'*

Rocco switched off the radio, glad someone else was having a tough day. After checking in by phone to the office, to make sure there hadn't been an outbreak of gang warfare while he was asleep, he decided to go to Paris. He had two reasons for making the trip: one was to see Santer and catch up with the long-promised lunch, the other was to dig around for whatever information he could find on Ardois – or was it Rotenbourg? Stefan had been very cagey. They were the only names he had, but they were better than nothing. He rang Santer and agreed to meet him at a restaurant within the Clichy area, then set off for the capital.

On the way, he remembered to call in at the village café to arrange drinks for the men putting in the pipes to his house and that of Mme Denis.

The owner, Georges Maillard, greeted him at the door. He brought the smell of last night's beer and cigarette smoke hanging in the air around him, and a stained roll-up hung from his lip, unlit. He was a large man with uncontrolled hair, a professional beer belly and a two-day beard, and in Rocco's limited acquaintance with him, seemed to wear a permanent air of disillusion.

'My licence is all in order, Inspector,' he grated automatically. 'Glad to hear it. But I'm not here about that.' Rocco explained about the workmen Delsaire had hired to connect the water pipes, and handed over some money. 'If they come in, this should cover a few drinks each.'

Maillard's eyebrows rose a notch or two, and his expression brightened. 'That's very generous of you, Inspector. And there's no "if" about it; they'll have smelt the money the moment you took it out of your pocket.'

He peeled off two notes and handed them back. 'You won't need that much. This'll see them happy enough.' He stuffed the money in his shirt pocket and rubbed his face with a meaty hand. He looked uneasy and glanced past Rocco's shoulder before speaking. 'Um… since you're here, Inspector, there's something I need to talk to you about. It's a bit delicate.' He backed away inside and closed the door.

At the far end of the bar room, a man was setting up a large white screen held in place on wires. A projector stood on the floor by the bar, trailing wires, alongside a stack of film reels. The man nodded at Rocco but said nothing.

'It's all right – he's deaf. It's film night tomorrow night. You should come – it's a Fernandel double – his *Don Camillo* stuff. Supposed to be excellent.'

'Thanks,' said Rocco. He'd seen some of the posters on walls and telegraph poles around the village. The idea of sitting here watching a scratchy film on a wobbly screen, surrounded by locals catching up on the latest gossip had its merits, but not right now. 'Maybe next time. What's on your mind?'

'Right. Well, these men have been coming in over the past couple of days. Three of them. Never seen them before, but I don't think they're from anywhere around here. They have a few drinks, a laugh, chat, the way customers do. But I've always had the feeling they were waiting for something… as if they were checking me out, you know?'

'You think they're planning to rob you?' Rocco had an idea how tight margins were for bar and café owners, many of whom had other lines of business to keep themselves afloat. But he couldn't imagine Maillard's place

– even if it was the only café in Poissons – being a target for robbers.

Maillard shook his head. 'I don't think so.' He swept a hand around the interior, which was clean, but had seen better days. The decor probably hadn't changed in three decades and the last coat of paint had been varnished over by years of cigarette smoke. 'Hell, look at the place. You see cash coming out of the walls?' He shrugged fatalistically. 'Anyway, the last time they called, they told me they'd got a whole load of drink going cheap from a restaurant gone bust in St Quentin. Wine, spirits, beer – all good quality.'

Rocco had heard it a hundred times before. 'Let me guess: no paperwork, no questions asked?'

'Right. And cash in the hand.' He rubbed fingers and thumb together.

Rocco was frowning. Investigating the back-door peddling of cut-rate alcohol wasn't strictly his problem. But living in such close proximity in a small village like Poissons meant he couldn't simply ignore it as if it didn't exist, especially if he was being asked for help. 'It's a long way to come from St Quentin,' he said, 'to sell cheap drink. It must be a good deal.'

'I know what you're thinking,' Maillard sniffed. 'I must be the only café owner in Picardie to pass up such an offer. Well, don't get me wrong, I'm not pretending to be a saint, and I'm not averse to making a few francs on a deal if I can. But these three are different; they don't look the sort to take no for an answer, if you know what I mean.'

'Have they threatened you in any way?'

'No. Not as such. But I felt threatened. Is that the same thing?'

'Near enough. Why – what happened?'

'One of them had a gun. I saw it under his coat – like I was meant to.'

Armed peddlers of hooch? It wasn't unknown, but usually in the cities, not all the way out here. Somebody must be desperate to unload it. 'How did you leave it with them?'

'They're coming back this evening about seven – with a van. They said to have the cash ready.' He shrugged. 'Like I have any choice in the matter.'

'Does anybody else know?'

Maillard shook his head. 'Are you kidding? If I'd told some of the soaks around here, they'd think it was Bastille Day and New Year all in one. I'd have a queue back as far as the *Mairie*.'

'Good. Keep it that way. I'll call in around seven.'

# Chapter Twenty-one

As Rocco was on his way to the city, a meeting was taking place in an annexe not far from the main Interior Ministry. There were three men present: Josef Girovsky, Marcel Levignier and the man called Delombre. A guard on duty outside the door was to ensure that there would be no interruptions.

'I am reliably informed,' Girovsky began accusingly, 'that the policeman Rocco is still taking too much of an interest in our business.'

Levignier shifted in his seat. 'I don't see how that can be; he's been instructed to finish his investigation and move on. In any case,' he added primly, 'there is nothing for him to see. The patients have been moved on and the place is empty.'

'And Drucker is beyond reach,' said Delombre softly. His eyes glittered as both men turned to look at him. He was enjoying the moment but ended their suspicions by conceding, 'Not that far beyond reach, sadly. As for Rocco, I'm sure I can put a more permanent stop to his investigations if you want me to. Just say the word.'

'No,' Levignier murmured. 'Not yet. We cannot go around killing policemen for doing their job. It would arouse too much interest, and we don't need the heat.'

'As you wish,' Delombre replied with a shrug. 'But once gone, the problem's over. Period, as the Americans would say.'

'Can't you simply order him to stop?' Girovsky put in forcefully. 'He's a public servant, isn't he?'

'Like us, you mean?' Levignier gave a dry smile. 'Actually, it doesn't work like that. There are lines of command, layers of authority. I can't order him to do anything, even if I wanted to... although,' he added dryly, 'I might sometimes try. All I can do is suggest.'

'Then suggest. Suggest he stops his infernal digging! You talk of lines of command. Can't you lean on his senior officer?'

'Of course.'

'Would it stop him?'

'Yes, it would. He would have to obey.'

'There's a "but" in there.' Girovsky looked frustrated. 'Thank God I don't have to run my businesses this way.'

Levignier adjusted his jacket sleeve and wondered why he was having to justify his actions to this self-important idiot. Probably because this idiot could, with his current exalted position within French industry and a long list of important 'friends', get Levignier shoehorned out of his job if he so chose. He sighed and explained, 'Men like Rocco are like hungry dogs: they will obey a direct order, but they never lose the hunger. Rocco would always wonder why he was taken off a live investigation, why he wasn't allowed to finish his job. It would be like an open sore, always there. Eventually, someone would listen to what he had to say.'

'So what the hell do we do? He's going to ruin things if he's allowed to carry on. Discussions are approaching a critical stage and we cannot afford distractions. The

Chinese are paranoid about any bad publicity getting in the way of future trade deals. A hint of scandal right now would derail everything we've achieved so far. And the Americans and British are waiting in the wings to scoop up anything we drop.'

'They know the details of the discussions?' Levignier queried. 'I thought it was still highly confidential.' His tone was waspish, as if realising that he was not as well-informed as he'd thought.

'They're bound to know something by now. Nothing stays secret for long where international trade is concerned – especially something of this magnitude.' Girovsky straightened his tie with a fussy movement of his hand. 'What the Americans don't look for, the Taiwanese will almost certainly suspect and make capital out of, given a chance. They stand to lose too much to let it lie without a fight.'

'Which is why action has been taken against a certain party – action, I remind you, that was instigated by yourself and your colleagues.'

'It was drastic, but necessary.' The Pole waved a hand as if anxious to brush the subject away. 'And don't pretend that you don't stand to gain considerably in status and position if all goes well in the next few days and weeks. I know how these things work in government corridors. We're not so different, you and I.'

'I know very well what I am,' Levignier said shortly. 'And it's nothing like you.'

Girovsky's mouth twisted. 'Touchy, I see. Well, never mind. I have no illusions, even if you do. These plans, if realised, will see France race ahead of our competitors and take a lead in the arms race for the next twenty years. The figures are eyewatering and the country needs this deal in particular. The Chinese are the future, believe me.'

'That's quite a sales pitch,' said Levignier. 'But you don't have to convince us, Mr Girovsky. We do what we are told, which means whatever is in the best interests of France. Don't forget that.'

Girovsky nodded. He took a deep breath, as if realising he'd been making too much of the statement. 'Of course. Forgive me – but there is so much riding on this for all of us… it makes me forget myself.' He glanced at Delombre, who had remained silent while the scene was played out. 'But I do not discount this gentleman's… contribution. So far we have kept everything under control. But having a rogue policeman nosing around because of other elements could bring the whole edifice crashing down. As I said, the Chinese are highly sensitive to bad news and will not hesitate to back out if there is any embarrassment threatened.' He looked keenly at Levignier and said heavily, 'You mentioned the best interests of France; well, let me remind you, the consequences for France if these negotiations fall through are too dire to contemplate.'

'For France… or for you?' Delombre murmured nastily. Girovsky flushed with indignation. 'I resent that! I, too, work for the glory of France, not for lining my own pockets!'

Levignier stopped further discussion by simply raising a hand. He was silent for a few moments as he thought the matter through. He knew when he was being played, but knew also that there are some games you cannot afford to win. And Girovsky, backed by many high-powered friends, was playing a winning hand with his use of patriotism as a driving factor. 'Very well. We'll stop him another way. The only way.'

Delombre brightened immediately. 'So I get to bag a cop after all, then? That would be a first.'

'Enough,' Levignier growled, without looking at him. 'This is no joke.'

'So what are you proposing?' Girovsky queried.

'You'll see. We'll appeal to his baser instincts, let's leave it at that.'

The Pole looked mystified, but acquiesced.

Delombre, on the other hand, sat back. A faint smile was edging his lips, as if he knew that his services were not going to be called off for long. He could tell by the desperation in the atmosphere, especially with the Pole. Levignier, too, was more anxious about this affair than he had seen him before, and had a great deal to lose. Talking would only go so far. Then action was needed.

It was why he was here, after all.

## Chapter Twenty-two

'I'm overworked and underpaid as usual, since I'm sure you'll get round to asking eventually.' Captain Michel Santer picked up a portion of bread and tore off a length of crust. 'But my wife quite likes me this week and my dog thinks I'm his real father, so what can I complain about?'

He and Rocco were in a small family-owned restaurant near the Guy Môquet métro. It was just far enough away from the Clichy *Commissariat*, and in an establishment guaranteed not to attract any of his police colleagues. Not that he or Rocco had anything to hide; but he knew enough about the way his friend worked to judge that discretion was often the safest bet.

'Job-wise,' he continued, chewing the bread, 'things are going to hell, though. There's not enough budget, courts are logjammed, which makes bringing cases take forever; we're facing another influx of workers from the south, not all of them interested in real work; and we've had two kidnaps, three bank jobs and a number of gang-related killings all in the last ten days. I tell you, the world's going insane. Why can't people withdraw money from the banks in the usual way?' He grinned at the old cop joke. 'How about you – still enjoying lousy roads, empty fields and the smell of cows on heat?'

'Compared with what you've just described, I'd rather have what I've got, thanks. And, as far as I know, cows don't go on heat. Who's been kidnapped?'

'Oh, some junior diplomat outside an apartment near Rue Legendre. Not his own place, incidentally, but belonging to a young woman who is most definitely not his wife but the niece of a senior army officer with strong Catholic morals. Daft bugger.'

Rocco grinned. 'The officer or the diplomat?'

'Both. The other kidnap was an industrialist's wife taken along Avenue de Friedland. Both lifted off the street in broad daylight, no reliable witnesses, no descriptions, smooth as butter. The Ministry are pointing the finger at a gang of Sicilians with a known modus operandi: lift someone high-profile, send back a body part along with something the family will recognise to show it's serious, then wait for offers.'

'Sounds extreme. Does it work?'

'Christ, yes. You'd be surprised how much is paid without argument on the strength of a gift-wrapped finger in a dinky little *Galeries Lafayette* box.'

Rocco had seen similar tactics before. In France, crimes with a sense of style somehow appealed to a certain section of the population. Outrageous bravado, a hint of carnival or *théâtre*, suitably laced with a snub to authority, usually did the trick and earned the criminals a degree of sympathy. But it only lasted so long before their excesses began to take over.

'We had the first two a couple of months back,' Santer continued. 'They both turned up alive and kicking in a warehouse out near Roissy – minus a finger each. Of course, we get the blame for not catching the kidnappers or preventing it in the first place, but some people just set themselves up for it.' He gave a wry smile. 'The press, of course, have given the gang a name: *Les Lafayettes* – which is going to do nothing to stop or help catch them.' He shook his head. 'They'll end up having songs sung about them, you watch. Are you going to tell me what you're up to? Not planning on knocking off *Monsieur le Président*, are you?' He chuckled and reached for another piece of bread. He was referring to Rocco's earlier investigation into an assassination attempt on President de Gaulle, which had come close to finding Rocco himself embroiled in the affair and accused of taking bribes.

Rocco poured them both some water. 'I'm looking for information on a man named Ardois, possible first name Simon. He was between forty-five and fifty-five, probably worked for the government in some capacity.'

'You make that sound like the past tense, as in deceased.'

'He got himself killed.' Rocco described the man's death in the therapy pool, and the likelihood that the name Ardois might be false. 'I'm stumbling in the dark on this and not likely to get any help from official sources.'

'Why's that?'

'Because the place he was at is a government sanitarium. Very few patients, or whatever they call them, which is why I think he was a state employee.'

'I've heard about those places. Not for us lowly drones, though, are they? I hear they've got a couple near Bordeaux. Think of all that peace and quiet… and St Emilion. God, it's not fair.' He shook his head sadly and sipped some water, then pulled a face and signalled for the waiter to bring the menu. 'So, in short, you thought I might be able to use my many contacts to do your work for you, is that it?' He gave Rocco an arch look. 'You think I carry a crystal ball in my pocket?'

'I figured that if anybody in the whole of Paris would know who to ask, it had to be you.'

'Flattery is the subversive tool of the idle seducer.'

'Very profound. Who said that?'

'I did.' Santer looked pleased with himself and mildly surprised. He scanned the menu briefly, then closed it with a snap and said, 'I don't know why I'm looking at this – I know what I want: *ragoût de sanglier* with spinach. And I'll have some of that Merlot you keep at the back.' At the waiter's lift of an eyebrow, he added, 'Yes, I know it's a little light to go with the boar, but my friend is paying and I feel like being unconventional today.'

'Very good, sir.'

'Oh, and a slice of that Mimolette cheese. Haven't had it in a while and since it hails from up north, not far from where my friend works, I might as well show support for the poor disadvantaged region. I'm also watching my weight.'

The waiter looked at Rocco, who signalled that he would have the same, and departed in a flourish.

'Where do they get their balls, these people?' Santer murmured, staring after him. 'I swear, if de Gaulle himself walked in here and ordered the same, that idiot would show the same disdain.' He shook his head. 'Where was I? Oh, yes. How important is this man… Ardois, was it?'

'Yes. There are two people dead already and another one's missing, probably also dead. I'm trying to find out who killed them. Unfortunately, ISD have other ideas.'

'That bunch of hooligans? Christ, stay away from them. They're not nice.'

'You know them?'

'Only what I've heard, which isn't good.' Santer sat back. 'I knew a couple of undercover cops once who stumbled on a case of corruption in the customs service. Stuff was coming into the country that should have been stopped, with big payments of cash changing hands in sports bags late at night making sure that certain officials would look the other way. They followed the trail and claimed it went all the way up to the headquarters building here in Montreuil. Then ISD homed in on the case and pulled rank. The two investigators objected to being frozen out just as they were zeroing in on their man, but it did no good.'

'What happened?'

'They got posted to some backwater patch – a bit like you only not so interesting. It turned out ISD were working on a connected case... or so they claimed, and theirs took precedence over the cops'. After that it went very hush-hush. Personally, I wouldn't want to get on their bad side. They play rough and don't much care who knows it. However, if they get away with it, it means the Minister must like their style and they get results which makes him look good.'

'I'll bear it in mind.' On impulse, he said, 'There's another name you could try: Rotenbourg. Same first name.' He explained about Stefan's slip of the tongue.

Santer scribbled both names on a piece of paper and stood up. 'With names like this, he could have come from Alsace or somewhere along the borders. I don't know anyone over that way, though. Give me two minutes and I'll get someone on checking the files here in Paris. It might take a while.'

'Don't worry, it's a start. He might have had some connection to Paris, even if only for work or residency purposes. But don't spend too much time on it and tell your man not to stick his head above the ramparts.'

'Never fear, he won't.' He looked across at a waiter hovering by the kitchen door. 'Tell him to get that wine over here. I won't be long.'

Rocco smiled and beckoned the waiter over. 'Will do.'

–

They were just enjoying coffee when the waiter approached and said there was a telephone call for Santer. The captain jumped up and went to take it, and came back after two minutes with a folded paper napkin which he dropped alongside Rocco's plate.

'My man had to ring a couple of people, but he found no male with the name of Ardois fitting your description and age range. But he did find a Rotenbourg, first name Pascal. He lives down in the fourteenth *arrondissement* near Montrouge. Nothing special about him, though.'

'How did he find the name?'

'From the incident records. Rotenbourg's car was broken into and vandalised seven months ago, and reported to the local station for insurance purposes. Nothing of note since.'

Montrouge. Rocco knew the area vaguely. He looked at the napkin on which Santer had scribbled the man's name, followed by an address and telephone number. It was worth a visit, if only to discount the possibility that another family member might have been sequestered in a state-run institution guarded by a military guard.

# Chapter Twenty-three

Later that afternoon, *Commandant* Levignier was at his desk, scanning a report on a group of disaffected council members in a group of islands in the Pacific known collo- quially as a 'Dom Tom' – *départements et territoires d'outre-mer*. It was one of France's overseas territories over which ISD had a watching brief, and he'd blocked all calls while he dealt with it. Some of the Dom Toms, as distant as they were, needed swift intervention by *gendarmes* from time to time, to avoid trouble escalating.

When his internal phone rang, he snatched it up ready to reprimand his secretary.

It was Delombre.

'The Pole's been trying to get hold of you. Says it's extremely urgent.'

'I know. I've been out of touch because I'm busy. What does he want now?' Levignier was getting tired of the way Girovsky seemed to think ISD were at his beck and call. Unfortunately, 'the Pole', as Delombre liked to refer to him, possessed a lot of influence in both the Inte- rior and Foreign Ministries, and right now, when French commercial interests were looking up and expanding, that was unlikely to change anytime soon.

'He's asking about our guest's other half, and still pissing himself over that cop, Rocco. One of his spies says he's been asking about the little pervert, Devrye-Martin, and a cop he thinks might be working at Rocco's instigation has been checking records for the names Ardois or Rotenbourg. He thinks he got the address in the fourteenth *arrondissement*.'

Levignier dropped the papers he was reading. Mention of both names brought a nasty stab of alarm. The fact that Girovsky had the ability and resources – without doubt somebody inside the Establishment – to keep tabs on matters that were not his to worry about was concern enough. But Rocco's interference this deep and his ability to come up with information leading to Rotenbourg was far worse. 'What sort of questions? And how the hell did he find out about the names?'

'We told him, didn't we?'

'Not Girovsky, you fool – Rocco.' But Delombre was right: it had been a mistake telling Girovsky about the Clos du Lac and its secrets. Not his fault, though, he reflected. Some middle-ranking secretary with a loose lip in the Ministry had blabbed about the precise function of the facility, thinking it would impress the Pole into keeping his mouth shut about the man they called Ardois. In doing so, he had also let slip the fact of Devrye-Martin's existence and background. It had clearly been enough to make Girovsky dig deeper for his own ends.

'Rocco's just a typical nosy cop,' Delombre continued. 'He's been asking questions. It was inevitable that someone would talk. For my money it's that nurse, Dion. She looks the sort to have opened up to him in a big way.' He sniggered at the double meaning, and Levignier winced with distaste. There were some people he would have wished not to work with, but Delombre was too good at his job to get rid of. For now, anyway.

'The nurse won't have talked,' he replied. 'And Rocco's no ordinary nosy cop. You shouldn't underestimate him. What does he know?'

'He found the name and where the family lives. Apparently he contacted a cop in their home town, and asked if he had a photo. I checked with records, and they said all photos of Devrye-Martin had been suppressed from police files. But the cop asked the local newspaper if they had one. Nobody thought of that.'

'Why the hell would he want a photo?' Then he knew why. On the night of the murder, Rocco had been in the pool house with Devrye-Martin. The man had wandered there by mistake, apparently. Drucker had assured him that Devrye-Martin was so drugged up he wouldn't have known his own name, let alone anybody else's. And if Rocco had learnt anything from him, he'd have been all over them before now, demanding details. No, however he had discovered Stefan's real name he clearly didn't know enough about him to make a real fuss.

But a photo was different – especially to an observant police officer. It meant he'd be able to identify the patient. And that meant a dead man come back to life, now living inside a government facility.

'Has he found one?'

'One of the editor's assistants did. She didn't know anything about the case and thought she was helping the police. She couriered it direct to Rocco.'

'Damn. How did Girovsky get to hear about it?' The Pole's private spy network was in danger of making the men at the Quai d'Orsay look like amateurs. Not for the first time he wondered at the blurring of lines between state and private security, and where it would end.

'The editor contacted the family and they rang their lawyer. He went to the Ministry. I think Girovsky's got an insider.'

Levignier made a mental note to investigate that. Not that it would surprise him. But whatever his importance to France's industrial and commercial future, the Pole was seriously pushing his luck if he started interfering with matters of state. 'Very well. Leave it with me.'

'I could always,' Delombre reminded him, 'arrange for a slight accident. Even businessmen have been known to trip over paving stones.'

'Don't be ridiculous,' Levignier replied automatically, his mind racing ahead with an idea. 'Tell him… tell him we'll let Rocco have his man.'

'Won't the family object?'

'For the greater glory and honour of France and our future, and with his sordid little history? I'm sure they won't mind making a small sacrifice.' Levignier nearly chuckled at the irony of a man like Devrye-Martin being useful to anybody. 'I might remind them how much money they'll save in the long run.'

'Couldn't he expose the others?'

'How so? He's a pathetic nobody with nothing on his brain but his perversions. He knows nothing about the others. They were all drugged and docile, remember? Besides, I don't mean we'll actually let Rocco have him, as such. That would be asking for trouble. We'll simply allow the inspector that illusion, then take it away from him before he gets too close.'

'I don't follow.'

'Let Rocco have the photo. It will keep him diverted. Not that he'll find anything. But I'm more concerned about his interest in Rotenbourg. I have an idea which should stop Rocco in his tracks.'

'Like what?'

'Well, if we can't get him warned off officially, how do you think an accusation of sexual assault will go down on his record? Maybe that will take his mind off his job.'

'Clever. You using anyone I know?'

'No.' Levignier had deliberately not brought Delombre in on this, or his little army of dubious undesirables who would do practically anything for money. Besides, he already had in mind a person who had the qualities and background that were ideal for bringing off what he'd planned, and he didn't want Delombre getting involved. In addition, the girl he was thinking of was a little special, and he wanted to see how susceptible she was to taking some extra-curricular orders.

'What do you want me to do in the meantime?'

'Nothing. The plans go ahead. You stand by in case of emergencies.'

'I usually do. Does that include our woman guest?'

'Not yet. Everything there is under control. She's being kept quiet, but her husband hasn't cancelled his talks yet.'

'Cold-hearted bastard.' Delombre sounded almost impressed.

'He won't be for much longer. If we have to, we'll use the Sicilian trick.'

'Can your men handle that?'

'They'll have to. If not, you may have to go in and help them.'

'Sure. Let me know when and where.'

Levignier thought about that. He'd deliberately kept Delombre out of the kidnap plan because the man didn't do subtlety; he much preferred violent action leading to final solutions. While that method had its place, it was too soon yet. But if things weren't resolved, he might have to get Delombre to finish it all for good. And that meant everybody. Kidnappers and victim.

'Do we know where Devrye-Martin is?' Another urgent problem, but this one was definitely Delombre's number to deal with.

'No. Nobody's seen him since he walked out of the halfway house he was taken to after leaving the Clos du Lac.'

'Careless. How did it happen?'

'Everyone thought he was heavily sedated, like the rest. Apparently not. We know he's not in Evreux, but he's got a couple of friends who share his passions. They might help support him if he stops getting money from his family. We're keeping an eye on them.'

Levignier thought about it for a few moments. From rumours on file about Stefan's earlier activities, it seemed certain that he had been peddling his photographs to fellow 'enthusiasts' in France and all the way up to Holland before he was discovered. Now he was out from under his family's care, and likely to find it difficult to obtain any more of their money, it was likely that he would try to get back into his old trade. Either way, if Rocco got to Devrye-Martin first, it could all get very messy. Bad enough that a former dead man accused of taking pictures of naked children had come back to life, courtesy of the state; even worse if that same man had discovered anything of consequence about his former housemates and their reasons for being at the Clos du Lac. A man like that was highly likely to trade information of that nature to keep himself out of trouble. 'As soon as you locate him, go see him.' He allowed himself a cold smile. 'Make it an aftercare visit.'

'Meaning?'

'You know what I mean. Soothe his pain. Make it permanent.'

## Chapter Twenty-four

By the time Rocco arrived at the address Santer had given him for Pascal Rotenbourg, it was late afternoon. Traffic on the main streets was building into the frantic hustle that Parisians seemed to hate and enjoy with equal measure, and he wanted to get clear of the city before it got too bad. But he needed to check Rotenbourg's address on the off chance that he was in.

The six-storey building occupied a corner site, midway down a tree-lined street, with shops at ground level and apartments above. Metal balconies ran the length of the second and fifth floors, and windows promised almost floor-to-ceiling views out across the park on the other side. The area seemed prosperous and was just enough off the beaten track to have a sense of calm, in spite of the traffic not far away.

Rocco parked his Citroën and walked into the building, nodding at a concierge cleaning a large brass handle on the open front door. Inside, against the rear wall, stood a bank of mail boxes. Rotenbourg was on the fourth floor, accessible by a clanky lift with concertina gates, a relic from earlier in the century.

'Can I help you?' The concierge had followed him inside. He was in his sixties and light on his feet, with the springy stance and bent nose of one who might have done a few years in the ring in his youth. His eyes flicked rapidly over Rocco and he nodded, making a quick assessment. 'You're police?'

Rocco nodded and showed him his card. 'I'm off my patch here,' he told the man, 'but I'm trying to verify some information about a case I'm working on. It could be a wrong lead, but these things have to be checked out. Just ticking boxes, that's all.'

The man shrugged. 'Fair enough, Inspector. We've all got a job to do, right? What name are you after?'

Rocco told him, and the man nodded. 'I know Pascal. He's not in, though. Went out this morning, early. You want to leave a message?'

'Sure. Can you ask him to call me?' Rocco felt the beginnings of an easy lead slipping away. Whoever the non-swimmer had been, it clearly wasn't Pascal. He took out another card and handed it over. 'What does he do, this Pascal?'

'Do? I'm not sure. He's retired from business, lived here about ten years, quiet, minds his own, comes and goes – you know how it is.'

Rocco sensed that he'd got as much information out of this man as he was going to volunteer, but asked, 'Does he have a brother?'

'I don't know. You'd have to ask him. He never says much about his background and I don't ask. Why, is there a body?'

Rocco smiled and thanked him, and headed back towards Amiens.

–

At ten to seven, Rocco walked through the door of the café in Poissons, and nodded at Maillard, who was drying glasses behind the bar. A pungent fog of cigarette smoke hung in the air, and the voice of an excited talk-show host was fighting a losing battle with a volley of shouts from the far end of the room and a fan clattering noisily in one corner.

'Drink?' Maillard jerked his head at the row of bottles behind him.

'Make it coffee,' said Rocco. He preferred a clear head when dealing with unknowns, and a cop who was seen to drink didn't instil confidence in the general public. In this case they were six men, all with the spare, weathered look of farm workers. Two were playing a noisy game of *Babyfoot* watched by four others slouched on chairs against the wall.

They nodded at Rocco, but said nothing.

'They're not here yet,' Maillard murmured softly. He poured a cup of coffee, black as treacle, and placed a slim glass of cognac alongside it, and a box of sugar cubes. 'On the house. Cognac, too.' For good measure, he opened a jar of gherkins and placed a fork on the counter, and tapped the lid of a large jar of pickled eggs.

Rocco nodded his thanks but passed on the eats. 'Will these men be any trouble?' He didn't know any of them, but his cop's instinct wondered if they were known to the drink sellers and might pitch in to help them.

'Not this lot. They know who you are, so they'll behave.' He smiled grimly. 'If they don't, they've got a long way to walk to find another place to drink.'

'Good. Just act naturally and don't look at me when they come in.'

As Rocco leant on the bar sipping his coffee, the outside door opened and three men walked in. They had the rough look of country men, but there was something about them that set off his internal alarms. The first man was short and stocky, strutting in as if he owned the place. Confident. The leader. He was wearing a pair of very shiny shoes with pointed toes. Definitely not country-style. The second man was tall and whipcord thin, in need of a shave and carrying a long shopping bag which might have contained a baguette. He looked edgy.

The third was the gunman. Rocco recognised the signs immediately. He was wearing a coat, and had one arm clamped across his middle. He was heavily built and watchful, and his eyes flicked around the room, taking in the other customers before arriving on Rocco, who was leaning heavily on the bar with a coffee cup in his fist. The glance didn't linger, but moved on to settle on Maillard.

'Gents.' The bar owner spoke automatically, but his nerves showed in the lick of his lips and the flick of the cloth across the counter.

'Set them up,' said the short man, carefully lighting up a Stuyvesant from a new packet as if it were a sacred ritual. The lighter looked like gold, expensive. 'Your best whisky all round. Big ones. We've got business to discuss, right?'

Whisky, thought Rocco. The drink of choice for criminals like this. As if they'd know a good whisky from a jar of paraffin.

Maillard went through the motions and slid three full glasses across the bar. The first two men took theirs and sipped as if they had all the time in the world. The third man reached past them and picked up his glass, throwing it back in one go.

A bad sign, Rocco reflected. A gunman who drinks like that is an amateur. Dangerous.

'Hey. You.' It was the stocky man. He was looking at Rocco, standing square on, crowding him. 'You mind giving my friends and me some space? Go drink some-where else. We want to talk in private.'

'He's OK,' Maillard said quickly. 'He won't say anything.' He was clearly worried that Rocco might be too far away to stop anything blowing up in his face.

'I don't care if he goes and plays the "Marseillaise", I don't want him here.' The man pushed at Rocco's shoulder. 'Go on, get lost.'

The bar had gone quiet. The men at the far end of the room were standing still, the click of a final ball rumbling into a pocket chute the only sound.

Rocco straightened up and looked down at the man, who seemed to realise belatedly how tall he was, and moved back a step. In the following silence, he heard a rasp of material, then an ominous metallic click. The hairs on his neck prickled, and a glance at Maillard's shocked expression told him all he needed to know.

He turned his head. The gunman had produced a short, double-barrelled shotgun from under his coat. It was a *lupara*. Easy to hide and popular for use on bank jobs, to intimidate. It had no range to speak of, but in a crowded place like this, it would be horribly indiscriminate and deadly.

'He said move, big fella,' the man murmured, his words sliding together. Clearly the whisky hadn't been his first drink of the day. As he spoke, the barrels lifted, catching the overhead lights and revealing a faint layer of oxidisation on the metal and a network of scratches.

An old weapon held by an amateur, Rocco thought. But still dangerous. He guessed that the drinks deal had been a bluff; they were here to take whatever they could get. It made him wonder how many other places they had hit today. The Bonnie and Clyde tactic: select an area, go for the easiest targets, hit them one after the other, then get out. Quantity before quality, the sign of limited aspirations.

His attention veered to the man with the shopping bag. He'd been silent throughout, not moving, just watching the play develop. Another danger. Yet his hands were empty of weapons.

Time to end it.

Rocco nodded and muttered thickly, 'OK, OK, no need to get rough. I'm leaving.' He pushed himself away from the bar like a man exhausted, and stepped towards the door. Past the stocky man who was now grinning, stepping alongside the man with the shopping bag. As he went to move past the gunman with the *lupara*, he turned and ground the barrel of his service pistol hard into his neck, just below the earlobe. Up close the man reeked of drink and cigarettes and an overlaying aroma of stale sweat.

'This is a MAB with seven rounds in the magazine,' Rocco said softly. 'Move a muscle and I'll use the first one to decorate this room with your brains.' He flicked a glance at the shopping bag man and said, 'You'll get the next.' Finally he looked at their leader, whose mouth had dropped open in shock, the Stuyvesant dropping to the floor at his feet. 'Then you.'

It was overdramatic, the language of cheap gangster films and barroom bravado. But it was something the three men understood.

Yet still the man with the shopping bag made a move. His hand slid down inside the bag. Before he could touch what he was reaching for, however, Claude Lamotte stepped through the doorway and rested the tip of his Darne shotgun against the man's shoulder.

'I wouldn't do that, my friend. You'd never even hear the noise this thing makes before your head bounces round the room like a dead chicken.'

Moments later, all three were sitting in chairs, hands and feet tied together by two of the farm workers with rope from Maillard's back room, while another stood over them with a raised billiard cue.

Rocco called the office in Amiens and arranged for a team to come out and collect the men, while Claude searched them for weapons and identification. It didn't amount to much: a couple of cheap knives and a set of brass knuckledusters, and some documents showing the men to be from Cambrai in the north. The shopping bag contained an ancient revolver pitted with rust. And a baguette with a chewed end.

Amateurs.

'Hey, Inspector,' one of the farm workers called out. 'Is it true you stuffed a live grenade down Didier Marthe's pants and made him run into the *marais*?'

'No,' Rocco replied. He knew the man wouldn't believe him. There were already some lurid stories circulating about how he'd dealt with the former Resistance worker who'd tried to blow him up. After this evening, the rumours would only get stronger and more colourful.

'Seriously?' one of his friends urged. 'I'd have paid to see that, the little shit.'

'Seriously. I made him walk, in case he tripped and hurt himself.'

'Mother of God,' Maillard breathed later, as the three robbers were untied and led out to a police van. 'You had me fooled back there, for a moment. I thought… Never mind what I thought.' He looked a little tight around the eyes, and reached for the whisky bottle. He poured shots for everyone in the bar and sank the first one himself, then pushed one each across to Claude and Rocco. 'Glad you were here, Inspector. Anytime you want anything... well, let me know. I owe you.' Rocco drank his in three sips, then said, 'You don't, but thank you. You did well, Georges. Stay safe.' He bid goodnight to Claude, who looked as if he'd suddenly had hero status conferred upon him, and waved to the other patrons, then went home to bed.

# Chapter Twenty-five

Next morning, after a brisk early run down the lane and back to shake the cobwebs loose, Rocco arrived at the office to find Massin waiting for him. The *commissaire* flicked an imperious finger and led him upstairs to his office. He told Rocco to close the door before retreating to stand behind his desk.

'Inspector Rocco, would you mind explaining why you were in Paris yesterday?' Massin stared at him for a second before sitting down, his authority imposed. 'Only I feel you may have forgotten that your transfer here last year means you no longer have to work the Clichy district. Or can they not cope without your valued assistance?'

'I should have spoken to you first, I know,' Rocco conceded mildly. He wondered how Massin had found out. 'But I had a lead to follow up on and I didn't want to leave it too long. You were out.'

'Yes, I was. Part of the reason I was out was because I was having my ears chewed off by my superiors from the Ministry, due to an investigator under my control finding it impossible to follow orders.' He tapped a rapid drum-beat on his desk, then said more evenly, 'I hear you and Lamotte apprehended three men last night in the course of an armed robbery. Well done. Was it anything to do with the Clos du Lac business?'

'Thank you. But no. They were gutter rats looking for an easy hit.' He brought Massin up to date on his investigations into the sanitarium deaths, carefully omitting any mention of Rotenbourg and concentrating instead on the possibility that one of the inmates had been Stefan Devrye-Martin, who was supposed to have died in Thailand. 'As soon as I have a photo, I'll be able to prove it.'

'I see. That could prove… awkward for someone to explain.'

'Someone in the Ministry, certainly. It would have needed a signature to get him in there.'

'In that case,' Massin reached down and slid a brown envelope across his desk. It was addressed to Rocco. 'I think this might be what you're waiting for. I picked it up from the front desk.'

Rocco opened the envelope and slid out a large black and white print. It showed a fat man climbing out of a car. In the background was a flurry of pennants and bunting, and a crowd of people dressed in summer clothes. The man was grinning at somebody off to one side, a lock of hair damp with sweat clinging to his face as he heaved his corpulent body out of the passenger seat. Around his neck was a professional-looking camera.

Rocco handed over the photo. 'That's him.' Stefan had lost a lot of weight since the picture was taken, and his hair was shorter. But there was no mistaking him: it was the man he'd talked to in the pool house.

'And he's supposed to be dead, you say.'

'According to Captain Antain in Evreux. Blood poisoning following an accident.'

'This is serious. Extremely serious.' Massin placed the photo on the desk and took a turn around his office, lips pursed. Rocco knew instantly what he was thinking: Stefan had been hiding in a government facility; if his 'death' were true, then they were faced with what amounted to possible state-sponsored deception.

'I'd like to sit on this for a while,' Rocco said, giving Massin a way out of reporting this to his superiors. Instinct told him that if this went up the chain of command, it might disappear and never be mentioned again.

'Why?' Massin sounded unsure, no doubt weighing up his options to find the least damaging one.

'I still think the death of the security guard, Paulus, is tied in with the murder at the Clos du Lac,' he added. 'It's too coincidental that they died on the same night.'

'How so?' Massin sounded distracted.

'Paulus either helped kill him and was then disposed of to keep him quiet, or he saw what was happening and the killer was forced to deal with him. The business about a crime of passion is a nonsense.'

Massin lifted his eyebrows. 'Why? Do they not go in for that sort of thing around Poissons?'

It was the nearest Rocco had ever come to hearing Massin make a joke. 'I'm sure they do,' he replied dryly. 'But crimes of passion in the countryside involve shotguns, axes or knives – maybe poison. Not nine-millimetre pistols. And Paulus was navy-trained; he wouldn't have been easy to fool or overcome.'

Massin lifted his chin and stared at the ceiling. 'So he was killed by someone he knew or trusted?'

'I believe so.'

Massin looked down at the photo. 'So where do you go from here? How does this "dead" man walking figure in all this?'

'I think he might know more than he was letting on when I met him. According to nurse Dion, he didn't always take his medicines and was in the habit of wandering the corridors at night, looking for anything he could pry into or steal. She described him as highly manipulative. I'd like to find him and see if he saw anything.'

What he didn't say was something that would have had Massin flying into a panic: that if Stefan Devrye-Martin was hiding in the Clos du Lac with official connivance under an assumed name, who were the other patients whose names were not their own? And why were they being hidden?

'Inspector Rocco?'

A call had been put through to Rocco's desk. The caller was Pascal Rotenbourg.

'Speaking. Thank you for calling, Mr Rotenbourg. I'm sorry to disturb you on what might be an irrelevant matter, but I wonder if you can answer a question for me?'

'Of course. How may I help?' The man sounded cultured, his voice calm and measured. Not normally the case, Rocco thought, when members of the public had messages to call the police and expected bad news.

'Do you have any male family members, by any chance?'

A momentary hesitation, then, 'I do, as a matter of fact. A younger brother. What is this about, Inspector?'

'Could you tell me his name?'

'Yes. It's Simon.'

## Chapter Twenty-six

The woman felt faint when she came to this time. The food supplied by the man had been plentiful and edible, pasta and fruit, but she'd had no appetite beyond a slight nibble to show willing. It was obvious the men were looking after her for a reason, yet that made little difference to her situation.

She was still a prisoner.

She tried to work out how many days it had been since she'd been taken. It felt like a lifetime already, but she knew she was suffering the effects of dehydration and fatigue. She tried to relate it to her inner sense of time and the regularity of food, then by bodily functions. On the first night of captivity she had been provided with a hospital bedpan of uncertain vintage, and water to wash herself. But the trauma of being kidnapped and the ever-present fear at what might happen to her since then had played havoc with her system, obliterating any kind of feel she might have once possessed for her own body's functions. It could have been anywhere between two and five days, she couldn't tell for sure.

Leather Jacket had remained all but mute, keeping his conversation to instructions about when to move, what to do, what not to do. He had not repeated his earlier threats, but she doubted that was out of kindness. His tone of voice seemed to be that of a man who was comfortable with himself and certain that he would not be disobeyed. A man doing a job.

The harsher threats might come later.

He was a soldier, she thought at one point. Or had been. But in post-war France, like the rest of Europe, soldiers were common enough, so what did that tell her?

She tried to judge where they might be, but she was finding it hard to marshal her thoughts. The stuffiness in the van was at times intense, until the man opened the door and allowed in some fresh air. But for all the good that did, in terms of seeing her surroundings, she might as well have been sealed in a cardboard box.

The van had been moved three times now, a mobile prison cell. But never far. A few streets, perhaps, or kilo-metres, she couldn't tell. It started up, it moved, she was thrown around, and all the time the man sat in the back with her. He never answered her questions, never said anything to show her the slightest comfort. But then, he never actually mistreated her, either.

It was her one consolation. Surely, if he ultimately meant her harm, he would care little about how she fared physically or mentally. But did that mean she would be allowed to one day go free?

She felt greasy and grubby; the first from not being allowed to do more than cat-wash, the second from being thrown around on the dirty mattress and the metal floor of the van. And each time the vehicle moved, it set up a curtain of dust which she could taste even through the hood that was always over her head. As for her hair... she thought with a grim sense of the banal what a waste of money that had been. Going to Marcel, only to have these men throw her around like a parcel moments after leaving the salon, must rate as some kind of wicked joke. Maybe, she reflected sadly, that should tell her something.

–

Levignier thought long and hard before making his next two phone calls. The first was slightly risky and could blow up in his face. But news from a reliable contact had confirmed that Rocco was closing in on a possible source of information, and where he would be later that evening. In addition, Levignier's own emotions were driving him to ignore the minimal risks. Partly it was the desire to win, and the awards that would bring if men like Girovsky kept their part of the bargain. He hadn't set out on this plan out of a desire to be the loyal servant, expecting no reward for himself; the Pole had made it very clear what he could expect if Levignier played his part and the negotiations with the Chinese went as expected. But this particular idea had been fuelled by recalling an image of the person he was thinking of, who worked not two hundred metres away from his own office, several floors down. He dialled an internal number which got him the research section of the Ministry.

A woman's voice answered. Cultured, smooth, like silk on bare skin.

'Marcel Levignier,' he said, his throat suddenly dry with excitement. 'I have a job for you. It's very important.'

He described what he wanted done, that it needed her attention right now and how he couldn't entrust the task to anyone else. The agreement was immediate, if slightly wary, as he'd expected. She wasn't, after all, a case-hardened officer. When he was asked about risk, which he'd also anticipated, he added smoothly, 'Don't worry.

There's no danger, I promise. It's not that kind of job. But since you ask, I have arranged to have two of my men close by at all times, watching.'

'So I just find out who this man is and what he's doing?'

'That's all. You've been trained on constructing chance encounters?' He knew the answer to that one.

'Yes.'

'Very well. Make the contact, talk, a drink, maybe coffee – somewhere public, of course, with lights. But be discreet.'

'Of course. Is he likely to be suspicious?'

The basic training course for all low-level officers, he remembered, with its bullet points of steps to consider when making a first 'cold' contact. It was kids' stuff, really, and he could have recited the questions she was asking like a rota. Still, at least she was remembering the lessons.

'He has absolutely no reason. Trust me.' He read out Pascal Rotenbourg's address in Montrouge, and gave a detailed description of Rocco so that she couldn't make a mistake, then said, 'Go there at seven forty-five and wait. Be discreet, but when you see him arrive, check the area and see where he goes. Remember the training. The rest is up to you. Afterwards, ring me and I'll tell you where to come. I want a personal report. This is not for paper or telephone.'

'I understand.' Her voice ended on a tone of uncertainty, but he ignored it. He knew why: a personal field report was a rarity, and lifted this task above the merely mundane.

He put down the phone, for a brief moment wondering if he hadn't oversold the assignment or misjudged this person's abilities. But the situation was too serious for hesitation; risks were necessary to achieve success, and he had to get Rocco out of the picture in a way that did not suggest Ministry interference in his police duties. Next, he dialled another number and gave the man who answered the same address. He outlined what he wanted done.

'How rough do you want it?' the man asked.

'As rough as you feel necessary,' Levignier purred. 'Rocco won't be happy to see you, that's for sure. But don't let that sway you. Use your own judgement.'

# Chapter Twenty-seven

There was no sign of the concierge when Rocco arrived back at the apartment block in southern Paris. It was eight in the evening and the streets of Montrouge were quiet. He buzzed to gain entry, and announced his name into a speaker box. When the door clicked, he made his way up to the fourth floor, his footsteps echoing on the tiled stairs. He kidded himself that he needed the exercise, but knew it wasn't that. Something about the ancient lift raised the spectre of being caught in a confined space, with no way out... another reminder of his time in the suffocating jungles of Indonesia.

A neat, slim man in his sixties was standing at the top of the stairs on the fourth-floor landing. He was comfortably dressed in expensive slacks and a short-sleeved shirt, with leather slippers on his feet. He nodded and extended his hand. 'Inspector. I would like to say welcome, but I have a distinct feeling this is not the right occasion. Please, come this way.'

He turned and led the way into an apartment overlooking the front of the building. It was neat – like the owner – and almost spartan in appearance, with no clutter, few ornaments and only a few shelves of books to relieve the cool colour of plain walls.

'I break with common practice and have coffee at this time of the evening, Inspector,' Rotenbourg announced.

'I find it helps me sleep, although I'm always being advised otherwise. Will you join me or would you prefer something stronger?'

'Coffee's good, thank you.' Rocco made a show of checking the books while Rotenbourg disappeared through a doorway into a small kitchen. He hadn't got far before the man returned moments later with a tray piled with cups, saucers and a battered metal percolator with a glass top.

'My mother's,' Rotenbourg explained easily. 'Makes the best coffee this side of Morocco. You've given me a good excuse to use it for more than just myself.' He indicated a chair. 'Please, sit down and help yourself.'

While the ritual pouring and addition of cream and sugar went on, they were both silent, until Rotenbourg put his cup down and said, 'So. This is not good news, I take it?' His manner was wary, Rocco noted. But wary and composed. He hoped it was going to make things easier, although time would tell, depending if he had got the correct Rotenbourg or not.

He explained about the death of a man in the therapy pool of a sanitarium, glossing over the lack of his identity by saying that there was a question of confidentiality, but that he wanted to move things along a bit faster. He added that a member of staff had let slip the name, but that it had not been possible to confirm it through any official channels.

'I'm sorry if it seems indelicate,' he added, 'but there are times when rules and regulations get in the way of resolving a case such as this.'

Rotenbourg nodded. 'Bureaucrats love to surround themselves with words and safeguards,' he acknowledged.

'Pity the rest of us who have to live with the results. How did you find me?'

'I used to work out of the Clichy commissariat. They helped.' When Rotenbourg frowned, he went on to explain, 'You had some damage done to your car, I believe.'

The other man's face cleared. 'Ah, that. I'd almost forgotten. Some street kids, I believe, although they never found out who did it.' He examined his fingernails. 'Tell me, did you get a look at this unfortunate person?'

Rocco nodded. 'I did. But I'd be lying if I said I could describe him.'

'I'm not surprised.' He turned to a small side table and picked up a photograph in a frame, lying face down. He handed it across and said, 'Is this him?'

Rocco stared at the photo. The man smiling out at him was in his fifties, slightly heavy around the jowls, with thinning hair and frameless glasses. The resemblance to Pascal Rotenbourg was clear in the eyes and around the mouth.

It was the man Rocco had seen in the pool at the Clos du Lac.

He handed the photo back. 'I'm very sorry.'

Rotenbourg took the frame and studied it for a few seconds, then brushed his fingertips across the glass before putting it back on the table, this time face up. He picked up his coffee and took a sip. Outwardly he seemed unaffected by the news, but Rocco could see a pulse beating in his forehead.

'How did he die?'

Rocco hesitated only for a second, then gave the details of the Clos du Lac and the swimming device that had caused his death. Although Pascal Rotenbourg would probably never find them out for himself, he felt he owed it to the man to be honest.

Pascal listened without expression all the way through. After a few moments silence, he said, 'And the official conclusion is what?'

'That I can't tell you.' Didn't want to, was what he wanted to say. He was hoping this man could give him a lead, no matter how tenuous.

'You're thinking it was suicide? It sounds… complicated.'

'Possibly. I'm afraid I've seen more complex methods, though. Any drugs he was on could have contributed, of course.' He continued apologetically, 'Is it possible your brother was suffering from depression?'

'My brother Simon worked for the Ministry of Foreign Affairs, Inspector. To me, that kind of stifling environment would have certainly been depressing. But Simon was nothing like me. He loved his work. I'm not sure what he did exactly, but it was mainly in the area of overseas trade.' He smiled thinly. 'He wasn't a spy, in case that's what you're thinking.'

'I wasn't, but it's good to know.'

'But spying is what he finally did. What probably got him killed.'

The words dropped into the room like a thunderbolt, and Rocco, about to take a sip of his coffee, froze. 'I'm sorry?'

Rotenbourg stirred in his chair, and for the first time allowed some emotion to cross his face. 'I don't mean he got caught digging his fingers into our defence files or taking photographs of documents and turning them into microdots, Inspector. Nothing quite so mundane. But he was threatening to reveal some information that he had stumbled upon. I believe that is why he was squirrelled away in some secret place such as the one you just described.'

'Can you tell me what he found out?'

'Certainly, although I doubt that you as a state employee will be able to do much with it. However, it might make me feel a lot better knowing that a man who relishes bending the rules to get to a solution also knows what Simon did.' He dusted imaginary lint off his trousers and continued, 'My brother and I were never very close; we had different paths, different aims. I ran my own business in the clothing industry for many years, while he preferred the safety of the government sector.' He gave a thin smile. 'Much good it did him, from what you now tell me… although I can't say I'm surprised.'

'Why not?'

'Well, in spite of our differences we kept in touch. About six months ago, Simon came to see me. He was very… disturbed, I think the word is. He had discovered evidence of a conspiracy within the Foreign Affairs Ministry to direct trade negotiations away from certain countries in favour of others, drastically affecting certain industrial figures here in France and overseas. Now, you might say isn't that what the Ministry is supposed to do?' He shrugged. 'To an extent, yes. As long as France does not lose important trade deals which endanger jobs here, that is their primary concern.'

Rocco was already getting a sense of something nasty in the woodshed, but he didn't want to jump to conclusions. 'Which countries are we talking about?'

'One being favoured was communist China versus Taiwan. The Taiwanese were already unhappy at the signals they were getting. According to Simon, the deals being discussed were mainly defence issues.'

'Arms?'

'Correct. Along with a few add-ons, like agricultural machinery and engines to please the doves on both sides. The other country favoured was Russia, although I don't know who was disadvantaged. He never got round to telling me. His main concern was that important figures in what he called the "grey" government – the civil service, in the Quai d'Orsay and Place Beauvau – were working rather too closely with certain influential industry leaders to steer talks along, shall we say, chosen routes.'

'Wouldn't industry overall have been the winners?'

'Some of them, absolutely. But where there are winners, Inspector, there are always losers. Take my own commercial sector, clothing. For every deal I won, one of my competitors would lose out – and vice versa.' He gave a slow, emphatic shrug. 'It's the way of the world. Next time, one of us would have to sharpen our pencil accordingly and hope to redress the balance. But what if I had managed to gain an advantage over my competitors by enlisting the help of government figures who should have remained neutral in the matter?'

'It would change things.'

'Of course. And what Simon told me about wasn't a deal for a few thousand shirts or dresses; he was talking major trade agreements, of the kind that companies live and die by and countries such as ours will do almost anything to secure.'

'You're talking about collusion at a high level… in return for what? I can see what it would be for the industries concerned, but why would the government employees seek to steer the negotiations?'

Pascal held out his hand and rubbed his fingers together. It produced a faint rasping sound in the silence of the room. 'Money, what else? Money and influence – even the promise of jobs in the private sector, if that's what they wanted. Help sign off a trade deal worth many millions of francs and you could expect substantial rewards for your efforts.' His face twitched with bitterness. 'I might not have been very close to my brother, Inspector, but the idea that he was silenced for profit makes my soul ache.' He sighed. 'Sadly, the people working for money or power are the easiest to understand. I've met plenty of them in my time, and business thrives for them and because of them. It's the ones working for duty who frighten me most. The patriots.'

'Why?'

'Because they're the most relentless in their aims, the most committed. And our country has more than its fair share of men who will do anything – *anything* – under the thin and misguided veneer of their patriotic duty. Even murder.'

'Are you serious?'

'All I can tell you is what Simon told me – and what subsequently happened to him. He took his concerns to his superiors, and laid out everything he knew. Names, dates, details. They did nothing, merely told him that they would investigate. Then he began to notice small things. Things that frightened him.'

'Like what?'

'He was being followed. Here in Paris, then when he travelled overseas. His mail was delayed, and he began to notice odd sounds on his telephone line. Friends found themselves being questioned about him, then rumours began to circulate about his reliability and suitability for the job. For a man who had reached a level of some responsibility it was akin to being attacked in public and having his sanity questioned. In the end he broke. Or, at least, that's what they said. That's when he came to see me. Shortly afterwards, he was suspended and confined to a secure hospital just outside Paris.'

'Were you able to see him?'

'Only under supervision, and never for long.' He shifted in his seat. 'I say this not to insult you, Inspector, but have you ever considered just how close we are to living in a police state?'

Rocco said nothing. He already knew there was no answer that would satisfy this man. And there were many like him who were level-headed and sane.

'Everything hinges on control through power: the army, the paramilitary machine, the police – even the fire brigade. And worst of all, the invisible army of bureaucrats.' His mouth twitched. 'Do you ever come up against them – the men in suits? I would hazard a guess that you do.'

Rocco nodded, remembering the various grey men with whom he'd butted heads. He allowed a few moments to pass, but it was clear that Pascal was done.

'You're saying you think your brother was silenced by the state because he knew things that he shouldn't.'

Another shrug. 'Possibly. Probably. Actually, I'm saying he was silenced by certain elements working *within* the state because he was willing to question what was going on. And questions like that are not permitted.'

'Do you have any proof of this? Anything at all?'

Rotenbourg sighed. 'Simon didn't leave me a dossier of facts and names, if that's what you mean. But he did tell me something interesting. The last time I saw him before he was moved on – undoubtedly to this Clos du Lac place you mentioned – the escort who was with us all the time during my visits was called away for a telephone call. It wasn't long, but it gave me a chance to ask Simon what was really going on. He was having trouble organising his thoughts by then – I'm pretty sure because of the drugs he was being given to calm his nerves. But he managed to tell me that there was a plan in place to force an important industry figure to abandon nego-tiations with the government of Taiwan and switch to China instead. This individual favoured Taiwan because he didn't trust the Chinese – and he was digging in his heels on the matter and looked like taking senior govern-ment figures with him. It was threatening to destabilise the whole series of negotiations, so a plan was hatched to use "extreme methods" to change this man's mind. It was Simon's emphasis on those words, not mine. The economic figures, he said, easily justified the means to those involved, although the French government itself would not have been aware of anything underhand.'

'Who was this man?'

'I never found out. Our escort returned and I was asked to leave.' He stared out of the window for a long moment, before turning back to Rocco. 'That was the last time I spoke to my brother.'

'Do you have anything to support your belief that he was killed? I'm not saying I don't believe you, but it's a question we have to address.'

Rotenbourg nodded emphatically. 'Absolutely I have proof. The one single thing that tells me his death wasn't an elaborate and sickly form of suicide, Inspector, is that Simon had a pathological fear of water. It had been with him since he was a child. He would no more have considered climbing into a harness such as you describe and drowning himself than he would have contemplated swimming *La Manche*.'

Rocco felt a wash of something approaching relief. The angry conviction in the man's voice was unswerving. He had his lead after all. His problem, however, was proving anything.

'If you can find the man,' Rotenbourg continued, 'this industrialist Simon spoke of, then I believe you will find the truth.'

# Chapter Twenty-eight

As Rocco walked back downstairs, thinking about what Pascal Rotenbourg had said, his nose picked up a subtle hint of perfume in the stairwell. Pleasant. Expensive. It was a subtle reminder of his wife, Emilie. He experienced a familiar moment of regret, then it was gone.

He stepped outside the front entrance of the apartment block and walked along the pavement towards where he'd parked his car. He was glad of the feel of fresh air on his face and the sense of space around him. He'd left Rotenbourg with a promise that he would do what he could to find his brother's killer. But they both knew it was going to take phenomenal luck to turn up any firm information – and then to process it through the system.

'I know what the machine of state is like, don't worry,' Pascal had said, escorting Rocco to the door of his apartment. 'I have no illusions about that. Greater injustices than this have been covered up, I'm sure.'

There were few people about and then only some distance away at the far end of the street. Across the way, the park was in darkness. This place, Rocco thought, was like a small oasis in the world of noise and movement just a block or two away. It was probably the quiet that allowed a faint sound of music to drift through the air. Melancholy and slow, it added to the atmosphere that he had known so well before his posting to rural Poissons-les-Marais, and he wondered if he would ever entirely lose his feel for the streets of the city. Maybe after a few more years, he conceded, but not yet.

His thoughts were interrupted by movement as the slim figure of a woman stepped out of a car just ahead of him. The door closed and the woman turned, then stumbled, dropping something to the pavement. Without thinking, Rocco bent to retrieve it. At the same time, the woman did the same, and they bumped shoulders.

'Oh, my God!' The woman was startled and stepped back, her heel twisting beneath her on the paving stones. She would have fallen had Rocco not grabbed her arm.

'It's all right,' he said quickly, reassuring. 'No need to be alarmed.' He handed her the small purse she had dropped. 'I'm sorry to have frightened you.'

'No – thank you,' she said quickly, turning her head and flashing him a smile. In spite of her surprise, her voice was soft and melodic, and he saw in the half light of the street lamps that she was tall and slim and elegantly dressed, with short blonde hair. As she took the purse, her fingers brushed his, and she placed her other hand on his arm. 'I'm sorry, but I think I've broken the heel of my shoe.'

Rocco looked down. The heel was bent at a critical angle, leaving the woman teetering on one foot. He knelt and checked, but the damage was beyond anything he could do to fix.

'Is it ruined?' She leant over to see, a hand resting on his shoulder to steady herself. A couple of dress rings, he noticed automatically. No wedding ring. Her skin smelt of soap and another, faintly familiar fragrance he couldn't quite place.

'Sorry. It's beyond salvage. If it was a horse, I'd have to shoot it.' He stood up, glad she couldn't see his face in detail. He felt like an idiot. Her hand stayed where it was on his shoulder, so that they both ended up standing close together. Rocco felt a momentary confusion. 'Umm… Can I help you back into your car, or do you live somewhere close by?'

'Actually, just two streets away,' she said. 'I had to park here because I was late back.' She looked coy and added, 'but I shouldn't really tell a complete stranger that, should I? My father would be *so* angry with me, even though I'm not exactly a little girl.' She gave a light laugh, showing small, perfect white teeth. 'Although I suppose we're hardly strangers, are we? You did, after all, save me from falling, so that puts you in the realm of a knight errant, don't you think?'

Rocco reached for his card and showed it to her, to allay her fears. Some instinct, however, made him doubt this woman was the kind to be alarmed too easily.

She stared at the card, tilting it to read it under the weak light. 'You're a policeman?' Her eyes widened. Then she appeared to recover and leant back to survey his dark clothes and shoes with an expression of obvious approval. 'But you're not in uniform.'

'No. I'm an inspector.'

'A detective? I've always wanted to meet a real detective! It's my lucky day, after all… well, other than for my shoe, I suppose.' She flicked back a stray lock of hair, uniquely feminine and natural. 'Still, there's no serious harm done, is there? Typical of the streets of Paris, waiting to trip the unwary… or bring salvation to the fallen.'

Rocco felt a small dig of unease. He had the feeling she was trying too hard. But why?

'So, would you like me to help you further, or…?' He left the rest unsaid. The soft smell of her was beginning to tickle his senses.

'Well.' She looked along the pavement in the direction he had been walking, to where a wash of light was flowing across the street from a bar beyond a large patch of shadow formed by a broken street light. 'Perhaps you would let me buy you a drink, Inspector, as a thank you for your gallantry? Or maybe a coffee – unless, of course, you're on duty?'

'Actually, I'm not, but—'

'Very well. It's the least I could do.'

'I don't think so.' His attention had been caught by a curl of cigarette smoke issuing from the window of a dark Renault near the patch of shadow.

'How about dinner, then? We could get to know each other.' Her voice was soft, gently insistent. 'You could tell me about some of your more interesting cases.' She leant in closer, her grip firm on his arm. He thought the look in her eye suggested that dinner was not what she was talking about.

The driver's door of the Renault clicked open, and two figures inside began to move. The pale oval of their faces were bland and indistinct. Two men. Big.

In the same instant the memory of where Rocco had come across the perfume before came flooding back.

It was inside the foyer of the apartment block where Pascal Rotenbourg lived. It had reminded him of Emilie.

'Why would I want to do that?' He gently released her hand from his arm and stepped back. The car passenger had one leg out of the car, his foot on the ground. Waiting.

'Because you're a policeman and a gentleman and I'm a lady?' She gave a slight lift of her shoulders and tried to smile, but there was a sudden tone of doubt in her voice. She glanced fractionally sideways, a small reveal, and Rocco knew he'd been right.

'I wish,' Rocco murmured enigmatically. 'But I'm afraid it's only partly true.' He wondered who this woman was working for. Whoever it was, if they were prepared to try entrapping a police inspector in a street set-up, they either had the weight to carry it through or were ready to take even more drastic measures if it failed. If so, he doubted that waving his police card would put them off.

He stepped back and walked unhurriedly to his car, slipping a hand into his pocket for the reassuring feel of his gun.

—

Rocco pulled in to the kerb at the first café he saw and went inside. Flashing his card, he walked through to the telephone in the rear and rang Santer's home number.

'Sorry to disturb you, Michel,' he said, 'but I just got accosted in the street in Montrouge by an attractive blonde. She broke her heel and I saved her from falling over.'

'Typical,' Santer muttered. 'Bloody country hicks come into town and have all the fun. Why are you telling me this? Is it to make me feel inadequate?'

'I think it was a set-up. It felt too contrived. And there were two men watching from a parked car.' He gave Santer both the car numbers and a description of the woman. He hadn't seen the men clearly enough for any useful details, but they would probably be leg-men, anyway, called in to do a job and forget it. He also doubted the numbers would lead anywhere, but it was worth a try.

'All right. I'll see what I can find out. It'll have to be tomorrow, though, as I've got a date to go promenade with my dog. If I don't go now he'll explode with horrible consequences.'

Rocco disconnected and thought about warning Pascal Rotenbourg that he was probably under surveillance. There was a risk with it, in that Rotenbourg might easily take umbrage and go to the press with his story. If so, Rocco's career goose would be well and truly cooked. But if his instincts about the woman's perfume were correct, then Rotenbourg had a right to know.

He went back out to the car and drove back to the apartment. There were no signs of watchers, but he knew that was misleading: unlike the entrapment team he'd seen earlier, any surveillance professionals would be out of sight.

He pressed the buzzer to Rotenbourg's apartment. It took a while for the man to answer. He sounded groggy with sleep. 'You should watch your back,' Rocco told him, and gave him a brief description of his encounter on the street.

Rotenbourg sounded surprisingly calm. 'You lead an exciting life, Inspector,' he murmured, his voice steady, even over the tinny intercom. 'But thank you for the warning. Would you like more coffee?'

Rocco declined and released the button. He'd had enough for one night. Time to get back home. As he drove, he flicked on the radio and caught a news broadcast. It confirmed in part what Santer had mentioned.

'*Police are still refusing to confirm that a kidnap victim taken off a street in the eighth arrondissement is the wife of a notable industrialist. A spokesman for the police has said that no details can be released yet, but they are expecting to make an announcement shortly. In other news, trade talks with the People's Republic of China in Peking have been interrupted by objections from Chinese negotiators, who are unhappy with what they call "shadow discussions" with Taiwan. Members of the French Ministry of Foreign Affairs say they hope to resolve this shortly and resume talks—'*

He switched it off again. Kidnaps and trade, it seemed, were a growth industry.

## Chapter Twenty-nine

'Not losing your touch, are you?' Levignier addressed his remark to Jacqueline Roget as she stepped inside his apartment a stone's throw from the Jardin du Luxembourg in central Paris. His tone was only mildly accusatory in spite of his frustration at the failure of his plan to hobble the inspector. It was a small setback, and one he had not anticipated. But he had no desire for a fight with this woman, who was not as fully trained in security-related duties as other more direct-action members of the department, but infinitely better connected. The truth was, although she fulfilled certain assignments for his department, and he had a clear and definite authority over her, she was no lackey. Yet that knowledge alone, quite apart from her attractiveness, filled him with excitement. 'I thought this one would be easy for you.'

Her eyes flashed momentarily at the implied dig, but she shrugged fatalistically. 'Maybe your Inspector Rocco doesn't like women,' she commented.

'You think?' The thought actually hadn't occurred to him, and he made a mental note; it might be an angle worth investigation. People with what society regarded as peccadilloes were always more vulnerable to pressure than others. Maybe this would be Rocco's.

His hope was short-lived.

'Actually, I don't. Quite the opposite, in fact.' She was holding a broken shoe, the heel hanging off at an angle. She was now wearing a pair of flat pumps. 'I broke my shoe. These were my favourites.'

'That's not a problem, my dear. Send the bill to me personally.'

She dropped her purse on a Louis Quatorze table in the hallway and lifted carefully tended eyebrows. 'Thank you,' she murmured coolly, 'but I do this work because I want to – not for the money. I also enjoy what I do… but I would like to do more.'

'I'm delighted to hear it.' Levignier interpreted that to mean much more than real work, and decided to call a truce. Now was not the time for business talk, anyway. He took her arm, leading her through into the front salon. Like the rest of the apartment, it was elegantly furnished with antiques and fine glassware, a legacy from an uncle in the Foreign Service who had loathed the countryside and preferred to stay in the city where he was assured of every luxury money could buy. Levignier didn't have quite the same level of finances, but the apartment was his for free, which gained him certain advantages, such as the attentions of certain young women. Like Jacqueline, he hoped. He had never tried to push beyond their professional relationship before, but he was sure there would be little resistance from her. As he knew well, power carries its own aphrodisiac.

He poured drinks and shrugged off his jacket. It had been a long day. He had been waiting for news of Rocco's potential downfall. Accused of assaulting a distraught and very convincing Jacqueline Roget, daughter of a senior member of the French diplomatic corps and therefore above reproach, it should at least have put a dent in the inspector's investigations long enough to have drawn attention away from anything to do with the Clos du Lac. He made a mental note to call off the men he'd instructed to deal with Rocco. They had missed their chance. He would have to think of another tactic for dealing with him. Especially now he had tracked down the dead Rotenbourg's brother.

'You sure you saw Rocco come out of the apartment block?'

'Yes.' Jacqueline took the glass he handed her. 'As soon as I got the call from your men, I went round and checked upstairs. I could hear voices from inside. How did you know he was going to be there?' She sipped her drink, eyeing Levignier carefully.

'That should not concern you.' Levignier tasted his own drink and reflected not for the first time that Jacqueline, considering her rather limited position in the security world, seemed to have an insatiable appetite for information. She appeared to have little hesitation in asking how things were done in a world where methods and explanations were rarely discussed unless among fellow professionals of a certain level. It made her dangerous, he decided, if she ever chose to switch allegiance. In fact, she probably already knew far too much than was good for her. Or himself, come to that.

The thought made an extra frisson run through him.

'So what do you want me to do now?' she asked, glancing around the room with a faint frown. 'I thought you wanted to discuss the next approach.'

He smiled, a predator's response. 'We don't have to discuss that now, do we?' He stepped in close and touched his glass against hers, managing to brush her forearm with his other hand. He noticed it raised goosebumps on her soft skin. 'Work can wait until tomorrow.' His throat thickened at her nearness, and he felt a rush of heat pushing him on. It was the thrill of the chase. The last girl who'd come here had been less wary, but far more... accommodating. Yet somehow, less alluring. Less of a challenge.

Then she was moving away from him and placing her glass on a silver coaster.

'I'm sorry, but I really can't stay,' she said, and moved towards the door. She paused long enough to pick up her purse.

'Wait.' Levignier was feeling an unaccustomed loss of control over the situation. This hadn't happened to him before and he felt a ripple of irritation. She should have been willing to do anything, not be walking away from him.

'I'll see you tomorrow,' she said calmly. When she turned to look at him, there was no mistaking her air of quiet confidence. 'I must go home. I promised to call my father. I haven't talked to him in a while.'

Mention of her father the diplomat, a tough and powerful figure from the old school of French diplomatic circles, was enough to stop Levignier in his tracks, his ardour dented. He hadn't reached his position without knowing who he could tangle with and who he couldn't. And Roget *père* would be the wrong person to cross.

'Of course,' he conceded smoothly. 'I should have realised you'd be tired. It can wait.'

He watched her leave, then reached for his private telephone directory. There were always other young women eager to advance in official circles, keen to do whatever extra-curricular work was expected of them.

Perhaps Jacqueline Roget would take a little more time to come round to his way of thinking.

# Chapter Thirty

Her mobile prison had moved again.

After an interminable period of inactivity, with no sounds to connect to the outside world, Leather Jacket had opened the door and told her to lie down. Moments later, the engine had started and they had rumbled over what seemed like a patch of rough ground, before picking up speed. She had lost track of time, slipping between wakefulness and fractured sleep, her head spinning as if she were drunk. Then the van had slowed and stopped, and the engine had been turned off.

Silence.

She had waited a long time before hearing footsteps. The door had opened and Leather Jacket had placed a cardboard box on the floor by her side. She had leant over and felt the contents. It held fruit, bread and a plastic bowl of what smelt like rice and vegetables. She was becoming quite adept at telling what she had by smell and touch, she thought. Much more of this and she'd know what was coming before it reached her.

'What time is it?' The question came without thought, a touch of normality, as if she had woken alongside her husband on a normal day and all was well with the world. She went hot, oddly embarrassed at sharing such an intimate moment, although she doubted Leather Jacket would have made the connection. She had the distinct impression, although she could have been wrong, that there was no Mrs Leather Jacket waiting at home for him.

'Early,' he said shortly. 'Or late. What's the difference?' She nodded, and felt for the bottle of water in the box.

What difference indeed? Late or early, she was always thirsty in this bloody cell. As her fingers found the smooth shape of the bottle, she paused. Her stomach jumped.

Toothpaste. She could smell fresh toothpaste on his breath. And the air coming in from the outside was cool and moist.

Signs of morning.

She smiled inside her hood. It was only a small victory – a tiny one in the grand scheme of things. But to her, right here and now, an important one.

'What's up – not hungry?' the man demanded, misinterpreting her hesitation. 'I can take it away if you like, throw it in the hedge. It's all the same to me.'

*Hedge.* Was that another clue? Were they near a park?

'No. Leave it, please. I'm stiff, that's all. I need time to loosen up.'

There was a familiar clank as he placed an empty bedpan on the floor, and she heard him grunt as he lifted the one she had used, then backed out of the van, closing the door behind him.

She no longer felt any embarrassment at the deeply personal nature of the exchanges. Since he had chosen to put her through this, he could put up with the indignity of handling her soils twice a day. She had even developed, after the initial desire to scream with frustration, an ability to deal with her panties and stockings as efficiently as her constraints allowed, while blind and bound and trying not to spill the bedpan as it filled. At least the man had finally agreed to untie her legs, which had helped. And at least, she decided, if his mind had ever veered in that direction even for a moment, he surely couldn't feel anything like a physical interest in her. Not now.

She ate an apple and nibbled at the rice and vegetables, sipping water to help it down. Her throat was still raw, but not as bad as after the first day. She was adjusting. She wondered if she was becoming institutionalised. And what her husband was doing. He must be going out of his head.

As usual, the man had given no explanation as to why they had moved again earlier, merely saying that she should lie down and be ready. She had done so at once; small rebellions or demands were sensible in her view, to at least demonstrate in a small way that she was no weeping wallflower. But allowing herself to become injured through her own stupidity was ridiculous. Besides, she was still waiting for that slight chink in his armour, that little gap that might allow him to say something that would tell her where they were and what they were going to do with her.

But there had been one development: she had heard a conversation between the two men, this time from the other side of the bulkhead panel between the back of the van and the driver's cab. It had been brief but revelatory.

'...had orders to move... a nosy cop coming to see why we're... here.' It had sounded like Leather Jacket, although she couldn't be certain.

'At last. Getting fed up with... glad to get rid... no longer our problem.'

'... we must do... handover... don't want them sending that crazy legionnaire bastard after us.'

They stopped talking. Moments later the van rocked slightly and the rear door opened. It was Leather Jacket.

'I have something for you,' he said.

She heard the hiss of released gas and the glug of liquid. *He was pouring her a drink.* He took her hand and pressed a bottle into it. It was cold and pear-shaped, with beadings of moisture down the sides. She recognised the smell of citrus.

'Freshly opened,' he told her. 'Frankly, I got sick of seeing you drink tepid water.' He loosened the drawstring on the hood and held a cup to her mouth. She felt the glorious liquid fizz across her tongue and down her throat, and threw all caution to the wind. It was such a relief she nearly cried. She gulped the rest like a child given a rare treat.

Soon they were on the move again. The earlier exchange between the men had told her very little, save that they, Leather Jacket and the driver, were scared of somebody – and it wasn't the police. Whoever they answered to, she decided sleepily, lying back and feeling her eyes begin to close, it sounded as if he would not put up with failure.

She yawned and wondered who the crazy legionnaire was. Maybe Robert, who knew some very strange people with dangerous eyes and quiet manners, had some even crazier legionnaires who might get her out of the living hell she was in.

It was only as she found herself drifting off that she realised the noise and movement of the van were receding, leaving her with a dull, drifting sensation, and the citrus drink had left her with an unusually bitter aftertaste in her mouth.

# Chapter Thirty-one

When Rocco arrived at the office next morning, he found René Desmoulins waiting for him with a knowing grin.

'Some snoot from the Ministry was asking after you,' he said. 'He called twice, demanding to know when you were in. Have you been annoying them again?'

'Only a little. Did he leave a name?'

'No. I asked, but he got shy. He said he'd call back.'

'How do you know he was from the Ministry, then?'

'Because he sounded like he'd got a stick up his arse and refused to leave his name.' Desmoulins smiled. 'As my old maths teacher used to say, "QED".'

Rocco nodded his thanks and went to his desk. There was a note to call Michel Santer. He dialled the number at the Clichy commissariat, and got put through.

'You move in mysterious ways, don't you?' said Santer. 'The Renault came up blank. We all know what that means.'

'Official,' said Rocco. Or criminal, although he doubted that.

'That's my boy.'

'And the woman?'

'Now that's where it gets interesting. According to the records, the driver's name is Jacqueline Roget. She's the daughter of a career diplomat who's served most of his time overseas. She works for the Interior Ministry, although I haven't found out which section. I floated the name around and it seems she has various friends at Place Beauvau, but nobody special.'

The Interior Ministry. Like a bad penny, forever in the background. He shouldn't have been surprised, given the way they operated; any and all means were permissible in the interests of the state, even, it seemed, using the seductive offspring of one of their own to spring a trap. Only it hadn't quite worked in his case. As before, proving it would be next to impossible. He was willing to bet that one of the young woman's 'friends' was Marcel Levignier.

'There's something else,' Santer continued. 'I think your Mademoiselle Roget is playing two sides of the same street.'

'How so?'

'I had a rare moment of inspiration, and ran the car number past a friend of mine who works on buildings security in and around the Quai d'Orsay. Her car has been logged in five times over the past two months at an annexe to the Pensions Ministry. He didn't say it directly, you understand, but he gave me that squinty look.'

'What?'

'The look that says they have nothing to do with pensions. He sort of hinted they might be part of the DST.'

The DST (Directorate of Territorial Surveillance) was the domestic intelligence agency responsible for, among other things, counter-espionage and the protection of national technology and industry.

'Is he sure?'

'Well, she's quite nice to look at, and he remembers faces. I know Bobo well – he's good at that kind of stuff.'

Rocco thought it over. He wasn't sure what it told him other than that Jacqueline Roget, she of the fragrant perfume and the broken heel, mixed with some very devious people. It was not impossible for people to work for both agencies, either on loan or semi-permanently. But which one had set her on him last night? He couldn't believe the DST would have an interest, although nothing was beyond them. The ISD, perhaps?

'You're getting in deep again, Lucas,' Santer warned him. He only called him Lucas when he was worried. 'If they're going to these lengths to do whatever it is they're trying to do, they must have their reasons.'

'Or they have something to hide.'

'I don't even like to think about that. Hiding things is their job. Is whatever you're working on worth it? Can't you simply enjoy the benefits of a quiet, rural existence and homely country girls?'

'I'll be fine,' Rocco replied. 'Thanks for the help.'

'I'm serious. If you were an important figure in the government or, say, the military, I'd say you had just missed being drawn into a honeytrap last night. Think yourself lucky, my friend: had you not had the resistance of a monk, not to say the romantic soul of a peasant, you could now be compromised... or worse.'

–

Rocco put the phone down and thought over what Santer had said. He didn't think the DST or Levignier's group would sink to the outright murder of a cop; but they would almost certainly try to put him off an investigation if it suited them.

His phone rang.

'Inspector Rocco?' The voice wasn't one he recognised, but it carried the authoritative ring of someone accustomed to being heard. The caller Desmoulins had mentioned?

'Yes.'

'Why are you making enquiries about the Devrye-Martin family?'

The question threw him for a moment. Not about last night, then. He said, 'Who's asking?'

The man batted the question aside. 'Let's just say that it's enough for you to know that I represent the Ministry of the Interior. I say again, why the interest in this family?'

'None of your business,' Rocco replied easily. He put the phone down and waited. He had no doubts that the call was indeed from the Ministry, but he wanted to see how long it would take the man to call back.

Two minutes went by before it rang again.

'Is my name good enough for you?' It was Levignier of the ISD. He sounded tense. 'Speak to my colleague, Inspector Rocco, or face sanctions.'

Rocco thought about it. Pursuing an investigation wasn't an offence, but disobeying Ministry orders was. He said, 'What kind of sanctions?'

'Let me see. How about suspension for obstruction and lack of cooperation to start with, along with unprofessional conduct? Then, since you will subsequently become a civilian, criminal prosecution for interference in official matters that do not concern you. Does that sound enough?' There was a thump as the handset hit a desk. Moments later another voice came on. It was the first man again.

'Let me repeat my question, Inspector. Why the interest in this family?'

Rocco thought about it. If they were asking this, they knew he'd made enquiries about the family, and therefore Stefan specifically. So why were they being coy about mentioning his name? Still, it meant an alarm had been tripped somewhere along the line between him speaking to the policeman in Evreux, and the request being put to the local newspaper. Someone somewhere had been tipped off.

Captain Antain in Evreux hadn't been exaggerating: the Devrye-Martin family had influence, and they had evidently used it.

'The name appeared on some property recovered from the Clos du Lac,' he answered neutrally. 'I was following a lead in relation to the killing of André Paulus, the security guard at the sanitarium. Levignier knows about it. Ask him.'

'One moment.' There was a hollow sound as the phone was covered, during which Rocco could hear only a murmur in the background. Then the man came back. 'There is no connection, Inspector Rocco. I think you are wasting your time.'

'You can't know that. Nobody can.'

The man ignored him. 'The Paulus death must have been due to an unrelated matter, outside the sanitarium. I think we can all imagine what that might have been. You should concentrate your energies on pursuing that avenue. If you cannot find a solution, the case should be abandoned until more evidence is forthcoming. I'm sure you must have other important duties to attend to.'

The line went dead. Rocco put the phone down. The message was clear.

He'd been warned off.

# Chapter Thirty-two

Rocco picked up one of the photography magazines and leafed idly through the pages. Being reminded of Stefan had set him thinking about what the man might know... and where he might be now. In some state-sanctioned hideaway, no doubt, courtesy of his family's influence. He tossed the magazine aside, frustrated by the tangle that was opening up before him. He had no illusions about the workings of government departments. To most of them, the furtherance and protection of the state underlined everything they did. But he also knew that every barrel held at least one rotten human apple who saw nothing wrong in misusing the power of the state machinery, whether in some perverse interpretation of their duty to the country or for their own criminal or career ends.

The magazine had landed on the edge of his out tray, and had balanced in such a way that the pages began to flick over in slow motion. He watched it, wondering where to direct his attentions next. Stefan or...

The pages stopped turning. Settled back and lay still. The uppermost photo was a startling picture of sand dunes in the early morning, the black and white showing the contrast been shadow and light, smooth sand and ragged peaks. A sidebar gave the technical details of the snapshot, from the camera and film used, down to the settings, lens size and the time of day taken.

And something written in hand along the inside margin. He reached forward and tugged the magazine towards him.

The writing was faint, in pencil, and hard up against the crease in the spine. Not so much hidden but tucked away where it would not be easily noticed. He turned the magazine sideways and worked his way through the scrawl, letter by letter.

12 bis, Rue des Noces, Pontoise.

He sat up. Glanced at the map on the wall. He knew Pontoise. It was a commune in the Val d'Oise, on the north-western outreaches of Paris. Small enough to be ignored and nudging close enough to the capital to hide within its shadow. He'd been there a few times following suspects on the run from Clichy. The town was a short car ride or train journey from the capital to make it a first stop for desperadoes who didn't quite fancy their chances out in the countryside. Other than the criminals he'd chased down, he remembered the place for its contrasts of an elaborate and historic cathedral and the gloomy narrowness of some of the backstreets where he'd been forced to trawl for runaways.

But why would Stefan have written such an address in one of his magazines? He checked the front cover again. Recent enough to make his nerves tingle.

He pulled the phone towards him, intending to ask the front desk to get the number for the Pontoise police, then thought better of it. If the note in the magazine meant what he thought it did, talking to the local police could be a mistake. Not that he suspected them of anything underhand; but if any word that had been put out to watch out for anyone seeking information on the occupants of the house in Rue des Noces carried official clout, they would have no option but to report it.

The problem was, treading on a neighbouring district's toes could provoke a lot of questions over jurisdictional discourtesies. And Massin would hate that.

Tough decision. He picked up his car keys and looked across the room to where Desmoulins was scratching out an arrest record. He looked bored and restless. Rocco waited until the detective's sixth sense pricked him into looking up, then nodded towards the car park at the back and waved his keys.

Desmoulins dropped what he was doing and reached for his gun and jacket.

'I need someone to watch my back,' Rocco explained, when they met up outside. 'But this is slightly outside our area,' he warned him.

'Slightly?'

'Well, a lot.'

'Fine by me,' said Desmoulins happily. 'That paperwork's driving me insane. I'd much rather be out there doing something constructive. Who are we going to shoot?'

They climbed in Rocco's car and he briefed the detective as he drove.

–

Number 12 *bis* had a ratty-looking door adjacent to a butcher's shop not far from the town's railway station. Rue des Noces was a misnomer, Rocco decided, looking at the depressed state of the buildings and the general air of gloom caused by the dark brickwork and lack of colour. If any weddings had taken place here recently, they had got off to a poor start.

He drove past the house and turned into a side street out of sight. Parking his car outside would have been like sending up a signal flare; if Stefan Devrye-Martin was inside, as he was hoping, he doubted the man would be keen on receiving visitors.

They climbed out and walked back to the corner. The street was quiet save for a couple of old ladies in traditional black, shuffling along clutching shopping bags.

'There's an alley two doors along,' Rocco said quietly. 'I'll take the front door, you see if there's an exit at the back. And watch yourself.'

'Got you.' Desmoulins sloped away, hugging the buildings on the same side of the street as number 12 *bis*, hands in his pockets and trying to look as if he belonged. Rocco gave him a few seconds start to get into place, then followed.

He arrived at the door. Close to, it showed peeling paint and a filthy pane of frosted glass behind an ornate metal grill. Dark-blue metal shutters covered the downstairs and upstairs windows, and the brickwork was in need of some attention. He counted to ten, then knocked firmly and waited. Seconds later he heard the scuff of footsteps approaching.

'Who is it?' The voice was wary, but familiar. It was Stefan.

'Simon,' said Rocco. 'Simon Ardois.'

'*What?*' The door flew open. Stefan stood there, mouth open, dressed in a sloppy jumper and stained slacks, with a pair of ancient leather slippers on his feet. A cigarette hung from his lower lip, held in place by a line of dry nicotine-stained saliva. The jumper was riding high on one side, revealing an expanse of belly covered in hairs and a red rash. Rocco didn't like to think what the cause of that might be.

Stefan did a double take on seeing Rocco and tried to slam the door against him. He would have found it easier to stem an incoming tide. Rocco jammed one foot against the door and put his hand against the man's chest, gently but firmly propelling him backwards into the hallway. It was like pushing a giant, sweaty marshmallow, and far less pleasant. He made a mental note to wash his hands afterwards.

Stefan's legs pumped rapidly as he tried to keep his balance. He bounced off the wall behind him, his torso wobbling, and blinked in shock. The cigarette detached itself from his lip and dropped to the linoleum-covered floor. His mouth moved in protest but only a squeak came out. Rocco kept up the momentum, steering him past a flight of uncarpeted stairs piled with boxes, into a long, narrow front-to-back room untidy with clothing, dirty plates and mismatched furniture, all layered in dust. A small kitchen ran off to an extended part of the building. It was as squalid as the rest of the place, and the feel of grease hung heavy in the atmosphere.

He pushed Stefan towards a sofa strewn with an array of photographic equipment – lenses, tripod, bags and a camera – and forced him to sit. Then he went to the rear of the room and peered through the window. A tiny yard strewn with rubbish ended barely three metres away in a high wall and a gate, opening, he guessed, onto a passage for access.

'You're not an easy man to find,' said Rocco. 'Are you shy or just trying to hide something? Like the fact that you're supposed to be dead.' He returned and stood in front of the sofa, preventing Stefan from getting to his feet.

'I don't know what you mean.' Stefan rubbed his chest where Rocco had pushed him. His mouth was slack with shock. 'What are you talking about? You can't do this to me – you've no right.'

'Why not?' Rocco walked round the room, studying the contents. The place was what some might charitably call minimalist, meaning sparsely furnished, with the sofa, a couple of chairs and a table bearing a battered typewriter and a box of envelopes. He flicked through them. They were blank. 'Because your family says so?'

'Huh?'

'You heard.' He turned and faced Stefan. 'You think you're untouchable because your family has influence, don't you? You'd better get wise. You're not untouchable and you're not as invisible as you might think.' He leant forward. 'What, for example, would the good citizens of Evreux say if they knew you were not only alive and breathing, but back on French soil? You think they'd be understanding, just because your family has friends in high places? I wouldn't bet too much money on family connections if I were you; I've got a feeling you might be on the verge of becoming an expendable commodity.'

'You're not making sense.' Stefan struggled to get up but Rocco prodded him with a finger until he subsided again. 'This is illegal, what you're doing!'

'You're probably right. But not as illegal as what you've been up to.' Rocco leant over and picked up the camera from the sofa. It was a Nikon, and looked very expensive. A long cardboard box lay alongside it. He opened the end flap. The box contained a telephoto lens of the kind he'd seen used by photojournalists in Indochina, and more often by horse racing enthusiasts. 'Nice piece of equipment. Expensive. What do you use it for?'

'That's none of your business.'

'You think?' He dropped the lens back in the box, eliciting a squeak of protest from Stefan. 'I'm not making judgements; I'd just like to know, that's all. Why – what's the secret? Or is there something you don't want me to know?' He tipped up a hard-backed chair to shake off a pile of magazines and sat down opposite Stefan. He looked at him with a faint smile and counted to twenty. Silence was always a great way to loosen tongues, he'd found, especially with the guilty. 'Come on, Stefan. There's no need for us not to be friends, is there? Help me out here.'

'Why should I? We have nothing to talk about.'

'Really? See, you haven't even asked what I want. That's a bit of a giveaway in my profession.'

Stefan merely looked sulky. He shrugged. 'All right. So I like taking photos. What's wrong with that?'

'Photos?'

'Landscapes. Pastoral stuff.' His lower lip was trembling and he was breathing rapidly. Rocco wasn't sure what the man's normal colour might be, but he didn't look healthy. He hoped he wasn't about to have a heart attack on him.

'Don't get excited. I'm not really interested in your decadent little hobbies, Stefan. I'll leave that to others.' It was a lie, but he felt no guilt about it. If he could find anything on this man, he would. But for now Stefan appeared to be protected from any further action.

'What do you want, then? Why are you here – and why pretend to be Simon Ardois?'

'Because it was quieter than the alternative.'

'Huh?'

'Kicking down your front door. Now, let's stop messing about. I want to hear everything you can tell me about the Clos du Lac and the people in it.'

# Chapter Thirty-three

Stefan tried to look blank, but succeeded only in looking guilty. 'I don't know anything about the place.'

'Really?' Rocco reached out and gripped the front of his jumper between his thumb and forefinger. The material felt greasy. Stefan tried to pull away, but couldn't. 'What was it you said to me that night at the Clos du Lac? *Lots of secrets in this place… but I've got a few of them tucked away.* Have I got that correct?'

'I don't remember. It must have been the drugs they had me on. Like I told you, they have all kinds of side effects… make me imagine things.'

Rocco let him go, and Stefan shrank back into the sofa. 'Of course – the drugs.' He reached into his coat pocket and took out the photography magazine. Unrolled it. Stefan recognised it instantly and his eyes widened. 'But you see, I know different. I found this little item in one of your hiding places.' He flicked through it until he came to the page with the address written in the inside margin. 'You know a lot about what went on at that place, don't you? All the little secrets you picked up on your nightly forays around the house when you were supposed to be sleeping. The nurse told me you used to avoid taking your medication.' He rolled up the magazine and slapped it into his palm with a loud smack.

'That's rubbish. She was lying!'

'Really? Like the night we spoke – were you sleep-walking?'

'I don't know… I didn't know what I was saying,' Stefan muttered, trying to edge away along the sofa. A dribble of spit crept over his lower lip. He wiped it away with his sleeve.

'But you do remember talking to me.' He noticed Stefan's jumper had sagged at the neck, revealing a lot of throat and part of his upper chest. Before Stefan could stop him, he reached out and tugged the material to one side.

It revealed the dark outline of a stylised tiger on the skin between his throat and shoulder. The tiger looked angry, as if about to attack.

'Nice. Get that done in Thailand, did you?'

'No.' Stefan pulled the jumper back into place. 'What's it to you, anyway?'

'Where was it done?'

'Here in Paris, if you must know. I've never been to – where was it – Thailand?'

'Where in Paris?'

'Huh?'

'Where did you get the tattoo? Which shop? What street? How much did it cost?'

Stefan's lower lip flopped at the speed of the questions, and he looked around as if hoping for a way of escape. 'I don't know – I can't remember. It was years ago.'

'Two years? Five? Ten?'

'Six… about that.'

'Not long after you went to Thailand, then? How did they do it – long distance?' Stefan said nothing, so Rocco pressed him. 'It's on record, Stefan. That's why we keep them, so we know where everyone is. Or did you think you were going to be allowed to move around the world for the rest of your life without anyone knowing?'

Stefan's face went stiff for a moment as he analysed the question. Then he seemed to deflate. His chin settled on the rolls of fat around his throat and he shook his head. 'They said I wouldn't be harassed like this.' His voice was a whisper, resentful.

'They?'

'My lawyer. He said there was an arrangement… that I had immunity if I… if I helped them out.'

An arrangement. That could only mean one thing: they had done a deal in return for immunity from prosecution. It happened all the time.

'You gave up some names. People with the same line of interests.'

'Yes. No – not the same thing at all.' He looked angry. 'All I did was sell photos. The others, they were into… extreme stuff. I wouldn't do that.'

'Of course not. Yet you provide the material for them and their kind.' Rocco felt like smacking him, but it wouldn't have helped. He'd come across sick individuals like Stefan before; they had built-in defensive measures that helped them shut down when attacked. Whatever they did could be justified in their own minds, and only the rest of society was at fault. Physical assault and threats were like hailstones off a brick wall. 'You faked your death in Thailand. Did your lawyer arrange that, too?'

Stefan nodded. 'I had no choice in that. They said I had to… that my family was suffering and there was a danger that I might be recognised as people travelled more.' He reached across to a tobacco tin and opened it. He took out a roll-up and a tin cigarette lighter and lit up. The smell of lighter fluid was strong in the room. He blew smoke into the air and flicked off some ash. 'I didn't want to go along with it, but they made me.'

Everybody else's fault, not his. Rocco recognised the tactic. 'Did they help you back into the country too?'

'Yes.' He sucked at the cigarette, consuming half its length, and coughed. 'My mother was ill. They said it was the only way to do it… to get me back into the country. After that I'd be kept in places like the Clos du Lac until they decided it was safe to let me go where I wanted.'

'But not home?'

He looked miserable. 'No. Not home. People had circulated stories about me. It was all lies – I wasn't doing anything wrong.'

'And your mother?'

'She's fine. But I can't see her, either. It's so unfair.' His chins wobbled, but Rocco wondered how much of this was an act, and whether his mother had ever been truly ill, or if it had been part of the 'arrangement'. He let it slide. There was nothing he could do about it right now, and he had more important matters to deal with. Clearly Stefan had no real concept of what he'd done to have made him such a pariah, and saw only the injustice to himself.

'So why here? This isn't a government place.'

'I wanted to be free, that's all.' Stefan stubbed out the cigarette in a saucer on the floor. 'They transferred me to a place near Rennes, but it was worse than the Clos du Lac, so I walked out. A friend said I could stay here as long as I liked.'

'Generous friend. How do you support yourself?'

For the first time, Stefan let slip a hint of something from beneath the mask of misery he was wearing, and a brief smile touched his lips. But he said nothing.

Rocco remembered how Inès had described him as manipulative. He glanced at the box of envelopes on the table.

'You're selling photos again. Isn't that what you used to do – before you got caught?' He picked up the box containing the telephoto lens and flipped it in his hand. 'You realise, I hope, that the "arrangement" your family lawyer came to is null and void if you're arrested and convicted of a fresh offence?'

No response. But there was a flicker of something in Stefan's eyes.

Rocco looked at the magazines he'd tipped onto the floor. Most were old and battered, well-thumbed. But one looked brand new. He bent and retrieved it. It was the same title as the one in his pocket, but the current issue. There was a sticky label on the back. It had no name, just a customer number. The address was to the family house in Evreux.

He tossed it back on the floor. 'Your family knows where you are, don't they? They're still helping you out. And you a dead man, too.'

Stefan remained mute.

There was a knock from the kitchen, and the back door opened.

It was Desmoulins. He was holding a skinny youth by the arm and carrying a small holdall in his other hand.

'This one just snuck in by the back gate. I think he might have something to show us.' He dropped the holdall by Rocco's feet. 'Take a look – but you might want to wash your hands afterwards.'

Rocco glanced at Stefan. The man had gone pale and was licking his lips, trying hard not to look at the bag or the youth. The bag contained three large brown envelopes. They each held a banded pack of black-and-white photographs. Most were postcard size, with one pack slightly bigger. Rocco lifted them to his nose and sniffed. Freshly developed. They had been taken somewhere on a beach, and he realised the children running around and playing on the sand and in the surf were mostly Asian, with just a handful of white westerners. Most were naked, innocently playing and oblivious of the man with the intrusive camera.

Rocco looked at Stefan. 'You've been busy. You brought back some of your work with you. Is this what the envelopes on the table are for? Your latest customer mailing?'

Stefan sneered. 'You didn't find them in this house. I don't know what he's doing here, do I?' He still wasn't looking at the youth, but he was now sweating heavily.

'You're absolutely correct. We didn't find them here. But how long do you think your little friend is going to hold out to questioning when we take him in and lean on him? An hour? Two hours? A day?' He looked at the youth. 'What do you reckon? We could put you in a cell overnight with a couple of lifers. They'd enjoy that.'

The youth looked terrified. He tried the same kind of sneer as Stefan, but couldn't quite pull it off. 'Go screw yourself, *flic*,' he muttered. 'I don't have to talk to you.'

Desmoulins cuffed him behind the ear. 'Watch your language, you little maggot. You're facing jail time.'

'What's your name?' Rocco asked. 'Help us and we'll help you. But you'd better be quick.'

'Alain Préault,' the youth muttered. 'But I'm just a messenger – I was paid to bring the bag here. I didn't know it had any of that shit in it.' He nodded at the photos and threw a malicious glance at Stefan. '*Sale putain!*'

Rocco caught Stefan's eye. 'Well, there goes one line of defence already. You ready to talk?'

Stefan took a deep breath, then nodded. 'Let him go first.'

Desmoulins looked at Rocco, who nodded, and escorted the youth to the back door. With a warning to keep his mouth shut, he pushed him out the back and told him to get lost.

'What do you want to know?' Stefan muttered. He'd lost what little bravado he'd had, and Rocco guessed he was aware that if Alain Préault developed a loose lip, it wouldn't take long for news of Stefan's line of business to get around the neighbourhood. When that happened, he'd have to move again.

'Who were the other patients, and why were they being held at the Clos du Lac?'

# Chapter Thirty-four

Stefan, it seemed, had managed to make himself a duplicate key to the filing cabinets in Drucker's office, and over a period of several nights had trawled the files uninterrupted, scavenging information which he had hoped one day to sell. Of the five residents, two had been genuine government employees being treated for stress, according to the records, and sedated throughout their stay.

'But that was a lie,' Stefan muttered. 'They were like zombies. I tried talking to them, but it was as if they'd been lobotomised. Then I saw their history notes.'

'What did they say?' Rocco asked.

'A lot. Some kind of shell shock, according to the notes, and severe intestinal problems due to bacteriological infections. They'd been attached to our embassy in the Central African Republic, on "strategic affairs", and got taken hostage by rebel groups opposed to French activities in the region. They were tortured until a ransom was paid, but only after they'd had both hands amputated. The notes said that could never be made public, probably because it would reflect badly on the embassy negotiators for having delayed paying up.'

'Who else?'

'Apart from me, you mean? Well, there was just one. His file name was Tourlemain. Jules Tourlemain.' Stefan grinned without humour, showing nicotine-stained teeth.

'How's that for a made-up name? You'd have thought they could try harder than that.'

'But you got his real one, of course.' Stefan was keeping the best for last, which was where the bartering would begin. This was just a taster.

'What's it worth, Rocco? You can't expect me to give up what I know without something in return. Without my help you'd have nothing. And don't tell me that slimy worm Levignier will help you. He's part of this whole business.' He gave a sly smile, like a kid wanting to trade secrets in the schoolyard, building up what he had ready for the big reveal.

Rocco decided to play along with him. 'Give me a flavour, as a sign of good faith.'

Stefan blinked a couple of times, then glanced at Desmoulins. But there was no help there. 'All right. I know what Simon Ardois is. Was.'

'So do I,' said Rocco roughly. 'He's a dead man.'

'OK. What he used to do, then. His real name was Simon Rotenbourg. He was a civil servant working in the Ministry of Foreign Affairs, on trade matters.'

'Go on.'

'He wasn't a patient, though. He was a prisoner. He'd been accused of spying.' Stefan sat back and waited, a hint of smugness around his mouth.

'I know.'

'What?' Stefan looked stunned. 'How could you?'

'Because I spoke to Pascal, his brother. He told me all about the trade talks. Is that all you've got?'

'No. Wait… that's not all.' Suddenly Stefan was desperately trying to justify what he had, searching for something else to trade, his chins wobbling as he became more animated. 'I spoke to him one time,' he said quickly, leaning forward, 'in his room. The nurse had gone downstairs and left his door open. All he could tell me was that he'd tried to expose a massive case of fraud by government negotiators backed by big industry, but nobody would listen to him.' He reached out a hand. 'Listen, this is true, I promise. He was mumbling… something to do with the Chinese being a preferred partner to Taiwan, and officials in the Foreign Ministry being paid to swing the vote towards Peking. I couldn't make much sense of it… but it was like he'd cracked under the pressure. But it was most likely the drugs they'd put him on to keep him quiet.'

So Pascal had been right.

'Not that he would have been surprised by what happened in the end,' Stefan finished. He seemed suddenly drained, as if he'd used all his energy to get the words out.

'What do you mean?'

'I got into his room again two nights before he was killed. He was virtually immobilised with drugs and couldn't get out of bed. He'd soiled himself and was rambling on about how they were going to kill him. It was the only way they could keep him quiet, he said, to shut him up for good. He said it was going to be a quiet execution, and there was nothing he could do to stop them.'

Stefan looked shaken by having to recount the incident, a line of sweat beading his forehead and, for the first time, Rocco believed what he was saying.

'Did he say anything else? Who was doing it to him?'

'No. I said he should tell Drucker. I mean, I was trying to help him out but what did I know? He said Drucker was a patsy, scared of his own shadow, that he was there as a public face. But he was resigned to his fate. He was just waiting for the moment when they came to kill him.'

It sounded too brutal, too authentic to be made up, or be the result of some drug-induced fantasy. There were some things, Rocco reflected, that simply didn't need embellishing. This, he guessed, was one. Whether Rotenbourg himself had imagined the threat or not, Stefan had believed him sufficiently not to try colouring it further. Because of that, it carried the chilling tone of reality.

'But you didn't hear or see anything else that night?'

'No, I told you at the time. I never heard a thing until I woke up with all the shouting and noise. But that wouldn't have been from the pool, would it?'

'No. It wouldn't. But now you've had time to think about it, is there anything else you can remember?'

Stefan shook his head. 'No. I didn't know anything until I saw Simon in the pool... and you standing there.' He looked up, his eyes wet. 'For a moment, when I first saw you there, and the body, I thought you were the Angel of Death.' He looked down at his hands, which were shaking. 'God, I'm so sick of all this.'

'So, tell me the rest,' said Rocco softly. 'Get it off your chest.'

There was a brief hesitation, then Stefan said, 'The other patient, Tourlemain; he wasn't a nice man. He pretended to take his drugs, too, but not all the time.' Stefan's voice had dropped, as if he'd run out of the will to barter further. 'I hated him. Or maybe I was scared of him. He was a brute... a bully. The security guard, Paulus? He was there to keep him in line... and protect him.'

'Explain.'

'Tourlemain boasted once that his life was in danger... that he'd got a big price on his head and there were people who'd like to see him dead. He acted as if it was something to be proud of. He was a gangster. I don't know about these things, but he had this aura… a kind of power. He scared me – and I think he frightened Drucker a lot, too. Every now and then some men would come to talk to him. They'd take him into a back room and be there for a couple of hours. The day before, they'd reduce his drugs so he could talk, but give him just enough to keep him subdued. And Paulus would be there, of course, to lean on him.'

'Who were the men who came to see him?'

'I don't know. We were all kept out of the way when they came. But I recognised the type.'

'Type?'

'Cops. But not ordinary ones, in uniform.' Stefan looked at him. 'Men like you.'

'So who was he?'

Stefan hesitated one last time, then gave a huge sigh. 'The name in the record file said Bruno Betriano.'

Rocco's blood went cold at the name, and Desmoulins swore quietly in the background. No wonder Stefan and Drucker had been scared of him. Bruno 'The Bear' Betriano was a ruthless gang leader born and raised in the slums of Marseilles. He'd long had a brutal grip over much of the trafficking through that port of drugs, people and arms, and had been bad news for years, a thorn in the side of the authorities and competitors alike. Yet the police had had little success in bringing him to book, for which there was, to most observers' minds, only one rational explanation: Betriano had local politicians and policemen in his pocket. Yet nothing had been proved.

He was untouchable.

And like Stefan Devrye-Martin, he was supposed to be dead.

'What happened to the others in this new place?'

'No idea. Probably where I left them. I didn't believe what we were being told, not after seeing the way Simon ended up, so I left. As soon as everyone was asleep I walked and kept walking. I had some money and managed to contact a friend, and ended up here.' He sighed. 'Fat lot of good it did me.'

'Did they say why they'd moved you from the Clos du Lac?'

Stefan shook his head. 'Not really. But I heard one of them saying that they needed to clear the place out and start afresh… and something about getting one of the rooms ready.'

'Ready for what?'

'I don't know. But I bet some other poor bastard was going to find out soon enough.'

–

While Rocco was questioning Stefan, a telephone call was being patched through to an extension in the depths of the Interior Ministry. It was picked up by Delombre.

'Where are you?' he said, when he heard the name of the caller, then listened as the man told him about keeping watch on Rocco as he'd been instructed, and how Rocco and another man had driven fast from Amiens to Pontoise. They had parked out of sight before entering a house in the Rue des Noces, Rocco via the front, the other man through the rear.

'When was this?'

'About thirty minutes ago.'

Damn. Delombre swore silently. There could only be one reason for Rocco to have gone anywhere at high speed. Devrye-Martin. Had to be. And he'd had more than enough time to lean on the little fat man and squeeze whatever he knew out of him. This business was fast running out of control. Levignier should have let him deal with Rocco earlier, for once and for all.

'You should have called sooner. They're still there?'

'Yes. Sorry, but I'm working alone—'

'Forget it. Did you see who they called on?'

'No. Whoever it was kept too far back, like he was frightened to show his face. Or her. I'll ask around.'

'Don't bother.' Delombre smiled, grimly satisfied in one respect: Rocco had led them right to Devrye-Martin's door, just as he'd hoped.

'What do you want me to do?' his man asked.

'Stay on them and call me when they leave. Don't blow your cover.'

He put down the phone and checked a wall map, then dialled an internal number. After issuing brief instructions, he opened a desk drawer and took out a semi-automatic pistol in a holster and strapped it on.

About 30 kilometres to Pontoise. Allowing for traffic, his men should be there in less than half an hour. It might be tight, depending on how much talking Devrye-Martin was doing.

But even if Rocco left before they got there, there was only one road he could be taking back to Amiens. It was time to apply a bit of pressure to the country cop; to frighten him into backing off. And no matter what Levignier said, if things got a little heated in the process, and someone caught a bullet... well, too bad.

As for himself, he was in no hurry. Pontoise was a leisurely drive away. It was time to do what he was good at.

That was to make sure the little pervert Devrye-Martin never spoke to anyone ever again.

## Chapter Thirty-five

'So what were they up to in that sanitarium?' said Desmoulins, as they drove back towards Amiens. 'Assuming it's true about Betriano.'

Rocco shrugged. 'There's only one thing: it was a government safe house. Two embassy employees with no hands and severe traumatic problems; one pervert who faked his death with official knowledge and sold out his mates; a problem employee in the Foreign Affairs Ministry who knew too much... and a gangster who reportedly died in a fight, but didn't. No wonder they're all on drugs; if word got out who was in there, and that it was all with official collusion, it would be enough to bring down half the staff of the Interior Ministry.'

And if Levignier and his department had even an inkling of what Stefan knew, he didn't rate the man's chances of staying free for very long.

'So what do we do?'

While he'd been talking, Rocco had been watching their rear mirror. He'd now seen the same car pop up three times on their tail. It was a dark-blue Peugeot, ordinary-looking and unremarkable, with three men inside. But something about the way it sat squat and firm on the road was disturbingly familiar. It was a pursuit vehicle and it was following them.

'We've got company.'

Desmoulins checked the mirror and came to the same conclusion as Rocco. 'It looks official. You think they're after us?'

'I'm certain of it.' What he didn't know, however, was what their intentions were. Right now, he decided, might be a good time to have the car radio Massin kept trying to have installed in his car.

He checked the road ahead. They were approaching a huddle of houses. It was hardly big enough to qualify as a village, but the end wall of the first building on the right was bare of windows, and held a giant handcrafted Ricard advert. It was a café, a whistle-stop for farmers and truck drivers.

He began to brake and said, 'Go in and call Godard. Give him our location and ask if he'd like to send out a couple of men for a training exercise.' *Sous-Brigadier* Godard headed up the local unit of the *Gendarmerie Mobile*, the equivalent to the CRS – the riot police – who were responsible for, as he liked to put it, anything involving trouble.

Desmoulins smiled. 'Christ, Lucas, they'll post you to a mud hut in Gabon for this.' But he jumped out of the car as soon as Rocco stopped and walked into the café.

The pursuit car had stopped, too, and was sitting three hundred metres back.

Minutes later, Desmoulins came back out, carrying two yellow bottles of *Pschitt* soft drink and a paper bag of brioches.

'Late breakfast and a bit of cover,' he explained. 'We're cops, after all; we eat on the move.' He handed Rocco a brioche and said, 'Godard said bless you. He's sending three men to do an intercept. Give them time to get moving and they'll wait for us the other side of Beauvais and do a stop-and-search on those clowns behind us.' He unscrewed the *Pschitt* and took a drink. 'Teach the buggers to follow us.'

'Did you tell him they're probably official?'

'Yes. He said all the better and don't worry about it.' He grinned. 'I think he gets easily bored when things are quiet.'

They finished their drink and brioche, allowing the minutes to drift by. If the car behind them gave up and left, they could call off Godard's men. If not, the plan was still on.

Rocco dusted off his fingers and started the engine, and got back on the road. The pursuit car stayed where it was. But ten minutes later it was back, a recognisable dot in the distance, matching their speed.

'They must know who we are, wouldn't you think?' said Desmoulins.

'In this thing? Bound to.' There was no mistaking Rocco's car, which Levignier would have seen at the Clos du Lac. The Traction was big, black and impossible to hide. It made surveillance for the men in the Peugeot an easy job.

Through Beauvais and out the other side, all the time with the Peugeot just in sight, they reached a straight stretch of road with little traffic. A car coming the other way blew past. It was unmarked and unremarkable, but Desmoulins raised a discreet hand and the driver flicked a finger to show he'd seen them. They were members of GM – Godard's *Gendarmerie Mobile*.

'The unit leader's name is Patrice,' Desmoulins commented. 'They say he eats barbed wire for breakfast.'

Rocco let his speed drop gradually, allowing the Peugeot to draw closer. Behind it, the car containing the

GM officers had turned and was coming up fast. The road in each direction was clear.

The men in the Peugeot didn't know what hit them. The GM car drew level, then hit the siren and slammed on the brakes, slewing to a stop across their front and driving them into the side of the road. Before the men in the Peugeot could react, the doors of the GM vehicle sprang open and three men in black uniforms without insignia jumped out, guns drawn.

It was all over within seconds.

Rocco eased to a stop and reversed to within a hundred metres. Then he and Desmoulins got out and walked back down the centre of the road towards the Peugeot.

The men inside watched them come, their hands in plain sight.

The GM car engine was ticking quietly in the silence as it cooled. The Peugeot's engine had cut out, its nose tilted over the edge of a drainage ditch where the driver had been forced to pull it round to avoid a collision. Two of Godard's men had snapped open the doors and were standing with their weapons trained on the occupants, while the third, the one Desmoulins had called Patrice, was checking the boot. He was tall and heavy across the shoulders. He turned as Rocco arrived and gestured at the inside.

'Take a look, Inspector. You think we can charge them with carrying dangerous items in public?'

Rocco looked. A special short-barrelled shotgun lay nestled in a metal box, with two boxes of spare cartridges and three tubular objects with ring-pulls. Smoke canisters. Behind the box lay a sledgehammer and a large tyre iron, and a box containing two gas masks with filter tubes on the front. Siege equipment.

'It'll do for a start,' Rocco agreed. 'Unusual equipment for changing tyres.'

Patrice nodded. 'I've seen canisters like these before. They look new – experimental. Wish we had them.'

'No doubt you will one day. Who are these three?'

'They don't want to say.' Patrice smiled. He was as tall as Rocco, with a broken nose and some serious scar tissue around one eye. The smile gave his face a malicious twist. 'Perhaps they're shy.'

Rocco nodded. 'Get them out and down on the ground.' Patrice turned and ordered the three men out of the car.

They hesitated for a moment, until one of his men grabbed the nearest – the driver – and yanked him out from behind the wheel like plucking a feather. The other two followed without argument and were quickly ordered face down on the road where they were patted down. The search produced three wallets, three automatic pistols and a large clasp knife. Patrice stripped out the magazines before throwing the guns onto the back seat of their car. He tossed the knife into the ditch and handed the wallets to Rocco.

Rocco told the driver to stand up. The man did so with a grunt. He was in his late forties, overweight and looked crumpled, as if he'd been up all night.

'Who are you and what are you doing?' Rocco asked.

'We're on official business,' said the man. 'And you're in deep shit.' He glared at the others. 'Just like the rest of you. Bunch of fucking cowboys.'

'Hey.' Patrice gave him a gentle slap on the back of the head. 'Easy on the insults, fella. We're sensitive types. Have you filed a movement report for this area?'

The man scowled. 'Have we what? What's a movement report? We can go anywhere we please.'

'Not according to bulletin GN 0345 issued last year. It states that all security personnel have to advise regional offices of their presence on-territory. Failure to do so renders the offender...' he paused meaningfully and looked at the other two men on the ground '...and those under his command, immediate severance from the service and suspension of pension rights.' He turned and looked at Rocco with a wink. 'Isn't that so, Inspector?'

'So I gather.' Rocco opened the man's wallet. An official card inside named him as Daniel Bezancourt, team leader of a security detail in the ISD.

'Hey – wait!' It was one of the men on the ground, looking over his shoulder at Rocco. 'What's that shit about us losing our jobs? You can't blame us for that – we were just following orders.'

Rocco squatted down beside the man. 'Really? Whose orders would that be?'

'Shut your mouth, *imbécile*!' Bezancourt snapped.

'Can't you see they're pulling your dick? There's no such bulletin.'

'Let's talk.' Rocco grabbed the man's arms and yanked him to his feet, and marched him away several paces out of earshot. The man was short and squat, and his face didn't reach Rocco's chin. He was forced to tilt his head back to look at him. Whatever he saw seemed to frighten him. He flinched.

'Now then,' Rocco said softly, 'just between you and me, whose orders?'

'I can't tell you,' the man muttered, eyes flicking back towards his colleagues, who were both watching intently.

'Of course you can.' Rocco let go of him and dusted down the man's shoulders and straightened his jacket collar. He took out the two remaining wallets and checked the photo inside. 'Gerard Gautery?' The man nodded. 'Good. Now look, Gerard, I mean, if it was Commander Levignier who gave you the order, what's the secret? He's your boss, isn't he?'

Gautery stared up at him, eyes flicking between Rocco and his team leader, trying to figure out who represented the bigger danger. He evidently decided it was Rocco.

'You know him?'

'Of course. We spoke only the other day, as a matter of fact – at the Clos du Lac.'

The name was clearly familiar to Gautery and he relaxed. 'Oh. Well, in that case it was Levignier, yes. Well, sort of.'

'What do you mean, sort of?'

'He's got an assistant, named Delombre.' He swallowed and threw another glance towards his colleagues. 'He's a creepy guy – only I never said that, right?'

'Never heard of him. What does he look like?'

'I don't know. I've never seen him up close.'

'But you know he's creepy.'

'Yes. But it's not just me that says it. Some say he's an ex-Legion battle freak who spent too long in the desert fighting the Arabs, and it went to his head. He doesn't walk so much as float. Eyes like a dead fish.'

'Sounds a charmer. And he works for Levignier.'

'That's right.'

'Fine.' Rocco patted him on the shoulder. 'That's very helpful. You can rejoin your colleagues.'

Gautery scurried away to stand alongside Bezancourt, who threw him a venomous look, while Rocco pointed to the third man still lying on the ground. Desmoulins hauled him to his feet and marched him across to Rocco, who repeated the same questions. This man was made of sterner stuff, however, and confirmed his own name but nothing else.

'Tough nut, huh, Mr...' he consulted the last wallet '...Mr Cropeq?'

'Tough enough.'

'So where does your name come from – eastern Europe?'

'Hungary, if you must know.'

'Nice country, I'm told. Cultured. You enjoy your work?'

'When I'm allowed to do it.'

The message was clear, and Rocco smiled and patted the man on the shoulder so that the others could see. He'd kept him talking long enough; Bezancourt wouldn't know which one had said anything. An old cop interview trick. 'Of course. My apologies. Thanks for your help. You can go now.'

Cropeq hesitated, as if unsure, then turned and walked away.

'You mouthy pricks,' Bezancourt muttered darkly, but clamped his lips shut when Patrice stepped up and gave him a warning look.

'Let them go,' said Rocco, handing the men their wallets. 'Make sure they go back to the city.' He gave Patrice a nod of thanks, adding, 'Good work.' This was to ensure that if any flak should come their way, it was clear that Rocco had been issuing the orders.

'You going to tell me what that was all about?' said Desmoulins, climbing back in the car.

'I got a name,' he replied. 'And I fired a warning shot. Now I just need to wait for the reaction.' He also needed to find out who this Delombre character was. From the way Gautery had described him, he wasn't good news.

# Chapter Thirty-six

Delombre parked in a side street between two canvas-sided delivery trucks and switched off the engine. He knew where his man would have been stationed, watching the house where Devrye-Martin was hiding, and he was no longer there. Just as well; Delombre preferred to work unseen, even by his own contacts.

He checked his weapon, sliding it out of the holster with a faint rub of worn leather, then put it back. He shouldn't need it, but you never could tell. Next he went to the boot and took out an overcoat and hat, both anonymously grey, which he put on, then lifted out a cardboard box advertising cooking oil. He made an adjustment to the box, then made his way through the streets to the Rue des Noces, walking past the house and limping noticeably. He caught his reflection in a glass-panelled door; saw the image of an ordinary man with a bad leg – an *ancien combatant* maybe – carrying home a few groceries. It would do.

He circled the block and approached the house along the rear alleyway, counting off the windows. He was mostly in shadow cast by the brick walls and outhouses at the rear of each property. He saw a single moth-eaten dog but no people.

The back gate to 12 *bis* was ajar. He paused and listened, thinking he heard a rumble of voices from inside.

Problem one: Devrye-Martin had company. Problem two: he didn't have time to hang around before someone noticed him. In a place like this, strangers stood out and were likely to be challenged.

He made a decision based on his training. Once on target, never go back. It was a simple maxim and had worked well enough for him in the past.

He pushed through the gate and walked up a cracked concrete path in a festering pit of a yard, and used his shoulder to nudge open the rear door. He was in a kitchen, the atmosphere rank with the smell of greasy food and cigarette smoke. A trace of gas lingered in the air, and he saw a blue canister beneath a cheap stove, with a rubber tube connected to two burners.

The voices were louder, coming from the next room. An older man was arguing about not having enough money, and another one – younger – was saying he wanted in on the business or he'd drop a few words to the police. Thieves falling out by the sounds of it, but Delombre didn't care. It might even play into his hands.

He crossed the kitchen, the soles of his shoes making a sticky sound on the filthy linoleum floor, and stepped through the doorway. He was in a living room. Two men. Stefan Devrye-Martin, fat and pallid as a large *boudin blanc*, rifling urgently through a box of photos on a table, and a younger man, leaning against a wall nearby, sucking on a cigarette. He was rail-thin and dressed in cheap trousers and a crumpled leather jacket. Probably a cheap street thug – or Devrye-Martin's boyfriend.

The youth saw him first and nearly swallowed his cigarette. But he was quick to recover. He jumped forward, whipping out a cut-throat razor from his jacket pocket and pushing Stefan aside for a clear field of fight.

'Oh, please,' Delombre muttered tiredly. He pulled his hand out from the hole he'd made in the bottom of the cardboard box. He was holding a small pistol fitted with a home-made suppressor. The youth was barely three feet away from him when he pressed the trigger. The .22 calibre bullet made a spiteful snapping noise as it left the gun, like breaking a stick to feed a fire. It hit the youth low in the left eye, killing him instantly. Delombre stepped aside as the body's momentum carried it forward, and watched as it slumped to the floor, a tremor going through the frame before going quite still.

'Damn, that was neat,' he said softly, and looked at Stefan, cowering against the table. 'I constantly surprise myself, you know? But the kid was quick, I'll give him that. Close friend of yours?'

'Who the hell are you?' Stefan whispered, eyes fastened on the gun. Then he looked at the dead youth. 'Why did you have to do that?'

'Sorry. Bit of a habit of mine. Something to do with a wretched childhood, I expect.' Delombre blew away a wisp of smoke coming from the suppressor, like a modern-day cowboy, and smiled. 'So, what are we up to here, then, Stefan?' He moved closer to the table and picked up a handful of photos, flicking them to the floor one by one and humming tunelessly. 'Not quite my thing, I have to say. Poor composition, lousy lighting and altogether a bit cheap. Your mummy must be very proud of you.'

'What's it to you?' Stefan was breathing in short, forced bursts, his face beaded with sweat. He had dropped the photos he'd been sorting through and was now clutching his chest with a pudgy hand, screwing up his cheap, stained T-shirt.

'Actually, it's not. You and your sort can burn in hell for all I care. Which, by the way, is a fate you'll be meeting sooner than you'd probably anticipated. Although,' he reached out to touch Stefan's face with the tip of the suppressor, 'you've been there already, haven't you? On paper, at least. Neat, I have to say. I might have to try that myself one day.'

'What?' Stefan winced. He tried to back away from the gun but there was nowhere to go. 'I don't know what you mean.'

'Blood poisoning in Thailand, wasn't it? Usually, you get septicaemia out there and you're dead meat. Must have been one of those miracles the Church likes to talk about. Never seen one myself, but there's always hope. What did Rocco want?'

'Huh?'

'Rocco, the irritating country cop. What did he want?'

'He—nothing. He was asking questions.'

'About what?' Delombre had gone very still. It made him look all the more dangerous.

'Things.'

'What sort of things? And just so you know, you take too long over this and I'll start shooting holes in your fat bits. And let's face it, I can hardly miss from here, even with my eyes closed, can I?'

Stefan swallowed hard. 'He was… he wanted to know about the other people in the Clos du Lac. It's a sanitarium.'

'Thank you. I know what it is. What did you tell him?'

Stefan shrugged. 'What could I tell him? I didn't know who they were any more than they knew me. It was all kept confidential. Anyway, I was on drugs most of the time.'

'Liar. Get your tongue cut out.' Delombre chanted the words softly, slowly. Menacing.

'I'm not, I'm—'

'OK, now let's backtrack. That's polite talk for this is your final chance, you *pustule*.' Delombre placed the tip of the suppressor against Stefan's ample stomach and pushed. It went in quite a long way, and Stefan yelped but didn't move. 'Now, I know there's a technical school of thought that says if one pulls the trigger of a gun with a fat pervert on the end, the gun will explode. It's something to do with blowback or reverse concussion – I'm not really that interested. But it means I ruin a perfectly serviceable little gun – and my hand in the process, which would seriously annoy me. Or you go pop like a giant *crème caramel*.' He gave a stab with the gun. 'Are you a betting man?'

'OK… OK.' Stefan held up a hand. 'Rocco wanted to know who the others were. He was threatening to expose me, so I told him what I knew.'

'Which was?'

'You know who they are.' Stefan looked sick, his voice low.

'I know, but I so love to hear your voice, daddy.' Another prod of the gun. 'Who?'

'I told him… Betriano and Rotenbourg. But not the others—' Stefan went very still, and his eyes opened wide, as if a switch had been flicked in his head. 'It's you!' he whispered, going paler than ever.

'Uh-oh,' Delombre murmured. 'The fat man knows something.'

'It's you!' Stefan repeated, looking horrified. Delombre blinked. 'I beg your pardon?'

'You. The therapy pool… your voice… I recognise –
*it was you who killed Simon.*'

'Ah. *That.*' Delombre understood. 'So I did. But how
did you know? Weren't you all comatose on drugs?'

'No. I was outside… your voices carried.' Stefan
coughed heavily, his breathing suddenly louder, and slid
sideways to sit on a chair. 'You forced him into that
harness and lowered him. I heard him choking.'

'Yes, so did I – and I probably had a much better view
than you, too. Did you like my handiwork?' He took the
gun out of Stefan's stomach and peered along the barrel,
one eye shut, swivelling to aim at the central light bulb.
'I like to be inventive, you see. It's my small attempt to
elevate a fairly mundane action to the level of art.' He
smiled coldly. 'With you, sadly, I have neither the time nor
the inclination. Still, one does what one can.' He bent and
peered in mock concern at Stefan's face. 'You really don't
look good, do you know that? Heart trouble, I suspect.
Ah, well, we all have to go sometime.'

With that he stepped back alongside the cardboard box
and pushed his free hand into the top. He produced a litre
bottle of liquid and flipped open the lid.

The smell of gasoline permeated the room.

'What are you doing with that?' Stefan's mouth went
slack and he glanced towards the kitchen door in desperation.

In response, Delombre flicked the bottle and a tiny
drop of gasoline hit the centre of Stefan's chest, spreading
out through the material.

'God, I'm getting better at this. Did you know,' he
said conversationally, 'that this is the easiest way to get
bits of cork out of the neck of a bottle? None of that gross

sticking in a finger, or fiddling with a corkscrew. Just flick it.' He went to do it again.

'Stop. *Wait!*'

'No, really. A wine waiter in London showed me how. Amazing. I mean, what do they know about wine, huh? Bunch of cretins.' He flicked again, and another wet blob hit Stefan's body. 'You should have stayed where we put you after you left the Clos du Lac. You'd be OK now. But you had to go off and do your own thing, didn't you? Back to the business you know so well.' Then, as he stepped forward to repeat the process, Stefan gave a loud gasp and sank back, his mouth opening and closing like a fish.

Delombre stopped. He hadn't been so far off the truth. The fat man was having a massive heart attack.

'Oops,' he said. 'Silly me. Bit too much pressure there, I think. Never mind.' He recapped the bottle and replaced it in the box, then checked the fat man's throat for a pulse.

Nothing. Damn, that was quick.

He immediately became all business. Leaving everything in the room as it was, he unscrewed the suppressor and wiped the gun clean. Then he placed the gun in Stefan's hand and adjusted the fat man's chair to align it slightly with the dead youth's body. He was reluctant to lose the gun, which was a handy little hideaway weapon, but it had served its purpose. He could get another easily enough.

'Such a shame,' he breathed, studying the layout of the bodies, 'when friends fall out.'

Next he carried the box through to the kitchen and placed a saucepan on one of the burners. He poured a measure of gasoline into the saucepan, taking care not to spill any, then turned on the gas and carefully lit a match, touching the flame to the burner. He stepped back to review his handiwork one last time, then turned on the second burner, but without lighting it.

Then he picked up the box and the bottle of gasoline, and quietly let himself out.

## Chapter Thirty-seven

Back in Amiens, Rocco rang *Sous-Brigadier* Godard and thanked him for the use of his men.

'My pleasure,' Godard assured him. 'Always happy to have an excuse for a training exercise. And my men don't much like Ministry gorillas so it made their day. Will there be any comeback?'

'I doubt it. If there is, blame me.'

He put down the phone just as Rizzotti appeared at the door. The doctor looked tired, but pleased with himself.

'Milk,' he said without preamble, and handed Rocco a lab report. 'Heavy on the cream, apparently. Dangerous, too much of it.'

Rocco stared at him, his thoughts clicking slowly into place. Lab reports? Then he had it: of course, Drucker's house. The powerful smell of bleach.

'So it wasn't blood?'

'Not a trace. The lab technician decided to check the empty bleach bottles first and noticed the smell of sour milk. He rang me before he started testing, just to show off. He was correct: cow's milk, crusted around the base, probably where – Drucker, was it? – had placed one of the bottles on the floor while cleaning up.' He shrugged. 'I'd have used neat bleach, too, had it been me. The smell of stale milk never goes away – especially in summer.'

'Thank you. That's good work.'

Rizzotti fluttered his eyebrows. 'Well, we try to please.' He turned and walked away, whistling happily.

Rocco sat down and stared at the report. So Drucker was still alive.

—

It was early evening by the time Rocco left the station. He'd written up a report on what Stefan had told him and left it on Massin's desk. Even he could see that much of it was supposition and would be open to demolition by those involved: a secretive government-backed safe house hiding two damaged embassy personnel, a faked dead man – no, two faked dead men, one of them a high-profile gangster, the other running from a sex scandal – and a Ministry spy who'd threatened to blow the lid off high-level official wrongdoings in international trade negotiations? It was surely the stuff of fiction, and he could already hear the arguments. He couldn't see himself getting much headway out of the gangster's presence at Clos du Lac, or even the injured and traumatised embassy personnel. Both would be dismissed as being there in the interests of the state and of justice. But Stefan's presence and the death of Rotenbourg would certainly cause severe ripples in the Interior Ministry, especially if he could prove that ISD personnel were involved. And if Stefan was prepared to make a statement, it would add considerable weight to the argument.

He'd rung Michel Santer with the name Delombre, and asked if his security contact, Bobo, could find out anything about the man.

'What am I?' Santer had muttered, 'your private investigator? This is going to cost me, you know.' But he'd murmured the man's name as he scribbled a note. 'OK, Delombre. I'll see what I can get.'

'He's probably ISD,' said Rocco, 'so be careful.'

'Thanks, Rocco. Now you tell me. Anyway, I'm always careful; you're the one with the death wish. I'll call you as soon as I can.'

Rocco hoped he was quick. He'd managed to stay out of Massin's way while compiling his report. But he knew it wouldn't be long before the *commissaire* might bow to official pressure from on high and pull him off the investigation. The only way to prevent that was by presenting him with a solid collection of evidence that couldn't be ignored or swept under the carpet by Levignier or whoever was controlling him.

Thoughts about the sanitarium made him decide to swing by the Clos du Lac. Seeing the place once more might prompt some useful ideas. As he'd found in the past, revisiting the scene of a crime, even long afterwards, sometimes acted as a kind of conduit to clarity of mind. And right now he needed all the clarity he could get.

–

There were three cars in the car park this time. A good sign. As Rocco climbed out of the Citroën, he noticed a figure standing in a covered gap between the main building and the poolhouse, watching him. It was a man, dressed in a dark suit.

Rocco nodded but got no response. The man turned and walked out of sight.

Rocco went into the lobby and tried the door. It was locked, but through the glass panel he saw an imposing figure approaching across the foyer.

'Yes, sir?' A man stood blocking the entrance. He was almost as tall as Rocco but wider, and dressed in a dark suit, with short-cropped hair and signs of a fading tan.

Rocco recognised professional security personnel when he saw them, and wondered if the man and his colleague were more of Levignier's attack dogs.

He decided to keep his approach formal, and held out his card. If this was the way they wanted to play it, he'd go along with it. But only so far. 'I'm looking for Miss Dion. Police Inspector Rocco.'

The man glanced at the card without much interest. 'She's busy.'

Rocco sighed. 'I'm sure she is. But she will see me.'

The man was adamant. 'She won't. You'll have to make an appointment.'

He began closing the door when footsteps sounded on the tiled floor behind him.

'That's all right, Jean-Pierre,' said a woman's voice. 'I'll deal with this.'

It was Inès Dion.

Jean-Pierre stepped aside, but didn't move far. He turned and glared at Rocco, his hands crossed in front of him. It was a stance meant to intimidate, showing off the width of his shoulders and the bulge of a weapon beneath his jacket. It wasn't subtle or even professional, but to anyone other than Rocco, it would have been effective.

Rocco ignored him and looked at Inès. She looked surprisingly fresh, with a focused look about her that had been absent the last time he saw her. She wasn't exactly smiling, however.

'You're looking well,' he said.

'I received new orders,' she said without blinking. 'Shape up or lose my job. I decided that falling apart wasn't going to bring André back, as much as I would like it, so I decided I might as well carry on.'

'So this place isn't closing?'

'Evidently not. In fact, we're expecting two new arrivals today. Private paying customers.' She stole a glance at her watch. 'The first of a handful, I think.' She gave a brittle smile. 'The Clos du Lac is still open for business.'

'Private or government?' He nodded at Jean-Pierre. 'Why the gorilla with the gun?'

She shrugged. 'The rules are the same: we aren't told who the patients are, and we don't ask. There are private clinics in Switzerland operating in exactly the same way with expert security. Rich people demand the best.'

The response came across as practised, almost automatic, and he wondered if she wasn't just using the rule book to hold herself together. Looking closely, he could see the strain in her eyes still, like a dark shadow lurking in the depths. He'd known plenty of cops who'd looked the same; on the brink of cracking up after a particularly stressful time, they'd sought safety in ritual, in the rules. It was easier that way. He'd probably done it himself, too, after Indochina, and must have been a pain in the neck to those who knew him. People like Emilie, his wife, for instance. Now ex-wife. She'd stuck it for as long as she could, even after he'd joined the police. Finally, with a comment about exchanging one set of dangers for another, she'd left. It happened.

'What happened to Drucker?'

'I don't know. I haven't heard. I think he's been moved on.'

The hum of a car engine approached along the road and her eyes flicked past him.

'Because of what happened here? That's harsh.' But typical of some government departments, Rocco thought. Especially those with secrets to hide. Clear out the dead wood, paper over the cracks and start all over again.

Inès turned as the crunch of tyres on gravel heralded the arrival of a vehicle. 'I'm sorry, Inspector, but I think the first of our new patients is here. You'll have to excuse me.'

Inspector, he noted. Not Lucas.

'Late in the day, isn't it, to move medical cases?'

'I don't dictate times or dates.'

He turned as a Citroën DS ambulance swept into the car park. It had a simple blue cross on the bonnet and ruched curtains along the side windows. Two men up front, no expressions. Business-like.

'I must ask you to stay back,' Inès said, with no trace of apology. 'We are expected to be discreet, I'm afraid. Part of the rules.' Then she stepped past him and walked across to the ambulance as the attendant and driver climbed out and went to the rear door. Inès spoke to them briefly, indicating the front entrance.

Rocco watched as a stretcher was slid out from the back and the driver snapped the wheels into place. A blanket was covering a shapeless form, held secure on the stretcher by two straps. He couldn't tell whether it was male or female. Just for good measure, the attendant had drawn a lightweight veil across the patient's head.

Inès turned and stared at him. It seemed to be a signal for Jean-Pierre, who moved across and stood in front of Rocco, close enough to share his body odour and partially blocking Rocco's view of the car and patient. Rocco resisted the temptation to drop the big man where he stood. It was time for him to leave. He walked to his car and got in. When he looked back, Inès and the two attendants had disappeared inside with the stretcher, leaving Jean-Pierre by the front door, watching him.

Rocco felt his hackles rising. This wasn't over.

## Chapter Thirty-eight

'It was clumsy.' Josef Girovsky slapped a firm hand on the polished surface of the conference table in the Interior Ministry annexe. He glared at Levignier but his words were directed at the man sitting at the far end of the table. Morning coffee stood undisturbed on a trolley near the door, the talk too urgent for it to have tempted anyone.

'It was necessary.' Delombre looked relaxed and unconcerned, as if discussing the deaths of two men was something he did every day. 'The kid came at me with a cut-throat razor. I had to stop him. And the fat man had a heart attack. I know I'm good, but even I can't arrange that.'

'You still shot one of them,' Girovsky reminded him. 'That's a bit obvious, isn't it?'

'Yes, and I arranged the scene so that it'll look like an argument that went too far. The cops will never be able to trace the gun, and they'll assume it belonged to the pervert. The kid came at him with the blade and he shot him. It's a simple scenario and they'll read it like a book.' He gave Girovsky a cool glance. 'Not that I have to justify myself to you.'

'All right, let's stick to the facts,' said Levignier, interposing a calming word between the two men. He wasn't so much concerned with anything the industrialist might say that could damage Delombre, but the other way round;

he knew what his man was capable of if the Pole pushed him too far. 'What's done is done. At least we now know what Rocco had learnt – and it's too much.'

'You should have stopped him sooner,' Girovsky muttered.

'We tried. He's been lucky,' said Levignier.

'I meant for good, not some half-arsed girl trap. Mother of God, if I ran my businesses in such an inept manner, I'd go bankrupt.'

It was an old argument, and one Levignier was sick of hearing. But it was one of the penalties of having to work in conjunction with this man. To change the nature and course of the discussion, he asked, 'Where are the negotiations with the Chinese so far?'

Girovsky sat back, content to be on his own ground. 'They're moving forward, but the topic of aircraft manufacture has come up again. They don't like the discussions with Taiwan and are suggesting it could cause irreparable hurdles if those deals go through.' He sniffed. 'Unlike in other matters, when it comes to trade deals and Taiwan, Peking does not believe in talking in convoluted circles.'

'What's the likely outcome?'

Girovsky shrugged. 'All bets are off, as the Americans would say. They'll go elsewhere and we lose everything.' He stared down at the table. 'And all because of the ego of that bloody man, Bessine.'

Levignier barely hid a wry smile. When it came to egos, Girovsky was up there with the best of them. But desperation was also at play. If he gave the word, he knew Girovsky would leap at the chance of him sending Delombre after Robert Bessine, the aircraft manufacturer and Girovsky's bitter industrial rival. They had each been storming about the world stage for years like trumpeting elephants, both eager to win huge contracts and outdo each other. But Bessine was currently holding firm, even now, by insisting on talking with Taiwan on the supply of jet fighters and commercial airplanes, much to the fury of Peking… and many people involved in the current round of trade negotiations on the French side, like Girovsky.

'We have to be extremely careful,' he said calmly. 'If we rush, we fail.'

'But you hold all the cards, surely, ever since you—'

'Don't say it.' Levignier's voice was soft, but cut through Girovsky's anger like a knife. Although he was certain the room was secure, what Girovsky had been about to blurt out would, if overheard, be enough to see them all put away for life. His eyes glittered dangerously. 'We have that situation under control.'

'Really? I hope so.' Now even the Pole sounded uneasy, as if realising that what had been set in motion in the past few days had taken them all beyond redemption.

'Absolutely. The subject is now housed in a facility where nobody will find it.'

Girovsky sniffed and looked up. 'I heard talk of a special task force being set up to do just that. Is it true?'

Levignier wondered how much to say. He was becoming concerned at Girovsky's limited level of patience, and his dubious ability to keep his information and opinions to himself. If he was sounding off in here like this, who knew what he was saying to his close confidants higher in the Ministry or elsewhere. But leaving him out of the sequence of events completely would only expose Levignier if the idiot began blabbing to his business friends – or worse, initiating some kind of drastic action using his own people.

'It's true that a small search team has been put together, yes. But they won't find anything. They're too few and too late.'

'How can you guarantee that?'

Levignier shrugged. 'We have our ways. In any case, this city is very large and a handful of men can't search everywhere.' He paused while searching for the correct words. 'The point was made from the very start by those much more senior than me that impulsive action on the part of the police would only lead to a drastic reaction by those on the opposite side. Hence the small team which, I remind you, benefits us all. The less they accomplish, the better.'

'He means if there was a city-wide search, the crazy idiots would panic and kill her,' Delombre put in bluntly. If he was concerned at upstaging Levignier or using direct language, he didn't show it. He shifted in his seat and stared hard at Girovsky. 'Why don't we stop pissing around? This is what you wanted, isn't it? A chance for a power play? You knew what you were asking for as a means to change the course of the talks, and this is what you've got. Now you just have to sit back and be patient.'

Girovsky's lip curled and his face flushed. He slammed a hand down on the table and stood up, sending a pen skittering onto the floor. 'And what if I choose not to, Mr whatever-your-name-is? What if I decide to stop "pissing around" as you so inelegantly put it, and tell that maniac Bessine that his wife has been kidnapped by men accustomed to killing and unless he stops talking to Taiwan, she won't be coming home again? *What if I do that?*'

Delombre smiled, and glanced at Levignier, who said nothing but waved a hand, a simplified form of shrug. Taking it as a signal to continue, Delombre said softly,

'Well, you can do that, Mr Girovsky. Of course you can. But if you do, I can guarantee you that she won't be the only person not going home again. Where will your trade advantage be then?'

'Gentlemen… enough.' Levignier spoke quietly but firmly, cutting off an outraged protest from Girovsky. 'Nobody is going anywhere near Bessine, least of all you.' This last was directed at Delombre, before he turned to address the businessman. 'In fact, a message has already gone to him which will quickly establish the ground rules.'

Girovsky blinked at the roundabout message he was hearing.

'Ground rules? What the hell does that mean? This isn't some minor civil service matter we're talking about – this is business!'

'It means that as soon as he receives confirmation of the situation, we can expect to hear by return that all the hurdles, as you put it earlier, will be cleared out of the way, and your – our – plans can go ahead.'

'But will he do the right thing? What if he digs his heels in and goes ahead with his talks?'

The idea had not been given voice before, and Levignier had a momentary feeling of uncertainty. What if, against all perceived odds and expectations, Bessine went ahead, risking his wife's life? It would be a disaster. And there were people in positions of power who were counting on that not happening; people who would soon decide to cut themselves loose of Girovsky and anyone else who might be able to talk of what had happened.

People like himself.

But then he took reassurance from the fact that, unlike Girovsky, who preferred money and business deals to any woman, Robert Bessine had a much-celebrated relationship with his wife and would do anything for her, no matter what the cost.

'Oh, I feel sure he'll do the right thing.' He stood up, signalling Delombre to stay where he was. He had a job for him to do. 'At least, he will if he wants her back in one piece.'

## Chapter Thirty-nine

'Rocco. You were in Pontoise yesterday afternoon, were you not?' It sounded like a question, but since Massin must have already read Rocco's report, it clearly wasn't.

Rocco sat up in his chair, clamping the phone to his ear. He'd had a sleepless night and insufficient coffee to snap him fully awake yet, and the dead atmosphere of the office wasn't helping. 'That's correct. I went to interview Stefan Devrye-Martin.'

'I see. And how was he when you left him?'

Rocco experienced a frisson of unease. It was the kind of circumlocutory question Massin liked to ask which, if he wasn't careful, could land him in trouble. Yet what sort of trouble? Beyond the usual felon's protests when suspected of almost any crime on the planet, Stefan hadn't complained about his treatment yesterday. So what had changed the situation?

'He was fine. We talked, he told me what he knew about the Clos du Lac, and I left. It's all in my report. Why?'

'Because Stefan Devrye-Martin, he of the faked death in Thailand, really *is* dead this time.'

Rocco felt the ground drop away beneath his feet. 'What happened?'

'A fire gutted most of the house, although a local doctor thinks Devrye-Martin might have had a heart attack. But there was a second deceased person present; this one with a gunshot wound to the head. His name was Alain Préault, a local thug and petty thief. The neighbours said he and Devrye-Martin – not the name they knew him as, of course – seemed to be friends. I was hoping you might be able to shed some light.'

'No. I can't.' It was a set-up. He knew it, could feel it in his bones. People like Stefan and Préault didn't fall out – or if they did, Stefan wasn't the sort to win out over a streetwise thug. There was surely only one question to be answered. 'What about a gun?'

'Well, that's where it gets interesting. Devrye-Martin was holding a small calibre handgun. A Unique, according to the local captain – a pocket gun. The barrel had been machined to take some kind of screw attachment.'

That could mean only one thing: a suppressor. A killer's close-up weapon. But that didn't make sense. Unless…

'It wasn't Stefan who shot him,' said Rocco with certainty. 'I doubt he's ever held a gun in his life, much less had the balls to kill a street thug with one.'

'What are you suggesting?'

'Someone else was there. Someone who went to clean up a mess.'

There was a brief silence, then Massin said, 'I think I need an extra paragraph or two for your report, Inspector. You had better come up with something concrete – and quickly. This is beginning to look ugly.'

Rocco was surprised. 'You're going to send it in?'

'Is there any reason why I shouldn't?'

'Because I thought you, along with ISD, wanted me off this case.'

'I don't control ISD, Inspector – and they do not control me. In fact, I resent their interference. But they have influence in the Ministry and clearly have their reasons for shutting you out of the investigation into the death in the therapy pool.'

'Reasons which need to come out.'

'That may be true. But we're running out of time with this and I'm not sure how much longer I can delay them. Sooner or later, they will get their way and the case will be closed... or you will be compromised.'

'What does that mean?'

'I've had calls suggesting that this Clos du Lac business has been blown out of proportion by an officer seeking to make a reputation for himself and get posted back to Paris where he really wants to be. Is that true?'

Rocco didn't hesitate. A few months ago, he'd have said yes. Back then, anything was better than this rural backwater where a man could feel himself dying of inactivity, away from the hustle and sheer speed of events and the adrenalin rush of high-level crime. But now he felt differently. Occasional contact with Michel Santer was good for his spirits, but it wasn't a precursor for going back. He liked it here.

'No. It's not. But it confirms what I suspect: there's some kind of conspiracy here. How deep, I don't know, but there's a lot more to this than I've uncovered.'

'I hope you're right. If it's a safe house – an elaborate one, I grant you – for people being held by the justice system, even if outside the normal rules, then we have no case.'

'I don't think it's as simple as that. Bending a few rules doesn't get people killed. If there was anyone who'd be a target for a professional killer, it would be the gangster, Betriano. There must be a long line of people on both sides of the fence who'd love to stop him getting to court and spilling his guts. But the dead man was a civil servant who'd threatened to expose a scandal about foreign trade deals.'

'Maybe. Just remember this, Inspector, in case you ever feel like going back to Clichy: Paris has plenty of Inspector Roccos, whereas this region needs the one it's got.'

The phone went dead, leaving Rocco certain that just before the connection was cut, he'd heard something like a smile in Massin's voice.

The phone rang again. He snatched it up. 'Rocco.'

It was Santer. He sounded serious. 'Lucas, your information's correct: there is a man named Delombre who works for ISD. Bobo says he's a tough guy – *un dur* – and not one to mix with. He's Levignier's errand boy, but he seems to come and go as he pleases.'

'So what is he – a mercenary?'

'Could be. He's been around a fair bit recently, according to Bobo, so something must be cooking. Watch your back, my friend.'

Rocco replaced the phone. It was no surprise that ISD were using outsiders – if that's what this Delombre was. There were all manner of reasons to use part-timers, or 'deniables', with no links to officialdom. It just made Levignier's scope of activities all the more interesting, especially if Delombre had some authority over people like Bezancourt and his men.

The phone again. It was proving to be a busy morning. 'Rocco.'

There was a brief pause, then, 'Inspector. It's Jacqueline Roget.'

It took a moment or two for the name to click into place.

'Have you had your shoe mended?' He wondered for a split second how she had found him, then realised that with her connections, it couldn't have been simpler.

'I still owe you a coffee, Inspector. Remember?' There was a hint of a smile in her voice. 'But most of all an apology. I'm in the *Augustine*. I'm hoping you can spare me a few minutes.'

The *Augustine*. A nice restaurant here in the town centre. Five minutes away on foot. If he cared to go.

He started to tell her that he was too busy, but the phone was already dead.

# Chapter Forty

'It's a long way to come for a coffee,' he said, easing into a seat across from Jacqueline Roget. There were no other diners yet and the place was silent, save for a waiter laying tables for the lunchtime trade.

'Worth it, though. I hope.' There was no trace of coquetry in the words, and Jacqueline's expression was carefully neutral, save for a slight pulse in her throat. An attack of nerves or was this another attempt to entrap him? 'In any case, my aunt lives not far from here; I thought I'd call on her at the same time.'

Rocco waited as she poured coffee from a silver pot, and added cream when he nodded. It gave him a chance to study her. She wore a dark-green silk blouse beneath what looked like a jacket of soft doeskin. A gold necklace hung at her throat, disappearing beneath the blouse and offset by the remains of a tan. She looked even more attractive than she had the other evening, and he detected a look of humour in her eyes that street lights would have masked.

She edged the sugar bowl towards him and sat back, hands folded in her lap. 'Don't you know it's impolite to stare?'

'It's even more impolite to deceive an innocent man.'

A smile touched her lips. 'OK. I deserve that. May I call you Lucas?'

'Of course. May I call you Jacqueline?'

'That would be nice.'

'You said something about an apology.'

She frowned, although whether at the change in tone or remembering the business that had brought them together, he wasn't clear. 'Yes. That. I'm sorry about the other evening. It was crude and clumsy, and I should have had nothing to do with it.'

'So why did you? Or were you following orders?'

'Yes.' No hesitation. It sounded like the truth. 'I was instructed to find out why you were visiting Pascal Rotenbourg. I was told you were a policeman, but acting in a private capacity. Was that true?'

'No. I don't have a private capacity. Who are you working for?'

She looked away. 'You know I can't tell you that.'

'Fair enough. Let me throw a name in the air. If you don't run screaming out into the street, I'll know I'm right. Is it ISD?'

Her mouth opened in surprise. 'As I said—'

'I know. You can't tell me.' He waved a hand to indicate their presence here. 'Is this just another assignment for you? Is the waiter your backup in case I start throwing crockery? Because this is tiresome and Levignier should know better.'

He began to rise, but Jacqueline lifted a hand to stop him.

'Please, Inspector. Lucas? Don't go.' Her cheeks were red, and he wondered if she was as tough as he'd first thought. 'I came here to apologise.'

'Why?' He sat down again.

'Because I feel I was used… to get close to you. And that doesn't mean,' she added quickly, 'what you might think. I don't do that sort of work.'

'I'm pleased to hear it. What do you do?'

She glanced across at the waiter, before leaning forward slightly. 'Nothing very important. Liaison, mostly, between departments and government, and research, of course. Occasionally, as a go-between… and sometimes a means of gathering information.'

'Like the other evening?'

She smiled briefly. 'Well, that didn't exactly scream success, did it? I decided to act innocent, and it was the only scenario I could come up with at short notice.'

He nodded and took another sip of coffee. It was lukewarm. 'And the heel – whose idea was that?'

She frowned. 'Nobody's. It broke, really.' She stared at him. 'You think I did that deliberately?'

'Yes. I'm sorry. What about the two men in the Renault?'

For the first time, she looked angry. 'They were supposed to be there to make sure I was safe. I didn't realise until you saw them how it must have looked. I'm sorry.'

'Two apologies.' Rocco smiled. 'I'm impressed. Your father clearly taught you well. All part of the diplomatic service culture, I suppose.'

'My fath—?' She sat up. 'How do you know about him?'

He pushed the cup away. 'Because I'm a cop. I ask questions and I find answers. What else did Levignier tell you?'

'God, was I that bad?' She had the good grace to look sheepish. 'He told me that you were investigating a death and he wanted to know more, but couldn't find out through the usual channels.'

'And you accepted that?'

'Of course. Much of our work is by its nature confidential, even secret. The moment we show an official interest, it ceases to be so.'

He nodded. It sounded reasonable… at a stretch. 'But you don't know why he's taking an interest? Or why me talking to Pascal Rotenbourg is something to concern him?'

'No. It's not as if Levignier confides in me. I simply follow orders.' She looked away in confusion. She had a very nice profile, he found himself thinking. Soft skin, slightly tanned, no blemishes. He remembered the smell of her perfume.

Then he realised she was staring at him.

'I'm sorry.' It was his turn to feel confused. She was looking very grave. 'I don't wish to sound rude, but you haven't said why you felt the need to apologise. You could have said nothing, and I wouldn't have given it another thought.' He realised how ungallant that sounded and added, 'Well, maybe a little.'

She gave a trace of a smile before replying, then said, 'Levignier has always been… remote with me and others on my level. But there has been talk – the way there always is talk around any office.'

'What about?'

She shrugged. 'About men, and what they do… or say. He has a reputation for going after young interns.'

'And you?'

'Until the other evening, no. I knew him, of course, from contact with other officers and from a remark he made about my father, whom he claimed to admire. But I wasn't aware that he had singled me out in any specific way. I receive my orders from a head of department.'

'But this time?'

'He called me himself and gave me my instructions. It was unusual, but at the time I didn't think anything of it. I assumed it was the normal way to test employees in the field ready for other assignments.' She toyed with a gold bracelet on her wrist. 'He told me what I had to do, and insisted on having my report in person that evening, after I'd... we'd... met. I had to go to his apartment in Robineau, near the Jardin du Luxembourg.'

'Expensive place to live.'

'Yes. He has family money, I hear.' She shivered slightly, and he asked if she was cold. She shook her head. 'No, it's... just that when I got there, it was as if he already knew it hadn't been a success, and wasn't interested, anyway.' She looked straight at Rocco. 'I'm sorry – this must seem silly to you, but it was creepy. I think he wanted – no, expected – me to stay the night. As if it was part of my duty.'

'What did he say?'

'That's just it. He didn't. But he was very close... and touching me, whereas before, nothing. I know when a man is trying it on, Lucas. The signals were very clear and he even sounded a little drunk, although I don't think he was.'

'What happened?'

'Nothing. I felt uncomfortable, so I decided to get out. I haven't seen him since.' She paused, then added, 'And the men he sent to be with me that evening. They were not there for my security after all.'

'How do you know that?'

'I saw one of them three days ago, walking into our building. He was wearing a visitor's badge, which told me he wasn't a direct department employee. I asked a colleague if he knew him, and he said I should not involve myself. He said this man does "arm's length" work for the department. When I asked what kind of work, he wouldn't say, but hinted that men like that do not play nice. I took that to mean they use violent methods.'

'And you're OK with that?'

'How could I be? It doesn't sound right but I'd be a fool if I pretended governments don't use irregular methods. Governments and the people working for them.'

'You mean Levignier.'

'Yes. He's a patriot and makes no secret of it. Duty is everything to him.' She nudged her coffee cup a centimetre or two away. 'I'm glad you didn't have to see what he might be capable of. But you should be careful.'

'Why? Does he carry a grudge?'

'No.' She shook her head. 'That would be too personal. But I hear he has a man who does.'

'What's this man's name?'

'Delombre. But that's all I know about him. People tend to avoid him – he has that kind of aura.'

'I'll bear it in mind.' That name again. The man was in danger of becoming a bogeyman. 'So what now?' He knew he was probably being dense, but he still couldn't see why Jacqueline was here, other than perhaps to assuage a sense of guilt about the other evening.

'Now, I'm going to visit my aunt.' She stood up, a fluid movement full of grace, and smoothed her skirt. 'I've already paid for the coffee. It was my treat, after all.' She gave a fleeting smile. 'I hope there are no hard feelings.'

'None at all.'

Rocco instantly felt… what did he feel? It was odd. As if he'd missed something important, something crying out for attention. He stood, too, nearly upsetting the table and making the coffee cups rattle.

Jacqueline walked to the door, then turned suddenly and said, 'My aunt Celestine lives in Poix. Do you know it? She joined an artists' community there many years ago, but it's long been disbanded. She lives near the church, in a house with a small turret. She's my family's black sheep.' She stopped speaking. 'Sorry. I'm gabbling.'

Rocco felt a tightness in his chest. He glared at the waiter, who had moved to open the door for them. The man scuttled away out of earshot, grabbing a tray of cutlery as he went.

'I know Poix – but not well. How long are you in the area?'

Jacqueline lifted an eyebrow, and he detected a glow of amusement in her eyes. 'A couple of days. Not more.' She leant forward suddenly and kissed him, a brush of soft skin against his cheek. Her breath was warm on his face and he enjoyed the sensation of her nearness.

Then she was gone.

Across the street, a man bent over a street map at a café table looked up surreptitiously as Jacqueline Roget emerged from the *Augustine*. He dumped the remnants of his marc into his coffee and swallowed it in one. He got ready to leave, making sure he remained in the shadow of a parasol, and watched as Roget strode down the street, admiring her long legs and neat figure. Some men were born lucky, he figured wryly, and this man Rocco must have been conceived under a magic star. Quite how he came to be friendly with a woman like Jacqueline Roget of the ISD was a mystery, but that was somebody else's problem to sort out, not his.

He ducked his head as Rocco himself came out of the restaurant and stood scanning the street. He doubted the inspector would pick him out, even this close. He'd been working surveillance for many years, in all manner of settings, and had never been made yet. But he still didn't want to take the risk. From what he'd heard on the grapevine, Rocco wasn't a man to tangle with.

As soon as Rocco was on the move, the watcher stood up and walked inside the café, heading for the telephone on the back wall.

# Chapter Forty-one

'Yes.' Delombre picked up his phone and listened. The call was from his man in Amiens. He'd been ordered to stick close but not be seen under pain of death. Rocco was on the move again.

Christ, what was it this time? He couldn't be interested in tracking down the other former inmates of the sanitarium; the gangster was a legitimate state witness and the two embassy people were in state care for their own health. With Devrye-Martin taken care of and unable to talk, that took the skids from under the idiot cop's feet.

'He went to a restaurant? So what? I said anything important, you fool, not his lunch appointments.' He was about to slam down the phone when his man mentioned a familiar name.

'*Who?*'

'Jacqueline Roget. I know it was her because I used to work in the same section of the building. She was waiting for him and they had coffee. Looked very cosy, too, at the end.'

'Give me a minute.' Delombre turned and stared through the window. Roget. She was a gofer, a junior officer attached to ISD, but with no direct-action responsibilities. He knew Levignier had had his eye on her for a while. The man had a weakness for young women in the department. It would be the ruination of him one day.

But what the hell was Roget doing meeting with Rocco? Then it came to him: Levignier's idiot plan to incriminate the cop in an allegation of rape: he'd gone all secretive about who he was planning to use. It had to have been the Roget woman. And that plan had failed.

Now she was turning round to bite him.

He spoke into the phone. 'Stay with Rocco, you hear? Keep me informed of his movements. If you get seen, I'll come and shoot you myself.'

'Yes, sir. Should I advise Levignier?'

'No. You don't advise anyone, least of all him. This stays with us.' All his instincts were telling him that Rocco, the country cop, the one he'd misjudged, was on the verge of kicking all their lives to hell and back. What an idiot he'd been. The bloody man was like a shark, sniffing out his prey from miles away, then zeroing in.

But it was too late for recriminations. He was going to have to make a decision that should have been made several days ago. And if Levignier didn't like it, that was too bad.

But first, he needed to see what this interfering cop looked like.

'Give me a place where we can meet,' he told the watcher, and made a quick note of a café in the centre of Amiens, near the cathedral. 'Fine. Three p.m. Be there or leave a note if you have to move.'

He dropped the phone back on its rest and swore long and fluently. Then he dialled Levignier. He needed to find out what was happening.

'Has the bulletin gone out yet?' he asked him. He was referring to the official intelligence bulletin from the Ministry, alerting selected police districts to the possibility of the kidnappers having moved their way.

'An hour ago. It should be reaching the stations anytime now, having gone through several different hands. Why? Problem?'

'Not at all. I was just checking to see where we were on this.'

'You agreed to it, Delombre. I hope nothing goes wrong.' Levignier's words were calm enough but laced with accusation. The tone suggested that while the real servants of the state were above being judged, men like Delombre stood to lose a great deal in the event of failure.

Delombre fought to keep his temper. He had no doubts that if the ball went out of the park, as one of his past commanding officers had been fond of saying, he would very quickly find himself shouldering the burden of blame. The idea of having to go underground for a long time didn't bother him particularly, but he knew what the final consequences would be: having a man just like himself, trained and motivated to do one thing and do it well, coming after him. It could only ever end one way.

'Nothing will go wrong,' he said calmly. 'We just need to keep the police distracted for a while, that's all. If they're looking for her elsewhere, they won't bother searching here, will they?' What he really wanted to say was that it would keep Rocco distracted, but that would be to admit that the damned man was getting too close. And after all his assurances to Levignier and Girovsky that it wasn't going to happen, he couldn't afford to put himself in that kind of danger. If Levignier didn't take direct action, he knew that Girovsky eventually would.

'If you say so. Our man is almost there, but it just needs a little while longer – and a reminder.'

'How so?'

'Well, I've been thinking, perhaps a word from our "guest" to show that all is still well might give him the impetus he needs. A sort of lovey-dovey connection, if you wish.'

'What kind of word?' God, Levignier and his mind games. The man was obsessed with convoluted plans to achieve his ends. Delombre favoured more direct methods – such as the kind he'd used with Devrye-Martin.

'A message containing a personal detail, to prove she's still… viable. I believe it should tip the balance of his judgement in our favour.'

'You want me to prepare her?'

'If you would. But don't hurt her; we need her alive and able to talk, not damaged or dead.'

'How long do you want this to go on? What if talking doesn't work?'

'Then she's no longer of any use to us, is she? Before you do that, though, I suggest you acquaint yourself with the search team as soon as possible. They're in the Pantin area – you'll get their location from central command. Find out what they're doing and put them off digging further. The intelligence bulletin should help. It would be embarrassing if they happened to stumble upon our two furniture removers, wouldn't it?'

'Very well. What if they're close?'

'In that case, cut to the chase and deal with the removers. You've got the address?'

'I have. Any specific orders?'

'They need to be retired.'

'Oh, goody.'

## Chapter Forty-two

Rocco walked back to the office, his mind in a whirl. At one point he stopped and turned. He'd got the odd feeling of something in the air, as if he were being watched. It gave him an itchy feeling in his shoulders. It wouldn't be the first time in his career that he'd been under surveillance, nor the last. But there was nobody obvious in sight.

What had just happened? He was confused. Had he just been played by an expert, or had Jacqueline Roget genuinely wanted to apologise to a target she'd never met before the other evening? And had the reference to her aunt's house been an invitation – or had he mistakenly taken it as such and blundered over the line of acceptable behaviour?

He was still trying to figure it out when he was met at the door by René Desmoulins waving a sheet of paper. It looked like one of the Urgent Response bulletins issued by the intelligence section of the Interior Ministry when they wished to poke the entire country's police force into a buzz of activity. Behind Desmoulins the building was a rush of voices and hurrying feet.

'There's a flap on,' said the detective. 'All hands on deck. Godard's been ordered to call in all his men.'

'Not being invaded again, are we?'

'Even worse. The Interior Minister has gone public about a recent kidnap victim. All regions are on full alert for signs of her, but we're the hot spot.'

'Do we have the victim's name yet?'

News reports over the past couple of days had been long on drama but short on detail. No doubt the authorities had been anxious to keep the victim's name out of the limelight for fear of a reprisal killing or instigating copycat crimes, but it probably wouldn't have made much difference in the end. It rarely did.

'Véronique Bessine, wife of the aircraft manufacturer, Robert Bessine.' He read from the bulletin as they walked into the main office. 'She was lifted after leaving a high-end beauty salon in Paris several days ago. Nothing's been heard since, but they believe she's been taken out of the city and they've got three addresses in our region where they think she might be being held.'

Rocco recalled two kidnaps being mentioned by Santer; a junior diplomat and an industrialist's wife. It seemed a lifetime ago. Evidently Mme Bessine rated a higher degree of official concern than a junior diplomat playing footsie with an army officer's niece.

'The Minister and Bessine were at university together,' said Desmoulins, interpreting his thoughts. 'I read it somewhere. I suppose that would account for the response level.'

'Why wait so long to tell us?'

'It says the decision was made in the best interests of the victim and her family, but now they've decided they can't wait any longer and all efforts must go to getting her back. Their words, not mine.'

'If she's still breathing.' As Rocco was well aware, kidnap victims rarely lasted more than a couple of days before they became a liability, or the kidnappers panicked and decided to cut their losses. Anyone held this long and still alive would be very lucky indeed.

'So who are we up against – Sicilians?'

'They haven't released that information.'

'Probably means they don't know.' He reached into his desk drawer for a spare shoulder holster. He hated the things, but there were times when they were useful. He strapped it on beneath his coat and checked his MAB. Full magazine and spare. If they found the woman and he needed more ammunition than this, they'd be in the middle of a bloodbath.

He noticed Desmoulins was holding a slim, buff folder with an official stamp on the front. 'What's that?'

'Oh, yes. Nearly forgot.' Desmoulins flipped the folder open. Inside was a sheet of paper. 'Brest sent this over. It's a summary of André Paulus's record – or at least the bits that aren't a naval secret. He was a cop, like you said – actually a navy provost under the *Gendarmerie Maritime*. The file wasn't much help so I wangled my way through to the operations office in Brest and spoke to a former colleague.'

'Go on.'

'Paulus was a career man. Single, confirmed bachelor, no ties or family – ideal for that life, by the sounds of it. Good at his job, according to his friend, but not a high-flyer. Liked to be mates too much, although not a party-goer. He served all over, liked to move around, volunteered for anything with some action, knew his way around the block. Then suddenly, he gave it all up.'

'Why?'

'For love, apparently. Met a woman and fell like a lovesick calf. She moved away from Brest and persuaded him to follow. His mates tried to stop him, but he wouldn't listen. He dropped out and the last they heard he'd got a job in security through the military employment office. They arrange jobs and training for ex-service personnel.'

'And the woman's name?' Rocco knew already, but needed confirmation.

'A navy nurse named Dion. When I say she moved, she was transferred onshore to what barrack-room gossip called "special duties".'

'The Clos du Lac.'

'I'd say, yes.'

Damn, thought Rocco. Wheels within wheels.

He was interrupted from further thought by *Sous-Brigadier* Godard striding into the room, followed by two of his men, one of them the tall and dangerous-looking Patrice, who grinned in acknowledgement. All were dressed in black and fully armed. Godard held a slip of paper in his fist.

'We've had a briefing from the Ministry via *Commissaire* Massin,' he said, and waved the paper. 'There are three places we've been told to hit, in the following order.' He walked over to the wall map and studied it briefly, then took three coloured pins and stuck them in the fabric. Roye, 25 kilometres east of Amiens. Doullens, less than 20 kilometres to the north. And Neufchâtel-en-Bray, 30 kilometres to the south-west.

Rocco studied the pins and their locations. It was like a three-spoke wheel, with Amiens at the hub.

'Where did these addresses come from?'

Godard shrugged. 'The criminal intelligence section in the Interior Ministry. They've been keeping an eye on likely suspects and seen them move out here at various times. They believe things might have got a little too hot for them in Paris, so they've come out looking for somewhere quiet to hide.'

'Here. Around Amiens?'

'Yes. Why?'

He shook his head. Now wasn't the time to question the likelihood of kidnappers choosing the Somme and Pas de Calais region to hide their victims. But something about this didn't ring true. Most kidnappers prepared their hideout well before the event and stayed put while they waited for the ransom to be dropped and collected. Moving a victim around too much was risky: there was always someone on the lookout, whether a nosy neighbour, a local cop on the alert or a kid with an active imagination and too much time on his hands. To ship a victim out of Paris this long after the kidnap meant they had been disturbed or the nature of the game had changed in some way.

'Why can't we hit them simultaneously?'

'I suggested that, but they said it would be too noticeable all going off at once and might make the kidnappers jump the gun.' Godard raised his shoulders. 'I tried but they wouldn't listen.'

'Are they sending any men out to help?'

'No. They said we should handle it ourselves. Same with other regions, apparently.'

In other words, Rocco thought cynically, let the regions take the flak if the victim ended up being killed in the process. The only credit to be gained would be if Mme Bessine was recovered alive and well, in which case it would reflect well on the Ministry's 'hand's off' approach and their confidence in the local police. Some things never changed.

'Right, where's the first one?'

'The nearest is Doullens. The location is a small farm just outside the town. Been abandoned for two years, according to the locals, but rented recently by a transport business in Paris. No other details, though. Ideal for keeping someone quiet, I'd have thought. We can be there in twenty minutes. I've sent a couple of men out to take a quiet look. They won't be seen. If that turns up blank, then I figured Roye, followed by Neufchâtel.'

'You've got men out there, too?'

'Yes. They'll call in if they look good.'

'Fine. Let's get on with it.'

Rocco followed them out to the cars, making a mental note that he needed to speak once more to Inès Dion. He had a feeling that she might have an interesting story to tell.

## Chapter Forty-three

When Delombre arrived at the unoriginally named *Café Sportif* in the centre of Amiens, his contact, named Ferrand, was sitting behind a cold beer with a wary expression, eyes on the door. The only thing sporting about the place, Delombre noted, was a large colour poster of French cyclist Jacques Anquetil, mounted in a glass frame on the rear wall. It looked more like a shrine than a celebration, and he reminded himself to figure out one day what it was about the Tour de France that aroused such passions in the nation.

'Someone killed your dog?' he muttered, and ordered coffee. Something about Ferrand's expression told him they weren't going anywhere soon.

'He's gone,' Ferrand muttered.

'Gone where? Why didn't you follow and leave a note?'

'Because the place was in an uproar. Every cop in the town must have been there, *Gendarmerie Mobile*, plain clothes, auxiliaries, the lot. It was like somebody jabbed a stick into a hornets' nest and they all woke up with a screaming headache. Before I could do anything, they were all up and gone. I didn't see Rocco, but I think he was among them.'

Delombre had a good idea what the fuss was about. Levignier's intelligence bulletin must have stirred them into action. Well, that was something, at least.

'Is it worth going after them? Somebody must know where they've gone.'

'I doubt it. We'd probably get jumped on. You've got the official muscle – can't you ask at the station?'

'I could, but I don't want to.' Walking into the police station meant he'd leave a trace and he didn't want Rocco picking up on his presence. The man seemed to have a sixth sense for trouble and Delombre didn't need the problem right now. 'What does he look like?'

'Rocco? He's big, tall – taller than you, has dark hair cut short and usually dresses smart, like an undertaker. Long black coat and trousers, shiny shoes, looks expensive.'

'So he's a fashion model.'

'Yes, but they say don't let his looks fool you. He's got a pair of shoulders on him and can handle the rough stuff.' Ferrand toyed with his beer. 'I hear he used to work with the anti-gang units before transferring out here, and he's been involved in a few incidents since he arrived.'

'What kind of incidents?' Delombre didn't plug into the office chatter much; he did his work and left the gossip alone. Any stories circulating about cops were usually blown out of proportion by the cops themselves, eager to gain some good publicity as hard men and a chance of promotion on the back of it along the way.

'He stopped an assassination attempt on de Gaulle not long ago. A bunch of English gangsters were involved and he put them down. End of story.'

Delombre lifted an eyebrow. Perhaps he should start taking more notice of gossip. He'd clearly missed some- thing here.

'You're saying he's a hotshot?'

Ferrand hesitated, as if wary of singing Rocco's praises too much. 'He's a hunter. I've seen him at work, the way he checks out the scene when he's out and about. He doesn't miss much.'

Delombre smiled and pushed his coffee away untouched.

'But he missed you.'

'Yes. He missed me.'

This Rocco sounded like a challenge. But not right now. If he was pumped up by the thought of taking down a kidnap gang, he'd be even more on the alert than usual.

'Very well. We'll give this one a miss. Stay on him for another twenty-four hours, but well back, you understand? I don't want him picking up a sniff that he's being watched.'

'He won't.' Ferrand said it without boasting; he knew how good he was.

'Let me know anything you hear, then stand down.' He stood up and walked out, leaving Ferrand sitting at the table.

—

The farm looked deserted. It was situated at the end of a long track meandering through flat fields some two kilometres outside the town of Doullens, the house and buildings nestling against a backdrop of trees. From a distance the place looked forgotten in time, abandoned to nature, with long, flowing grass on the track in, and tendrils of ivy crawling across the front porch and through a broken pane of glass in the door.

Rocco studied the place through binoculars, paying particular attention to the windows at the front and the outbuildings at the rear. Wooden shutters hung at the window on the left, secured by what looked like a heavy chain. But the door and right-hand window were uncovered, suggesting that somebody had been inside recently. A tramp, maybe?

He checked the chimney, but saw no sign of smoke. Didn't mean a thing.

'My men reckon it's empty,' said *Sous-Brigadier* Godard, sliding up alongside him. 'They've been watching for a couple of hours and haven't seen a thing.'

'What are your instructions?'

'To report back and wait. No movement until we get word to go from Massin.'

And until Massin gets word from the Ministry, thought Rocco sourly. Everybody wants their say in what happens now.

'Is there a back way out?'

'Only on foot. We checked that first.'

The place reminded him of the farm owned by Thomas Portier, yet in an even worse state of disrepair. He could see why someone seeking isolation might choose it as a hideaway, but only if they were a painter or writer – or seriously antisocial. For anybody dragging a kidnap victim along with them, especially a high-profile one like Véronique Bessine, there had to be plenty of places far more convenient they could have found. Out here was putting a stretch on the term remote, and its very location, with no secondary way out, also made it vulnerable as a trap. What he couldn't understand was how the intelligence unit had heard about the place being used.

'Have your men spoken to any locals?'

'Only some old guy in a field down the road. He says nobody's been here for a long while. The land is poor and the house would be easier to knock down than restore. Mind you, he said a few uncomplimentary things about morons from Paris throwing their cash around to get in touch with the land, but I don't think he was talking about anyone coming here.'

'But he wouldn't know if someone had turned up while he was away.'

'True. But my men took a close look at the track. There's been nothing on wheels down there for months. It rained less than a week ago, and the ground here is soft; even a nun on a bike would have left some kind of sign. There's nothing.'

Rocco studied the line of the track leading up to the front door. It was straight and narrow, bordered by a ditch and a wire fence each side, both overgrown. The track surface itself was lost in a sea of moving grass, mesmerising and lush. Anyone inside the house would have a devastatingly clear shot all the way down, with nowhere for an approach vehicle to go but back. And going back would mean ending up in the ditch.

Or dead.

'Seems a shame not to try something,' said Godard. 'We've trained hard for this stuff; just never got to use it yet.'

Rocco looked up at the sky. The afternoon was rolling on, bringing a grey sky studded with heavy cloud. If they left it too long, anybody in the house might decide to cut their losses and try to get past them once the light fell.

He looked behind their position. They were on the edge of a bank bordering the track, where a bend offered them a slightly elevated spot from which to see the house. The rest of Godard's men, the uniforms and other police units were all out of sight at the top of the track where it met the road to Doullens.

He studied the chimney on the house. It had a tin pot protruding from the stack, battered by the elements and blackened around the upper rim. It would make a hell of a noise if it took a bullet. But any action like that was Godard's call.

'That chimney,' he said casually, 'is a heck of a target.'

'That's what I was thinking,' Godard agreed. 'And the noise would scare the shit out of anybody inside.'

'Long shot, though. It would have to be a good man to hit it from here.'

Godard took a look through the glasses. 'Are you kidding? I could hit that myself – and I'm not the best. Still, if there is someone in there – and with Bessine?'

'I'd lay good money that there isn't. Send two of your best men down the track as close as they can get to the front door. As soon as they're in place, get your sniper to take a shot, and the other two go in hard.'

Godard nodded slowly and pursed his lips. 'I can do that.' He added, 'See the last fence post on the right, just before the track opens out into the front of the house?'

'Yes.'

Godard gave a short whistle. Immediately, a man's hand slid up the fence post, then disappeared again.

'Patrice. There's another man on the left.' Rocco smiled.

'You had this planned.'

Godard returned the smile. 'What – you think we sit round all day polishing our boots? Give me three minutes and the chimney's gone. Wait for my whistle but don't stand up until the shot's been made.' With that, he slid back down the bank and disappeared back along the track at a jog, using the lay of the land.

Rocco waited, hoping he was right. If Mme Bessine was being held in there, he was making a serious mistake. Yet every fibre of his body told him this place was empty. Somehow the intelligence unit had been handed false information. It happened.

He heard Godard's warning whistle and focused the glasses on the chimney pot. The shot when it happened took him by surprise, and came from no more than twenty metres behind him.

The pot exploded in a cloud of thick soot and a shower of twigs, probably an old bird's nest, and tumbled down out of sight on the far side of the roof.

Instantly he saw the tall figure of Patrice leap up out of the grass and sprint across the front yard, closely paralleled by another man in the same black uniform. Both carried handguns. Patrice made it to the porch and ran straight through the front door, taking it off its hinges. The other man dodged round the side, both of them calling out their positions to each other.

Moments later, they reappeared through the front door.

They looked relaxed.

Patrice signalled with a shake of his head. Empty.

# Chapter Forty-four

'Empty as in never used,' Patrice told them as they approached the front door. He looked disappointed at the lack of action and nodded at Rocco, adding, 'There's some stuff in the back room, but it could have been left by a vagrant passing through.'

He led them through the front of the house, which was bare of furnishings, the ancient plaster walls showing the wooden lathes beneath in large patches where damp had wreaked its worst over the years, and into a rear space which had once doubled as a kitchen and workroom, with a shallow stone sink in one corner and an old knife grinder beneath a broken window.

'Christ, I haven't seen one of those in years,' said Godard.

He pushed the stone wheel, but it was jammed solid.

In the corner away from the sink lay an old army greatcoat and a filthy towel. Alongside was a battered spirit stove. A metal mug with chips out of the enamel had a layer of black covering the base and sides.

Rocco bent and sniffed at the spirit stove. He'd used one like it in the army for a while. The familiar tang of spirit made his nose twitch and brought back memories of long waits for anything to heat up, usually battered by wind and rain. The mug had a dark residue in the bottom which could have been coffee. The greatcoat was filthy.

He checked the pockets. A crumpled cigarette packet. Empty.

He toured the room. Damp had penetrated the floorboards and eaten into the walls, and black spots of mould were scattered across the ceiling. There was no electric wiring, but a stub of a candle on the windowsill had grown a white fuzz, like a rabbit's tail. The sink had harvested a layer of leaves and twigs, as had the floor, no doubt blown in through the window.

He turned back to study the greatcoat.

'What's up?' asked Godard, reading his expression.

'It's too neat. The greatcoat hasn't got any mould on it and the spirit hasn't evaporated.' He tried to think what it reminded him of and immediately got it: it was like a museum exhibit he'd seen in Paris once, dedicated to the war in the trenches in 1918. It was just stuff left lying around, genuine enough but not real. 'No vagrant would leave the coat, even at this time of year. And the stove would bring a few francs if he was desperate.'

Godard nodded, pursing his lips. 'But why – and how come there's no signs of entry along the track?'

Rocco shrugged. 'It was a distraction, to keep us occupied. Checking this place out thoroughly would take a couple of days if we got a full team in here. As to how, one man could have carried this stuff across the fields without leaving a trace. We'll probably find the same set pieces in the other two locations.'

Godard nodded. 'I'll get in touch with my men. You want them to go straight in?'

'Yes. But tell them to be careful. This could just be a feint.'

'I'll do that.' He turned and left, ushering his other men with him, leaving Desmoulins with Rocco in the kitchen.

'Are you sure about this?' said Desmoulins. 'I don't mean you're wrong, but why would anyone risk doing this? If it's not the kidnappers being really clever, how did the intelligence section get the information in the first place?'

Rocco shook his head. He didn't answer. But he didn't much like the ideas that were forming in his mind.

–

By the time they returned to Amiens, calls had come in from Godard's observers in the other two locations at Roye and Neufchâtel. Both were isolated properties outside the towns, and had been under surveillance without any sightings of vehicles or potential kidnappers. Both had offered good potential as hideouts for the kidnappers and their victim.

Both were empty save for some tell-tale items.

'Same results,' Godard reported. 'A few bits and pieces to suggest a bolt-hole, but nothing elaborate. It's the sort of crap you can pick up at any flea market for a few francs, mostly ex-military.' He scratched his head. 'Whoever did this didn't have much imagination, though. I mean, why bother if it wasn't going to fool us for longer than two minutes?'

Rocco had been going over the possibilities, and had come to one conclusion. 'It was both a delaying tactic and a distraction. They knew we'd have to wait before going in, while keeping the houses under observation. They also figured we'd spend even more time going over the stuff we found with a magnifying glass looking for clues, because that's what we do. Both options take men and time.'

'Distracting us from what, though?'

'From getting too close, maybe?' Desmoulins threw in, but without looking convinced. 'If so, I wish the kidnappers would let us know for sure how close. That poor woman must be going out of her mind.'

'If she's still alive,' said Godard, with feeling. He, like all experienced cops, knew that after a certain amount of time, things did not look good for kidnap victims. He looked at Rocco. 'I need to debrief the men. What do we do about a report?'

'Leave it to me. I need to think about it. Are the three sites secure?'

'Yes. All locked up tight. Give me a shout if you need us again.'

Rocco signalled for Desmoulins to follow him, and walked into the main office, which was temporarily empty as the search teams sorted themselves out, some signing off, others returning to their normal duties.

'I think you were right both times,' he told the detective quietly. 'We are getting too close. But this stays between us until we figure it out.'

Desmoulins nodded. 'Of course. But if that's the case and we're close to finding her, shouldn't we call in the big guns, let the Ministry know?'

Rocco hesitated. He still wasn't sure, but the thoughts he'd had earlier wouldn't leave him alone. The main problem was, if his suspicions were correct, he'd have to prove it before speaking out. But to do that, he'd be taking one hell of a risk with somebody's life.

'Where's that bulletin you had earlier? It might help if we knew who was behind the kidnapping.'

Desmoulins pulled it out of his pocket and handed it over, saying, 'It was thought to be Sicilians at first. Then someone suggested it could be a group opposed to trade deals with the Chinese Republic – that's the lot in Taiwan, not their bigger cousins. Bessine's currently in talks with their government on the supply of fighter jets and other airplanes.' He shrugged his broad shoulders. 'I'm no student of international politics, but it doesn't sound much like any Sicilians I've ever met.'

China.

Rocco scanned the bulletin quickly. He couldn't see any connection, either. He wondered if the suspected kidnap group was affiliated to either side, since each would have their own reasons for ensuring a disruption of talks over the supply of warplanes. He sat down, trying to organise his thoughts. Pascal Rotenbourg had mentioned the Chinese, based on his brother Simon's fears of high-level collusion to influence trade talks; Stefan Devrye-Martin had mentioned them, too, also based on claims voiced by Simon. And Simon had claimed that 'extreme methods' were going to be exerted on a senior industry figure to force him to change the direction of his negotiations.

Could it be possible, he wondered, that 'extreme methods' could include kidnapping an industrialist's wife?

'There's a big sticking point,' he said finally. 'What if telling the Ministry could be signing the victim's death warrant?'

'Eh?' Desmoulins stared. 'What – you mean… No!'

'You asked the question yourself: how did the intelligence section come up with the information on these locations in the first place?'

'Yes, I know, but I was just sounding off…' He stopped. 'Jesus, that's crazy. But why would they do that? Surely they must have known somebody might figure it out.'

'Human nature,' he replied. 'You give a bunch of cops the most obvious but most ludicrous suggestion for a guilty party, and they'll spend days running round in circles trying to find an alternative, simply because they won't want to contemplate the truth. None of us does.'

'Fair enough. But that still doesn't explain why.'

'They knew we'd find nothing, but didn't care. We weren't meant to. It took us away from what we were doing, because that's all somebody needed.'

'Somebody?'

'Somebody in the Ministry... or an outsider with contacts inside that they could use to disseminate the information.' He was thinking about Levignier. He'd have the means. And he'd already displayed his contempt for the rule of law by spiriting away the dead body from inside the Clos du Lac. But would he conspire openly with a kidnap – and if so, to what end? If not, there was someone else who might be a prime mover: the shadowy figure behind him, with the power to command Bezancourt and his men to follow Rocco.

The man known as Delombre.

Desmoulins said, 'The Ministry. Christ, you don't exactly pick the easiest enemies, do you? What do we do now?'

Rocco picked up his telephone and dialled Massin's internal number. He was going to make a report, and Massin would do the rest. 'We let them think we're going to investigate all three locations.'

Desmoulins smiled, recognising the tone in Rocco's voice. 'Then what?'

'Then we'll do the exact opposite.'

# Chapter Forty-five

Inspector Leon Drueault was halfway through a snatched cup of coffee in the Pantin *commissariat* and checking a local map of the area, when he was told he had a visitor.

He swore mildly. It had been a very long day, and it wasn't over yet. Worse, nobody other than his commanding officer and a very select few were aware of his presence here. Even the officers and few remaining staff on duty upstairs hadn't been brought in fully on the act, merely told that a special task force was operating in the district and to give them a wide berth. He and his men had deliberately dropped off the edge of the planet as far as the rest of the Paris force was concerned, to allow them to operate without hindrance.

If someone had tracked them down here, it had to be somebody from higher up the chain of command.

Someone with clout.

'Tell them I'll be out when I finish my coffee,' he said bluntly, without turning from the map. His men were in a corner on the other side of the room, taking a well-earned break, while he was trying to read the local map to find where, in a haystack of places to hide, the kidnappers might now be holed up with their captive. The truth was, he was trying to stem a mild case of panic, because so far they were in the dark, with no further clues or sightings.

'That's all right, Inspector,' said a voice from the door. 'No rush.'

Drueault spun round and saw a tall, slim man walking across to meet him. He was dressed in regulation suit and tie, confirming Drueault's suspicion that he was from the Ministry, but there was not much about him that identified him as a desk man. In fact, Drueault thought he walked too much like an athlete. Or a soldier.

He put down his cup and extended his hand. 'My apologies. We've been up all night chasing ghosts. I didn't mean to be rude, Mr...?'

'Delombre,' said the visitor. His grip was firm without being competitive, yet Drueault suspected he could have applied far more pressure had he wanted to. There was something about this man that spoke of an interesting history. And danger.

'Very well, Mr Delombre. What can I do for you?'

Delombre produced an identity card. 'First things first, eh? Mustn't forget the basics.' He turned and looked at Captain Detric, Sebastien, and Ivrey, the third team member, who were watching to see what happened, hands wrapped around breakfast bowls of coffee. The table top in front of them was sprinkled with crumbs from the crusty sandwiches they had been eating. They all looked drained and pallid, and were dressed in ordinary street clothes, more like workmen than cops.

Drueault inspected the card and handed it back. 'Fair enough. You're from ISD. Now I am worried. What brings you out here? I didn't think many people knew our location.'

Delombre gave a tiger's smile. 'Then you can count me in as one of the favoured few, can't you?' He nodded at the map on the wall. 'Any clues as to their location yet?'

'Who are we talking about?' Drueault kept his face blank.

'Cute,' Delombre murmured dryly. 'I must remember that. The people who kidnapped an important person's wife a few days ago from Avenue de Friedland.'

'Not yet. We're following a trail all the way across the north-east of the city. Whoever they are, they're staying on the move, but so far they're keeping a step ahead of us.'

Delombre tilted his head to one side 'You think there's a pattern?'

'Definitely. We believe they're using a furniture wagon, possibly with a defective exhaust system or an old engine. There have been sightings all across here.' He swept his hand across the map from left to right. 'The last one was yesterday right here in Pantin, but they've either gone to ground somewhere since or moved out.'

'So you have no idea where they might be, then.'

Drueault blinked at what might have been criticism. 'Ideas, no. A couple of guesses, perhaps. But that's all they are.' He flicked a glance at his men, who were listening intently while pretending not to.

'Well, we'll have to go with that, then. Your best guess.'

Drueault hesitated. Voicing his beliefs to a suit from the Ministry, especially one from ISD, was risky. If his suspicions proved flawed, and the kidnappers turned up a hundred kilometres away with a dead captive, he could wave goodbye to his career. He had heard about ISD's methods in the past, and they didn't care about leaving bodies lying in their wake.

'They've been using abandoned or unoccupied buildings so far – places nobody would think to look. But only for short periods. I think they've opted to stay on the move deliberately. The moment they pick up a whiff of interest, they simply move on and find somewhere else to park. In fact,' he was taking a real punt here, but he didn't really care, 'the closer we get, the more I believe they've had a number of such hideaways scoped out from the very start.'

It was Delombre's turn to blink. 'Is that so?' He turned and looked at the other three in the corner. 'Do your men share those thoughts?'

'Why don't you ask them?'

'We'll save you the trouble,' said Detric, stretching out his legs before standing up and walking across to join them. He looked tired and cranky and not a bit in awe of Delombre. 'We do all think the same. This was pre-planned; the pickup, their method of transport and the bolt-holes they're using. Nobody but an idiot would drive a furniture van around Paris day after day with a kidnap victim inside and take a chance on finding any old place to stop. They knew what they were doing, where they could go and what places were safe.'

'You talk like a soldier...?'

'Captain Detric. I used to be, yes. Now I'm a cop.'

'Excellent.' Delombre looked past him at the other two men, then turned back to Drueault. 'So, assuming your little team of bloodhounds is on the right scent, Inspector, where does that put these people now?'

Drueault very nearly shrugged, but thought better of it. The use of his rank had been a near reminder by this man that a casual response wasn't permitted. It also told him that Delombre didn't share his belief and was saying so openly. What he couldn't understand was why he was choosing to do it in front of his men. Normal rules of command etiquette dictated that any disagreement with officers was voiced at a discreet distance so as not to undermine the chain of command.

'They're still here,' he said. 'Probably no more than two kilometres from where we're standing right now.' In spite of his confidence, he was keeping his fingers crossed mentally. It was risky, but this stranger was beginning to piss him off.

'Really?' Delombre's eyebrows rose slowly in open disbelief. 'What on earth makes you think that?'

'Instinct. Experience.'

'Ah, of course. Gut feel – the policeman's crystal ball.' A glimmer of something approaching malice danced in the other man's eyes. 'I thought that had died out along with seances and seaweed. Is that really all you've got?'

'Pardon me?' Drueault felt the sting of the verbal slap. He saw Sebastien and Ivrey stand up, and gave them a signal to hold fast. If Delombre was looking for a fight, he didn't want to drag them into it.

'You heard me, Inspector. You're chasing shadows all right – but shadows of your own device. Why on earth would these people stay within the city area, with all the police and security personnel we have available to search for them, when they could be a hundred kilometres away in the middle of nowhere? It makes no sense.'

'Because they're not country people,' said Detric.

'Sorry?'

'They're city, not country. Driving a big truck around this city the way they've been doing takes skill. They haven't got stuck in side streets, they haven't hit anyone apart from a badly parked bike, they've avoided random street stops by traffic cops and they seem to know where they're going.' He gave a wise-guy smile. 'As the boss said, they're still here.' With that he turned and walked away, and sat down with his back to Delombre.

The ISD man watched him go, then turned to Drueault. 'So, you've got men who are loyal to you. That's admirable. Take a round of applause, Inspector.'

He reached into his jacket and took out a folded sheet of paper. Drueault recognised it as an intelligence bulletin. He'd seen enough in his time.

'What's this for?'

'According to latest information, sightings of known faces in the kidnap-and-ransom business have been made in four places. One south of the city near Orléans and three to the north. None of them is less than an hour's fast drive. Longer in a truck. That means they couldn't have been anywhere near here when you say they were. You've been chasing nothing, Inspector.' He slapped the bulletin against Drueault's chest. 'Or are you saying your instincts and experience have greater merit than up-to-date intelligence from the Ministry?'

Drueault took the paper but didn't bother reading it. He had no idea why this man seemed intent on provoking him, but it was obviously what he was trying to do. However, nobody but a fool argued with intelligence bulletins – at least openly. The information in them was not infallible, but it was culled from a variety of sources and more often than not proved correct.

Delombre turned and walked over to the door, then paused. He surveyed the men one by one, then said, 'Seems to me you'd best stand down, Inspector. Get back to the kind of police work you understand.'

# Chapter Forty-six

A house with a small turret near the church in the town of Poix. Rocco found a space outside the church and parked his car, then checked the area on foot until he saw a narrow, two-storey building behind an iron railing. It had a vaguely fairy-tale tower looming defiantly into the night sky out of one corner, as if added for a dare by some previous owner. He couldn't see much detail, but he decided that anybody who could live with that had to be an interesting character.

He hesitated before approaching the front door. This could be painfully embarrassing or simply painful. He had no way of knowing if Jacqueline Roget had given him a detailed location of her renegade aunt's house in Poix deliberately, or whether he was about to make a complete donkey of himself.

There was only one way to find out.

He stepped up the short path and used the brass dog's head knocker, and heard the sound reverberating inside. A light came on as a door opened, and suddenly she was standing there, looking out at him.

'Why, Inspector,' Jacqueline said, quickly tucking a stray lock of hair behind her ear. 'What a surprise.'

'I, uh… I hope this isn't too late?' he murmured, feeling a prize idiot. 'I was in the area, so…' He shrugged and felt his ears go hot.

'*Bring the inspector in,*' called a voice from the rear. '*You can't leave him standing out there like a carpet salesman when he's come all this way!*'

It was Jacqueline's turn to be embarrassed. She smiled and stood aside. 'You'd better do as she says. She's got second sight, and ears like a bat.'

'*I heard that!*'

Rocco followed her down a long hallway, carefully skirting plant stands leaking long strands of greenery, and two large and elegantly fragile-looking porcelain jardinières.

'Limoges,' whispered Jacqueline. 'Break those and she'll poison your drink.'

'I will not,' said the voice. 'They're clever fakes made by an old lover of mine in Nancy many years ago. Not worth a centime unless you're a fool.'

They entered a conservatory room with a sloping glass ceiling, and the speaker was revealed as an elderly lady in a Chinese-style brocade jacket and plain trousers, smiling in greeting from the depths of a high-backed wing chair.

The room was a mixture of plants and furniture, as much garden as living area and studio, with a collection of easels and painting materials at the back, showing splashes of vivid colour lit by a glass or crystal chandelier balanced on a tall pair of wooden stepladders.

'Forgive the mess, Inspector. I don't have much time for cleaning, and there are better things to do with life than primp the place for visitors. Would you like some sherry?'

Without waiting, she picked up a decanter and filled a slim glass, and held it out to him. 'I'd take a seat if I were you. By the time Jacqueline closes her mouth and jumps into action, you'll be exhausted.'

'Thank you.' Rocco took the glass and sat down on the end of a settee alongside another plant pot, this one with metal handles and covered in large china flowers. He felt it move as his elbow caught it a glancing blow, and watched it rock for a moment before settling down. 'Sorry,' he said. 'Another fake?'

'No, that's an Edouard Gilles from the late nineteenth century. Break that and I *would* poison you… and bury you in the back garden.' Her eyes glittered and he didn't know whether to take her seriously or not.

She raised a glass and sipped, then said, studying him openly, 'I have to say, I wasn't sure if my niece had invented you or not. You sounded far too good to be true.'

Rocco sipped his sherry. It was dry and excellent, although he was no expert. 'I hope I don't disappoint, then.' He glanced at Jacqueline, who sat on the other end of the settee glaring daggers at her aunt.

'Oh, she was singing your praises, don't worry.' She ignored her niece with a knowing smile. 'Inspector this, Inspector that, Lucas the other… I was getting quite worried.'

'Why?'

'Well, I thought it was all an invention. I don't mean she's lost her mind, of course, but she's always been so intent on a career, like her father, there's been no time for boyfriends, although how you call it a career to be a typist in the civil service, I don't know.'

She gave a sweet smile of pure mischief and took another sip of sherry.

Lucas glanced at Jacqueline, who gave a minute shake of her head and a pleading look, and he nodded.

'Actually, I never enquired what she does, Madame,' he admitted. 'We've only just met.'

'Of course you have. And please call me Celestine; "madame" is for old biddies. You'd better not hang about, Lucas; this is a whole new age we're in, you know. Young people don't stand on ceremony and go through long courtships these days. You'd better get in there quick before someone else does.'

'*Auntie!*' Jacqueline glared at her aunt and avoided meeting Rocco's gaze, then snatched up her own glass and took a drink, promptly causing a coughing fit.

Rocco reached out and grabbed the glass before she dropped it, then handed her a handkerchief from his top pocket. She gasped a thank you, then dabbed at her skirt and hand where droplets of sherry had landed.

'Good looking *and* a gentleman, I see,' Celestine murmured approvingly. 'Not bad, not bad at all. So, what kind of place do you live in, Lucas?'

He told her about Poissons, and the house behind iron railings at the end of a road into nowhere. 'I was lucky to find it. It suits me.' He said the last with an odd sense of realisation. It was something he'd never given voice to before.

'It sounds very pleasant.' She stood up, reaching for a stick. 'Well, my signal to go to bed.' She smiled as Rocco stood, too. 'Delighted to meet you, Lucas. Remember what I said about the Gilles?'

'Of course.'

'My niece is in the same category… although I've a feeling I don't need to tell you that. Come again, why don't you?' With that, she walked out, head up and back straight, pausing to lay a gentle hand on Jacqueline's shoulder.

'I'm sorry about that,' Jacqueline murmured softly, once the old lady was out of sight. 'She's impossibly blunt, as you can see. No wonder the rest of the family doesn't see her very often. But I think she's wonderful.' She eyed him cautiously. 'I hope you weren't offended.'

'Not if all she said is true, no.'

She smiled. 'I think that's definite. She's never asked *anyone* to call her Celestine on a first meeting before. You made a good impression.' She reached out and took back her glass, and waved the handkerchief. 'Sorry about the display. I'll wash this and post it back to you. It shouldn't stain. Hopefully.'

They sat in silence for a few moments, then Rocco said, 'I have a problem, which I'm hoping you can help with.'

'Really? A work problem?' A faint frown had touched the centre of her forehead, and Rocco felt the atmosphere cool a little.

He cursed inwardly. But it was too late to back out now, so he forged ahead. 'I have reason to believe that the man you told me about – Delombre – working in the Interior Ministry, may be involved in… a criminal enterprise.'

'Really?'

'Yes. I was wondering what else you know about him.' Christ, he thought savagely. Do I have to sound so much like a cop?

Jacqueline lifted her eyebrows. 'Does that mean you think I, too, might be involved, Inspector?' She put her glass on a small side table and dropped the soiled handkerchief alongside it. There was a finality about the movements that made Rocco's gut curl.

'No, of course not. I know this sounds as if I came here on business, but that's not true. I—'

'No.' She raised a hand. 'It's perfectly fine. I understand. You have a job to do. So how can I help?'

He wondered if there was any worse tone he could have heard in her voice, any more matter-of-fact delivery that could have made him feel lower than he did, as if his legs had been cut from beneath him. But the die was cast. He could only go forward. At this rate he was going to be receiving poison pen letters from Aunt Celestine in the next post.

'I need to know about this man Delombre. How close is he to Levignier? Does he have autonomy within the department?'

'What is this enterprise you suspect him of being involved in?'

'I can't tell you that – I'm sorry. It would be better that way.'

'What, you think because I'm a woman I can't handle bad news?'

'No. I didn't mean that.' He stood up, feeling the ground opening up further beneath him. This had been the worst of all bad ideas.

She said nothing, her eyes cool, unblinking.

He gestured at the door. 'I'll be going. Please thank your aunt for her hospitality.'

She nodded, the movement barely perceptible. 'Of course. Goodnight.'

Rocco stepped outside and threw his head back, breathing in deeply in frustration. Well played, moron, he thought angrily. That went superbly well, didn't it?

He walked back along the street and drove home.

–

He'd been indoors two minutes when there was a knock at the door.

It was Mme Denis. She was holding a plate draped with a square of linen. 'Present for you. Not all eggs have to be eaten as omelettes.'

Rocco lifted the linen cloth. She'd baked him a sponge cake. Decorated with tiny flecks of orange and lemon, and smelling of citrus, it was still warm from the oven.

'You didn't have to do this,' he said, and realised that this was an honour.

'Of course I did. I used a saucepan, two bowls and at least three spoons – and my cake tin. You think I'm going to miss an opportunity to have something to wash under my new tap?'

He'd forgotten about the pipes being connected, and smiled. 'That was quick work.'

'Yes, the men said they had orders from Maillard at the café to finish it double quick, otherwise there'd be no drinks for them all week.' She gave him a sly look. 'I suppose you wouldn't know anything about that, would you?'

He shook his head. 'Not me. Must be all Maillard's doing.'

'Really? You think I came down with the last rainfall? The village is abuzz with stories about how you and Lamotte arrested three robbers at the café. Maillard thinks you're the best thing to hit Poissons since the invention of the corkscrew.'

'He talks too much.'

'Maybe he does.' She lifted her shoulders. 'No matter. I might have to heat my water the old way, but at least I've got running cold.' She smiled with evident pleasure and looked past him. 'They haven't done yours yet, then?'

'Not yet.' There was the beginning of a trench across his front garden, and a hole bored through the front wall of the house, but no pipes. 'Would you like to come in for cake and coffee?'

'No. Never eat the stuff, myself. But you go ahead.' She reached out and briefly clutched his arm, then turned and walked back down the path.

Rocco put on some water and made tea. Then he cut a large slice of sponge cake and sat down to eat it.

Above his head, the resident guests continued their games in the attic.

# Chapter Forty-seven

Delombre left the Pantin *commissariat* and made his way through the streets to a small fish and vegetable market behind the railway station. He stopped periodically to check his back trail, conscious that with the falling light it wouldn't be hard for a follower to stay out of sight. He was pretty sure that Drueault, the search team leader, wouldn't try to check up on him, but distrust was an ingrained habit he found hard to lose. He distrusted cops most of all.

He cruised the area a couple of times on foot to make sure it was clear, sticking to the shadows, then slipped down a side street bordered on both sides by small businesses and lock-ups. The sound of beaten metal echoed from inside one building, and a man in greasy overalls was clearing up the components of a motorcycle spread on the pavement outside. Delombre walked round him and reached the end of the street, and saw a large furniture van parked up on the pavement near the intersection.

He couldn't see anybody in the cab. He tried the door. Unlocked. He closed it again and went to the back of the van and opened the rear door. It gave a creak of dry hinges, and a gust of foetid air came out, carrying a smell of overripe fruit and human waste from the bare interior. He stepped up and walked to the far end. The glow of a nearby street light showed signs of a large stain on the floor where something had been spilt, and a blackened banana skin lay curled like a dried leaf against the side wall. The clean-up job had been cursory at the very least, and he wrinkled his nose in disgust, wondering where Levignier got these people. Had they no clue at all? It wouldn't take much for somebody to call the local cops to have the van moved, and for the evidence inside to signal to even the dimmest trainee officer that a person had been kept captive inside here for some time.

A knuckle-rap on the plywood sheets lining the sides of the van received the dull thud of a filled space in return. At least that had been a job well done; whoever had prepared this space had known what they were doing.

He jumped down and closed the door, then walked back down the street and took a left. This time he was in a narrow residential street with washing airing over balconies and the high-pitched squealing of children at play inside. The few cars here were old and battered, in the way only Paris traffic could make them, and the buildings in need of decoration. Elsewhere a tinny radio was playing a rock number by a French band trying to sound American. Overlaying it all was the steady, muted buzz of people living in close proximity.

He stopped at a door halfway along the street. It opened on to a small tiled foyer. He stepped past a battered racing bicycle and down a narrow hallway lit by a feeble yellow bulb, then walked up a flight of stairs. The air smelt of tabbouleh and cooking oil, and musky dampness.

At the top of the stairs was a small landing. The overhead bulb threw a sickly glow over bare floorboards, the wood scarred and warped. A broken hard-backed chair covered in dust stood in one corner. There were two doors, one either side. One was open, the room beyond empty and bare, the other closed. The silence was intense.

He knocked on the closed door and waited. Tried the handle. It was locked.

He knocked again, muttered drunkenly, 'Hey, Dede, *mon pote*. You there?' No response.

He put his ear to the wood. There were no vibrations, no surreptitious movements. He thought about coming back later, but decided against it. Later was no good; he had too much to do. This needed finishing before he could move on.

He walked across the landing and through the open door, crossing the room and through another door at the rear. A window opened out onto a backyard with a gate sagging off the hinges. Beyond that, an alleyway disappeared into the gloom. He opened the window and peered down. Not much to see, just a square, box-like structure that had probably once housed coal or wood.

He returned to the locked door and put his shoulder against it. He pushed harder, felt it flex. Cheap wood, dried out and ready to pop. He pushed again and simultaneously jerked down on the handle. The door sprang open.

He was in a small, scruffy room furnished with two camp beds, army-style, a single leather armchair leaking stuffing, a radio on the floor, a couple of wooden packing crates and a standard lamp. Dirty cups had been left where they lay, rimmed with dried coffee, one stuffed with cigarette ends. Two empty wine bottles stood like bookends on the window sill, and on the floor beneath them two empty bowls showed the remains of a meal. A pair of underpants hung from the back of the armchair, and a single sock with a hole in the heel lay at the foot of one of the beds.

Kidnapper chic, thought Delombre, and tried not to breathe the foul air. They must have been holed up here all day, and finally broke cover and went out in search of more booze.

A door at the back led to another room, empty of furniture. There was an identical window to the one across the landing, but this one was screwed shut, the heads shiny and new.

The criminal elite: so untrusting.

He returned to the front room and took out a gun, a semi-automatic with an untraceable history, and checked the magazine. Then he reached in his jacket and produced a fat metal tube several centimetres long. He fitted it over the end of the barrel, checked to make sure it was secure, then used the tip of the tube to flick the underpants off the armchair.

The tube was a once-only suppressor, or silencer, made by a former military armourer in Moulineaux, in the south-west of the city. The man had left the French army under a dark cloud for allegedly manufacturing gun parts for collectors on army time. He'd cautioned Delombre that the silencer would take at most four shots before losing its effectiveness. But four was more than he'd need.

He went out and turned off the landing light, then sat down in the armchair to wait.

## Chapter Forty-eight

He'd been waiting an hour before he heard the sound of a car at the end of the street. Engine off, two doors closed, dull thuds in the night. Then, much closer, footsteps.

They'd moved faster than he'd expected, already coming in the front door and up the stairs together, noisy and obviously drunk. The landing light went on. It was gone eleven, and the area had fallen silent. Even before the two men arrived at the top of the stairs, he heard one saying how glad he was to have finally got rid of 'that bitch'.

Stupid, stupid, stupid. First leaving the kidnap vehicle out on the street, with enough evidence to put them on the guillotine; now prattling aloud about how clever they were.

Delombre picked up his gun and rested it on his thigh, facing the door. He was relaxed, sitting back in the armchair, but ready to move at a moment's notice.

The first man through the door wore a leather jacket and cowboy boots, and was sucking on a cigarette, backlit by the overhead bulb. He frowned at the open door, but drink had made him slow and careless.

Delombre flicked on the standard lamp.

'What the fuck—?' The man stopped, his boots making a loud rat-tat on the bare boards.

Delombre gestured with the gun for the man to move sideways. With his other hand, he held a finger to his lips.

The man did as he was told, blinking hard and swallowing, trying to work out what was happening. If he'd possessed any degree of courage, the sight of the gun had frozen his instincts solid. The cigarette fell and bounced off the bare boards in a shower of sparks.

The second man blundered past him, laughing at some shared joke, and was halfway across the room before he noticed Delombre sitting there in the half shadow cast by the standard lamp.

'Hey, *putain* – who're you?' he squawked, drunkenly aggressive. 'Get out of my chair!'

'Please don't call me names. We haven't been introduced.' Delombre's voice was soft, but carried a tone of menace that pierced the atmosphere in the room like an arrow. Unfortunately, the man failed to heed it.

'I said, get the fuck out of my *fuck*—'

Delombre shot him in the chest. The force of the bullet flipped him round sideways, the report no bigger than a loud slap. He landed in a heap on one of the army cots, and subsided with a sigh.

'Jesus!' said the man in the leather jacket, 'you didn't have to do that!' He stared at his colleague's body and swallowed hard, then turned and threw up noisily in the corner with a horrible hacking sound.

Delombre waited until he was done, then asked, 'What's your name?'

'Danny. It's Danny.' The man spat on the floor, trying to clear his throat. 'What's it to you, anyway?'

'You'll find out. Sit down on the other bed, Danny, and wipe your face. You've got sick all over your chin.'

Danny sat and dabbed at his mouth with his sleeve, merely managing to smear the vomit across his cheeks. He rubbed his eyes, his breathing coming heavy and fast, and stared once more at his friend as if he couldn't believe what he'd seen.

'So, how did it go, with your important guest?' Delombre queried casually, huffing on the side of the suppressor and rubbing at it with his sleeve to remove a speck of gunshot residue. He also noticed a stray strand of wool-like substance that the armourer had used to pack the baffles inside, and gently teased it out. It happened to these things, but not usually after a single shot. He'd have to speak to the rogue armourer about that. 'Did she behave herself?'

'What? You just shot my mate dead and you want to know whether she—'

'Yes, I want to know,' Delombre interrupted him. 'And if you argue with me one more time, you'll join your foul-mouthed friend in whatever version of hell you're both bound for.'

Danny nodded quickly and held up a hand. 'OK, OK. Sorry. We, uh… we did as we were told. To the letter. We kept on the move, kept her fed and watered, then delivered her as arranged to the farm near Clermont.'

'Go on.'

'She was fine. We made sure there was nobody else about, then took her out of the van and handed her over to the ambulance driver and his mate. She was still asleep… well, unconscious, really. But that was it. Job done.' He frowned. 'Are you saying she wasn't all right after that? Because if so, that's not down to us. She was good when we handed her over.'

Delombre ignored him. 'Did she see your face?'

'No, not once. I made sure of it. Not a glimpse. I kept the hood thing in place all the time.' He gave a sickly smile. 'I mean, it's not like I haven't done stuff like this before, right?'

'So how did she eat and drink?'

Danny explained how he had done it, lifting the hood just enough for the woman to take in food and liquid, but no more. 'There's no way she saw my face, honest.'

'Good. That's good.' Delombre looked down at the man's cowboy boots. 'Nice boots. You wear them all the time?'

'Yes, sure. Why not – I paid enough for them. I had them imported specially from Fort Worth in Texas.'

'Great. So they're – what, unique, then?'

'I'd say so. I mean, why pay top money to wear the same as every other mug?'

'How very wise. But – sorry, but I have to be sure – this woman you were holding, she never saw your face, not once? Or that of your deceased partner over there?'

'That's right. He stayed out of sight, mostly in the cab.'

'Yet each time you lifted the hood to feed her... she'd have had only a clear view downwards, right?'

'Uh... I guess. Yes.' Danny frowned, not making the connection.

'Downwards at your fancy *imported* and uniquely *identifiable* footwear. Isn't that correct?'

The question was met by a heavy silence, and Danny stared at Delombre, his mouth open as the implications of what he'd said sank in fully. He went very pale and stared at the gun, any remnants of drunkenness now instantly dissolved.

'I said, correct?'

'Hey... no, wait!'

'No, thanks. You're dismissed.'

The leather jacket jumped as the first shot hit home, then jumped again with the second. Danny groaned once and fell back on the bed.

As Delombre stood up, he heard the downstairs door creak, and a scuff of footsteps on the stairs. A whisper of voices fed upward as if through a funnel, and he felt the movement of air in the room. Somebody was trying to be quiet, but not because they were frightened of waking the neighbours.

Then came a sound he knew all too well: the rattle of a round being chambered.

# Chapter Forty-nine

Delombre switched off the lamp. It was probably too late, as they'd have already seen the glow from the street. He'd been careless, assuming the car noise earlier to have been these two morons returning from whatever bordello they'd been celebrating in. But it explained why there had been such a short time lapse between the car stopping and the two dead men arriving on the stairs.

They'd been followed. And he had a good idea who was doing the following. Divisional Inspector Drueault and his band of eager beavers had proven better than he'd thought. They'd found the truck rather than standing down as he'd advised, and followed the trail to this address.

He stood up in a fluid movement and grabbed the man in the leather jacket. Dragging the lifeless body behind the armchair, he propped it in place so that only the head, shoulders and arms were showing. Then he moved the standard lamp so that it would throw up a glow behind the dead man. It wasn't nearly enough of a distraction, but it would have to do. Hopefully, any cop coming through the door expecting trouble would see Danny's outline and shit himself.

He moved over to the door. He had perhaps twenty seconds left before the men downstairs came up in a rush, weapons out and ready to shoot. Once they got to the top he'd have no way out. He had to slow them down.

He took a deep breath and stepped out onto the landing.

The one named Detric was in the lead, already halfway up. He had his weapon in his right hand and was hugging the wall, trying not to make a noise. He looked up as Delombre appeared, but his gun was pointing away.

Big mistake.

Delombre shot him before he could bring up his gun, then reached up and swiped the bulb in one smooth movement. It popped and everything went black.

Men were shouting at the bottom of the stairs as their wounded colleague tumbled down among them. Delombre continued across the landing, flicking the broken chair down on top of them to add to the chaos, and through the open door into the empty flat. Two shots rang out behind him, but they were shooting blind, no doubt hoping to scare him into giving up.

He closed the door and hurried across to the open window, swinging one leg over the sill. Lowering himself easily, he hesitated for a second, then dropped. As his feet hit the wooden structure of the coal store, he pushed himself off and jumped to the ground, making no more than a hollow thump. The noise would be lost among the shouting upstairs and the two more gunshots that rang out as the remaining cops stormed the flat and came face to face with a desperado hiding behind the armchair.

At least Danny had finally done something right.

He looked out of the rear gate. The alley was dark and full of rubbish, but his eyes were already adjusting. The cops had made another mistake: they hadn't posted a man to cover the rear. Stuffing the gun in his jacket, he walked away in the dark.

Rocco's telephone jangled with what seemed unusual harshness, springing him from sleep barely minutes after he'd finally managed to nod off. He scrambled for the handset and dragged it onto the pillow. It was still dark outside.

'Hello?'

'It's me.' He sat up as if fired from a gun, throwing back the bedclothes. It was Jacqueline, her voice steady and calm. Just two words, neither of them clear enough to judge whether she was still mad at him or not.

'Hello, again.'

Her voice was cool, businesslike. 'The man Delombre? I called a friend of mine who knows everyone in ISD. He confirmed what I thought. Delombre is a contract employee for the department, and works exclusively for Marcel Levignier. He's a former Legionnaire and does not do office work. I asked for a description, and was told he's tall and thin, exceptionally fit, with fair hair thinning on top. I hope that answers your question.'

'Wait.' He didn't want her to put down the phone. 'Please. I owe you an apology. I'm very sorry. But I promise, I didn't come to your aunt's house just to ask questions. Well, not those questions, anyway. But thank you for doing this.'

The silence went on far too long, and he thought she'd hung up until he heard a faint sigh.

'Are you there?'

'Remember what I said about Levignier. He will do anything in the pursuit of duty. His man Delombre is a killer.'

There was a click as the phone went down.

# Chapter Fifty

Delombre arrived at the Clos du Lac just after nine. It was a cloudy morning, muggy with a promise of rain. He strode through the front door, past the large figure of a security guard who nodded in recognition and stood back.

'Where's the nurse?' he said, his voice bouncing around the marbled foyer. He made Dion's title sound like an insult.

'She's here.' Inès Dion appeared from the back of the building, heels clattering briskly on the tiles. She looked neat and in control, dressed in a smart two-piece suit. She nodded at the security guard. 'Thank you, Jean-Pierre, I'll deal with this.' She met Delombre's gaze without flinching. 'This is unexpected.'

'Get used to it. Where is she?'

Dion flushed slightly at his tone, but said nothing, merely turning away to lead him upstairs. She walked confidently, arriving on the landing and turning right along a carpeted corridor lined with gloomy paintings. She stopped at a door in an alcove and took out a key.

'Is she awake?' Delombre asked, 'or will I have to slap her to get her attention?'

'She's drifting in and out of consciousness,' Dion replied. 'Slapping won't do her any good. Sorry.'

Delombre looked her in the eye, trying to determine if she was being sarcastic. 'Pity,' he said, and waited for her to unlock the door, then pushed past her and into the room.

It was simply furnished, with shafts of light coming through the shutters across the big double windows. In the centre of the room was a single bed and a small, wheeled table holding a plastic water jug and a plastic glass. A woman lay beneath a blanket and bedspread, breathing irregularly. Her hair was spread across the pillow and a few damp strands pasted against the skin of her forehead. The air smelt musty, with a faint tang of sweat.

'Hasn't she been washed?'

'No. Why bother?' Dion walked over to the bed and tapped the woman on the shoulder. There was no response.

Delombre joined her. 'Good point, I suppose. Can she understand us?'

'She will when she comes round. What do you want her to do, exactly?'

'The easiest thing in the world: speak to her husband.' Dion's eyes widened. 'You're letting her go?'

He chuckled. 'Good God, no.' He turned away and walked over to the window, peering through the louvres into the outside world. All he could see, though, were mature evergreens shutting off any view of the surrounding countryside. 'It's been decided to give her poor besotted spouse a hint of hope, so he sees the error of his ways and stops talking to certain parties. For that we need her alert and chatty, not drugged or insensible.'

'I'll need time. The sedatives she was given were quite strong.'

He checked his watch and turned back to the bed. 'You have thirty minutes. I'm going downstairs for coffee. In the meantime, this might help.' He reached out and picked up the jug of water from the bedside table and emptied it over the sleeping woman's face.

Without waiting to see the reaction, he turned and walked out of the room.

He was halfway down the stairs when he heard the crunch of car tyres on the gravel outside, and saw through the glass panel over the front door a black Citroën Traction cruise to a stop in the car park.

'It's the cop,' called out Jean-Pierre, the security guard, from beside the entrance. 'The one called Rocco.'

–

The Clos du Lac looked quiet as Rocco got out of his car. There were just two vehicles in the car park: a small Renault he recognised as belonging to Miss Dion, and a light-blue Peugeot 404.

Alix Poulon climbed out the other side and looked around. 'What do you want me to do?'

'Listen to what she says, mostly. And watch her face and body language. You'll pick up on inflections that I'd miss. I want to know when she's lying.'

'When? Not if?'

'Both. But she's clever enough to use elements of the truth – how she sees it, anyway.'

He walked over to the Peugeot and looked through the window. There was nothing inside on view to show who might own it, no papers or clothes or a glaring sign giving the owner's details. It was too new to belong to a staff member, too impressive unless a visiting family member had been allowed access to a patient.

He walked over to the front entrance and saw movement behind the glass.

Jean-Pierre was standing on the other side, watching him.

'Lucas.' Alix said softly. 'To your right.'

He turned his head and saw a figure standing at the corner of the building. Another guard, as bulky as Jean-Pierre, but not as tall. The dogs were out in force.

'There are no visits allowed today,' said Jean-Pierre, swinging the door half open and filling the gap. 'Come back next week.' He began to close the door, a snide smile on his face.

Rocco waved his police card in the air. 'This is official business. You close that door and I'll come right through it and stamp all over you.' For emphasis, he flicked back his coat and showed his gun. 'You choose.'

Jean-Pierre hesitated a second, then stood aside, his face tight.

'There's a good boy. Now go get your boss – or would you like me to go looking for her?'

'That won't be necessary, Inspector.' Inès Dion's voice floated down the stairs ahead of her. She was walking down almost regally, head held high and composed, like a fashion model, Rocco thought.

'What do you want? I'm afraid we're very busy right now.' She saw Alix behind him and smiled briefly.

'This shouldn't take long,' he replied. 'Just a couple of questions.'

She considered it for a moment then gestured to a side room and led the way.

As Rocco followed her, he caught a glimpse of movement at the top of the stairs. He felt a strong urge to call out, but resisted it. No doubt another one of Dion's tame guards. The thought made the muscles in the middle of his back go tight.

-

Above them Delombre stood and waited, holding his breath. He hadn't counted on coming this close to Rocco. Thankfully the interfering investigator hadn't seen him. But the longer he was here, the more likely it was that something would go wrong.

He checked his watch. He would soon have to make the call to a prearranged number, so that Robert Bessine could hear his wife's voice. It was vital that the aircraft manufacturer got the message that all was well, and set in motion the cancellation of his talks with Taiwan. Anything less would be a disaster. Delombre had few fears about any man, and knew he was skilled enough to take care of himself in most situations; but he was no fool. He knew that if he failed at this late stage, so critical was it to success or failure, he wouldn't want to be around for Levignier's anger to show itself, or for one of Girovsky's private army of thugs to come looking for retribution.

He felt the back of his neck twitch at the recognition that he was not invulnerable, especially from those he served. It was a feeling he wasn't accustomed to, but he had to acknowledge the fact. There wouldn't be a frontal attack, he knew that, because that would be messy and cause waves. It would instead be a single man, perhaps two, as skilled as himself and probably younger, fitter, faster. He wouldn't see them coming, but he might hear their final move.

By then it would be too late.

While he waited for Rocco to leave, he pondered on his next move, after all this was over.

## Chapter Fifty-one

'You've never once asked after Mr Drucker,' said Rocco, taking a seat across from Inès Dion. Alix was standing off to one side, seemingly not part of the conversation, and from where she could watch Dion's face for reaction. They were in the library, surrounded by an expanse of bookshelves, the atmosphere sombre yet restful. Rocco could have spent some time in a room like this. He had never been an avid reader, but with all this room had to offer, he'd have been ready to give it a try.

For a second Dion didn't reply, a faint crease touching her forehead. Then she said, 'I didn't ask you, perhaps. Should I have done?'

'Didn't you wonder what had happened to him?' His gaze was on the small pulse beating at the side of her throat.

'Not really. I was too... upset with everything else that had happened.' She brushed a hand across her lap, a vague gesture that to Rocco resembled dismissal. 'He must have decided to move on. He could hardly have counted on this as having been his finest hour, could he?'

'Of course. I should have thought. Stroke of luck for you, though. Right place, right time, I suppose.'

'I wouldn't know about that. I feel fortunate, if that's what you're suggesting. But there's nothing wrong with taking advantage of circumstance, is there?'

'Of course not. Is that what André Paulus did?'

'I'm sorry?' The question appeared to throw her and she glanced at Alix, then away.

'Well, I gather he threw up everything to come here and be with you. Was that following circumstance? If so, it didn't do him much good, did it?'

'I-I'm sorry – I don't understand.' She looked stricken, her face flushed. 'What are you talking about?'

'According to his navy colleagues – former colleagues – he fell for you in a big way. From being a career navy man, he changed to a man in love and left the job he truly enjoyed. And then he was murdered. Shot twice with bullets, here,' Rocco stabbed twice at the base of his throat, 'and here. Apparently without any obvious attempt to defend himself. Odd, for an experienced navy cop like him. He must have been in the thick of his share of bad situations over the years, yet he never saw real trouble coming when it finally hit him. Why is that, do you think?'

'I don't know – how could I? What happened to André was tragic... horrible!' Her throat caught on the last word, and he saw a glimmer of moisture appear at the corner of one eye. She brushed angrily at her face and looked up at the ceiling for a long second, then back at Rocco. As she did so, a single tear rolled slowly down her cheek. She did nothing to stop it.

'Yes. It was,' he agreed.

'Is that what you've come to tell me, Inspector – that you're no further forward with finding out who killed André? For God's sake, how difficult is it? There must be somebody who knows... somebody local he may have run into... an argument, perhaps.' She looked beseechingly at Alix. 'You live locally, you told me. Don't rumours circulate easily in a rural place like this? Some-body boasting, perhaps, spending more money than they would normally?'

'No,' said Alix. 'Nothing like that.' And when Dion turned away, she looked at Rocco and nodded.

Dion was good, Rocco conceded. Exceptionally good. Unless he was making the biggest character assessment error of his life. But one thing he was certain about was her self-control and cool ability to put on a convincing act. Because he'd seen all this before: the grief, the angry flushes and the tears… then the switch to being composed and businesslike. And the red eyes on his previous visit were most likely less to do with grief at the death of Paulus than the result of some frantic rubbing as she'd climbed from her car to meet him.

He hadn't been entirely convinced then; he was even less so now.

Because he hadn't mentioned to anyone that André Paulus's wallet had been missing. So why did she mention money being spent?

'I'd agree with you, Miss Dion, but there aren't many people around here who carry nine-millimetre pistols, and fewer still who know how to use them with such precision.' He slapped his hands on his knees and stood up. 'How are the patients settling in, by the way?'

'Pardon?' Dion frowned and dabbed at her cheek.

'Your new arrivals – or, at least the one that I saw. How is he doing?'

She stood too, and nodded. 'Oh, that. Yes – he's fine, thank you.'

'Good. Well, sorry to have upset you. I hope not to disturb you again.' He turned and led Alix out and across the foyer, where Jean-Pierre was waiting by the door to let them out.

–

'That was pretty brutal,' Alix commented as they got back in the car.

'Maybe.' He started the engine and backed out of the space. 'What did you think?'

'About her?'

'Yes.'

'Well, I'm no expert, but purely from a woman's perspective, I'd say she was lying through her teeth. She was playing us.'

'Thank God for that,' he breathed. 'I thought it was just me.'

'Playing' was a good word to use, he thought. She had been playing them from the very start, through the aftermath of Simon Rotenbourg's murder, the discovery of Paulus's body, the search of the building. By staying to 'help' them with the search, she was able to steer them wherever she wanted... and away from anything incriminating.

But she must have played Paulus on an even bigger scale: persuading him to leave the navy and join her because she knew she could control him; luring him away from his post so the killer could enter the building... maybe even pulling the trigger herself. After all, who else could have got closer to him than the woman he loved and trusted?

'So what now?'

He was thinking about the guards around the place, the way they controlled every inch with such care and expertise, and the way Dion had reacted to his question about the new arrival. The 'he' that she had fastened on so easily, when every instinct told him that the only person in the place was a woman.

He saw Claude step out from the edge of the road a hundred metres ahead, and stopped to let him climb aboard.

Alix was surprised to see her father. 'What are you doing here?'

'Watching over you,' he said, brushing a stray leaf from his hair. 'I lost sight of you once you entered the building, but I had at least two of the guards in my sights all the time.' He patted the shotgun across his knees.

'How many did you see?' said Rocco.

'Three, unless they have others sleeping. They're good, too. Former military, from the way they move.'

'They would be.'

'So was the visitor.'

Rocco caught his eye in the rear-view mirror. 'Say again?'

'The visitor in the Peugeot. He arrived not long before you, walked in like he owned the place.'

'What did he look like?'

'Tall, thin, walked like he was on a long, slow route march.' In other words, like an ex-Legionnaire, Rocco thought. He remembered Jacqueline's description of the man. Delombre. It had to be.

He drove on. The momentum was gathering. Whatever was going to happen, it had to be today.

## Chapter Fifty-two

Rocco dropped Claude and Alix off in Poissons before heading back to Amiens. He found a note from Massin, waiting to see him in his office.

'I've been advised,' Massin said as soon as Rocco entered, 'that an undercover team of officers working in the Pantin district of Paris was attacked last night while raiding an apartment. One of them was shot and wounded, but not seriously. He was lucky. Inside the apartment they found two bodies, both male, both shot at close range.'

'Who were they?'

'Well, that's where it gets interesting. The undercover team had been following the two men's progress across the north of the city, although they hadn't managed to get a clear sighting or identify them. But they were certain they were driving a furniture van with Véronique Bessine inside.'

'But they didn't find her.'

'No, sadly, they didn't. What they did find is a large van parked in a street nearby containing ample evidence that a person was held captive for a number of days. And one of the men has a history of being involved in kidnaps, although no firm convictions.' He looked at Rocco. 'You don't sound surprised.'

'I'm not.' He hesitated, wondering how far he could take this man into his confidence. They had a chequered history, he and Massin, where trust had not been a high priority between them. But he couldn't see any way past this point without telling Massin what he suspected… and what he knew for certain. What Massin – who invariably chose the safe against the risky where his superiors in the Interior Ministry were concerned – chose to do next was anybody's guess.

He told Massin everything.

The senior officer looked aghast at first, then incredulous, then shocked when Rocco told him about the trade talks and the motive behind the kidnap of Bessine's wife.

'Rocco, I find this hard to believe,' he said at one point. He reached for the telephone. 'Do you want coffee?'

'Yes. Please.'

He ordered coffees, then told his secretary to hold all calls, no matter who they were from. 'Well, of course,' he conceded after a brief exchange, 'unless it's from *Monsieur le President*. But I don't think that's likely, do you?' He shook his head and put the phone down as if it might bite him.

He looked hard at Rocco, then held up a finger and stood up. He walked around his office, then sat back down again, clearly agitated. 'So let me understand this properly. All this… the killing at the Clos du Lac, the murder of the guard, and then of this supposedly already dead Stefan Devrye-Martin and his friend, and the approach to you by this Miss – Roget, you say? Roget, yes – on the orders of this Commander Levignier of ISD, and now the killings in Paris… they're all linked to this kidnap, which has been carried out by, you suspect, Levignier's people in order to frustrate trade talks between Bessine's people and Taiwan.'

'In favour of Peking and other industrialists here in France, yes.'

'Incredible. It doesn't seem possible. Why—' He broke off at a knock on the door, and leapt up to admit his secretary carrying a tray with cups and a fresh brew of coffee. She handed the tray over before being ushered out again, but not before glancing at Rocco with a look of incomprehension.

'Who else knows about this?' he queried, stirring sugar into his cup.

Here it comes, thought Rocco. This might be where it gets stamped on.

'Desmoulins, Lamotte... and *Gardienne* Poulon,' he conceded, adding, 'they all know bits and pieces – Desmoulins probably more than the others.'

'Good, good.' Massin drank some coffee, then took another walk around his desk, tugging at his jacket. 'We need to keep this contained.'

'Pardon?'

'I don't mean swept under the rug, Inspector. I mean between a select few officers.' He sat down and gave Rocco another hard stare. 'Can you get her out of there – the Bessine woman?'

'I think so.' Rocco held his breath. This was unexpected. He didn't know what to say. Thank you seemed inappropriate.

'You'll need men – good men. I'll speak to Godard. He's got some excellent officers under his command. And whatever resources you need from here. But you'll have to be discreet. If word leaks out about an operation being planned...' He shook his head and didn't finish. Natural caution rearing its head again, thought Rocco.

'So,' he said quickly, before there was a change of heart, 'you're ready to go with this?'

'Of course. I should have my head examined, I know. But if we had not had the... uh... experiences that we have, you and I, then I would now be calling the Ministry for advice.' He stared into his coffee. 'But we all know that would be a disaster. When are you planning on going in?'

'Tonight, after dark. There's a back way in, but we might have to play it by ear.'

'Not sooner?' The implication was clear: what about the kidnap victim – if indeed she was in there?

'They'd see us coming. The guards look as if they know what they're doing, and they must have a fall-back plan in case of a raid. Darkness gives us the edge.'

'Well, that's your... speciality. But you have my full authority.' He picked up the telephone and said, 'I'll speak to Godard, Canet and Perronnet. I can't hide this from them, but I know they will be discreet and support us where necessary.' He nodded and began to dial, and Rocco took it as his cue to leave.

–

Rocco found Desmoulins churning through some paperwork, and said quietly, 'What are you doing this evening?'

'Nothing. Why?'

'Come to my house, eight o'clock. Don't tell anyone.'

Desmoulins looked at him, eyebrows raised. 'Are we going hunting?'

'Something like that. Dress for the occasion.'

'You bet.' Desmoulins looked excited, and began to attack the paperwork with renewed vigour. 'See you later.'

Rocco picked up the phone and rang Claude.

# Chapter Fifty-three

A light mist was hovering around the lake like a shroud as Rocco and Desmoulins made their way around its perimeter, keeping the water to their right. Claude had assured them that the ground here was solid enough, as long as they didn't stray too close to the reeds.

It was two-thirty in the morning, and the air was still, carrying the metallic aroma of water and rotting vegetation. A cloudy sky ensured no moonlight, and there was a promise of rain in the air. Poor visibility wasn't ideal, but it favoured them rather more than the guards on watch.

They were both dressed in dark clothing, with smears of mud on their cheeks and foreheads, and even from a couple of metres away, Desmoulins merged like a wraith into the gloom.

The hours had ground past with agonising slowness following his talk with Massin, expecting to hear at any moment that the kidnappers had been caught somewhere else with their victim, or that the raid was off. But first Godard had sought him out to discuss plans and personnel, then Canet and even Perronnet had appeared to give him a subtle nod of support.

Now he was here, Rocco felt calm and ready for what lay ahead. His nerves were on edge, but that was a necessary part of any armed operation. He paused every few metres to scan the ground ahead. He had a clear image of the area in mind from a previous sighting: the grassy area ran flat for about fifty metres, before reaching a line of trees standing like sentinels in the dark, their tips just visible against the slightly lighter sky. They were poplars, lining the canal and planted by the same man who had designed the Clos du Lac, no doubt to add order to the view on offer.

He had no reason to suspect that the new security arrangements had placed a scout out here this far from the buildings, but he wasn't about to take chances. Jean-Pierre looked the sort to shoot first without asking questions, and he didn't want to increase the risk to Desmoulins or Claude, who was approaching on the far side of the sanitarium, by exposing them to a trigger-happy thug with an attitude problem.

He looked to his right, across the lake. Two of Godard's men were over there somewhere, approaching on a similar course, while Godard and two more men had control of the road running past the Clos in case anyone tried to leave. All had military experience and were skilled at moving around in difficult terrain.

A burst of activity betrayed a waterfowl skittering away through the reeds, and Rocco sank down instinctively, Desmoulins doing the same. They waited until the bird had splash-landed out in the centre of the lake before continuing.

As they neared the trees, Rocco looked for a flash of white in the gloom. It would be a marker post put in place by Claude earlier, to show the location of a foot-bridge across the canal. From the other side it was only a short walk to the lane running past the Clos. He was counting on the guards keeping a close eye on the lane itself, running from the road out of Poissons, rather than expecting any approach across the rougher ground around the lake and the canal. If they got that far without being spotted, they were in business.

The ghostly shape of an owl drifted by overhead, and other noises in the dark showed how easily disturbed were the creatures of the night. Rocco slowed his pace, feeling his shoulders beginning to tense. It brought back memories of other times and places when he'd sought to become part of the world around him when all his nerves were screaming to be somewhere else. Then it had been jungle, vivid and claustrophobic, deadly in every sense; not the benign French countryside of the Somme valley. Yet with what he sensed might be waiting in the form of Jean-Pierre and his colleagues, the danger was no less real, no less final.

He reached beneath his coat and checked the comforting feel of the MAB semi-automatic. It was no guarantee or protection but going in without it would have been suicidal.

Claude had instructions to wait when he got into position, having first scouted the general area around the sanitarium. They would meet up near the back door to the pool house, which was a blind spot for the guards, and decide on a point of entry once they knew what they were up against.

'What exactly are we looking for?' Claude had asked over the phone.

'The guards,' Rocco had replied. 'Where they are, how far they move.' He told him of the new arrival on the stretcher, and that gaining fast access to the inside was their first priority. 'Who do you think it is? Another dodgy criminal hiding from justice?'

'Bigger than that.' He'd paused before saying it, the words suddenly seeming ludicrous. But it was too late now. 'I think they're holding Véronique Bessine, to put pressure on her husband and derail his trade talks.'

There had been a stunned silence from Claude, which Rocco had made no effort to fill. There had been plenty in the news already about the kidnap; Claude was a cop and would see the problems they were facing.

'You better not get yourself shot, Lucas,' Claude breathed, 'that's all I can say. Otherwise Mme Denis will cut my balls off.'

'You'd be the lucky one. Think what she'll do to me.'

Desmoulins stepped up alongside him, and Rocco sensed him pointing in the dark. 'Over to the right,' he whispered. 'Is that your marker?'

Rocco saw a faint glimmer several paces away. They were on target.

'That's it.' He led the way and found a short post embedded in the soil, with a splash of white paint on the side facing the lake. Beyond it lay the footbridge over the canal.

They moved apart and approached the bridge on a parallel path. Rocco paused and listened. If a guard had been posted anywhere out here, this would be a logical spot. But he couldn't hear anything.

The footbridge was made of wood, narrow enough to allow two people side by side across, or a farm animal, but nothing bigger, and rising in a curve to allow canal barges underneath. Rocco felt the first rise of the ground beneath his feet, followed by the dull, hollow scuff of the wooden ramp. He trod carefully, one hand on the balustrade to steady himself as he crossed, then down the other side, stepping off quickly to one side to wait for Desmoulins.

He heard a clicking noise from behind, and the soft scrape of a footfall. Godard's men, also approaching the bridge.

Five minutes later, they were crossing the field below the Clos, heading for the doorway to the pool house.

# Chapter Fifty-four

'They're coming.' Delombre took out his gun and checked the magazine. He was standing in the kitchen with Inès Dion and the guard known as Jean-Pierre, and listening to the night sounds beyond the window. They had been ready to leave, to scatter, having made sure there was nothing incriminating left behind. Now every instinct told him that they'd left it too late. 'They wouldn't dare,' murmured Jean-Pierre. 'They can't know for sure if she's here or not. Anyway, we're ready for them.'

Delombre looked at him with contempt. 'If you really believe that, you're an idiot. They'll come because they know. It's all they need. They're not administrators, grey-suited *fonctionnaires* more accustomed to meetings and filling in forms; they're no different to you or me. Especially Rocco. Christ, I should have dealt with him earlier, like I wanted to.' He swore under his breath and stared out of the kitchen window into the darkness. It wasn't the only thing he wished he'd done differently. But it was too late now, all in the past. Regrets were for old men.

He slipped the gun into its holster and said to Dion, 'What was the plan to deal with the woman?'

'There's a flagstone in the pump room behind the pool.' Her voice was ugly and matter-of-fact, almost disinterested, as if playing at being tough. It made him want to slap her. 'It's been hollowed out. She'll go in there. Nobody will find her without demolishing the building.'

Delombre winced at her lack of emotion, and wondered where these people got their ideas. If the police thought Véronique Bessine was in here, they'd bulldoze the place in order to find her, dead or alive. And that bloody Rocco would probably be at the controls.

Ever since getting the woman ready to speak to her husband nearly an hour ago, things had been going from bad to worse. First it had taken a lot longer to bring her round, the combined results, Dion had insisted, of the sedatives she'd been given and her deteriorating mental and physical condition. Whatever fight she may have had in her to begin with had faded.

'Can't we give her a tablet or something?' The agreed time for the phone call impressed on him by Levignier and Girovsky was coming up fast. He was aware of the extensive use of Benzedrine and other stimulants in military circles, to keep troops and pilots going for long stretches, and could see no reason why they didn't use something similar to get Bessine awake and ready to talk.

'It would probably kill her,' Dion had said firmly. 'Then where would you be?'

Eventually, by a series of cold compresses and bursts of oxygen, Bessine had begun to show signs of coming to, first by asking where she was, then by struggling with surprising strength when she saw their faces.

Delombre recognised the desperate realisation in the way she fought: she was no fool and knew that now she had seen them, she wouldn't be allowed to go free.

'*Quiet!*' Delombre had hissed fiercely, his face so close to hers that he could smell the sourness on her breath. He shrugged off Dion's warning hand. There really wasn't time for niceties. 'Be still! Can you understand me? If so, say yes.'

Bessine's eyes flickered and grew wide as she struggled to think. Then she nodded weakly. 'Y-yes. I hear you.'

'Good.' He almost purred. 'Now, listen carefully. In a minute, you're going to speak to your husband, Robert. Do you understand?'

'What? He's here…?' She tried to sit up and Delombre held her arms in a vice-like grip until she subsided.

'No, he's not here. But you will talk to him on the telephone, understood? But only if you promise to behave.'

'Yes… of course.' She stared at Dion, standing nearby, then up at Delombre. 'I'll do it. Please let me speak to him.'

'There. It's very simple, isn't it? You do as I tell you, and we'll get on fine.'

'What do you want me to say?' Her voice was becoming firmer, more assured, Delombre thought, probably due to the promise of speaking to her husband, and an eventual happy outcome.

'Say anything you like. Preferably that you're well and looking forward to coming home.'

She looked as if she didn't believe him. 'Is that all?'

'Well, there is a little more. Tell him… tell him that the people holding you are allied to an extremist Chinese group and that he must cut off discussions with Taiwan. Immediately.'

'I don't understand.' She frowned and looked around. 'What has this got to do with China?'

'You don't have to understand,' he said coolly. 'Just do it. Now repeat back to me what I just said.'

She hesitated and licked her lips, and Dion stepped forward to give her a sip of water. It took three goes before she was able to parrot with any degree of clarity what Delombre had said, but eventually he was satisfied.

'By the way,' he warned her, 'if you deviate from this, if you try to describe our faces in any way, if you don't do exactly as we've asked, I will make one phone call.'

She looked at him but said nothing, waiting.

'That call will send a two-man team to your husband, and he will be dead before the hour is up. Are we understood?'

Véronique Bessine nodded. 'I understand.' But the phone call had never taken place.

First he'd called Levignier as arranged, using the extension in the kitchen, to signal that everything was ready and that the culmination of their plans was finally upon them.

There was no reply.

He rang Levignier's private number. No answer.

He tried the duty officer at the ISD headquarters. The duty desk knew of everybody's whereabouts – apart from his own, at least – and would surely be able to find Levignier.

'I'm sorry, sir,' said the man, 'but the commander hasn't been in this afternoon. Would you like me to take a message?'

'Wha—? No.' He slammed down the phone and stared at the floor, sensing a rising feeling of panic. This couldn't be happening. Everything was in place – *he* was in place – so where the *fuck* was Levignier? He was supposed to be in his office, coordinating the supposed call from the kidnappers! He took out a slim notebook and checked through the pages. Found the number for Girovsky. It went against all his instincts to even consider talking to the obnoxious Pole, but this was an emergency.

He dialled the number, found he was holding his breath.

'Hello?' A woman's voice. Elderly. Cultured.

'Is Girovsky there?'

'No, I'm afraid he isn't. He's gone to a meeting at the Foreign Ministry. Shall I take a message?'

'No, thank you.' He was about to put the phone down when a thought occurred. 'Why is he at the Foreign Ministry? My apologies, but I'm a work colleague. We were supposed to meet somewhere else.'

'Ah, I see. Well, it's all the latest news, I suppose. It's taken everyone by surprise, Josef says.'

'News?' He hadn't listened to a news broadcast since this morning.

'Yes. About the Chinese. They've changed their minds, apparently, about trade talks. The Foreign Minister's apparently in a dreadful huff about it – he's already flying home. I'm surprised you didn't know, being a colleague of Josef.'

She continued rattling on but Delombre was no longer listening. He dropped the handset on its rest and reached out and switched on a radio on the side, waiting impatiently for a news broadcast. When it came on, he felt the floor open up beneath him.

'*Chinese officials at the Foreign Ministry in Peking have called off trade talks with the French Trade Delegation with immediate effect, amid rumours that they have signalled a preference to rethink their strategy on international relations. This follows unconfirmed rumours of a split in the Chinese government on who should become a preferred trading partner during the coming decade. Early reports from French industrial leaders and officials is that this puts any talks firmly back with Taiwan, China's main competitor for foreign and export trade in the region, and returns to centre stage the aircraft manufacturer, Robert Bessine, whose group has already been in discussions with them for some weeks. There are doubts in some quarters, however, that Bessine, whose wife is at the centre of a kidnap rumour, will be able to deal with this development, which observers say will have a detrimental effect on French manufacturing if moves are not made immediately to—'*

Delombre switched off the radio.

It was over. Done. Levignier was gone. Girovsky was doing what Girovsky did best: looking after his interests.

He took out his gun. He felt better holding it, now things were this close. He said to Dion and her friendly gorilla, 'Bring the woman to the pool house – now!'

# Chapter Fifty-five

Claude was a dark bulk to one side of the pool door, calmly watching and listening. He was sitting with his back against the building, the Darne slung across his arms. Rocco squatted next to him. 'Anything?'

'Sure is. Any second now we're going to be in the shit.' He gestured behind him. 'Just heard someone shouting about the pool house. I think they know we're here.'

'If they did, they'd be shooting. How many guards?'

'I counted three, all armed, one with a sub-machine gun, the others with rifles and handguns. Didn't see the woman patient. Saw the nurse – and your friend in the Peugeot. His car's still out front.'

Rocco absorbed the news with pragmatism. The men inside were ready for war.

Moments later Godard's two men appeared and slid up to join them.

'They'd be good to have out behind the house,' suggested Claude. 'If anyone makes a break, it could be across the fields.'

Rocco nodded in agreement and the two officers slid away into the darkness.

Moments later they heard voices and a banging noise close by. It was the pool-house door.

Rocco pictured the layout of the buildings. If the guards knew they were here and came piling out through the back door right beside them, it would be debatable who'd come off worse. They could avoid that by going in the long way round, but that would bring them up between the two buildings – and right under the noses of the guards. There were too many lights to do it that way without being spotted like dancers on a stage.

'Have you tried the door?' He recalled Dion saying that the door was never unlocked.

'Just done it. You give the nod and we're in.'

Suddenly all the lights in the pool house went on, flooding over their heads and across the garden. Rocco and Desmoulins ducked instinctively, hugging the building. Claude, revealed dressed in his hunting gear of soft jacket, trousers and high, laced-up boots, and looking like a bandit, pulled a face and lifted his gun.

Then came a piercing scream and the sound of glass shattering.

Mme Bessine. It had to be. Rocco stood up and took out his gun, nodding at Desmoulins and Claude. It had to be now.

'Go!'

Claude grasped the door handle and pulled it open, while Rocco stepped through into the overheated chemical-ridden atmosphere of the therapy pool. They were in a small lobby with two doors. The one to the right was open, beyond which he caught a brief flash of startling blue from the pool, now brilliantly lit. The door directly ahead was closed, but the voices were coming from behind it, along with sounds of a struggle.

Rocco pointed at Desmoulins, then the door handle, then to Claude, with a motion for him to go through first. He thumbed his own chest and indicated the open door to the pool, then signalled for them to count to five before moving.

They got the message. Desmoulins took hold of the door handle, while Claude clicked his shotgun closed and stood ready to go through.

*One*. Rocco went through the connecting door and turned left, then left again. *Two*. He was by the main entrance. *Three*. A pane in the door had been shattered, with shards lying across the floor. *Four*. A trail of blood led away down a short passage to a doorway at the end marked Pump Room, where he could hear voices and a woman's muffled cries.

*Five*. A bang signalled the inner door being slammed open by Desmoulins, and Claude's voice telling everybody to stand still. The shotgun boomed and a woman screamed, followed by a thump. Then two figures came running from the pump room.

It was Dion followed by Jean-Pierre.

'Stand still!' Rocco shouted, although more as a warning to the others that he was here and not to come out shooting. Dion ran right at him, an animal snarl on her face, knocking his gun arm aside. Jean-Pierre took advantage of the situation to aim a shot at Rocco's head. It went wide, the explosion deafening in the enclosed space, and took out a large chunk of plaster from the wall behind him.

Rocco ducked and brought round his own gun, trying for a snap shot, but Jean-Pierre was too quick. He dodged out of the short corridor and was gone, his footsteps fading into the night.

But Rocco still had Dion to deal with. She turned on him, trying to claw at his eyes, her face purple with rage.

She began kicking out and shouting incoherently, a spray of spittle touching his cheeks.

Then suddenly she was gone, jerked clear by Desmoulins, who took her down to the end of the corridor. She turned and kicked him between the legs, then came the sound of a slap. Silence.

'Sorry, Lucas,' Desmoulins grunted. He was clutching himself and breathing quickly. Dion was lying on the floor, groaning. 'Mother of God, that hurt.'

'Where's Bessine?'

'In the pump room,' said Claude, producing a length of cord, which he tossed to Desmoulins to tie up Dion. 'They dropped her and ran.'

'Watch our backs,' Rocco told him. 'I'll go check on her.'

He stepped into the pump room. Véronique Bessine was slumped next to a square hole in the floor, about a metre deep. A flagstone with its underneath covered in dirt stood on its end nearby. The hole was just big enough to take a body, and once the flagstone was in place, it would have been easily missed.

Bessine was dressed in soiled underwear and a slip, and her body was bathed in sweat, one leg trembling. He knelt quickly by her side and pressed his ear to her mouth. She was breathing, but it was horribly light. He checked her pulse. At least she had one, but that, too, seemed worryingly weak. He took off his coat and wrapped her carefully in it, telling her that she was safe and that he was a policeman. He wasn't sure if she heard him or not. Then he carried her through to the small lobby, where he lay her down against the wall.

Two shots rang out from somewhere in the main building, and elsewhere a car's starter motor turned over with an urgent whine.

'The Peugeot,' said Claude calmly. 'Won't do him any good.' He took out a jumble of leads and tossed them into the corner. 'I disabled both cars.'

Rocco smiled and checked that Desmoulins was fit and ready. Dion, he noticed, was gone. 'Where is she?'

'I tied her up and put her in the hole,' said Desmoulins. 'A small taste of her own medicine.'

'You sure she won't get away?'

'Not unless she's Houdini's daughter.'

'Good. We set?'

They left the pool house, Rocco jogging across the car park, his shoulders twitching uncomfortably as he passed under a flare of light from a security lamp at one corner, the other two running across to the main entrance which was lit inside by a single light.

The Peugeot was empty, the driver's door hanging open.

The same with Dion's Renault.

Rocco joined Claude and Desmoulins, waiting inside the entrance lobby. The house was silent, the marbled foyer deserted and inviting. Rocco held up a warning hand, remembering the feeling he'd had before of being watched from the landing. It was like a fairground shooting range; the moment they stepped into the open they'd be easy targets for anyone waiting up there.

He turned and looked around. A stout walking stick was leaning against one corner. He lifted it out, and with a signal for both men to stay back under cover, slid it across the foyer floor, before stepping back behind the shelter of the doorway.

A flash of movement came from up on the landing, and a figure dodged into the open and began shooting. The yammering bark of a sub-machine gun was deafening in the confined space, and plaster and brickwork showered around them and across the floor of the foyer, and a cloud of dust rose in the air. The moment it stopped, Claude and Desmoulins stepped forward in unison and fired a volley into the shadows at the top. The sound of the shots seemed puny in comparison – even the shotgun – and brought a shower of plaster, mouldings and wood splinters bouncing down the stairs towards them.

'*Merde*,' Claude muttered in frustration. 'I thought we'd got him.'

Then a tall plant stand toppled out from the shadows, followed by the figure of a man. Both thumped to the floor, and the man's sub-machine gun clattered down the stairs, tumbling over and over towards them, the overhead light flashing on the gleaming ugliness of the barrel.

'*Down!*' shouted Rocco.

# Chapter Fifty-six

Delombre was in a mood to kill. At the top of his list was Rocco, the interfering cop he'd underestimated so badly. That realisation alone was like a savage worm eating away inside him, knowing that he should have been better than this. How could he have allowed himself to be beaten so easily? He should have been back in Paris by now, reaping the benefits of a job well done, instead of fleeing like an escaped prisoner into a land of bogs and water, of cow pastures and ploughed fields, where the eyes of every inbred country yokel would be on the lookout, hoping for a reward by bagging him.

He swore bitterly as he stumbled in the darkness, his city shoes useless on the slippery grass, and felt the sticky moisture of God knew what sort of filth seeping over the rims to wet his feet. Right alongside Rocco and sharing in his hate was Levignier, the willing architect of this whole plan, and Girovsky, the scheming money man and whining little Pole who stood to gain most, even though the initial idea had failed. No doubt he would even now be insinuating himself alongside those other industrialists in Bessine's team, to grab a share of the proceeds from the talks with Taiwan, a born survivor.

He felt a pain in his chest, and slowed his mad dash; it wasn't the agony of injury, however, that was hurting, but the more vicious bite of resentment and failure. Of knowing he had allowed himself to be sucked into a world he knew nothing about, where silky words and veiled promises counted for everything... and nothing.

He had, quite simply, backed the wrong horse.

He stopped for a moment to look back across the field to the house. Flickers of movement showed against the lights flaring from the building. It wasn't much, but enough to tell him that going back wasn't an option. The building was now lit up like a carnival, and more men would be arriving as they called up reinforcements. The chance of stealing a vehicle now was remote at best.

He was now the object of a manhunt.

He scanned the darkness, hoping to see a sign of the other guard, Jean-Pierre. The man had been the first to run, which had come as no surprise. Too full of himself to be truly experienced in close-quarter combat, the coward had buckled the moment real bullets had started to fly.

Delombre moved deeper into the dark, and smelt water nearby, rank and tangy. He trod carefully, and realised he was by the canal he'd seen on the first night he'd come here. He conjured up a mental picture of the map he'd used while planning his entry to the area, and worked out the position of the lake on the other side of the canal, with the lane he'd followed on the moped somewhere off to his right. He debated going that way, but ruled it out; the cops would have it covered. Instead, he recalled the map showing details of two small farms, one near where he'd dumped the moped.

Farms meant vehicles; it was his only way out of here.

He veered to his right and saw the shadow of a bridge against the water. Once he was over this, he'd be away from the road with no way back. But his instincts pulled him towards open country, where he knew he could hide more effectively than any search party could uncover him. If Rocco or any of his men came too close, he'd make them regret it.

# Chapter Fifty-seven

The moment the sub-machine gun came to rest on the bottom step without spitting fire, Desmoulins jogged across the foyer and up the stairs, ready to shoot at anything that moved.

'One man,' he called back. 'Dead.'

Rocco grunted. One down, two plus Delombre to go. Fewer if the earlier shooting had been on the side of the angels. It had. Moments later a soft whistle came from the front entrance and one of Godard's men covering the field came in.

He slid a hand across his throat and held up a single finger.

It left Delombre and one other.

They covered the rest of the house with care, leapfrogging each other to check every room and cupboard. It took several minutes, the search sweaty and frenetic, the way all house clearances are, each man expecting at any moment for a door to swing back in a blaze of gunfire.

But they found nothing, ending up back in the foyer, crunching through the fallen plaster and mouldings.

'Weird that there are no other patients,' said Desmoulins, checking his weapon.

'Not really,' Rocco replied. 'This was strictly for the Bessine job. After what happened here before, they probably didn't want to risk having anyone else around.'

'So where are the bad guys?'

'Out there somewhere.' Rocco nodded towards the front entrance. It was bad news. A mix of open country, marshland, trees, the canal and the lake, it would take a small army to search the area effectively, and the darkness wasn't in their favour. Too much chance of shooting at shadows… or each other.

And Delombre would know that.

He beckoned to Godard's man and said, 'Call an ambulance. The Bessine woman's in the lobby at the back of the pool house where we came in. She needs urgent treatment. Ask *Commissaire* Massin to get word to her husband. The nurse is tied up in a hole in the pump room. Don't untie her or she'll ruin your sex life. She's part of all this.'

The man nodded and went in search of a telephone, while Rocco debated what to do next.

'We could wait until morning,' suggested Desmoulins. 'Get more men in and flood the area.'

Rocco nodded, but he didn't like it. These men needed catching. Delombre, especially, with his experience and training, could cover a lot of ground in a few hours. His options were limited, in that he was in unfamiliar territory and needed transport to get away, but that meant heading for a farm or a village. And the nearest village was Poissons.

'It's risky either way,' he said. 'Claude?' He was happy to defer to the one man who knew the area best.

'I reckon they'll go for the lake,' said Claude calmly, checking his load and settling his jacket around him. 'The road's too open and the fields up behind here lead nowhere. Down by the lake and canal, it's a small jungle. They'll count on being able to hide until they find a way out of here.'

Rocco nodded in agreement. It was a jungle all right, and one he'd seen at close hand. But two men in the dark were as dangerous as ten, and he wasn't about to send anyone out there to find them who wasn't used to the terrain.

A clatter of footsteps heralded the arrival of several men, and Godard appeared through the door.

Rocco said, 'There are two men on the loose, both armed. We've searched the buildings, but they might have doubled back.'

'No problem. We'll run a sweep of the area.' He looked around and saw his man using the telephone. 'We heard a small war going off. Is anyone hurt?'

'Only Desmoulins' pride,' Rocco said with a grim smile. 'The three of us are going out to look for the two men down by the lake. Keep your men up here, will you? We don't want to exchange fire with our own.'

Godard looked as though he was about to argue, then nodded, seeing the sense in not having too many guns out there. 'OK. But if you want more, we're here.'

'Got you.' With that, Rocco turned and led Desmoulins and Claude out into the night.

## Chapter Fifty-eight

Once he was across the footbridge, Delombre found himself in the quiet and funereal atmosphere surrounding the lake. From the solid ground underfoot of the field leading down from the house, and the immediate area around the canal, he felt the springiness of a different kind of terrain, and the tug of vegetation against his legs, the night's moisture soaking through to his skin. Urgent bursts of movement in the dark preceded him as waterfowl moved to avoid his approach, slapping at the surface of the lake, and the rustle of reeds and grass betrayed larger animals, perhaps fox and rabbit, slipping further into cover until he passed.

He ignored them all and pressed on, knowing that each one could potentially betray his whereabouts to anyone following.

He spun round at a curse in the gloom, his gun swinging up.

'*Wait – it's me!*' It was Jean-Pierre, clumsy and unsure, swinging a weapon above the tall reeds as he emerged from cover by the lake. He was breathing as hard as if he'd run a marathon, and his movements were echoed by a sloshing sound from soaked boots and lower legs.

Delombre considered pulling the trigger anyway; this idiot was going to get him killed if he couldn't move more quietly than that. But he relaxed his finger. Maybe he could use him.

'What the hell are you doing? I thought you'd gone.'

'I tried, but I didn't know what to do.' He sounded like a petulant child who'd run out of games to play during the holidays.

Delombre thought quickly. Letting this oaf stick close by meant certain capture, even death. The police would have flooded men into the area by first light, but he didn't discount the idea of that bastard Rocco coming into the *marais* after him, eager to finish off what he'd started. Then he had an idea. 'Are you any good with that thing or do you use it to frighten small girls?'

'What, this?' Jean-Pierre swung the weapon up and Delombre grabbed the barrel. He recognised it as a MAT-49 sub-machine gun with a long 32-round magazine. Out here, good for spraying holes in the air; but the followers wouldn't know that.

He pointed back at the footbridge. 'You've got control of anyone coming over here if you hold the bridge. I'll go round the other side of the lake and across the canal further down, then double back up the other side and shout when we're clear to go. There are vehicles at the sanitarium – we can be in Paris before midnight. Can you do that?'

Jean-Pierre nodded, and Delombre saw his teeth flash in the dark. 'No problem. It'll be a duck shoot. But don't go without me, will you?'

'Are you kidding? After this I might need a good right-hand man.' Delombre clapped him on the shoulder, then slid away into the dark, shaking his head.

–

Progress for the three officers in pursuit was slow, with Claude leading the way using dead ground and a hedgerow for cover, and listening for the movement of waterfowl in the night. Any sudden upsurge would mean a man was nearby. They crossed the field immediately below the Clos du Lac, then slowed as they approached the canal, Claude whispering caution.

Rocco called a halt and said, 'If there's trouble, it will be at the footbridge. It's the only way across and Delombre is ex-Legion; he'll know all about ambushes and fighting in rough terrain. We need to flush him out first.'

'I know a bit about fighting dirty, too,' Claude said. 'Let's spread out along the bank, me in the centre with the Darne, you two twenty metres either side. When I make a signal, let's see if we can get him to move.'

'What sort of signal?' asked Desmoulins. 'You put one foot on that wooden bridge and he'll hear you.'

'Don't worry, I don't intend to do that. Wait and see – and be ready.'

Rocco and Desmoulins moved away, while Claude edged closer to the canal and the footbridge. He was listening to the sound of water, which was slow moving here, sluggish and gentle, swirling occasionally as it encountered a fallen branch or a landfall in the bank. But he knew that if he was able to isolate that noise, any alien sound would stand out.

He stopped a few short paces from the bridge, knowing he couldn't be seen among the tall grass. This was his terrain, as familiar as his own garden, with every stretch of water and marshland embedded in his memory through many nights and days of patrolling; and he would defy any man to be able to use the cover here more effectively.

He hunkered down and breathed easily, giving time for Desmoulins and Rocco to get into position. While he waited, he took a slim, half-litre bottle and a handkerchief from the inside pocket of his hunting jacket. He took out the cork and tore the handkerchief in half, then stuffed the material into the neck of the bottle, leaving a good length trailing down the outside.

He was ready. He took out a lighter. Holding the bottle in his left hand, he snapped the lighter's wheel and lit the trailing end of the handkerchief. It flared instantly, the material now soaked in spirit. Without hesitation, he pulled his arm back and hurled the petrol bomb high in the air, then rolled sideways, grabbing his shotgun.

The flame arced over the canal and fell to earth on the other side of the footbridge. But Claude didn't watch it fall. Instead he watched for movement nearby.

When the bottle landed and burst, there was a cry of dismay and a figure stood up just a couple of metres from the spreading flame, caught in the flickering glare. It was Jean-Pierre. He was holding a sub-machine gun and yelling at a tongue of fire burning on one leg of his trousers, where some of the burning spirit had splashed him.

Claude shouted, 'Police! Drop the gun!' He fired a round into the air, the shot echoing across the *marais* and sending up a frantic clatter of birds from the trees and reeds around them.

But Jean-Pierre was beyond listening. Instead he looked about wildly, trying to locate the source of the voice. Then he swung the sub-machine gun and sent a burst of bullets spraying across the canal, spitting harmlessly into the night.

Two shots sounded from either side of Claude, and he saw Jean-Pierre step sideways, like a dancer. He dropped the gun, then his legs refused to carry him further and he fell over without a sound, and lay still.

# Chapter Fifty-nine

Delombre stopped and looked back as the blast of a shotgun shattered the night. A flash of flame with an orange tail curved gently through the air. It burned brightly for a few moments, then came more gunshots before the flame was swallowed by the dark.

He swore quietly. They'd fooled the guard with a silly trick to get him to show himself. But it had worked. A kid could have done better.

He turned and increased his pace as much as he dared, aware that they couldn't be far behind. The ground softened beneath his feet, and a squelching noise sounded as he felt the sucking action on the soles of his shoes. He veered left, keeping the lake to his right. One foot sank deep, and a spray of water flew into his face, momentarily blinding him. He tasted iron on his tongue, brackish and foul, and spat it out, a layer of grit coating his lips. He veered right, trying hard to breathe more easily. This was taking too much out of him. Fitter than most men half his age, he could run almost any distance without stopping. But this terrain was killing him.

He saw the gleam of water and moved left, then left again. He was going back towards the sanitarium, and realised that the lake here was jagged in its outline, and he'd somehow stumbled onto a small promontory, and was now in danger of being boxed in.

He stretched himself and pushed harder, his lungs beginning to ache and his leg muscles screaming at him to stop, to rest. But he couldn't. He powered on, and found the lay of the land beginning to pull him back to the right, away from his pursuers.

He was going to make it!

A shot sizzled through the air in front of him. 'Give it up, Delombre. There's no way out.' *Rocco*.

Delombre stopped, floundering now, bewildered by this crazy terrain, the mud, the water and the dark... and the man who wouldn't give up. Then he saw movement, a patch of paleness as a figure appeared in the corner of his eye.

He turned and fired three times, back once more on the Legion's commando training ground, shooting at targets, the hot sun on the Gulf of Tadjoura, in Djibouti, baking his shoulders through his shirt and the instructors screaming out their orders to both lead and confuse.

But this was no training ground, and Delombre realised that there would be no end to the day and a shared truck ride back to camp for cold drinks.

This was for real.

He heard another shout, but didn't recognise the voice.

Rocco had outplayed him, bringing other men with him. Men who'd been prepared to come into the night after him.

He moved backwards away from them. He could outrun them. They were only police, not former men of the Legion like him. Then one foot sank deep into soft mud and he lost his balance, pitching over on his back. He scrambled up immediately, feeling the softness beneath him and the wetness soaking into his clothing. He dragged his leg out of the ooze, and felt his shoe come loose. In panic, he dropped his gun. He scrabbled around and by a small miracle, found it again. Brushing it against his body to clean off the filth that caked it, he made his way further to his right, feeling the pull of reeds and long grass clutching at his legs. He sobbed in frustration, cursing softly, determined not to let it stop him.

Then he realised the men were no longer following. He paused and looked back. He thought he could see them, indistinct shapes in the gloom, watching and waiting, and he wondered what they were planning. One of them shouted, but he couldn't make it out above the sucking noise around him, and the sudden splashing of cold water that seemed to be up around his thighs. Just then the ground lurched beneath him and his waist felt cold and wet.

He was sinking.

—

'Can you see him?' said Rocco.

'No.' Desmoulins cleared his throat and spat out a mouthful of dirty water where he'd fallen, gulping in whatever had risen to greet him. Rocco had reached down and hauled him upright, before pushing on towards the frantic splashing noise coming from near the lake.

'Stop,' warned Claude. 'Don't go any further.'

'What's up?' Rocco thought he saw a movement, but it could have been his imagination or marsh mist or a swarm of mosquitoes. The quality of darkness here was confusing.

'He's in the mud swamp.'

'What?'

'It's a soft bog – a mudflat covered in a few inches of black water. It's fed by the lake and a couple of springs, but it never drains off. It's pure mud, like soft chocolate.' His voice sounded flat, dull, as if imparting something that had no good end. 'Even cows have gone missing in there. Not a trace of them ever found.'

'*Bastards!*' Delombre's voice floated out of the darkness, and more splashing echoed across the lake, less frantic now than before. Gunfire split the night as a volley of shots echoed across the water.

The three men ducked, although none of the shots came near. They didn't return fire.

'Can't we do something?' said Desmoulins. 'I know he's a killer, but…'

'No.' Claude's tone was final. 'He's too far out. Believe me, you go out there and we'll lose you, too.'

'What are his odds?' said Rocco. He was breathing deeply, like the others, and stank of mud and rotted vegetation.

The splashing stopped. Seconds later there was a renewed burst, but weaker now. Then silence.

'Not good.' Claude's voice was pragmatic. 'We won't know until morning – maybe not even then. This place doesn't often give back what it takes.'

–

Out on the mudflat, Delombre had given way to utter exhaustion. He tossed away his gun. It was no use to him now; all his shells were gone and his enemies were out of sight and beyond reach. He hoped he'd managed to take at least one of them with him with that last volley, and that it was Rocco. Bloody man.

The watery ooze was now up to his chest, its relentless sucking power drawing him deeper and deeper, the more he struggled. Something moved against his leg, wriggling frantically, then was gone. He began to shiver, goosebumps rising on his upper chest and shoulders, but it wasn't the cold. A gentle pressure was gripping him, and he could feel the wetness moving inexorably upwards towards his neck and face, claiming him centimetre by centimetre.

He coughed as the foul stench of mud filled his nostrils, and tried one last time to lift his legs, to push himself up from whatever certain horror lay beneath.

But it was no good. He was too tired.

He sighed. It shouldn't end like this. Not for him. But there were some things you couldn't control.

With a final defiant curse at the fates, he emptied his lungs of air, then lifted his arms and made his body go rigid, and allowed himself to sink smoothly beneath the surface.

## Chapter Sixty

Rocco arrived home and left the car out in the road. He felt too tired to open the iron gates and drive inside, and with a long day of paperwork and briefings ahead of him, there were better things to worry about. Like catching a couple of hours sleep. He checked his watch. Already nine o'clock. He'd promised Massin a full report at midday.

He'd sent Claude and Desmoulins home, and left Captain Canet and a fresh team of officers to finish off at the Clos du Lac. Medics had taken away a bruised and bewildered, but otherwise increasingly lively Véronique Bessine, swapping his coat for a blanket, and her husband, no doubt accompanied by half the cabinet and the media, was on his way to Amiens hospital to meet her. Dion was on her way to a high-security cell and a lot of questioning.

He went over to the pump and kicked off his muddy shoes and trousers, dropping his jacket to the ground. He got the pump flowing with a few deft strokes, and washed off the mud and filth that had soaked through his trousers onto his legs and feet. The ooze was black, like coal dust, and the rank smell took him right back to the last few moments of the chase as Delombre vanished in the dark. He left his soiled things outside, ready to take to Madame Drolet at the co-op for cleaning, and went indoors and changed into fresh clothes and shoes.

The phone rang.

'Inspector?' It was Georges Maillard. 'Sorry to trouble you, but I heard you go by. There's somebody down here you should see.'

Rocco walked down the road to the café, the smell of stale water replaced by the tangy aroma of cow droppings from the farms along the way. Cows, he decided, were better than swamps.

Maillard was waiting for him at the café door, scratching his belly and yawning. He waved a thumb towards the side of the building, which edged on to a stretch of green space beneath a line of chestnut trees.

'There's someone here arrived more than an hour ago and woke me up asking directions to your place. I knew you weren't in, so I told her she should wait here. I gave her coffee and kept an eye on her, and last I saw she was asleep in her car. Nice model. She's not bad, either.' He smiled knowingly, then added more seriously, 'Sounded bad, during the night. Anyone hurt?'

'Nobody who didn't expect it. Does this woman have a name?'

'I asked, but she said she wanted to surprise you.' He fluttered his eyebrows, then turned and went inside, humming tunelessly.

Rocco walked round to the side of the café, and saw a sporty-looking cream Renault Floride parked beneath a tree. Jacqueline Roget was curled up behind the wheel, asleep.

He tapped gently on the window. She came awake instantly, looking up and smiling when she saw who it was, and wound down the window.

'You realise I could arrest you for violating local parking laws,' he told her sternly.

She grinned and yawned, then opened the door and climbed out. She was dressed in a jumper and slacks and looked surprisingly fresh, considering where she'd been sleeping and the time of day.

'Sorry, Officer,' she said meekly, then added, 'I remembered what you said about your house being at the end of a road, but I wasn't sure which one, so I stopped here to ask directions, just in case.' She fluffed her hair into place and straightened her jumper. 'The owner, Georges, was very sweet. He said there had been shooting just outside the village during the night, so it might be best if I stayed here until you got home. There were a bunch of other men here, talking about it. He told them to watch their language and they asked if I was any good at *Babyfoot*.' She smiled knowingly. 'I thrashed them. I used to beat everyone when I was at college but I didn't tell them that. Georges is a big fan of yours, by the way. He thinks you're tough.' She frowned and looked him over. 'The shooting. Are you all right?'

'I'm fine, thanks. You want to drive me to my place? Only our every move is now being closely monitored.' He was referring to the curtain twitching in the café's end window. Give it a couple of minutes and the entire village would know he'd got a lady visitor who beat everyone at *Babyfoot*.

He directed her down the lane and led her inside, where he put the kettle on and excused himself while he bagged up his dirty clothes. Jacqueline watched for a moment, then picked up his shoes and began to clean off the mud.

'You don't have to do that,' he protested, but she shooed him away.

'I used to clean my father's boots when he came in from fishing. I became quite expert. Besides, if you leave these too long, you'll ruin them.' She studied the inside label. 'They're English. Expensive.'

'It's a weakness I have.'

'Well, I'm pleased you have at least one.' Then her eyes became serious. 'Was the shooting to do with Delombre?'

'Yes. He got away.' He guessed that might not be accurate, but they wouldn't know for sure until later this morning when they dragged the lake.

'You weren't hurt, though.' It was a statement, a reassurance, and said with relief.

'No. I ducked.'

She frowned slightly. 'Please don't joke.' She put his shoes down and began to stuff them with newspaper.

'Sorry. It's a coping mechanism.'

'Yes, I know.' She brushed her hands, then looked up as a skittering noise sounded across the ceiling. 'You've got fruit rats! I love them – they're so cute, with their little Zorro masks.'

'I didn't know they wore masks.' He tried to recall the things Claude had said about them. Razor-sharp teeth was one. Not masks, though. Another species, maybe.

'The little ones do. Aunt Celestine has them, too. You won't try to get rid of them, will you?'

'I'm not sure I could, now,' he replied. 'In fact I'm thinking of adding them to the rent book. Would you like some cake?'

'I'd love some.'

He cut two slices and put them on plates. They sat and ate in silence, and Jacqueline expressed her approval by having a second slice.

'My neighbour,' he explained. 'She doesn't think I eat enough.'

'Lucky you. It must be nice being surrounded by people who think so highly of you.' She dusted crumbs off her fingers. 'Would it be dreadfully bad for your reputation,' she added carefully, 'if I stayed here today? Only I have a lot of thinking to do. This place feels so peaceful.'

Rocco felt the last of the cake go dry in his mouth, and his heart began pounding faster again. Actually, he decided, it hadn't slowed much in the first place. 'We'd have to keep one foot on the floor and drink lots of tea.'

She smiled and blushed. 'Of course.'

He explained about having to report to Massin, and the likelihood that Interior Ministry people would descend on Amiens in droves, in the wake of the kidnapping and shooting. 'I don't know when I'll be back.'

'That's all right. I'll only stay a few hours. Then I have to go back to the city.'

He asked, 'Does your aunt know you came?'

'Of course. I told you, she's the family black sheep. She approves.'

'And you're taking after her?'

She looked down. 'No. Not really. My father thinks I'm a lot like her, especially doing the job I'm doing. Was doing.'

'"Was"? Is that what the thinking is about?'

'Yes. I resigned. I decided that all the skulking around and being secretive wasn't really me, nor was being expected to make late-night visits to a senior officer's apartment. So I rang my supervisor yesterday evening. He told me there's a big reorganisation going on, so I shouldn't make any rash decisions, but I said it wouldn't make any difference.' She bit her lip. 'Levignier has disappeared. Did you know that?'

'No. I didn't. When?'

'Sometime yesterday. My supervisor told me that a security guard saw him being picked up outside the office by two men in a car. He didn't come back. What do you think that could be about?'

Justice, Rocco thought instinctively. A clean-up operation to make sure none of what had happened over the past few days ever got out. Levignier was probably discovering the hard way that even being near the top of ISD was no guarantee of protection against failure. It had so many ramifications, failure, especially allied to official circles; one of them being its cast-offs getting scooped up like rubbish in a dustpan.

'I'm sorry I was so touchy at my aunt's,' she said after a while, and another cup of tea. 'About the questions, I mean. I don't know what came over me.'

'It's what I do,' he explained. 'Ask questions. But I'll try to keep them appropriate to the occasion in future.' He realised immediately how that sounded, but suddenly didn't mind. It was an unusual concept, the future.

She was smiling, a delicate crease forming in the middle of each cheek. She said, 'I might keep you to that.'